Death in the Garden of England
A Mrs Hudson Mystery

Susan Knight

Paperback ISBN 978-1-80424-175-2
ePub ISBN 978-1-80424-176-9
PDF ISBN 978-1-80424-177-6

Published by MX Publishing
335 Princess Park Manor,
Royal Drive, London,
N11 3GX
www.mxpublishing.com

Cover design by Brian Belanger

for Patricia McCarthy

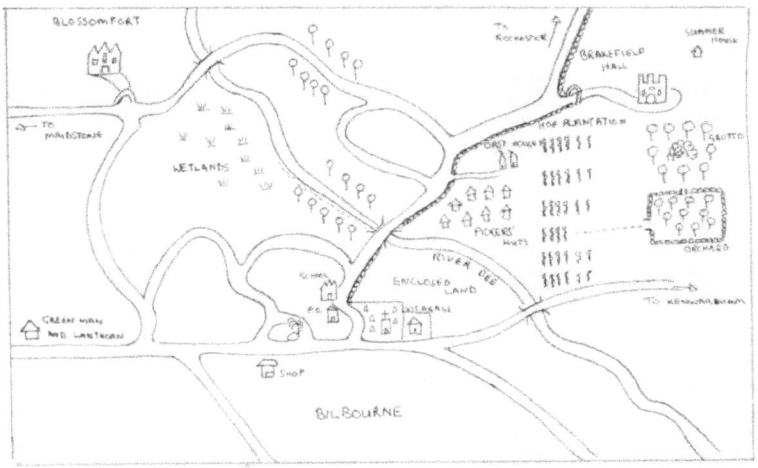

Map of Bilbourne drawn up by Eleanor Hazelgrove

CHAPTER ONE

'They've found him at last!'

Eleanor burst into the upstairs parlour where I was sitting quietly, having just returned from Rochester.

'They've found him. Thank God for that.' I smiled up at her.

'No, mama. I'm afraid it's not good news,' she replied. 'They've found his body... Oh, it is too horrible.'

I looked at her in disbelief. He's dead! I fell back, suddenly weak, clutching the arms of the chair.

'Mama, are you all right?... Oh heavens, I had no idea... I shouldn't have broken the news so bluntly.'

She fussed about me, searching through my reticule for the sal volatile that I always carry with me.

'I am all right,' Eleanor,' I assured her, gathering myself, for I seldom have use for those reviving salts. 'It's just... well, I was only talking to the poor lad a few days ago. Making plans for his future. To think now that he has gone for ever...'

She stared at me. 'Oh, mama,' she said. 'I'm so sorry. I should have been clearer. It's not Timothy they've found.'

'What? Not Timothy? Who then? Who?'

My readers must forgive me for thus upsetting the order of chronology by starting my tale in the middle. Indeed, Dr. Watson, who has started to show an interest in my little jottings, has already chided me for it and, chuckling, tells me that I am become quite the literary iconoclast. My reply is that a startling opening can only hope

1

to intrigue and tempt, and that this has been, successful or not, my intention here. However, I must now step back some weeks to explain how events led to the point described above.

Following my recent adventures in Paris,[1] I had returned to London, to my house in Baker Street, where Mr. Sherlock Holmes, the renowned detective, has his lodgings, along with his friend and associate Dr. Watson. Perhaps it was the strain of the past terrible weeks in the French capital, but it soon became evident that my health was not as it had been previously. I, who have always prided myself on my vigour, was become subject to sudden weaknesses. Dr. Watson, bless his good heart, examined me and concluded that, despite the blow on the head I had sustained during my sojourn away, there was nothing seriously wrong. It was simply that I was in need of a period of complete rest, something I was unlikely to enjoy in London.

'I cannot see you taking your ease here, Mrs. Hudson,' he said, smiling at me. 'You will be constantly searching to know what Clara and Phoebe are about.'

The aforementioned being my two maidservants.

'Clara,' he went on, 'is perfectly capable of holding the fort here if you can find somewhere to go and stay for a while, somewhere preferably with good clean country air where there are people to look after you... I believe,' he added, 'you have mentioned in the past that you have a daughter living in Kent. Indeed, I have had the pleasure of meeting her here on occasion. Perhaps now would be a good time to pay her a visit.'

I have, in fact, two daughters, although the thought of taking the arduous journey north to Edinburgh to stay with Judith, much as I love her and her young family, seemed just then beyond my powers. Eleanor's abode in the pretty village of Bilbourne in Kent, the aptly named Garden of England, was, on the other hand, little more than

---

[1] *See Mrs Hudson goes to Paris*, MX Publishing, 2022.

a relatively short train ride away. The prospect of a sojourn there appealed greatly. While my daughter came up to London occasionally to visit me, and to take advantage of the opportunity to explore the elegant emporia of Regent Street – a treat for her to view the latest fashions which she, an accomplished needlewoman, could then copy at a much cheaper price – I had only ever made the journey down to Kent once before, shortly after her wedding. Eleanor was married to George Hazelgrove, proprietor of the only shop in Bilbourne, a grocery store. Sad to say, they were not yet blessed with children.

'Thank you for the suggestion, Doctor,' I replied, thinking it would be good, in any case, to get away from the stifling summer air of the city. 'I shall write to Eleanor directly.'

Without delay I penned her a letter, making little of my health problems, although my canny daughter must have read between the lines, for she insisted on coming to town to accompany me back, despite my assertion that I could manage alone. In fact, I rather suspected that the good doctor himself had dropped her a line, recommending she fetch me.

Thus it was that on a sultry day in late August, I found myself packing my bags yet again, worrying all the time that I was laying too heavy a burden on Clara in particular, since it was barely two months since I had returned from France.

'Don't you be fretting yourself, now, ma'am,' that capable young woman assured me. 'We'll manage quite well here without you, and if Mr. H objects to Phoebe burning the toast, well, let him come down to the kitchen and prepare it himself.'

I should say here that, despite all our combined efforts, young Phoebe, although full of good intentions, continued to fall far short of the qualities demanded of a housemaid. But, because I was fond of her, and bearing in mind the neediness of her poor mother, burdened with an ever-increasing family, and a feckless husband to boot, I had not the heart to send her packing.

I made the mistake of expressing my worries aloud.

'You know quite well, mother,' said Eleanor, who had arrived the previous evening and who was at that moment delaying me considerably by helping me pack, 'that Clara is well able to look after the two gentlemen.'

My maid beamed. She and Eleanor, being of an age – the middle twenties – were good friends, despite their difference in status. Indeed, to look at them they could be sisters, similar in colouring and physique. Both my daughters take after my dear late husband Henry's side of the family, being tall and slender, like Clara, where I am small and somewhat plump, dark where I am fair (without, I am happy to say, having yet had recourse to put colour in my hair).

'The carriage is come, mum.' Phoebe tore into the room in her usual impetuous way, conveying the intelligence without refinement.

'Now I trust you'll be a good girl, while I am gone, Phoebe, and help Clara in every way,' I told her.

'Yes, mum.' She bobbed an ungainly curtsey. 'And I do hope you'll come back better, mum.'

To my surprise, I discerned a tear in her eye.

'I will, Phoebe. Come here and give me a hug.'

The poor girl, no beauty at all but an ungainly country lump of a lass addicted to yellow-backed tales of romance, was no doubt awaiting a swain to come and sweep her off her own two rather large feet. Just then, she happily gave me a great bear hug, while Clara embraced me more decorously, a reassuring smile on her face, though she too, as I knew, was worried about me.

'I'll be perfectly fine,' I assured them, 'and home before you know I've been away.'

'We'll see about that,' Eleanor said. 'You'll stay until you've got your strength back.'

Her over-solicitousness, grasping hold of my arm to support me as I walked to the carriage, grated on my nerves.

4

'I am not an invalid,' I told her rather sharply. 'Just in need of some peace and quiet.'

'Yes, mother,' she replied meekly. 'Still, you know, you're not as young as you used to be.'

'I am barely fifty, miss,' I retorted sharply. 'The Marquess of Salisbury is sixty-six.'

'Well, you aren't the Prime Minister. Not yet, anyway.' Eleanor laughed, adding. 'Though perhaps the country would be better off if you were.'

'At least women would get the vote,' I replied, mollified. 'It's scandalous that we still have no voice in the running of the country.'

Eleanor agreed with me. She is quite the revolutionary when it comes to women's rights, and supports the suffragist movement.

Friends again, for we cannot argue for long, we caught the Dover train from Victoria and, after an hour or so of travel, alighted at the intermediate station of Kenwardham, where a horse and carriage was waiting to take us inland to the village that was our destination. Our driver was a young lad covered in freckles, with a mop of ginger hair.

'This is Joe, mama,' Eleanor said. 'He helps out in the shop,'

'Help, is it!' the lad exclaimed. 'I do everything, I do. And little thanks or pay I get for it, neither.'

He chuckled merrily, and Eleanor joined in, ruffling his hair. Clearly Joe was one of the family.

Kenwardham is a flourishing port town on the Thames estuary with a charming medieval centre. The newer part had expanded considerably since my previous visit, well into the surrounding countryside, and I wondered at all the changes, the modern villas with their little front gardens, stretching for quite a distance along the tarmacadamed road out of town. I cannot say that I considered these lines of identical dwellings attractive, although no doubt their inhabitants were delighted with the conveniences of good plumbing and the like.

After finally leaving the town behind us, we found ourselves bouncing over inferior rough country roads for three-quarters of an hour or so, passing nothing more than the occasional farmstead or stone cottage and, visible in the distance, the distinctive round shapes of oast houses pointing their bent steeples to the skies, for this is hop-growing country.

At last, we reached Bilbourne, with its pretty village green surrounded on three sides by white-washed cottages – some thatched, some tiled with blue slates – a blacksmith's and a carter's. And in the midst of all, glorious behind new plated glass windows, was the grocery store that belonged to the Hazelgroves.

Since I was quite fatigued by the journey and ready for a rest, I was not of a humour just then to meet Eleanor's mother-in-law, who surged out of the shop door as we approached. I could tell that my daughter wasn't happy either, for I heard her mutter, 'What's *she* doing here?'

I had of course encountered Mrs. Hazelgrove senior before – Henrietta as she liked me to call her as if we were best friends – once in London at the wedding and again on my previous visit to the village. She was a small red-faced woman, round as a ball, with tight pepper-and-salt curls, a loud voice and overbearing manner, who took any opportunity to inform all and sundry that the Hazelgroves were of noble descent, Lords of the Manor in the West Riding of Yorkshire, no less, with a coat of arms she was always nagging her son to place over the shop, as well as on the side of the wagon used for deliveries.

'To let people know they aren't dealing with the hoi polloi here, you know.'

Easy-going George always laughed and replied that it was far from lords of the manor that the family found themselves today, and that anyway he wouldn't like to set himself up above his neighbours, while Eleanor scowled and under her breath whispered to me that it wasn't even as if Henrietta were a Hazelgrove herself, just a tanner's daughter from Maidstone.

'Here you are arrived now, Martha,' Mrs Hazelgrove senior said, stating the obvious, with the slightly condescending familiarity that had amused me in the past, but which I found jarring on a hot afternoon after a long journey. 'You look ghastly pale,' she continued. 'Eleanor, bring your mother inside instantly.' As if my daughter had every intention of running me around the green.

The woman fussed about me further, obstructing my passage and instructing Joe on how properly to carry my suitcase into the house, 'And do mind the stairs.' For the family lived over the shop.

Joe just grinned. He was no doubt used to her busybodying around.

George, built like his mother and a head shorter than his wife, a jolly fellow with rosy cheeks and incipient loss of hair, was busy with a customer in the shop, but greeted me warmly, and introduced me to the old woman who was just then purchasing a packet of tea. This Mrs. Gracie said she was delighted to meet dear Eleanor's mother, and that Eleanor was a credit to me, which pleased me greatly, indicating how much my daughter was liked in the village.

'I am sure,' George then said rather pointedly, looking at Henrietta, 'that you'd like to have a lie down, mother-in-law. Especially after Joe's driving.'

Did the woman take the hint? Not at all. She bustled up the stairs ahead of us, with every intention, it seemed, to settle in and treat me to all the local news. She and her husband ran the post office (coat-of-arms over the door, of course) and Mrs. Hazelgrove senior was ever less than discreet when it came to the doings of the small community in which she lived.

Eleanor was well able for her, however, without being rude. She conceded a welcome cup of tea to all three of us, during which time Henrietta started filling me in on the business of all sorts of people

I didn't know nor care about, and complaining at the same time that the tea wasn't strong enough.

'This gnat's water won't do your mother any good, Eleanor,' she remarked, using a somewhat startling image, hardly appropriate for an aspirant to the nobility. 'You should be able to stand the spoon up in it. Why you never leave the pot on the range to brew sufficiently, as I have advised you before, I shall never understand... Young women think they know it all,' she said, shaking her head at me.

In vain I protested that it was as I liked it.

'I find stewed tea too bitter,' I said.

'Not if you sweeten it properly.' She added another large spoonful of sugar to her drink. 'And can you not run down to the shop, Eleanor, and get some of those chocolate sponge biscuits I like so much.... You will love them, Martha, so creamy.'

'This home-made shortbread is enough for me,' I replied. 'Very tasty, Eleanor.'

Henrietta shook her head again and poured her tea into her saucer in the way of country folk, before slurping it up.

'And how,' she asked, her eyes glinting after this unattractive procedure was done, 'is that famous lodger of yours. Any fresh scandals?'

I shook my head and replied that I was no confidant of Mr. H, and that my knowledge of his activities was as much as could be gleaned from the accounts written by Dr. Watson. As much, indeed, as Henrietta could glean herself.

She sniffed. Clearly she was most disappointed in me, and at long last – no doubt despairing at my lack of response – took the hint, and was gone, instructing Eleanor downstairs in loud tones that carried up to me, to be sure and let me rest, for I was clearly not myself and indeed, in what passed with her for a whisper, looked to be not long for this world.

'You should prepare yourself, my dear,' I heard her utter, 'for the worst.'

I suppose she meant well, but she was undoubtedly trying, and it was with great relief that I took myself to the small but well-appointed room that was to be mine for the next while, and laid myself down on the bed.

CHAPTER TWO

In Bilbourne, and annoyingly considered by all around me an invalid, I had to adjust to a life of idleness, so very different from what I am used to. Indeed, Eleanor insisted I spend near enough a dreary week hardly out of my bed. Almost my only visitors were herself and George, apart from Bella, the ginger and white cat whose official function was to keep the rats and mice away from the grain bags in the storeroom, but whose greatest pleasure was to lie on my bed and let herself be petted. The local doctor, who checked in on me from time to time, was a feeble little man of such considerable age he had difficulty climbing the stairs to my room, so that I soon took to coming down to the shop to be seen by him in the office at the back.

This Dr. French, concurring with Dr. Watson that there was nothing fundamentally wrong with me – despite Henrietta's gloomy prognostication – simply prescribed a locally produced oatmeal stout to build me up, a tasty enough concoction, though whether it did me any good, I remain unconvinced. However, after days stuck indoors, I finally insisted that I be permitted to enjoy some fresh air. Thus, accompanied by my ever-attentive daughter, I had the pleasure of taking a few turns around the green with its little duck pond at one end where we could sit on a bench under the shade of a willow tree watching the charming antics of the waterfowl, while Eleanor introduced me to some of the various denizens of the village as they went about their business.

Of course, the arrival of a newcomer in their midst stirred the curiosity of the locals, for, as I have indicated, I was not well-known in Bilbourne. My fame had preceded my appearance, however, thanks, I suspected, to Mrs. Henrietta Hazelgrove, for after exchanging greetings with Eleanor, several of the passers-by asked after me in doom-laden tones that suggested they also believed my end to be nigh. I was able to reassure them cheerfully that I had no intention yet of venturing into that country from which no traveller returns.

I was far from being the only stranger in the village, however. It was the hop-picking season and thousands of people had descended on the county of Kent to help with the harvest. Bilbourne, with its nearby hop plantation, was one of their destinations. Although the pickers tended in general to stay out of the village, regular forays, as Eleanor informed me, would be made by the menfolk – and even by certain women also – to the Green Man and Lanthorn, the inn at the end of the village, where, she sighed, they often squandered their earnings as soon as they received them. George's shop – which stocked a much wider range of goods than a city grocery, serving as hardware store and newsagency as well – was also a frequent destination for the newcomers, although, as Eleanor explained, the Brakefields, who owned the plantation, provided basic accommodation and food for them.

'It's hardly lavish,' she said, disapprovingly. 'Communal sheds with straw to lie on and sleep, and pots of potage and black bread to eat. No wonder they come to us for extras.'

Again, as she told me with regret, it was often drink they were after, for George, as a licensed victualler, stocked bottles of a local brew, cheaper to buy there than in the Green Man. Sometimes, as we sat by the pond, groups of grubby children, often barefoot and in raggedy smocks, would run up the street and pile into the shop, clutching precious farthings to spend on sugar plums or toffee or brandy balls or humbugs, George often adding an extra sweet or two to the bag for the poor mites.

'His mother says he's too soft-hearted, of course,' Eleanor remarked. 'But it's so little for us and they have nothing.'

It pleased me greatly, even after Eleanor decided I was fit enough to be let out by myself, to amble around the green and then sit myself down for a while under the willow, to read a book or a newspaper, or watch the ducks. Now and then someone would join me for a chat, some curious to hear about London, some so completely cloistered by the boundaries of their little world that they could hardly see beyond it, clearly pitying me for not being a permanent resident. Henrietta Hazelgrove was such a one, if I was ever unfortunate enough to be spotted by her.

'Poor you. All alone with no one to talk to,' she'd say, flopping herself down beside me, quite disregarding the fact that I was engaged in reading.

'I must say, Martha,' she would continue, with an almost imperceptible degree of disappointment, 'you are looking better every time I see you. It must be the good Bilbourne air. I was quite afraid that you were in a complete decline, you know; you looked so wretched when you first arrived. Well for you that you came here in time.'

Then she would cast around for more subjects to discuss, being particularly rewarded if there was some scandal to relate.

'There goes that Betsy Warren one now with a swelling belly on her and she only two weeks wed.'

Or, waving warmly at the wife of the vicar, she would then turn to me in a whisper and inform me of the shortcomings of the lady's domestic arrangements.

'I am sure I don't know how poor Reverend Considine puts up with it. Their house is quite upside down you know, as you'll discover if they ever invite you to visit. I'm sure I'd be ashamed to bring people into such a muddle, but *she* doesn't care. It's not what

I call a good example to the rest of us.' Henrietta would draw herself up self-righteously.

Or seeing a certain fashionably dressed young man ride by on a fine white horse, she would exclaim, 'What would you in London call the likes of him? A dandy, is it? Well in my humble opinion that attire might be considered à la mode in Hyde Park, but it's hardy suitable around here, don't you agree? We're plain simple folk in Bilbourne, with none of your citified fancy airs and graces. A purple jacket, indeed! And I am sure I spotted a yellow rose in his buttonhole.'

I studied the man, as he rode off into the distance. 'Who is he?'

'The squire's heir, Freddie. Down to visit his father. Comes whenever he's short of money, I reckon, looking for a handout.' She shook her head. 'Probably headed for the inn, if I know him.'

'So there's a squire here?' I asked, ignoring the rest of her allegations against the youth.

'Oh yes, Martha. We aren't completely savage here, no matter what you think. We have our share of the gentry, too, you know. Yes, indeed. Squire Simister. He lives in that big old house near the Maidstone road.'

'Sinister? That's a strange name.'

She laughed heartily. 'No, no, Martha, Simister with an m, not an n. Good heavens! What are you like, seeing intrigue everywhere! You've spent far too long with your lodger and his escapades. Nothing of that sort goes on here, you know. No murder and mayhem in Bilbourne. We're law-abiding... well, most of us.'

Henrietta frowned deeply at a pair of shabbily dressed women making their way at that moment along the street.

'Pickers!' she said with disgust. 'I'll bet you anything you like, Martha, they are heading to George's shop. Haven't I told him over and over again not to let that sort in, but get Joe to take their orders at the door. But will he ever listen to me? Not at all... They're a light-fingered lot, I try to tell him. Well, all I can say is, he'll be sorry when half his stock goes missing… Luckily, the likes of them don't have much occasion to visit the post office. Most of them probably don't even know how to write their names, let alone pen a letter.'

It was extremely tedious to hear her go on like that, and I am afraid that if I ever saw Henrietta Hazelgrove before she saw me, I'd make sure to hurry off and hide.

However, most of the people I met by the duck pond were more engaging, kindly country folk, happy to pass the time of day without being too intrusive. Indeed, that was where I first met Timothy, of whom Henrietta would have doubtless disapproved. It was one late afternoon after the pickers had finished their work for the day, a setting sun infusing the scene with a golden light, gilding the tiny wavelets on the pond. I spotted a tall gangly lad – I supposed him to be aged about fourteen or fifteen – thin as a lath and unhealthily pale, following a group of younger children. While the others went into the shop, no doubt clutching a farthing or two, he stood uncertainly by the window, and then wandered over to the pond, crouching down near me to look at the ducks. Used to being fed, they came crowding to the bank hoping for crumbs. I was shocked then when the boy picked up a stone and flung it at them, missing them all, but causing them to scatter with angry squawks.

'Stop that at once!' I cried.

He turned a wan face to look at me.

'Sorry, m'm,' he said, shrinking a little as if he feared I would hit him.

'Why did you do that?' I asked. 'Whatever were you thinking?'

'Well, m'm…' He looked at me as if assessing what my reaction would be to his words. 'I was thinking how fat they are. How one of them would make a nice tasty dinner.'

'Good gracious!' I exclaimed. Then added, 'You're hungry?'

He grinned. I saw how he had lost some of his teeth and that the remaining ones were turned green. 'I'm always hungry, me.'

'Well, please don't think of killing a duck.' I paused and looked at him. Then reaching into my reticule, I took out a thrupenny bit, for indeed, he looked half-starved. 'Go and get yourself a hot meal.'

He took it, astonished. 'God bless you, m'm!' he said and scurried off towards the Green Man, where, as I had been told, he could get some chops or a good thick soup.

After that, if I were sitting alone, he'd come and crouch nearby. I suppose he was hoping for another coin, the which I always provided, and yet he took to lingering to chat a while before rushing off. In that way I learnt something of his history. An orphan, he had grown up in the workhouse, but had been taken on by the Brakefields, a year or so before, as a labourer on their hop plantation.

'I won't say they be cruel,' he said. 'But they could be kinder.'

Remembering what Eleanor had told me about the accommodations provided for the pickers, I asked where he lived.

'In a barn,' he said.

'Not in the winter, too, surely?'

'Yes, m'm. Summer and winter. It's warm enough with the straw. Warmer than the workhouse anyways.'

I feared they didn't feed him properly, since he was always hungry.

'Cook says I'm like a bucket with a hole in it. You can't never fill me up.'

Yet when he told me what he was given to eat – hunks of hard bread, scraps and peelings, the sort of leavings you might throw to a pig – I wasn't surprised he was famished.

'But there's soup now for the pickers, isn't there?' I said. 'You get some of that, don't you?'

He laughed. 'I have to wait till them have finished, and then scrape around the pot. Sometimes there's a bit left and sometimes there ain't.'

Yes indeed, his employers could be kinder, and I started to wonder if there was something I could do for the lad.

I mentioned him to George that evening, thinking maybe he could find some work for him. To my surprise, that good-hearted man frowned and shook his head.

'I shouldn't like to cross the Brakefields. I imagine they'd not take kindly to me for poaching one of their workers.'

'But he's treated like a slave,' I protested. 'They pay him nothing, claiming the wages cover his meagre board. It's quite scandalous.'

'Mother-in-law,' George replied gently, 'look around yourself. I'm sure you'll find armies of the poor who are treated as badly or worse than young Timothy, especially back in London. Will you try and save them all? You and the vicar's wife.'

'Mrs. Considine, do you mean?'

He laughed. 'She's an inveterate do-gooder like yourself. You two should get together.'

Now that was a thought. Though I had seen the woman, I had never spoken to her. Now I determined to search her out. Maybe she'd be more ready to do something for Timothy.

'She'll probably be at church tomorrow,' Eleanor said, adding, 'It's not that we don't care, mama. It's just that it's impossible to take on the woes of the whole world. We do what we can, you know.'

Give an extra humbug to an urchin, I thought, and appease your conscience that way. I, of course, took George's point regarding the enormity of the problem, but I could not help but remember the words of Our Lord, 'Inasmuch as ye have done it unto one of the least of these my brethren, ye have done it unto me.'

On the next day, the first Sunday in two weeks that Eleanor judged me well enough to attend, we dressed up in our best clothes to make our way to the village church of St John the Baptist, where the Reverend Considine was vicar. Of course, I had passed that ancient edifice several times before on my wanderings through the village, and judged it to be a delightful example of small-scale Norman ecclesiastical architecture, built of flint and stone, with a square tower surmounted by a spire. The interior proved to be plain enough, the white-washed walls adorned only with a few crudely executed but quaint paintings of biblical scenes. Someone had placed a bouquet of rust-coloured rudbeckia on the altar, simple flowers but turned beautiful as they caught the glow from the stained-glass window above them, depicting the crucifixion, Mary looking up at her blessed son, in his agony.

This was my first opportunity to view the local 'gentry,' as Henrietta Hazelgrove had described them. Indeed, that same woman insisted on squeezing her bulk into the pew next to me, stating bluntly, 'I vow you have got decidedly fatter in the weeks you have spent here, Martha.'

Mr. Hazelgrove senior, it seemed, was sitting towards the back, his usual place.

'But I just had to come up and join you, to see how you are.'

She went on to indicate, in an embarrassingly loud whisper, who was who.

'That man with the mutton chop whiskers in the front pew, he's the Squire. Simister, you know. Simister, not Sinister!' She nudged me sharply, and chortled.

I looked across at the large man in tweeds, the very image of a country squire, a head of thick sun-bleached hair crowning a weather-beaten face that sported a fine moustache, as well as the afore-mentioned whiskers.

'Freddie, you'll recognise from the other day. In a new jacket, I see. Hardly suitable for church, is it?'

Scarlet, this time. For once, I had rather to agree with my interlocutor.

'Is the squire's wife not with him, then?' I asked, regarding the empty space beside the two men.

Henrietta looked at me with something of a gloat.

'Dead!' she said. 'Long dead. Oh, there's a story there, right enough. I'll show you her tomb in the graveyard after. It's a sight to see.'

Before I could respond to that particular offer, Henrietta was distracted by the arrival of a new couple, accompanied by a small boy in a sailor suit and a young girl of about sixteen.

'The Brakefields,' she said with a sneer. 'King Thomas, Queen Lydia and their son Prince Randall. The girl is Eve, his daughter by a previous.'

Timothy's employers. I regarded them with interest. The man, undersized, thin as a stick, was considerably older than his wife, his scant hair like strands of steel atop a stern clean-shaven face. Sombrely clad though he was, it was yet clear that his coat was expensive and beautifully cut. Mrs. Brakefield was a haughty beauty, dressed in the height of Paris fashion, as I had recently observed it, her dark blue silk outfit sporting a skirt that fell from her wasp waist in generous folds, and with absurdly inflated sleeves on the matching jacket. Her cone-shaped hat meanwhile featured a bird positioned as if ready to take flight. The girl, Eve, shuffling along behind them, looked awkward, head down and shoulders bent, as if she would like to disappear. She tended to plumpness, though not unattractively so, with rosy cheeks and dark hair. The frilly outfit she was wearing did nothing for her, and made her seem bigger than she was. The boy I judged to be aged about seven, a little angel by the look of him. However, as they passed along, I saw him kick his half-sister hard on the shin. She flinched but said not a word. Indeed, apart from the boy pulling faces at us, the rest of the family looked neither to right nor left as they progressed in stately fashion up the aisle until they reached the top, taking their seats in the front pews across from the squire and his son.

'They have always to make an entrance after everyone else has arrived,' my companion whispered disdainfully. 'Everyone calls them the king and queen because of their high and mighty ways. But I could tell you a thing or two about *them,* oh yes indeed.'

Not right then, thankfully, for the organ struck up the notes of the first hymn – 'We Plough the Fields and Scatter' – and we all stood to sing it, George booming out a fine baritone while his mother made up in volume what she lacked in musicality.

The service ran along predictable lines, with a benevolent sermon from the Reverend Considine, a long lean man in his middle forties, his face as deeply creased as a deflating leather rugby ball, surmounted by tousled greying hair, as if he were in the habit of running his fingers through it in lieu of a comb. He informed us that we must reap what we sow, and urged us, therefore, to be kind to one another. It was hardly the stuff from which revolutions are born and the congregation listened, to my mind, with polite indifference. The service ended with the hymn 'All things bright and beautiful', after which we dutifully trooped out, the vicar waiting at the door to acknowledge each of us.

Eleanor, whom the Reverend Considine greeted warmly, presented me to him.

'I am delighted to meet you at last, Mrs. Hudson,' he said clasping my hand in his hard dry one. A man who works manually as well as spiritually, I thought with approval. 'Your fame precedes you!' he went on and, when I looked askance, added, 'I must confess to be an avid reader of Dr. Watson's accounts of your lodger's exploits.'

I nodded without enthusiasm, and simply replied that I was hoping soon to make the acquaintance of his wife.

'Ursula… She should be here somewhere.' He looked around vaguely.

'We'll find her,' Eleanor said, and started to draw me away.

'I should love to get a first-hand account about you-know-who,' Mr. Considine called after me, 'from… well, I won't say the horse's mouth – for you are clearly no horse, Mrs. Hudson – ha ha! – but you know what I mean.'

Oh dear. I am sure he meant no harm but I wish people wouldn't seek for gossip about Mr. H. It is so taxing always to put them off.

'Poor Reverend Considine, 'Eleanor said. 'Not the most tactful of men. As for his wife, I can't see her anywhere. She doesn't always attend the services. She has her own way of doing things, you know.'

'Never mind,' I replied. 'I am sure to bump into her soon enough.'

At that moment, I became aware of a pair of cool green eyes fixed upon me. They belonged to, of all people, the haughty Mrs. Brakefield, and I wondered guiltily if she had found out that I had befriended young Timothy, before dismissing the notion as absurd. Why should she care?

'Martha!' The strident voice that interrupted my thoughts as the Brakefields swept away to their coach, belonged of course to Henrietta Hazelgrove. 'Come along. I promised to show you that tombstone.'

'Another time, perhaps,' I replied. It did not strike me as seemly to go poking around in the churchyard for his wife's monument while the Squire was in the vicinity.

'You are tired, poor thing. I'm not surprised after all that standing up and sitting down and standing up again. I find it quite wearing myself.'

'You'll be coming to Sunday dinner, mother?' It was George who asked. He had just joined us after exchanging some words with a few others of the congregation.

'Yes, indeed,' Henrietta replied, to my dismay. 'Now that Martha is so much better.'

Eleanor hadn't informed me of this particular arrangement and gave me a rueful smile.

'I just hope we won't have a repetition of the roast pork fiasco of the last dinner,' her mother-in-law went on.

'There was nothing wrong with the pork,' George said, laughing. 'It was a fine joint.'

'It was dry and the crackling overcooked.' She sighed. 'I suppose I am just too particular for my own good. Still, your father agreed with me, you know, didn't you, Walter?'

'Well, now...' I suddenly recognised the little man hovering near us as Mr. Hazelgrove senior, whom I had met before and liked. He was a self-effacing individual in his early sixties, thin and stooped, with watery eyes and a tendency, even in summer, to a nose that dripped. Otherwise, he was every inch the village postmaster in his buttoned-up black jacket and grey trousers.

'Come now, mother,' George said. 'Father ate up every morsel on his plate, as did you, yourself.'

'We were simply being polite, weren't we, Walter?'

The roast beef, with its Yorkshire puddings and gravy, served for our dinner, evidently met with his approval, for though the man said little, he certainly did everything justice and even agreed to a second helping of the meat, looked on somewhat disapprovingly by his wife who pronounced the joint too rare for her taste.

'Just give me the end piece please, George,' she said. 'It is the only part well done. Oh, and one or two more of those roasted potatoes... Actually, you might as well add another, since they are so very small... And pass the gravy please, Eleanor. It could do with a little more salt, you know.'

She sprinkled that condiment freely over all.

However, if she, as she claimed (against all the evidence) ate little of her main course, she made up for it with the dessert, a sponge pudding oozing syrup. Indeed, she was so busy eating that she even stopped talking for a while, which enabled the rest of us to have our say, so the meal-time passed pleasantly enough. Mr. Hazelgrove senior, when finally given free rein to speak, even showed himself to be a man of no little erudition, being quite the expert on local history, explaining to me about the Iron Age Celts who settled in the

Weald of Kent, which the Romans apparently knew as Cantium. He urged me to visit the ruins of Richborough castle, thought to be where the Romans first landed.

'It's inland now due to coastal shifts, and set in the marshes, but it was once a prosperous port. You can even view the triumphal arch through which the Romans marched.'

He rubbed his hands together enthusiastically.

'To think that Julius Caesar himself...'

'Oh, for goodness sake, Walter,' Henrietta butted in, having cleared her plate at last, washed down with a glass or two of port wine. 'Would you ever leave off about your stupid Romans! You are boring everyone to tears.'

She yawned loudly, hardly covering her mouth.

'Not at all,' I said. 'It is most interesting.'

'How about a game of cards, mother-in-law?' Eleanor suggested, intercepting the hard look Henrietta was directing my way. It seemed the lady did not brook contradictions well.

'No, thank you, Eleanor,' she said. 'You all play cards if you want. I am far too fagged out.'

Whereupon she sat herself in the most comfortable chair in the parlour and soon fell sound asleep, while the rest of us played a hand or two of Newmarket, the relative silence punctuated by snores.

CHAPTER THREE

The next day Eleanor and I received an invitation to take tea at the vicarage that very afternoon, the which we were pleased to accept, although I rather feared that the Reverend Considine had every intention of taking the opportunity to quiz me about Mr. H and Dr. Watson, when what I really wanted was a quiet word with his wife.

In fact, the vicar, as that lady informed us on our arrival, had been called away at the last minute on urgent parish business.

'I was so anxious to meet you myself,' said Mrs. Considine, 'that I decided not to postpone your visit.'

Of course, I could not tell her how relieved I was at the absence of her husband.

Although Henrietta had warned me in advance about the chaos I would find at the parsonage, I must say that, though maybe not as orderly as it might have been, the room we were in, with its view over a large untidy garden to a meadow beyond, was comfortable and clean. Books and magazines were piled on every surface, it is true, wooden toys and a rag doll lay under our feet; the colourful covers on the sofa and chairs did not match and were in various stages of wear, but the paintings on the walls – landscapes and still lifes – showed considerable taste, and the whole impression was one of a pleasant domesticity. Our hostess, a little untidy herself, with wisps of fair hair falling from her topknot, her dress buttoned up crookedly, had a sweetly amiable face that pleased me greatly. We were Martha and Ursula (Eleanor already being on first-name terms with her) before many minutes had passed, nibbling on homemade gingerbread biscuits and sipping China tea from oddments of antique porcelain cups that had, she told us, belonged to her grandmother.

'I was hoping to meet you myself,' I told her after various pleasantries had been exchanged. 'Having recently become acquainted with an unfortunate young boy who works for the Brakefields, under what seems to me impossible conditions, I should like to do something to improve his lot, and I am given to understand that you occupy yourself with such cases.'

As I explained about Timothy, Ursula's expression became grave, and she nodded from time to time.

'I have of course seen the poor fellow,' she said at last. 'Though I had no idea he was being treated so badly, while you, who have just arrived have discovered it in a matter of days. I feel ashamed.'

'Not at all. I got to know him quite by chance.' I did not mention the attack on the ducks. 'For some reason, the boy confided in me… I should not wish,' I added, 'to interfere in village life or to antagonise the Brakefields.' (Much I cared about them except for George and Eleanor's sake!). 'However, in his case I feel that something needs to be done.'

'It is true that the Brakefields rather consider themselves above the law here, able to do whatever they like,' Ursula replied thoughtfully. 'They are not known for their charity, are they, Eleanor?'

'They take little part in village life, unless to preside over some event or other,' my daughter replied, adding, 'They are feared rather than loved.'

'Feared?' I said. 'That's a strong word to use.'

'Perhaps too strong,' Eleanor conceded. 'But those who have run-ins with them, live to regret it. Thomas Brakefield has an explosive temper and takes offence easily. He has a penchant for resorting to law when believing himself crossed. Moreover, his

24

connections among the local magistrates are only too willing to decide in his favour, whatever the rights and wrongs of the affair.'

'The squire, a good man on the whole, detests him.' Ursula added. Hardly words appropriate for a vicar's wife to utter, yet I appreciated her candour.

'Why?'

'Oh, over the years they have clashed on so many issues, the squire running the hunt over Brakefield land, for instance. Not the hop plantation, of course. No, the rough terrain which we all consider common land anyway but which the Brakefields have enclosed for no good reason. In fact,' she continued, 'you can see it from the window,' gesturing towards the meadow beyond the garden.

'It's not as if they use it for anything,' Eleanor said. 'George says they enclosed it out of spite.'

'Good heavens!' I exclaimed. 'I thought that practice ended centuries ago.'

'Well, Thomas Brakefield produced some document of dubious validity, seeming to prove that his father had rights to the land,' Ursula explained. 'Of course, his magistrate friends upheld his claim, and that was that.'

'It is said that anxiety over the hunting conflict drove the squire's poor wife to an early grave,' Eleanor added.

'An extreme reaction, surely,' I said.

'Not when you take into account the persecution and threats, none of which could directly be attributed to the Brakefields, of course, but who else would have done it? Susannah Simister was a gentle woman, much loved.'

'Threats, you say?' I was astonished to hear it.

'Anonymous letters, the poisoning of the dogs. We probably don't know the half of it,' Ursula said. 'Oh but, Martha, that was years ago. After Susannah Simister died, all that stopped. What remained was the bitterness.'

'But you see now, mama, why people tread warily around the Brakefields.'

'I do indeed. But what then of poor Timothy? Can anything be done?'

Ursula poured out more tea.

'Removing him from here completely would seem the only solution,' she said thoughtfully. 'To find somewhere safe for him to go. We could act in secret so it that appeared that he had run away by himself. They would surely not bother to pursue him... I am sorry to say that there are plenty more poor lads where he came from.'

'The workhouse.'

'Indeed. Or even from among the wretched poor here for the picking.'

Could such a safe place for Timothy be found? Surely it could. I would put my mind to it.

At that moment, three boys, come from school, burst into the room to greet their mother. The adage that children should be seen but not heard clearly did not apply in this household for Davey and Jamesie, who were twins, and their younger brother, Oliver, proved to be full of boundless high spirits, and bounced around us, treating us to the activities of the day.

'Miss Clements says I'm the bestest at reading,' boasted Oliver.

'The best, you silly, not the bestest,' and the twins roared with laughter. At which point, Oliver, poked one of his brothers in the belly – I am not sure which for they were very alike – so that he doubled up in pain while his twin proceeded to attack the perpetrator.

'Out!' their mother ordered. 'Out and fight or play in the garden. You can each take a biscuit with you.'

Instantly recovered, and friends again, they disappeared as quickly as they had come – disposing of the biscuits in the customary manner even before reaching the door – and soon we saw them tearing among the flower beds, which, I am sorry to say, did not benefit in any particular from the incursions.

'There's a school in the village then?' I asked.

'Yes, indeed. Until the boys are old enough to go to big school in Kenwardham. Those few that don't start working at eleven or twelve, that is.'

'Haven't you seen it, mama?' Eleanor said. 'It's in that brick building just up the hill from the Post Office.'

'I haven't ventured that far yet,' I replied carefully, the truth being that I avoided that part of the village, for fear of running into Henrietta.

'The teachers there are two sisters,' Ursula explained. 'Miss Jane Clements, and her sister, Miss Phyllis, who's an absolute darling. She's Oliver's teacher and also our very accomplished organist. Miss Jane takes the older children, and I'm glad to say is stricter with them.' She sighed and gazed out the window at her wild sons. 'They need the discipline.'

I picked up the rag doll.

'So who owns this?' I asked. 'Surely not one of the boys.'

'That's Emily's,' Ursula replied. 'Nurse took her out in her perambulator to keep her from disturbing us while we had our chat.'

'That's a shame,' I said. 'I do so love babies.'

'Do you have grandchildren then?' Ursula glanced across at Eleanor, knowing her to be childless.

'Yes. My daughter, Judith, in Edinburgh has three. Sadly, I get to see them only very rarely.'[2]

As for Eleanor, although her mother-in-law frequently bewailed the fact that so far there were no offspring of the marriage, it was a subject I myself avoided. I suspected that my daughter was longing for a baby of her own, in which case it would only add to her pain if

---

[2] See the story 'Mrs Hudson goes to Edinburgh' in *Mrs Hudson Investigates*, MX publishing, 2019

I raised the matter. It seems to me that too often there are those, like my maid Phoebe's mother, who, though ill able to afford them, can't stop having children, while others who are childless look on with envy. Just now, Eleanor said nothing.

Ursula was far too discerning to pursue the matter, and, after more inconsequential pleasantries, we were ready to take our leave.

'Oliver will be sorry to have missed you,' Ursula said, which confused me for a moment, until I realised that she was referring to her husband. 'You must come again. It has been such a pleasure.' She took my hand. 'And we'll discuss further the matter of young Timothy.'

Ursula's advice to remove him from Bilbourne preyed on my mind, until I thought to contact Mary Goodhart, mother of my godson, Martin, and a young woman I had once been privileged to help in her time of trouble, now happily married to a clergyman in the county of Hampshire.[3] I was sure that Mary and Felix would be able to find a situation for the lad, far enough away to be safe. I duly wrote to her straightway on the subject. And, as I anticipated, hardly had my letter reached Mary than her warm reply came back to say that certainly there was something suitable in Foxbridge for young Timothy. A local farmer, a man whose sound character she could vouch for, was looking for a willing lad to help out around the place. Timothy would be furnished with a room of his own and good nourishing food.

'Your poor little starveling will soon be strong and stout,' she added. I was deeply moved at her words and kindness.

All that remained was for me to impart the good news to Timothy himself, trusting that he would accede gratefully to the plan. In the meantime, to my considerable surprise, I received an invitation, nay one might well call it a summons, to call on Lydia Brakefield. What

---

[3] See the story 'Mrs Hudson and the Gentleman in the Next Room' in *Mrs Hudson Investigates*.

was that about? She assuredly could not have heard of our machinations regarding her young labourer, since I had told no one, not even George, and I was sure the same was true of Eleanor and Ursula. A carriage, the note said, was to be sent for me on the following morning. For me and me alone, the invitation not being extended to Eleanor, who laughed at the omission, and said that she should not have wanted to go anyway. For myself, I had no great inclination either, but hoped I might have occasion at least to meet with Timothy. It seemed unlikely, however: the hop harvest being in full swing, he was sure to be busy working in the plantation.

Eleanor wondered, too, at the reason for the invitation.

'Maybe Mrs. Brakefield, too, is a fan of your Mr. H,' she said. 'Extraordinary as that would be.'

'Oh dear, I hope not.' Yet what else distinguished me from the other females in the vicinity? I should just have to wait and see.

Meanwhile, the afternoon being fine and I feeling stronger, I decided to take a walk further out of the village than I had yet ventured. There were several tempting little lanes that called to me, and Eleanor was able to recommend a circular route that would not be too taxing.

'I am afraid I am not free to accompany you today, mama,' she said. 'Joe is away with deliveries, and, with George stocktaking, I have to serve in the shop.'

'That is no problem at all.' Indeed, I was happy to have some time to myself. The rooms above were small enough, so we were rather living on top of one another. Moreover, although Eleanor would be a charming and easy companion, I always find silence and solitude more conducive to the full appreciation of nature.

'Don't get lost,' she called out, as I departed.

I laughed. That was hardly likely to happen.

The lane she had advised me to take was bordered on both sides with blackberry bushes, the fruit now ripe enough to eat. Indeed, I was sorry I had not brought with me a receptacle in which to collect them, since I am most partial to a blackberry and apple tart, and would have been pleased to make one. Still, I mused, I can return another day, and meantime enjoyed plucking the berries to eat there and then, the sweet juices soon staining my fingers purple. At least I had removed my gloves, which otherwise would have been spoilt.

Occasionally the bushes thinned out, and then I had a view over fields golden with corn stubble – the harvest now mostly being in – or towards orchards where branches drooped under the weight of apples, pears and plums. The sun shone warm without being oppressive, and all in all I was delighted with myself, and even grateful for the slight indisposition, that had caused me to remove from the stifling air of city to this country idyll at such a fruitful time of year.

So absorbed was I in my musings, not that they were of any particular moment – I was thinking of Timothy and how happy he would be in the new surroundings I had planned for him, of Clara, wondering if she was managing to satisfy the demands of Mr. H (Dr. Watson would assuredly be content under any circumstances), how lovely it would be if Eleanor had a family (I had seen the longing way she had looked at Ursula's boys), how tedious it was for her to have Henrietta as a mother-in-law and yet how patiently she dealt with her – when it suddenly occurred to me that it was a long road that had no turning. I started to wonder if I had missed the lane that led back to the village. Surely not. Perhaps Eleanor's notion of a short walk in the country was different from mine. I proceeded for another while and then, indeed, came to a turn. It was to the right, however, when I was sure Eleanor had said 'to the left', but it seemed to swing back the way I had come so, as I thought, it must be the one to take.

Again I found myself walking between high hedges, this time of honeysuckle, the fragrant and delicate blooms turning now to red berries. Holly and ivy flourished there too, and brambles and ferns. So thick were the hedges, indeed, that little space was left for the passage of a carriage, and I soon observed grass growing along the centre of the lane. A sharp bend led me under trees on either side, arching over to form a tunnel, which now, as the leaves were starting to turn colour and fall, was carpeted in red and gold. Very beautiful, admittedly, but engendering in me at last a certainty that I had indeed gone astray. I would see what was round the next corner, before deciding what to do.

Suddenly, I was in the open, rough ground on either side of me and in the distance in one direction I could espy the distinctive crooked spires of the oast houses and on the other, a straight spire rising from a tower which I recognised to be that of the village church of St John the Baptist. It seemed very far away.

A wave of fatigue swept over me. I could hardly face the walk back for I knew now that I had indeed missed the correct turn and would have to retrace my steps, an undertaking I felt almost beyond me. Perhaps it would be quicker over the fields. At least I could keep my object in front of me and not get lost again.

I had resolved to do as much, and was making my way towards a gap in the hedge that led into the rough terrain, when a voice behind me said, 'I wouldn't go that way, if you value your life.'

I turned in shock and beheld none other than young Freddie Simister, purple jacket and all, mounted on his white horse, an amused expression on his face. His approach must have been muffled by the grass on the lane, for I had heard nothing.

'You aren't from around here, madam' he said, 'or you would know not to venture into the wetlands.'

'The wetlands?'

'It's all bog there. Ditches concealed by long grasses. Most treacherous, you know. Once you get in, it's the devil to get out. You could disappear in there, and never be found. Quite swallowed up.'

I must have looked utterly dismayed, for, in kinder tones, he asked, 'You wish to return to Bilbourne?'

I nodded. 'I got lost,' I said. 'I thought I would take a short cut.'

'Well, lucky for you, then, that I came along,' he said.

'Yes, indeed. Thank you for the advice.' I turned to go back the way I had come.

'It's a good hour's walk and you look quite fagged out, madam,' he called after me. 'Would you consider sitting up on Pegasus, here and I can then lead you back? He's a gentle enough beast, and despite his name not inclined to fly at all.'

I understood the mythical reference, but shook my head. I have never sat on a horse in my life, and felt most disinclined to do so at that moment.

'Thank you, but I will manage,' I said. 'I'll take my time.'

'No question of it, madam. I should feel responsible if you collapsed on the way.' He paused. 'Let you come with me to our place. It's just a few minutes down the road. You can take some refreshment there, and then we'll send you back in the pony and trap.'

It was a tempting offer for I felt I could not take another step.

'That is extremely kind of you,' I replied. 'I hardly like to impose myself.'

He laughed. He was a most attractive young man, despite his dandified dress. Gleaming black hair, rather longer than customary, framed the olive complexion of his countenance, and I particularly liked his dancing dark eyes. If I didn't know who he was, I might have taken him for an Italian or similar from the Mediterranean countries.

'Come along,' he said, jumping down from the saddle. 'If you won't sit up on Pegasus, then I will walk with you.'

He insisted on supporting me on one side, while loosely holding the reins with his other hand. In that way, we proceeded along the road, he trying to distract me with various observations I am afraid I barely took in. I was very annoyed with myself for my uncustomary weakness.

It was thankfully true, as he claimed, not far to the manor house, which proved to be a fine solid building dating, I supposed, from the Jacobean era, red bricks glowing under gabled roofs. Big and old, as Henrietta had informed me. Nevertheless, from the gate to the house was a goodly stretch, and almost more than I could manage, so that I was grateful for the young man's strong arm under my elbow. As we approached, Freddie gave a loud whistle that made me jump.

'My apologies for startling you, madam,' he said ruefully. 'A signal to the groom, you know.'

On cue, a young boy emerged from the side of the house where I supposed the stables to be situated. He took the horse and led it off, not before Freddie had slapped it on its hind quarters in a good-fellow-well-met kind of a way.

On entering the house, I found myself in a hallway full of mahogany, a hall stand, a chest, some upright chairs, all set on polished parquet flooring, a beamed ceiling over all. A fine wide staircase led to the upper floors. What struck me more and quite forcibly, however, was the strong though not disagreeable smell of... what? Leather? Tobacco? A very masculine smell anyway.

'Halloo, father,' Freddie called out, 'I've brought you a lady I found wandering lost in the lanes.'

'By God!' a loud, deep voice roared out. 'It better not be that tr...'

The large tweed-clad figure of the squire burst from a side room, holding a pipe and looking, I have to say, almost apoplectic, even ready for a fight, his thick fair hair rising in a great wave above his head. However, on seeing me, he softened instantly, his crest of hair even seeming to subside, the high colour fading from his face, and his lips curling in a smile, under that bushy moustache.

'Madam,' he said. 'What a delight. I do believe I had the pleasure of seeing you at church the other day.' He inclined his head.

'Never mind all that,' Freddie cut in. 'Poor Mrs. Hudson is near fainting away... Come and sit yourself down,' he went on, leading me into the room from which his father had emerged.

At first, I was too overcome to take in what I saw. A small library, was all I registered. I sank into the armchair indicated to me, and, with a trembling hand, took the glass of I knew not what that was offered, drinking a large draught of it. Sweet and powerful it was. A little too powerful. I coughed.

'Good Mariani wine, that is,' the Squire remarked, looming over me. 'It will soon set you on your feet again, Mrs... er...'

'Hudson,' said Freddie.

'Precisely.'

'Mariani wine?' I asked.

'Restores health, strength, vitality and... what else Freddie?'

'No idea.'

The Squire looked at the label on the bottle. 'Energy! That's the fellow. As drunk by popes, politicians, actors and inventors. Also by squires in darkest Kent. Am I not a walking advertisement for the stuff, Mrs. Hudson?' He pulled himself up to his full height, which in truth was very high, a fine figure of a man, as they say. 'Am I not full of health, strength, vitality and energy? What? Drink it up, Mrs. Hudson. Drink it up.'

'Thank you, but I should really prefer some plain water.' I had a sudden thirst on me that the sweet beverage could not quench. I was also hoping that Squire Simister, though evidently meaning well, would move a little further off, taking his energy, et cetera, with him.

'Water, Freddie, the lady wants plain water... Whatever the deuce that might be. See to it, will you.'

He addressed me as the young man left the room. 'If I ring for the maid, do you see, it will take forever. Anyway, it gives the young layabout something to do.' He chuckled, and then, seating himself down at the desk, busied himself with cleaning his pipe, in that

34

rather disgusting ritual I had observed Mr. H perform on many occasions.

'I hope you will excuse my somewhat uncouth welcome, when you arrived,' he said. 'By God! I thought the scamp had brought one of his… er… lady friends back with him. Young fellows, you know… Incorrigible!'

He filled his pipe with tobacco from a serviceable ceramic jar – no Persian slipper, for him! – while I took in more of my surroundings. Comfortable and brown, very brown, with wood panelled walls, wooden bookshelves full of leather-bound books, leather upholstered chairs, a heavy brown desk, brown velvet drapes at windows that looked out on a vista of lawn and trees. It was snug and homely. A good place to sit and read.

Freddie soon returned bearing a large tumbler of water. Hardly soon enough for me, however, with the squire staring into my face while puffing on his pipe, reminding me again rather forcefully of Mr. H, the squire's weed smelling nearly as evil.

'Now make sure that's water and not gin he's brought you,' the squire jested, winking at me. 'I wouldn't put any trick past our Frederick.'

'Fear not, Mrs. Hudson. It's good clean water from our well,' Freddie said. 'Never mind father's Mariani wine. This will pick you up.'

Truly, the water was cold and sweet, and I drained the whole glass.

'Hmm,' the squire said, still staring across at me with keen blue eyes under bristling eyebrows. 'So what brings you here then, Mrs. Hudson, heh? The truth now. Out with it.'

'Here to Bilbourne?' I asked. 'My daughter…'

'Not Bilbourne. Here to Blossomfort Manor.'

'Your son brought me here.'

'Is that it? Is that all? You weren't… spying, for example?'

'Spying?' I was utterly confused. 'On what?'

'Father, really!' said Freddie. 'Mrs. Hudson was out for a walk and got lost.'

'You mean to claim you weren't sent here by those Brakefield upstarts to see what I was about?'

'Good heavens!' I started to laugh, the energy indeed returning to me, whether from the sip of Mariani wine or the water I cannot say. 'I don't even know them.'

'Hmm.' He took another puff of his pipe, emitting clouds of smoke. 'So you say.'

'Although I have been invited by Mrs. Brakefield to visit her tomorrow,' I added. 'I cannot think why.'

'Aha!' The squire slapped the desk so hard it made me jump again. 'Aha! I knew it. The vixen wants to enlist you as one of her confederates. Don't go, Mrs. Hudson. Don't venture into the lion's den.'

A vixen in a lion's den was hardly a happy combination, but I was not about to correct the squire on his mixing of metaphors.

'I can assure you, sir, that I am well able to resist any attempt by anyone to enlist me as a spy,' I said. 'It is a mere courtesy invitation, I am sure.'

'Well, well. Hmm.' He looked at me quizzically. 'I should be most interested in hearing what transpires.'

'You mean you want me to spy for *you*!'

The squire leaned back in his chair, roaring with laughter. And when I say 'roaring', I mean it. If there was a lion's den around here, then surely I was well and truly in it. With his thick mane of sun-bleached hair, Squire Simister even bore some resemblance to that large feline.

'I wouldn't dream of asking,' he said. 'Just saying, that's all. Just expressing the view that it would be most interesting to find out what the baggage is up to. No good, I'm sure... But no matter.'

His pipe needing further attention, we sat in silence for a moment or two. Then Freddie stood up.

'I'll get the pony and trap to take Mrs. Hudson home,' he said.

'Oh, not yet, surely,' the Squire objected. 'The lady looks like she could do with some solid refreshments before she leaves. I happen to know there's a good hock of ham in the larder, and some over-ripe cheese. I'll wager a woman like yourself would do justice to the likes of that, Mrs. Hudson. Along with a hunk of fresh white bread and a draught of our own local beer. Don't tell me you aren't tempted.'

I started to shake my head.

'Ah now, be kind to me. It isn't so very often that an old widower like myself has the opportunity to entertain a pretty young woman...' Whoever did he mean? He was surely of a similar age to myself or perhaps just a year or two my senior. Neither of us old, though certainly not young either.

'Ha, you think I am flattering you, Mrs. Hudson. Not at all. Though I admit I have mislaid my spectacles.... Ah, here they are.' He put them on and made as if to study me. 'No, I was right the first time. A pretty young-ish woman.'

'Father, really!' Freddie said again. Then turned to me. 'You would like, I am sure, to go home, Mrs. Hudson.'

'The squire is most kind,' I replied. 'But yes. I should be grateful to return whenever it suits you to take me.'

'In that case,' his father replied, getting up. 'Who am I to detain you? But I trust you will visit us again. In fact, I absolutely insist upon it, madam. I have a fine cook in Mrs. Jefferies, whose steak and kidney pudding is without match.'

Seeing them side by side, I could not but marvel at the contrast between father and son, the one so broad and bluff and golden in the afternoon light, the other so slender, and dark as a raven. I could only imagine that the deceased wife had bequeathed her colouring to her son, for there was nothing in him of his father.

'Farewell, dear lady,' the squire said. 'And remember my warning. Beware the vixen. As for you, young fellow-me-lad.' He hardened his tone. 'Come straight back.'

'I hope my father has not given offence,' Freddie said, after helping me up into the trap. 'He has a great heart, you know.'

'I could tell,' I replied. 'Not at all. You are both most kind.'

'Oh no, Mrs. Hudson,' he said smiling, white teeth flashing. 'I am not kind at all. I only pretend to be.'

There was nothing to be said to that so we travelled on for a while in silence.

By now the sun was low in a lavender sky.

'What beautiful light,' I said. 'There is never anything like this in London.'

'There's a storm brewing.'

'Surely not.'

'Can't you hear it in the trees? The restlessness. We'll certainly have lightning and thunder later tonight.'

I glanced at him. I detected a restlessness in the young man himself.

'And heavy rain,' he went on. 'The harvesters won't like that.'

The road into the village took us past the post office, Henrietta seated on a bench outside, ever watchful of the comings and goings. I was amused to see her mouth drop open as we passed.

'Meddling old gossip,' Freddie said. 'That'll give her salt for her soup.'

'She's my daughter's mother-in-law,' I told him, as I waved back at her, amused to observe his discomfiture. 'Don't worry. She's no great favourite of mine.'

Freddie helped me alight at the shop, brushing aside my thanks, as Eleanor rushed out the door, looking at him in confusion.

'Mama, there you are at last. Are you all right?'

'This gentleman was kind enough to come to my assistance when I got lost,' I told her. 'Mr. Simister, this is my daughter Eleanor Hazelgrove.'

He laughed. 'Mr. Simister! No one calls me that. I'm just Freddie. And quite delighted, Mrs. Hazelgrove, to make your acquaintance, though of course I have seen you out and about the place.' He bowed, giving her an appreciative glance. 'Yes, indeed.' He remounted the trap.

'Eleanor,' he called out as he drove off. 'What a pretty name! I must remember to call in next time I need a bag of sugar'

We watched him leave. Not in the direction of Blossomfort manor, however. Quite the opposite way.

'Good heavens, mama,' Eleanor said, as we entered the shop. She was blushing from the encounter. 'Whatever happened to you?'

'I missed the turn and then came over all feeble,' I said, and explained more of my adventure.

'The wetlands! Oh, goodness, I should have warned you. They are very treacherous. Mr. Simister… Freddie… is right. You could have disappeared into them and no one would have known what had happened to you.' She gave me a kiss on the cheek. 'Thank God he came along. Anyway, mama, you should go and lie down before supper. In fact, why don't I bring it up to you? You are still convalescing, you know.'

I wasn't inclined to agree to that – not being willing to admit my weakness – until I saw Henrietta through the plated glass window approaching the shop hot-foot. I am afraid I ran to hide in the back office.

Of course, she had to ask how I came to be in the company of Freddie Simister.

'You know his reputation, Eleanor. Anything in skirts… I mean, Martha should be told of it or people will talk.'

Eleanor laughed. 'On this occasion, mother-in-law he was simply acting the Good Samaritan.'

Henrietta's eager voice again. 'Is that so? Where is Martha? I must talk to her?'

'She's resting.'

'Yes, but...'

At that point, I tiptoed up the stairs to my room and shut the door. Before lying down, I looked out the window and saw how the wind had picked up. How it was tossing the branches of the trees and tugging the leaves away. How the sky was become the colour of a fresh bruise. Freddie was right, a storm was brewing.

CHAPTER FOUR

I was up early after a reasonably restful night. Freddie's predicted storm had passed over us with a few lightning flashes and cracks of thunder, while the subsequent rain shower had lulled me back to sleep with its patter. By morning, a dazzling sun was streaming through my window and turning the puddles in the street into molten gold. The air smelt newly washed. I breakfasted with George and Eleanor, my son-in-law insisting I try some fresh Whitstable kippers, fetched by Joe from Kenwardham that very morning.

'Fat and juicy, mother-in-law. I'll bet you can't get the like of these in London,' he said.

I agreed they were very tasty, but replied that in Billingsgate market you could buy all sorts of fish almost as fresh as if they came straight out of the sea. 'Which kippers don't, of course,' I added.

George laughed and said, 'Well, well, mother-in-law, I see you won't ever admit the superiority of country living to the city. Nevertheless, I still say you can't get better than these.'

He helped me to another kipper and took one himself, Bella the cat displaying great interest in the proceedings, mewing and winding herself around our feet to remind us of her hungry presence.

'You'll get yours later,' Eleanor informed her. 'When we've finished.'

The cat wasn't consoled by that intelligence, and continued her sorrowful mewing.

'You could take a brace of these over to Lydia Brakefield as a gift from me,' George said. 'A tribute. I'm sure she'd be grateful.'

'George!' warned Eleanor, and he laughed merrily.

'As if that ladyship would bother picking meat off kipper bones,' he said. 'Although, now I come to think of it, she probably has a footman do that for her. Like she has them do certain other things.'

'George, that's enough,' Eleanor said again. 'He's terrible,' she added to me.

'I'm sure Martha is too much a woman of the world to be shocked,' he replied.

'Just because your own mother likes to spread unsavoury rumours, there's no need for you to repeat them here.'

'I'm sorry, my love. Lydia Brakefield is no doubt as chaste as Caesar's wife… Have another kipper, mother-in-law.'

I declined, considering to myself that was another point against country living. People have so little to think about, they start making up stories about their neighbours, or at the very least they embellish the facts to titivate idle imaginations.

'Eleanor,' I said, changing the subject. 'I'd like your advice on what to wear this morning.'

Of course, my good black bombazine would serve, but, the weather being warm, I judged it unsuitable.

Breakfast over, and George, looking a little sheepish after all, descended to the shop, while my daughter put the leftovers on Bella's dish for her to guzzle. Then Eleanor accompanied me to my room and checked through my sparse wardrobe. She agreed regarding the bombazine – 'Far too heavy' – and soon picked out a gown in grey-blue muslin.

I was doubtful. 'Isn't it too plain? Of course, I could wear my cerise silk, but that would surely be too fancy.'

To tell the truth, I had not intended to bring along the fine garment I had purchased in Paris – what use would I have for such high fashion in the countryside? – but Clara, with the foresight of a canny maidservant, had insisted on packing it despite my reservations.

'You never know,' she had said.

Now, Eleanor agreed with me that it would not do for a morning visit.

'The muslin will be just fine,' she said. 'I can lend you a shawl to go with it. Your black straw hat is stylish enough, along with your kid gloves… You know, mama, the woman might consider herself royalty, as mother-in-law says, but she is no such thing. And anyway, she won't be pleased if you outshine *her*.'

The which I considered most unlikely.

Eleanor made no mention of George's other disparaging remarks about Lydia Brakefield, so I didn't refer to them either.

The shawl was lovely, of black silk embroidered with a delicate pattern of red and purple flowers, and I exclaimed at its quality.

'George bought it for me in France, on our honeymoon,' Eleanor said. 'Sad to say, I have little occasion to wear it here. Though maybe for the harvest festival.'

As I already knew, that particular annual celebration was soon to take place, and I had been urged, even if fully recovered, to stay on, it being one of the highlights of the Bilbourne year. I had made no promises, for, of course, I had responsibilities elsewhere to my lodgers, but still, the prospect was a tempting one. I remembered with pleasure such festivals from my childhood, growing up as I did in a village like this one, memories that, seen from a distance of many years, were bathed in a golden light.

Dressed and ready at last, I went down just before the appointed hour to the shop where I sat myself upon a stool, to wait, greeting the various customers or observing out the window. No sign of the carriage. I waited. And waited. How very rude, I thought and, after a good three quarters of an hour had passed, according to my silver fob watch, I was about to go and change back into my comfortable cotton day dress, when a great coach drew up at the shop, a coat of arms not dissimilar to that of the Hazelgroves emblazoned on the side.

'Is that it?' I asked George in amazement.

'So it would seem,' he replied, amused, adding, 'your ladyship.'

'You're rather late,' I said to the coachman, a youth all skin and bones and disfiguring acne, in a green and gold livery far too big for him. He pulled a face as if to say, what matter. I'm here now, aren't I? You should be grateful for that.

It wasn't an auspicious start.

We drove off, I feeling most uncomfortable as every head turned to watch our progress through the village. At least Henrietta was nowhere to be seen this time.

It came as a relief, all the same, to reach open country, evidently Brakefield land, for we were passing a plantation where an army of pickers was at work, plucking the high-growing hops. Many of them there too paused and stared as us as we passed, though without any particular curiosity, while I looked out for Timothy, but of him there was no sign.

Unlike the authentically ancient abode of Squire Simister, the large house belonging to the Brakefields was a modern enough edifice trying to look medieval, of grey stone, with crenellated towers and turrets, arched mullioned windows and grotesque gargoyles. To my mind vulgar and ostentatious.

The boy-coachman handed me down from the vehicle with an insolent expression on his face, mirrored in that of the elderly and unprepossessing footman who opened the big heavy front door with its knocker in the form of a demon head. He could hardly be the inspiration for George's scurrilous innuendos, being a humpy-backed individual, with a face like squashed pumpkin and the bulbous red nose of a heavy drinker. He sniffed disdainfully as I told him my name. I supposed the servants considered me the woman who lived above the shop and thus not worthy of respect. As if I cared about them or their opinions. At least, he let me in.

44

The immediate interior of the house was as much a pastiche as the outside, calling to mind the setting for a novel by Mrs. Radcliffe or Horace Walpole, a suit of armour in the hallway, a cast iron chandelier, gloomy portraits fixing the incomer with unfriendly eyes, a metal bound wooden chest large enough to hold a pirate's treasure or a body but, I was sure, containing nothing more sinister than linen. I was much amused at such a bare-faced attempt to overawe, and wondered what sort of people would live here like this.

However, the footman showed me into a much more attractive room, a rosy parlour, the sun's rays passing through thin blinds to illuminate wallpaper of a delicate pink overlaid with a trellis pattern, pink upholstered chairs, everything most tasteful. And in the midst of all this pink, stretched out on a chaise longue, dressed in white, the porcelain-fine figure of Mrs. Lydia Brakefield. At a distance, and given the virginal nature of her dress, she looked like a young girl, but as I approached I could see that she was older than I had first thought, maybe even nearing forty years of age, although she presented herself well. In fact, a little too well, in what looked to be a studied pose, tresses of auburn hair tossed loose across her shoulders and breast, while she peered at me through those heavy-lidded green eyes. It was most strange, and again I wondered what was behind it.

'Forgive me for not getting up, Mrs. Hudson,' she said at last in low, world-weary tones. 'I am somewhat fatigued today.'

I smiled and nodded and stood looking at her.

'Oh, sit yourself down, do.' That rather impatiently.

I found a seat near her.

She passed the back of a thin pale hand across her forehead, a gesture that suddenly made me wonder if at any time Lydia Brakefield had been an actress, though possibly not a very good one.

'I must apologise, too, for the delay in fetching you here,' she said. 'My husband had to go to Kenwardham on business, you know, and took the pony and trap I was planning to send for you. It was only later I thought to use the coach.'

'That's quite all right. Though I admit I was getting a little anxious at the wait. Wondering what could have happened, you know.'

'Hm. Well, I said I was sorry.' That sharp tone again.

I sat up straighter and pulled the shawl around me. Self-appointed queen of the village she might be, but she would not intimidate me.

She studied my face, while I gazed at her, with a slight smile that was not reflected back.

'Oh, tea,' she said at last. 'Coffee, chocolate.'

She rang a bell, and the crabbed footman, who must have been waiting outside the door, for he entered instantly, actually said, 'You rang, my lady?'

Yes, it was just like being in a play the plot of which, however, I was ignorant.

'We'll take coffee in here, Jobbins.'

She had not asked my preference, and, although coffee was fine by me, I should have liked to be asked.

The footman inclined his head and withdrew.

'I was thinking we might take it in the garden only, you know, I am too fatigued to move.'

'It's a beautiful day,' I remarked, for something to say.

'Is it? Is it? Beautiful? Oh God, they're all beautiful.' She sighed.

'Unless they aren't.'

'Aren't what?'

'Beautiful. Unless it's cold or raining. There was a storm last night.'

'Was there?...Yes, yes, yes. I suppose I was thinking of Italy.'

There was no reply to that.

'It is most gracious of you to invite me here,' I said instead, 'to your most interesting house.'

'Oh, you like it, do you? It was my husband's late father Benjamin – the ugliest of the frights hanging in the hall – who was so enamoured of the Gothic that he added to the rather ordinary little house that was here before. Well, I suppose at least it can't be called ordinary now.'

Somewhat astounded at her slighting reference to her father-in-law, I waited for her to say more, but she simply waved that little white hand in the air and sank back into the chaise longue.

'This room is most attractive,' I said, finally. 'William Morris wallpaper, if I'm not mistaken.'

She looked more animated at that.

'Yes, indeed. I insisted that, if I had to stay living in this pile, on having at least one room of my own to retreat to, without all those ghastly faked medieval gimcracks. I adore the Arts and Craft movement, Mrs. Hudson. The Pre-Raphaelites, you know. I've been begging Mr. Brakefield to get Holman Hunt or one of that lot down here to paint me. Before I turn into an old hag.'

She put a hand up to her throat as if checking to see that it was still swan-like.

'Or let me go up to town to sit. That would be nice. Very nice. I should like that.'

Her heavy-lidded eyes nearly closed. Perhaps she was thinking of the pleasures of sitting still for hours, stared at by an artist, becoming a work of art herself. The pose she affected now made more sense. Though I was no expert, I had seen some of the works of the Brotherhood and judged that, with her russet hair and pale skin, Lydia Brakefield was quite the model for a Pre-Raphaelite muse. It seemed churlish to mention just now that those same artists were fond of pretend medievalism in their own way, as evidenced by their very name. I imagined a too clever remark of the sort wouldn't go down well with my hostess.

At that moment, the coffee arrived, brought in by a dumpy, wall-eyed maid. I couldn't help wondering, uncharitably, if Lydia

Brakefield surrounded herself with the ugliest people she could find in order to set herself off to even greater advantage, the way princes of old employed dwarves to make themselves look bigger and more powerful.

The coffee, served in thimble-sized china cups along with tiny macaroons, seemed to energise her somewhat (perhaps, even better, she should have imbibed some Mariani wine), and she actually sat up.

'You are no doubt wondering why you are here, Mrs. Hudson,' she said.

'Well...'

'You see, we have an acquaintance in common.'

I waited. I could not imagine whom it was she meant.

'Beatrice Trueblood,' she said at last. 'I met her last year in Deauville.'

'Beatrice!' I smiled broadly at the name. 'How wonderful. How is she?'

'Very well indeed.'

'No husband yet, then?'

'Oh, no. Beatrice values her independence too much.'

'Yes, I remember.'

I had been instrumental in extracting the young lady from a near-fatal situation. Indeed, she was the very first person ever to call for my assistance in such a case (Mr. H being otherwise engaged at the time), and for that reason I think of her with particular warmth.[4]

'I cannot remember now,' the languid lady before me remarked, 'how your name came up in conversation, but I recall how grateful she was for your intervention with regard to a certain unpleasantness... Ah,' she stirred her coffee with a pretty little silver spoon. 'Yes indeed. I think we were strolling together through a

---

[4] See the story 'Mrs Hudson and the Smiling Man', in *Mrs Hudson Investigates*.

street market where some blackamoor or other was selling ghastly masks, and she said they reminded her of you.'

'Indeed?' I was amused. 'Hardly flattering.'

'Oh no. Not, of course, that they looked like you. Of course not,' Mrs. Brakefield laughed just a little unpleasantly. 'No, as I understand, there was such a mask in her history.'

'That is so.'

I did not add that Beatrice had presented it to me subsequently, and that the horrid thing now resided in the attic, along with other unwanted objects.

'You see, Mrs. Hudson,' Mrs. Brakefield leaned forward confidingly. 'I am hoping you can help me, too.'

Ah, so that was it at last. I tried not to sigh. I had come down here for a complete rest and yet it seemed that was not to be.

'Help you in what way?' I asked.

'I have received a somewhat disturbing anonymous letter. I can show you.'

She reached under a cushion and pulled out an envelope, the which she passed to me.

I took out the letter and read as follows: 'You should take care of your daughter, Madam, even if she isn't of your blood. She has been consorting with unsuitable men.' It was signed, 'A friend.'

I looked up, puzzled.

'I don't understand,' I said. 'Whatever do you want me to do?'

'To find out if it is true, of course,' Lydia Brakefield said with some passion. 'And who this man is. Or men. So I can put a stop to it before her father finds out. It would send him into a fury and he would blame me.' Her eyes grew wider, as if anticipating her husband's rage

'Can you not just ask the girl?'

'Ha! Eve! She wouldn't tell me anything.'

Clearly their relationship was not a close one.

'Secretive little chit,' she added.

'So who is this 'friend'? Can you guess?'

'I have no idea. I have no friends here.'

No true friend would write anonymously anyway. She would sit you down with a cup of tea, and express her concerns to your face.

'Do you know who the man is?' I asked.

'Of course not. If so, I could deal with it at once myself.'

'But you might suspect someone.'

She looked at me, her sharp green eyes like glass from a broken bottle.

'Yes, I might suspect. Anyone in trousers for a start.'

That was harsh.

'Well,' I said, replacing my coffee cup on its saucer, 'I cannot see that I can help you, Mrs. Brakefield. I should not know where to start.'

'Ah, you underestimate your powers, Mrs. Hudson.' Suddenly the woman was all apparent charm. 'Dear Beatrice told me of your insights and your ability to create trust. Talk to Eve. Make a friend of her. Get her to confide in you.'

To act as a spy for her stepmother! How horrible! I could not help but recall the Squire's warning.

'I am sorry,' I said, standing up. 'It is quite impossible.' Her regard was anything but friendly, so I decided on an excuse, to temper my refusal. 'I am here to recover from an indisposition, you understand. I have been prescribed rest.'

'In that case,' she replied coldly, 'I am sorry to have disturbed you. I'll ring Jobbins to get the coach brought round.' She reached for the bell.

'Actually, Mrs. Brakefield,' I said, anxious at least to take some advantage from the situation, my thoughts turning to Timothy. 'I should be most interested in taking a turn around your hop plantation. I've never had occasion to visit one before.'

'Oh... But surely you are far too indisposed for that.'

'Fresh air is good.' I bit my lip. 'Perhaps… Eve could accompany me.'

Lydia Brakefield smiled then. 'Ah, how very discreet you are. I understand completely now,' she said. No, you don't, I thought. 'Yes indeed. What a very good idea. Please sit yourself down for a moment. I'll get Jobbins to call the child.' She reached for the bell.

It was some time before Eve could be found. In the meantime, the boy, Randall, joined us with his nurse. He was more angelic-looking than ever, all dimples and curls and the apple of his mother's eye, but very soon it became plain that he was a brat.

'Who's that woman?' he said, regarding me with dislike.

'This is Mrs. Hudson. Say hello, Randall.'

Instead, he stuck out his tongue, took a sugar lump, sucked it for a bit then took it out and replaced it in the bowl.

His mother laughed and when the nurse remonstrated with him, she interposed. 'Oh, Doris,' she said, 'for goodness sake. He is only a child. Come to mama, my pet.'

With a triumphant sneer on his face, Randall snuggled up to his mother. Now, although I don't believe in the regular beating of children to discipline them, if I had the minding of young Randall, he'd be given an occasional sharp rap on the bare leg with a wooden spoon for his rudeness, and be all the better for it. But that was not Mrs. Brakefield's way, and I doubted that Doris would dare to chastise the child as he deserved. Well, it was none of my business and yet I pitied the boy. An indulged child makes for a dissolute adult.

At that moment, Eve came in, a thick notebook in her hand. For some reason, shyness I suppose, she blushed crimson at the sight of a stranger.

'You called for me, Lydia,' she said. Not 'mother' or 'mama' then.

'Yes. Mrs. Hudson here would like to have a look around the plantation. I am far too fatigued to take her, so you might as well do it?'

The girl looked at me, and I smiled reassuringly. 'If it's not too much trouble, 'I said, looking at her notebook. 'I see that you are busy.'

Mrs. Brakefield burst out laughing. 'Eve busy! She's never busy. She has nothing to do except sit around and scribble God knows what all day long.'

'Of course, I'll take you,' Eva said in soft tones.

'Me too.' Randall jumped up. 'I want to go.'

'No, dear,' Mrs. Brakefield replied, no doubt thinking that the presence of the child would discourage confidences. 'You'll stay with mama.'

This would not do. Instantly, the child had a temper tantrum, stamping the floor and screaming, 'I want to go. I want to go.'

'No, Randall.'

'No' must have been a word the child seldom heard, for he only redoubled his fury.

'Why can't I? Why? You never let me do anything. I hate you.' He started pummelling his mother.

'For heaven's sake, Doris,' Mrs. Brakefield said, pushing him away with some force. 'Can't you control the boy? My God. What do we employ you for?' She smoothed her robe, while, without a word the nurse picked up her charge and carried him, still kicking and screaming from the room.

'Takes after his father,' she said, smiling again. 'Too much spirit altogether. Still, one wouldn't wish a child to be too quiet, would one?' Looking meaningfully at Eve as she spoke.

For myself, thinking of the stern and silent figure I had observed on Sunday in the church, I could trace no such spirit at all in Thomas Brakefield. However, various people had told me of his temper, and looks can, as I know well, be deceiving. The way one conducts oneself in the house of God may bear no resemblance to one's actions without.

CHAPTER FIVE

'Shall we take the coach?' Eve asked as we left the house.

That mighty contraption was still standing outside, although its unprepossessing driver was nowhere to be seen.

'I should prefer to walk,' I replied. 'If it's not too far.'

'This way then,' she said, turning from the gate. 'It's quicker through the orchard.'

I feared the young girl would resent having to act as chaperone, but she seemed content and even eager to accompany me. Not that she was talkative. At first, she answered my questions in monosyllables, looking down rather than at me. However, she soon relaxed, realising I intended only friendliness. I certainly had no intention of quizzing her in the way her stepmother wanted.

Whoever planned the gardens here had it in mind to reflect the Gothic character of the house. Once we left the open lawn and plunged into woodland, statues of mythical beasts and demons peered at us from dark shrubberies as if about to pounce. Between twisted trees, a stream struggled its way over rocks, finally tumbling down a small waterfall into a murky pool. I confess it gave me quite a turn to see the head of a crocodile emerging from the water even though I soon realised the thing was made of stone. Still, it was disconcerting, especially since its baleful green eyes rather called to mind those of the lady of the house.

'Horrid, isn't it,' my companion remarked. 'I am quite afraid to come here alone, even though I know it's all made up.'

'Made up?'

'It's not real. None of it. Not even the waterfall. My grandfather had it patterned after some book he'd read.'

'"The Castle of Otranto," perhaps? "The Mysteries of Udolpho"?'

Eve shrugged. 'I don't know. I don't read that sort of book.'

I mused again at the doings of those with more money than sense. Surely Mr. Brakefield senior could have spent his wealth on something more useful than idle fancies, on improving the conditions of his labourers, for instance.

From the waterfall, we soon came to an ivy-clad tower that Eve told me had been constructed ready ruined, and, passing by some tombstones, arrived eventually at a grotto.

'That's the hermit's cave,' Eve said.

It was covered in shells and set into the side of a small mound. I peered into its gloomy interior.

'So where is the hermit?' I asked, my tongue in my cheek.

Her reply was unexpected.

'Oh, they pay a man to live there when we have visitors to stay,' she said. 'He's terribly thin, with long hair and a beard, and dressed in a ragged robe, to look the part. Lydia likes to tell everyone he's there all the time, but he isn't.'

'I see.'

'It's wrong to lie, isn't it?' She had stopped smiling.

'Well, I suppose it's more of a joke. I don't suppose your visitors really believe it.'

'Hm… Well, I don't like him. He's certainly no man of God. I don't come here at all when he's around.'

'Does he frighten you then?'

She paused, scuffing the ground with the toe of her shoe.

'Not really. Well, once he said that I was a very pretty girl.'

'Which you are, my dear.'

She shook her head. 'I know I'm plain. Not like... Anyway, I didn't like him saying that to me. Coming up really close, and touching my face.'

'Not exactly what one expects from a hermit.' I smiled at her, despite my misgivings. 'And believe me, you aren't plain at all, Eve. You have a lovely face.'

She just shook her head again.

I imagined that her stepmother was behind the girl's poor opinion of herself. The father too, perhaps.

By now, we had reached a gateway set into a high stone wall. This led, as Eve told me, into the orchard, an altogether pleasanter place. The boughs of the trees were drooping with russet apples ripe enough to pick, windfalls lying on the grass, beset by bees and wasps, the humming providing a soft accompaniment to the stirrings of the leaves above them.

'Apples and damsons,' Eve said in response to my query, adding, 'I like to come here, especially in spring, when the blossom is out.'

'To write in your journal?'

She shrank a little. Had I overstepped the mark?

'Sometimes,' adding tentatively, 'and sometimes I write poems. Not very good ones. though.'

'Don't say that, Eve. I'd love to read them some time, if you'd let me.' Again, she looked wary, so I didn't press the point. 'I can well imagine being inspired here,' I went on, looking around. 'It's a lovely place. So peaceful.'

'Yes... mostly.'

'Not always?'

'Well just now, with the pickers about, some of them climb in and rob the fruit. Papa gets furious. He has a man on the look-out, but sometimes he comes in here himself, with a shotgun.'

'Dear me.' So here was the hitherto unseen side of the man. 'Perhaps,' I added, 'the pickers are hungry.'

'I suppose so...'

By now we had traversed the orchard and were faced with another high wall, another gate. However, to my eyes the rough cast of the wall looked to be easy enough for fit young lads to scale. And why begrudge them a few apples, when there was such plenty? Nevertheless, I kept that notion to myself.

Eve unlocked the gate, making sure to lock it fast again behind us.

'Papa would kill me if I left it open,' she said with a little smile.

From where we were now standing, a path led for some several hundred yards beside a field where horses were grazing, towards the distinctive forest of hop plants that comprised the plantation. I could see many people engaged in the harvest. Of young Timothy, however, there was still no sign.

As we drew nearer, the air became thick with a heavy though not entirely unpleasant smell, rather like that of a pine forest. Noticing our approach, a man in a cap stepped forward to meet us, a good-looking muscular fellow, his skin browned from the sun. He had a collection of sticks on a string slung across his chest.

'Miss Eve,' he said, nodding at my companion.

She blushed deeply and looked down.

He eyed me with curiosity.

'Mrs. Hudson,' she said, 'this is Stephen, our overseer and head tallyman.'

'You'll have to explain that to me,' I replied. 'In fact, you'll have to explain everything. I know nothing about hop-picking, Stephen. I'm here to learn.'

He grinned, revealing strong white teeth. How attractive he was. Could he be the unsuitable young man that Mrs. Brakefield feared had won the heart of her step-daughter? Eve stood awkwardly, still staring fixedly at the ground. As for Stephen, he was happy to lead us through the plantation, rather as if he owned the place, explaining as we went how the hop bines were trained to grow up strings stretched taut between poles set in the ground.

'Some say chestnut be the best for training but hops here seems to like the alder more.'

He pointed out how the men were pulling down the bines with long, vicious-looking forked hoes, so that the hops could be stripped off and gathered into baskets. This seemed to be work for women and children. I commented on the fact.

'Yes,' Stephen said. 'Whole families come down for the harvest.'

'Where from?'

'London… East End, mostly. There be locals, too, and gypsies, wandering from place to place, wherever there's work. Gypsies be very quick at filling the baskets. Quick at complaining, too, and trying to cheat.' He spat on the ground. 'They don't get nought past me.'

The stripping work didn't look to be too hard, and I said so.

'Here, have a go,' he said, pulling a fallen bine towards me.

'No.' Eve tried to protest.

'I should like to try it,' I said.

I removed my gloves, not to spoil them, and started to strip the cone-like fruit the way the others were doing.

'Ow!' A sharp spine on the stem had punctured my hand.

Stephen grinned.

'Not so easy, now, is it?'

I looked him in the eye. There was a challenge in his brown ones, even a glint of cruelty.

'You shouldn't have,' said Eve. Was she speaking to him or to me?

One of the women workers was looking at me with pity.

'Yes, love,' she said. 'Them prickles do be right nasty till your 'ands grow 'ardened to 'em.'

She showed me her own hands, blackened with juices.

'I'll survive, I think,' I replied, smiling back at her, padding at the blood with my clean handkerchief.

Meanwhile the woman continued to work at speed, stripping the hops and tossing them into a large basket. Beside her, a child, too small to reach the top of the basket and wearing a bonnet too big for her, was filling an open umbrella with the round green cones.

'That's right, Sarey, good girl,' the woman said, emptying the contents of the umbrella into the basket. 'We be near done with this one, as long as 'e don't squash 'em down.' She looked across at Stephen with dislike.

'Now then Nance,' he replied. 'As if I'd do such a thing to you. Ain't I your friend?'

'Hah.' She continued with the stripping, quickly and skilfully.

'So you fill the basket and then what?' I asked.

'That there's a five bushel basket,' Stephen said. 'Once it's full – and it's not quite yet, Nancy, no matter how you try and plump it up – I mark a notch on her tally stick and then she gets paid according to how many bushels she collects in a day.'

''Tis precious little I get paid, after all.'

He smiled an alligator smile at her. 'No one forces you to come here and work, my love,' he said. 'You can always stay in your East End slum if you object to the conditions here.'

'Fresh air's good for the kiddies,' she replied.

'How much do you get paid, Nancy?' I asked.

'Eight pennies for a full basket. If I'm lucky.'

'That's very little.'

'It's the regular rate,' Stephen said. 'They can take it or leave it.'

'It's still very little for so much work.'

'Who are you?' he asked, suddenly hostile. 'One of them do-gooder type, I'll wager. Poking your ignorant nose in. Trying to tell us how to do things.'

'Stephen!' Eve said. 'Mrs. Hudson is our guest.'

He looked sullen. 'They gets their shelter and food for nothing. They've no cause to grumble.'

Nancy laughed. 'That's right. Real luxury old Brakefield provides. A leaky shed with damp straw to sleep on, and a feast of 'ard bread and soup from scrapings you wouldn't feed to a pig.'

No doubt hearing raised voices, a man carrying one of those forked hoes arrived on the scene.

'Now, now, Nance,' he said in appeasing tones. 'Master Stephen does his best for us. There's many a farm where we'd be worse off than 'ere.'

He patted little Sarey on the head, and she smiled up at him.

'That's right, Nancy,' Stephen said. 'Listen to your old man.' He looked across at me. 'Bad times it be, Daniel, when womenfolk starts to raise their voices.' Then, as if to prove how decent was he, he added. 'That basket's full enough, Nance. Give your tally stick over here.'

He carved a notch into it, Nancy looking at me meanwhile with a grin on her worn face.

'What happens to the hops now?' I asked, also anxious to diffuse the bad atmosphere.

'They gets loaded on the ox carts and taken for drying,' Stephen said. 'If you want to see that, you'll have to go by yourselves. I'm busy here.' He moved off.

Oh dear. I had quite definitely rubbed him up the wrong way.

'Thank you, Stephen,' Eve called after him.

'My pleasure, girlie,' he replied, turning back with a wink. 'Always.'

Really, I thought, looking after him as he swaggered off, swinging his talley sticks, the man has no respect.

'Afore you go, m'm,' Nancy said, 'you should 'ave your shoes rubbed with 'ops for good luck.'

'Is that so?' I asked. 'What a charming custom.'

'Then she'll expect you to give a donation for the feast,' Eve put in. Her tone had an edge to it.

'A feast?'

'At the end of hop harvest. It's a tradition.'

'The only thing worth waiting for,' Nancy added.

'Oh, I see!' I reached for my reticule.

'No, that's all right, m'm,' Nancy said, with a glance at Eve. 'No need.'

'But I should like to,' I replied, pulling out a coin. 'How much should I give?' I asked the girl. 'Is a half-crown enough?'

'Far too much.'

I gave it all the same, despite Eve's disapproval, and lifted my skirts a little to uncover my shoes, so that Little Sarey could do the necessary. She giggled as she rubbed hops on my shoes.

'I hope that's plenty of good luck.'

'You may be sure of that,' the woman said. 'Several bushel's worth.'

'And this is for you, Sarey.' I pressed a silver sixpence into the child's hand.

'Well now, thank the kind lady,' Nancy said, nodding at me, but Sarey was overcome with shyness, and just looked up at me with big eyes. 'Now you must share that with Charlie... That's her brother, m'm.'

Sarey clutched the coin tightly.

'You shouldn't have,' muttered Eve as we moved off. 'It only encourages their sort to beg.'

Rather surprised at Eve's attitude, I was thinking that I should, in fact, have liked to give more to this needy little family.

'See what I mean,' the girl went on, as other pickers were drawing near, attracted perhaps by the chink of coins. 'Now they all want some.'

Of course, I know well that, as the Lord said, the poor are always with us, and that it is impossible to provide for everyone. Nevertheless, I resolved, if possible, to assist Nancy and her family at another time.

Leaving Daniel cutting down the bines with the sharp blade of his hoe, and Nancy and Sarey starting on a new basket, we made our way onwards, until we came to a clearing where several oxen were waiting patiently for their loads. Already the carts were piled with bulging sacks, ready to be taken to the nearby oast houses. I have to say it was a relief to move away from the plantation with its pungent scent that had started to make me feel dizzy. I hoped that I was not overexerting myself. It would not do to succumb to weakness again. However, since I was determined to visit these most unusual and pleasing looking edifices, I decided to soldier on.

Eve, who had been silent for a while, suddenly said, 'I should not have spoken to you like that, Mrs. Hudson,' she said, 'but, you see, I know what these people are like. I notice it all the time. You saw how that woman complained to Stephen.'

'No need to apologise, my dear,' I replied, although I thought her wrong. Nancy did not strike me as anything but an honest hard-working person, who only wanted to be paid a fitting wage. Still, I was Eve's guest, and did not wish to argue.

'How is your hand?' she went on.

It was stinging, and, although the bleeding had stopped, I was loth to replace my gloves in case they got stained.

'It's nothing,' I said. 'I will be fine.'

'You should clean and bandage the wound properly when you get back...' She looked at me timidly. 'Stephen isn't a bad man, you know.'

'You like him?'

'Well... yes, I suppose.' She was blushing again.

'He is somewhat outspoken.'

'Yes.'

'But very handsome.'

She said nothing for a moment, then surprised me again.

'There's Timmy!' she exclaimed, genuine pleasure in her voice.

I was also pleased, and indeed relieved, to see the familiar ungainly form of the youth I had been seeking for so long, employed in loading the ox cart, hefting sacks almost as big as himself.

'You know Timothy, then?' I asked the girl.

'Yes... Do you?' Now it was her turn to be surprised.

'I have spoken to him a few times in the village.'

'Oh... the village... Bilbourne, you mean.'

'Yes. My son-in-law has a shop there.'

'We shop in Kenwardham,' she said. 'Or Rochester, of course.'

I suddenly remembered how Henrietta had complained that the Brakefields turned their noses up at the local establishments.

'You'd think,' she had said, 'that with the Hazelgroves' noble antecedents we'd be grand enough for them, but no such thing. If only George placed our coat-of-arms over his shop...'

Clearly it was a very sore point with her.

Meanwhile, just now, the youth, responding to the girl's beckoning hand was trudging over to meet us.

'Hello, Timothy?' I said. 'I have been missing our chats by the duck pond.'

He shuffled his feet and looked under his lashes at Eve.

'Bin busy,' he said.

'Yes, I suppose the harvest takes up all your time and energy.'

'How are you, Timmy?' Eve asked.

He grinned at her. Oh, those green teeth!

'Have you robbed any more apples?' she went on.

He shook his head, 'Oh no, miss. Not no more.'

'You can if you like, you know. I don't mind *you* taking them. Although...' she hesitated, 'make sure Papa isn't around.'

I assumed that was how they met, Eve taking refuge in the orchard with her journal and the boy climbing the wall for scrumping purposes. I was amused to see that she had become veritably animated, while he stared at her with adoration in his eyes.

'I'd come when you're there, Miss,' he said. 'But 'ow'd I know?'

She frowned, puzzled.

'Perhaps you could leave a token somewhere,' I suggested. Maybe it was wrong of me, but I pitied the lonely pair. If Eve had made a friend of the poor lad, I was not about to discourage it.

'Of course,' she replied. 'A ribbon. I'll tie a ribbon on the gate…' She paused. 'I'll even leave the gate open for you, Timmy. How about that?'

'Tim! Tim!' a man roared across. 'Come back 'ere. Wagon's ready to roll.'

'Better go,' he said.

'That's our way, too,' Eve remarked. 'To see the workings… Perhaps Mrs. Hudson here can ride, while I walk alongside you.'

'Oh, Miss!'

Thus it was that I was raised up on to the cart to perch beside the hop sacks with only a little loss of dignity and a worry that my good muslin might get stained. However, my fears were offset by relief at being able to take the weight from my feet, the two young people chatting and smiling to each other, as Timothy led the placid beast along the dusty tracks towards the oast houses.

CHAPTER SIX

I have already mentioned how attractive I found these brick-built constructions, their conical roofs topped with tilted chimneys, like witches' hats.

On our arrival, Timothy helped me down from the wagon, and then immediately started loading the full sacks on to some sort of a mechanical hoist. This raised them on to a platform, or gantry, as Eve told me it was called, from which they could be carried inside. The boy had to be stronger than he looked, for, as I have said, they were bulky enough.

Leaving him working, we went within, to a long room with a narrow staircase leading to the upper floor. Huge bulging sacks were stacked at one end of this place while another empty one hung from a contraption in the ceiling, apparently in order to be filled from above.

I remarked on how hot it was.

'That's from the kiln,' Eve said. 'Oh, here comes William. He can explain it all better than I can.'

A wizened little man was approaching us, brown as the proverbial berry, with a shiny bald pate, and sporting a straggly red beard.

'Miss Eve,' he said. 'Good to see you.'

'This is Mrs. Hudson, William,' she told him. 'She's interested in how things work here.' She turned back to me. 'William's the most important man on the farm. He's our dryer.'

'Most important, is it?' William said. 'Now, now, Miss Eve. You do be giving me a swelled 'ead.'

'A dryer,' I asked. 'I'm sorry for being stupid. What exactly does that mean?'

'Well... just that William makes sure the hops dry properly,' Eve replied.

'You see, m'm,' the little man explained, 'them 'ops mustn't be let dry out too much. That'd make for bad beer, that would. See, there 'as to be just the right amount of moisture left in 'em.'

'So how do you know when they're dry enough?'

'Part by the feel of 'em and part by the smell. Come up, and I'll show you.'

He indicated the narrow wooden steps. With my long skirts, these were difficult enough to climb, and I was glad when William ran on ahead of me, then to extend a helping hand and support me up.

The floor here was almost completely covered with hops, a couple of men, stripped to their undershirts, carefully picking their way between the rows and spreading the cones out evenly with forks.

'This 'ere's the cooling room,' William explained.

It didn't seem cool to me at all, and I said so.

'Ha, well that's because you haven't been in the drying room yet.'

He led us to a door which he opened to let me peep in. The walls of the circular space beyond were lined with slatted wood, and, looking up at the cone shaped roof, I could see daylight beyond. We were under the chimney. A heap of green hops was drying here on, as William told me, a sheet of horsehair cloth.

'See, that's so the air can circulate properly.'

The heat was almost intolerable and the scent quite intoxicating. I remarked that I should not at all like to work under such circumstances.

'See, well, we're right over the furnace 'ere,' William said. 'All fire and brimstone.'

'What?'

'That's what we burn, m'm. Brimstone and anthracite. It'll get us used to the torments of 'ell, anyways.' He laughed merrily, revealing the fact that he had no front teeth at all and only blackened stumps for the canines, giving him the sinister appearance of a little elf, although he seemed perfectly amiable. 'See, the 'ot air passes through them 'ops and up out through the crookedy vent. That's 'ow they gets dry.'

As we moved back through the cooling room – which, as I said, wasn't much cooler than the other – I was taken aback to observe a mattress on the floor, with a chair beside it laden with personal effects.

'Does someone sleep here?' I asked.

William laughed some more.

'That'd be me, m'm. Don't I stay here all through September to keep an eye on things? Make sure them 'ops don't 'op it, like. Or, like as I says before, dry out too much and spoil the beer.'

'It must be hard for you.'

'Not at all, m'm. It's more of an 'oliday, like. A bit of peace and quiet away from the missus and the kiddies. With only Satan for company.'

'Who?' Had I heard aright?

He indicated a black cat, curled up on a mat under the chair.

'Good name for a cat what lives in 'ell, 'ain't it?' he grinned. 'Good ratter, Satan is. 'Is job's almost as important as me own.'

Eve reached towards the cat to pick him up.

'I'd love a pet kitty but *she* won't let me,' she said. The creature purred at her caresses.

'Well, don't you know you can 'ave a share in Satan any old time, miss,' William said. 'We're always 'ere, for now, anyways. 'Im and me don't plan to go away nowheres just yet.'

While William resumed the tour, Eve continued to hold the cat, stroking it and whispering to it. The poor lonely girl, I thought again. Meanwhile William was further describing the workings of the oast house, indicating how the hops – once dry enough but not too dry, remember – were loaded from this top floor into the hanging bag, or pocket, as he called it. It was a strange designation, to my mind, a pocket surely being a small neat thing, while this great sack could have accommodated Eve and me together with room to spare.

A couple of men were just now engaged in raking dried hops into the said pocket. They paused at William's request, thereby enabling Eve and myself to peer in and view the cones, now turned from green to brown. From time to time, William explained, the men would squash down the mass with the heavy metal hop press hanging over it until the pocket was as full as it could be. Then it would be removed from the sling, stacked with the others, and finally taken off to the brewery in Kenwardham.

'Where, after all's done, they be brewed into the finest sup of beer you'll ever 'ave the good luck to taste, m'm.' He smacked his lips at the prospect. 'A shame there's none 'ere for you to try, though o' course the Green Man 'as it on tap... Still, a lady like yourself would 'ardly be seen there, I s'pose.'

'Hardly,' I replied, smiling. 'Though my son-in-law sells ale in the shop in the village. I don't know if it's the brand you praise so much.'

'George 'Azelgrove, is it?' He grinned. 'A good man, that. Yes, 'e stocks it right enough. Though, mind you, the bottled stuff ain't a patch on the beer drawn from the barrel. All the same, better than nought, as the feller said.'

He particularised further on the process, though I have to say the technical side of the operation rather passed me by, with his talk of laths and cockles and the benefits of sulphur. What I had taken for chimneys he insisted were in fact vents, though I confess that I failed to grasp the difference. Again, the smell combined with the heat was making my head spin, and after a while I begged to be allowed to sit down.

William laughed. 'Yes, indeed. 'Tis like the Tropic of Capricorn in 'ere all right, m'm. You gets used to it after a bit.'

I had no intention of staying long enough to find out if that were so. Interesting as it was, I had seen enough, and, Eve finally reluctantly relinquishing her hold on Satan, we made our way outside, followed by William. Timothy was still at work, though he paused to talk to us.

'You will come to the village again soon, Timothy, won't you,' I said.

He nodded.

'Good, for I have a particular reason.' I would not say more in front of the others.

'And you must come to the orchard too, Timmy.' Eve smiled at him.

He nodded again, I have to say with more enthusiasm than he had shown me.

Suddenly we heard angry shouting. A figure was approaching us, horsewhip in hand.

'Papa,' exclaimed Eve, with trepidation.

It was indeed Mr Thomas Brakefield himself, lord of all, his face distorted with rage.

'What's going on here?' he demanded. 'Why are you all standing about loafing? Is this what I pay you for?' He pointed at Timothy. 'You, boy, get back to unloading that wagon right now.'

As Timothy scurried past him, Brakefield raised his arm and thrashed the lad hard across the back with his whip. I felt Eve flinch beside me, as if she too had been struck. Her father would likely have continued the chastisement, but William stepped forward and placed a restraining hand on his shoulder.

'Timmy,' William said. 'Back to work, lad.'

The boy didn't need telling twice but ran off. I understood he was used to blows.

'No need for that, sir,' I protested. 'Timothy works hard for you.'

He glared at me.

'And who the devil are you and what are you doing trespassing here?'

'My name is Martha Hudson and I am certainly not trespassing. I am staying in the village and was invited by your wife to call upon her today. When I expressed an interest in viewing the plantation, she very kindly asked your daughter here to show me around… Really, sir, you are most intemperate. Your behaviour and rudeness are quite uncalled for.'

It seemed Mr. Brakefield was unused to people talking back to him, for he regarded me with astonishment, as did Eve, while William grinned quietly.

'Well,' the unpleasant gentleman growled at last, no apology in his tone. 'That's all as maybe. But we've urgent work to do here and can't allow the whims of lady visitors to distract us. I'd be grateful, madam, if you could now go back to wherever it is you came from so I can converse with my man William here on important matters… Eve, take this person away.'

I turned to the dryer.

'Thank you, William, for sparing some of your precious time. It was all most instructive… Good-day, sir.' This last addressed to the master, whip still twitching in his hand, so that I could not help adding, 'I hope you are not intending to inflict that upon me, too.'

He muttered what sounded rather like an imprecation as I swept by him, with as much dignity as I could muster. The two men then disappeared inside the oast house.

Timothy was lifting another sack on to his shoulders, wincing as he did so.

'Are you all right, my dear?' I asked.

He nodded, but I thought I saw tears in his eyes.

'I'm so sorry, Timmy,' Eve said. 'Papa isn't himself today.'

Indeed, I rather suspected from various telling signs and symptoms that the gentleman had previously imbibed a fair quantity of spirituous beverages.

To me, she added, 'I apologise for Papa, Mrs. Hudson. He had no right to speak to you like that.'

I simply nodded. What could I say? The man was a brute.

Before we walked away, I pressed a shilling into the boy's hand.

'Remember the ribbon,' Eve whispered to him, and a half-smile flickered on the lad's face.

'I will, miss.'

Even though I had put a brave face on things, I confess I was shaken.

'I am not sure,' I said to the girl, 'that I can walk all the way back right now. I'll wait for the wagon to be unloaded and ride on that.'

'Indeed, you will not,' she said with more decision in her voice than I had heard heretofore. 'We'll take Papa's pony and trap.'

That conveyance was standing nearby.

'Are you able to drive it?' I asked, somewhat astonished.

'Of course. I'm an excellent horsewoman, you know.' She wasn't boasting. Just stating it as a fact.

'What will your father do with it gone?'

'It would do him good to walk,' she declared, a little spitefully. 'But don't worry. I'll bring it straight back. He'll be a while in there with William anyway.'

'Won't he be angry if he comes out and finds it gone? Perhaps we should ask him first.'

Eve shook her head as if to imply that, if we asked, we should not be let.

'I'll have someone tell him. Not Timothy. Papa always gets so cross with him.' She called to a man helping unload the sacks, instructing him to inform Mr. Brakefield, should he come out, that the lady was taken ill and had to be transported on the pony and trap,

71

but that Eve would return with it forthwith. The man nodded. He looked less than delighted with the errand imposed upon him, but Eve gave him a coin, and he grinned then, and tipped his cap.

'I fear that you will suffer if your father finds out,' I said.

'Well, he never beats *me*,' she replied. 'And sticks and stones, you know…'

I was pleased to see her show spirit. The further she was from that awful house, it seemed, the more lively she became. Of course, I was also grateful for the ride back to the village.

'I should love you to come in and meet the family,' I said. 'We have a cat, too. Bella.'

'Thank you but I must get back.'

'Another time then.'

She had a sweet smile.

'That would be nice… If I'm allowed.' She paused. 'Is that where you meet Timmy?' She indicated the duck pond.

'Yes. On the seat there under the willow.' I was on the point of telling her my plans to get him away from the farm, but she was in a hurry to be off. It also occurred to me that she would perhaps not be too happy to lose a friend.

We said our farewells, I reiterating my thanks before entering the shop, while Eve drove off at a spanking pace. I hoped she wouldn't get in trouble for helping me, the father having shewn himself to be such a brute.

Eleanor was, of course, agog to hear of my adventures, though not at all surprised at the treatment meted out to me.

'Thomas Brakefield is well known for his rudeness and rages, drunken or not,' she said. 'But tell me all from the beginning. We were mightily astonished that they sent the coach for you.'

I explained about that, and went on to describe my visit in detail, which, since my readers have already heard all, I shall not repeat here.

CHAPTER SEVEN

The next two days passed with neither sight nor sound of young Timothy, although each evening I positioned myself at the duck pond with a book in case he should turn up. It was a most unsatisfactory state of affairs – I was grown impatient to help the lad and felt frustrated – especially when Henrietta, inevitably, found me out there.

'I see this is your favourite spot, Martha,' she said, parking herself beside me. 'I suppose it is pleasant enough although I find I am a martyr to midgets.' I was taken aback until I understood that she was referring to the gnats flying about us. Midges. I did not correct her. 'They seem to have a particular love for me, for some reason.'

She fanned the air ostentatiously with her gloved hand. I hoped the vicious little insects would soon drive her away, but no such luck. She was determined to remain.

Meanwhile I kept an eye open for my young friend, wondering what I should do if he appeared. It would be just my luck. He would certainly not join me if he saw me with such a companion.

'I find it is a good place to read in peace and quiet,' I said.

Of course, Henrietta failed to take the hint.

'Yes, you always have your nose in some book, don't you, Martha,' she replied. 'Lucky for you. Most of us are far too busy for such indulgences... Though of course,' she conceded, 'you are recovering just now from a very dangerous illness. I suppose when you are at home with Mr. Holmes you are kept far too occupied for such idle distractions.'

'I always have time for reading. I do not consider it idleness.'

'Yes, but I suppose *he* makes lots of demands on you.' She looked at me searchingly. 'How fascinating it must be for you, with all that detecting going on around you. I should so love to pay you a visit and see for myself.'

'I am afraid,' I said with a smile, ignoring the broad suggestion, 'that, as I have mentioned before, I am not privy to the cases concerning Mr. H and Dr. Watson.'

'No, but you must see things, overhear things. You must, Martha, being so very, very close.'

I had a sudden comical vision of the round ball that was Henrietta come to Baker Street, crouched down, her eye glued to the keyhole of the gentlemen's chambers, straining to hear what was being said within.

'You are right,' I replied, trying to keep a straight face, 'I am kept far too busy to notice anything of the sort.' Then I relented a little, and pandered to her snobbery. 'Of course, I perforce encounter the illustrious visitors who come to the house, having to admit them and shew them upstairs, as I do.'

Her little eyes lit up. 'Oh, who, Martha? Tell me who?'

'I couldn't possibly reveal that, Henrietta. You do understand, don't you? Discretion is all.' I lowered my voice and spoke in conspiratorial tones. 'Just to say that some are very high up indeed in the governance of the country, some are noble, some even foreign royals.' And most are clerks and shopkeepers and governesses, as common as Henrietta and myself.

'Foreign royalty! Oh, I wish you could give me a clue. Just one.'

'You might read Dr. Watson's accounts, Henrietta. If you ever have time, that is. He reveals what can be revealed.'

She looked most discontented. 'It's not at all the same,' she said.

Of course not. What she wanted were the unwritten scandals.

Days slipped past, largely for me in the idleness so abhorred by Henrietta, since Eleanor would not permit me to exert myself in any way. However, one cannot read all the time, despite the attractions of Marie Corelli, Ouida and Mary Elizabeth Braddon, and I was tired of kicking my heels to no purpose. In truth, I was thinking of returning early to Baker Street, even before the harvest festival – assuming I could sort out Timothy's position before that – though I knew I was not yet fully myself.

The following Sunday, meanwhile, we prepared again to go to church. Indeed, I was looking forward to it, and not, I admit, for spiritual reasons alone. I was curious to observe the Brakefields, now that I knew so much more about them. As well as to see again bluff Square Simister, whom I liked. In fact, this latter gentleman greeted me as we approached St John's as if he and I were the oldest and best of friends. Freddie at his heels, sporting a pea green jacket, an amused expression on his face, nodded at me too, and more particularly at Eleanor.

'Mrs. Hudson,' the Squire bayed, 'I trust you are fully recovered by now from your recent ordeal.'

'I am indeed, sir. Thank you kindly.'

'Splendid, splendid… and less of the sir, if you don't mind. John Simister's my name and you can call me by it.' He rubbed his hands together. 'So there's no excuse now. You must come back with me today, and have that dinner I promised you.'

'Thank you. I am honoured, Squire,' I replied, taken aback. 'But you know we have a family dinner arranged already.'

'Nonsense. I am sure these good folk here can spare you. Isn't that right, Hazelgrove?'

'Well,' that worthy replied, somewhat abashed, 'if mother-in-law is of a mind…'

'You see!' The Squire turned back to me triumphantly.

'Perhaps,' Freddie said, 'Mrs. Hudson is worried about offending the proprieties, father. If only her daughter might accompany her...' He gave Eleanor another little bow and meaning glance. She blushed and clung tighter to George's arm, shaking her head.

'Oh,' I said, 'For myself, I have no worries regarding the proprieties.' I had, after all, revolted any pernickety Mrs. Grundies by much worse in Paris. 'However...'

'That's settled then.' The Squire marched off into the church before I could develop my 'however' any further, Freddie following, with a mock sorrowful salute to my daughter.

'Ho, ho,' said George, grinning. (He either didn't notice Freddie's attention to his wife, or didn't care about it.) 'It seems you have made a conquest there, mother-in-law.'

'No,' I replied. 'I fear the Squire is just another enthusiast wanting to hear about my famous lodger.'

But here comes another 'however': That was not what I really thought. Indeed, I was at a loss as to what was behind the offer, until I remembered how interested the Squire had been in the news that I was to visit the Brakefields. That must be it. He wanted to quiz me about them.

On entering the church, I was waylaid again, this time by Ursula Considine, who gestured to me to join her in her pew near the back. Eleanor shrugged acquiescence and continued up the aisle with George while I slid in beside the rector's wife. Henrietta, already installed at the front, must have queried my absence, for she addressed a word to Eleanor, and then looked back at me askance.

'Have you managed yet to speak to Timothy?' Ursula whispered.

I shook my head, explaining how I had seen him at the plantation but that being among so many others, had been unable to tell him of our plan.

'I let him know that I wished to talk to him, but so far he hasn't made an appearance.'

'Hm,' Ursula replied thoughtfully. 'Well, we'll wait a little longer. Then maybe I can help. One of my duties is to go among the pickers, to take them donations of food and clothes, and to encourage them to come to church.' She looked around herself ruefully. 'Few do, however.'

I looked about, too, and was surprised and pleased to see Nancy, little Sarey and an older boy – the brother, Charlie, was it? – seated not far from us. I waved at them and was rewarded with a similar gesture. Nancy bent her head to say something to Sarey, and the child rewarded me with a shy smile.

'You know Nancy, then?' Ursula asked, surprised.

'I met her at the plantation. She seems like a sound woman.'

'Yes, indeed. Salt of the earth.'

'Her husband isn't with her today.'

'No,' Ursula replied, shaking her head sadly. 'Doubtless he'll be down at the Green Man with the other men, drinking up the week's wages… Though,' she added hastily, 'Daniel isn't the worst of them by a long way. He doesn't beat his wife or children.'

Some recommendation!

Just then, the doors opened with a clang. It was the Brakefields, though this time Eve was missing, only the boy with them. The couple strode up the aisle as arrogantly regal as before, to the very front, while Randall, who was wriggling in his mother's hand, pulled faces at the congregation and stuck out his tongue.

'Now there's a child who might benefit from a few slaps,' I said, sotto voce.

'No, no,' Ursula replied. 'That's never right, Martha. Never.'

I had no time to argue before we were required to stand and raise our voices in the rousing hymn, 'Praise my soul the King of Heaven.'

After the service, having sat through another worthy but dull sermon exhorting us to consider the lilies of the field and not indulge in unnecessary excess (the Reverend somewhat oddly extolling the virtues of weaving cloth from nettles – some sort of mortification of the flesh, I assumed, strange in a Protestant church), I bade farewell to Ursula, each of us promising to let the other know as soon as we managed to track down Timothy. I was just then looking about for Nancy, to greet her, when I was waylaid by Lydia Brakefield, who swooped down upon me, her stony-faced husband lingering behind, while the boy kicked at a gravestone. The lady's most fashionable outfit of a vivid green silk, braided in gold, together with her ostrich-feathered hat, might have served as a counter to those simple field lilies mentioned by the vicar, not to mention an attire made of nettles. However, she displayed no consciousness, let alone Christian remorse, at so flaunting her extravagances.

'There you are, Mrs. Hudson,' she said. 'My husband has something to say to you.'

Thomas Brakefield stepped forward

'I understand I must apologise,' he said, without looking in the least contrite, 'for my intemperate behaviour at the oast.'

'Think nothing of it, sir,' I replied.

'Humph!' He looked quite as though he indeed thought nothing of it. Moreover, unlike the Squire, he accepted the 'sir' as a right.

We stared at each other in silence.

'Where is Miss Eve today?' I asked at last. 'I wanted to thank her again for her great kindness to me.'

'She is unwell,' Lydia Brakefield replied.

'Nothing serious, I hope.'

'Eve's locked in her room.' This was Randall, speaking with relish.

'Nonsense,' his mother replied. 'She has one of her headaches and has to stay in.'

'She's locked up,' the child insisted. 'You locked her up.'

'Randall!' His father's voice held a threat, though it seemed to inspire no fear in the boy who clung to his mother's skirt. She, he seemed to know, would protect him.

'Silly boy,' she said, stroking his hair. 'Such an imagination... Let us hope Eve may be well enough to come down this afternoon,' adding, with an attempt at a warm smile, rather belied by the coldness in her eyes, 'You see, to make up for everything, we must insist that you accompany us back today to partake of luncheon, don't we Thomas?' Her husband nodded, though without enthusiasm. 'You see, Mrs. Hudson, at Brakefield Hall, we eat in the French style, our main meal being in the evening. However, I am sure that there will be sufficient to satisfy your hunger with a cold collation, or something of the sort. I believe cook has prepared an excellent salmon mousse.'

Never mind the salmon, I knew she wanted to quiz me about Eve and her alleged beau.

Before I could reply, however, a roar rang out over the churchyard. 'Mrs. Hudson!' It was the Squire unceremoniously calling me. 'Mrs. Hudson. Over here for the rumble to Blossomfort.'

I smiled at the Brakefields. 'My thanks and apologies. It sounds perfectly delightful, but I am afraid I have a prior engagement.'

'With Simister!' Thomas Brakefield growled, glowering at me.

'The Squire has been kind enough...'

'I must warn you against having anything to do with that blackguard, madam,' he interrupted me. 'He is a rogue and a crook, not fit for civilised company. You must not go.'

'But you see, sir,' I replied calmly, 'I have already accepted the invitation. It would be most impolite to back out now, no matter how much of a rogue he is... though I have to say that Squire Simister has always behaved towards me like a perfect gentleman?' Unlike yourself, I could have added. It was cheeky of me, in truth, to express myself thus, but I deeply resented the man's tone of authority. Who was he to tell me what to do? 'Please to excuse me.' I started to walk away.

'Another time, then,' Mrs. Brakefield called after me. 'Soon.'

I looked back, giving a slight nod. The expression of rage I surprised on Thomas Brakefield's face rather chilled me. He would, no doubt about it, have grabbed my arm and dragged me back if he could have got away with it.

CHAPTER EIGHT

The Squire was chuckling.

'Oh yes indeed,' he said, 'you've put those two Brakefield noses out of joint. Those snouts. Ho!'

'That was certainly not my intention,' I replied. 'I merely told them what was true that I had a prior engagement.'

'Don't you know you were supposed to break it off? No one says no to his lordship. Still, you being a stranger here, you might get away without having a writ served upon you.'

'Don't be ridiculous, father,' Freddie said. 'He's just trying to frighten you, Mrs. Hudson. The Brakefields aren't that bad.'

'What! Not that bad! They're worse, far worse, as you should know well.'

Freddie just shrugged his elegant shoulders and winked at me. With Freddie as driver and the Squire and I seated behind, we were winding through the country lanes that I had walked before, eventually passing again those treacherous wetlands.

'Did you hear how old Jackson lost another sheep in there the other day, Freddie?' the Squire asked. 'Silly fool can't keep his gates closed, then wonders why they go wandering.'

'Did he get his sheep back?' I asked.

The Squire laughed grimly. 'Not at all. Those wetlands are hungry. They ate it up.'

I shuddered. The wetlands, so innocent-looking, yet proving so deadly.

On our arrival at last at Blossomfort, Freddie was sent to inform the staff that another place must be set at table. In the meantime, the Squire gave me a guided tour of what was indeed a most charming house, the which, though large, managed at the same time to be cosy and unpretentious. It was a house to be lived in rather than looked at, and I liked it very much, even if there were rather more antlers and deer skulls hanging up than I cared to see. Otherwise, everything was most tasteful, each room flooded with light from high windows.

I expressed my sincere admiration to the Squire.

'Well, Mrs. Hudson, the last time you were here you were hardly in a fit state to take in much.'

'It looks old. When was it built?'

'Yes, it's older even than I am. Dates back to 1621 when my ancestor, come up from Cornwall, was granted land here. Of course, there have been some additions since then. Yet what you see is largely what would have been here nearly four centuries ago.'

'Goodness! And you Simisters have been in residence ever since?'

'Indeed we have. Not like some other upstarts who only date their occupancy in the area for a couple of generations, yet now think they own the place.'

No need for him to explain whom it was he meant.

I stopped in front of a series of prints that depicted men in red jackets on horseback, pursuing a fox with a pack of hounds. They made me smile.

'Do you hunt, Mrs. Hudson?' the Squire asked.

'Not at all,' I replied. 'Such scenes always remind me of Mr. Wilde's witticism regarding "the unspeakable in full pursuit of the uneatable".'

The Squire frowned. 'Wilde! Isn't that the fellow that was imprisoned for...? Humph!... I'm not surprised he'd say something as d....d foolish as that, excuse my language.'

'Mr. Wilde's private behaviour might be considered vicious by some, Squire, and yet there is no doubt he is a great writer.'

'You are far too soft-hearted, Mrs. Hudson. And I reckon you know little of which you speak. The man is a degenerate…'

I was about to argue, when a bell rang loudly somewhere in the house.

'Ah, dinner time!' the Squire announced with gusto. 'I am starved and I hope you are too.'

It was hardly a condition to be wished for, but I knew what he meant and – poor Mr. Wilde forgotten – agreed that I was ready to eat.

One end of the well-polished table in the dining hall was set for three, the Squire at the head and Freddie and myself facing each other. I exclaimed at the porcelain ware, emblazoned with what I was informed was the family crest, an elaborate emblem featuring a medieval helmet surmounted rather threateningly by a pronged portcullis, the whole hanging over a turreted castle and surrounded by arabesques of foliage. A motto in Latin was inscribed below the crest: *Quasi summus magister*.

'What does that mean?' I asked the Squire.

'How the deuce should I know?' he replied, chuckling. 'I never thought it worth my time to study dead languages. Ask Freddie. He's the scholar, or supposed to be.'

'You know perfectly well what it means, father. "Like the highest master".'

'Yes, yes. That's what it means, but what does it *mean*? Makes no sense to me, nor to you either, Mrs. Hudson, I imagine.'

'The highest master, I suppose, is God,' I said. 'So the aspiration is most worthy.'

'Hubris, I call it,' the Squire continued. 'I certainly make no claim to resemble the Supreme Being.'

He shook his head, though, in point of fact, with his imposing stature and crown of golden hair, he might stand model for a pagan deity.

'Of course, it could also mean, "like a head teacher,"' Freddie went on. 'Though, since that doesn't apply to either of us, I am afraid, Mrs. Hudson, that the thing must remain a mystery.'

Freeing us, most thankfully, from such linguistic knots, Mrs. Jefferies, accompanied by a nervous-looking maid, entered at that moment bearing steaming and aromatic dishes. The cook-cum-housekeeper proved to be a friendly, homely body in her late fifties, and the meal she had prepared was as substantial as I imagined it would be, in several courses. A tasty asparagus soup was followed by poached snapper and a juicy roast of sucking pig, all accompanied by fine wine (not Mariani, thank goodness), with advice to leave some space for the sweet.

'Mrs. Jeffries' puddings,' the Squire told me, 'are *sine qua non.*'

I laughed. 'So you do speak Latin.'

'Not at all. Just the few phrases everyone knows. But eat up, Mrs. Hudson, eat up.'

I needed no further urging and ate with relish, as did the Squire, while Freddie merely toyed with his food. A collation of salmon mousse might, I felt, be more to his taste.

'Look at him!' the Squire said dismissively. 'Not a pick on him. No chip off the old block, him. Can't say I know where he was got at all.'

'You know I take after mama,' Freddie replied, adding to me, 'My mother's mother was Turkish.'

That explained his colouring.

'Yes, indeed.' The Squire guffawed. 'Your grandfather plucked her from the harem.'

Freddie shook his head. 'Don't believe a word he says, Mrs. Hudson.'

84

I feared that mention of his late wife might dampen the Squire's spirits, and indeed he seemed to become morose. Then suddenly he banged his fist on the table, causing me to jump and the crockery to rattle.

'Don't ever say those Brakefields aren't too bad, Freddie,' he bellowed. 'Didn't they drive your poor mother to an early grave?'

Freddie lowered his head and stared at the remains on his plate. He muttered something.

'What? What's that?'

'Nothing?'

I had heard him. 'It wasn't just them' is what he'd said.

'Are you planning to stay in the village, Freddie?' I asked, to change the subject on to what I hoped were safer grounds.

'I hope not!' his father exploded again. Then burst out laughing. 'I'd prefer not to be witness to his shenanigans.'

'I'll be returning to London soon to continue my legal studies, 'Freddie explained. 'When the Michaelmas term resumes, you know. Father is most insistent I qualify.'

'So that you can take those Brakefields on at their own game,' the Squire added.

Freddie sighed. 'I wish you'd just let it go, father. It does your blood pressure no good, you know to dwell so much on what you perceive as injustices.'

'Let Thomas Brakefield let it go! And that trollop of a wife of his.'

'Father!'

Squire Simister looked rueful. 'I apologise, Mrs. Hudson. Most uncalled for. Unparliamentary language and all that. I quite forgot Lydia's a friend of yours.'

'Hardly,' I replied.

'But she invited you to visit, and then again today.'

'Yes.'

There was a pause. Both men were looking at me askance. It was as I had thought. The Squire, and maybe his son too, wanted to hear more about their haughty neighbours. I stayed silent.

The Squire laughed. 'Ha! I see you are a woman of discretion, Mrs. Hudson. I like that. I like that a lot.'

Perhaps it was coincidence, or perhaps the housekeeper had some intuitive powers, but once again, at an awkward moment, Mrs. Jeffries re-entered with an appetising-looking summer pudding, bursting with raspberries and surrounded with whipped cream.

'I didn't trust Mabel to bring it in without dropping it,' she explained.

I smiled. 'I know the feeling, Mrs. Jeffries. My Phoebe is like that. I can't trust her with a simple plate of biscuits.'

She nodded back at me, setting the dish on the table.

There was no more talk of Brakefields or feuds for the rest of the meal, as we indulged ourselves in the sweet, along with a sup of Madeira. Then the Squire suggested a turn around the grounds.

'Really, father! I suspect Mrs. Hudson is quite worn out with all your chatter, and wishes now for nothing more than to return to her delightful daughter,' Freddie said, adding. 'I'd be most happy to drive her back.'

'Not at all,' I said. 'I should love a short walk in the gardens after that fine feast.'

'You see, Freddie. The lady isn't as feeble as you'd like to make out.'

In truth, I should have preferred a rest to digest the huge meal. However, I wished to keep Freddie far away from Eleanor. Perhaps the lad meant no harm other than idle flirtation, but I could see that his attentions discommoded her. Perhaps I could insist that the coachman drive me back instead.

The Squire took my arm in what was a more familiar gesture than I was quite comfortable with – like father, like son after all, perhaps. However, I felt I could not pull away without giving offence.

'I must apologise in advance, Mrs. Hudson. I know that you ladies love flower beds and such-like gimcrackery,' the Squire remarked as we set off. 'But I'm a simple fellow, and grass, bushes and trees are good enough for me.'

He was deliberately self-deprecating, as I told him, for the grounds were most pleasantly laid out, a sweeping vista leading down to a small lake, graced with willows and reeds.

'Thank you,' he replied. 'Originally the gardens were more formal, with all sorts of fancy folderols, greenery trimmed into unlikely shapes and so on. But I prefer my plants to grow naturally, don't you know.'

I largely agreed, though one must admire the skill of gardeners able to sculpt simple bushes into animal and other recognisable forms.

'The only original feature that remains is the maze.'

'How delightful,' I exclaimed. 'I adore a maze. Can I see it?'

'Indeed, you can, Mrs. Hudson, though I strongly advise against entering it. If you do, you know, you may not be able to find your way out again, and then you would be trapped here forever.'

He chuckled and squeezed my arm.

This time I pulled away, on pretend of searching for something in my reticule, drawing out a handkerchief, which I then waved in front of my face, as if to ward off midges.

The Squire made no attempt, I am pleased to say, to take hold of me again, and we continued our leisurely stroll round the back of the house where he shewed me a well-stocked kitchen garden. I expressed my delight.

'Mrs. Jefferies' domain,' he explained. 'We try to grow most of our own fruit and vegetables here, and as you can see, they are flourishing.'

'Is there a Mr. Jefferies?' I asked.

'There was, of course, sadly now deceased. She has a son and daughter, the girl married away somewhere or other, while the son, Joe, works in the village. In a shop, I believe.'

'Joe!' I exclaimed. 'Not Joe who works for my son-in-law in the grocery.'

'Ah, most likely. Yes, indeed. Now you mention it, Joe's with the Hazelgroves. A nice lad. Very sound.'

'He seems to be... True what they say, it's a small world.'

'It certainly is, especially round here. By God, you can't say anything about anyone in case they're related.'

I was privately sure that never stopped him from expressing his most decisive views.

Meanwhile, the Squire had paused to examine a large marrow.

'Quite a prize specimen, don't you agree, Mrs. Hudson.'

'Oh yes. A good size. Though I confess I am not partial to marrows. I find them too watery.'

'Not the way Mrs. Jefferies cooks them.'

I smiled. 'You are blessed in your housekeeper.'

'Don't I know it... I just wish...' His eyes drifted away.

There was a long pause.

'What do you wish, Squire?'

'Ah, no matter, no matter...' He shook his great head, as if to dispel sad thoughts. 'But tell me honestly, Mrs. Hudson, what do you make of young Freddie?'

'He seems most charming,' I replied carefully.

'Ha! Too charming! That's his trouble, the pup! Too busy charming people. It's about time he took his responsibilities seriously.'

'Whatever do you mean? What responsibilities?'

'Well, to carry on the line for one thing.'

'He's very young yet.'

'Nevertheless, I won't around be for ever. I'd like to be sure the succession is established before I go.'

88

I laughed. 'You look to me to be good for many years to come, Squire.'

He gazed into my eyes. His were as blue as I imagine the Mediterranean Sea must be.

'Do you? Do you indeed, Mrs. Hudson?'

'Certainly.' I edged away, in case he caught up my hand, as he showed some inclination to do. 'A fine marrow indeed,' I said. 'Do you have a competition here at harvest festival? If so, I suppose that you must be a winner.'

He was not to be distracted.

'Humph... Still, I wish Freddie took life more seriously. I suspect that he spends more time in London courting the ladies than he does on his studies, though without any serious aspiration to a suitable marriage.'

'What age is he? Surely not more than twenty-two or three.'

'Something like that... You are quite right, Mrs. Hudson. I should allow him to sow his wild oats.'

'Well, as to that...'

He clapped his hands, interrupting me. We had just exited from the kitchen garden through a gate in the wall.

'Here's my maze. Now, Mrs. Hudson, I'll lay odds that you've never seen a finer one.'

The maze was verily a sight to behold. Trimmed yew hedges higher than my head, nay higher than that of the Squire himself – and he was tall – covered an extensive area. A gap enticed one to go in, and I stepped forward.

'Remember my warning,' the Squire said. 'Enter at your peril.'

Resisting the temptation with some reluctance, I stepped back.

'Not because of what you said, Squire, because I should love to take on the challenge, but because I confess I am after all somewhat overcome after that splendid meal, and really should be returning home.'

'Aha!' He clapped his hands gain. 'I understand your little game, madam. You are hoping for another invitation.'

I shook my head in an attempt at a denial.

'Dear Mrs. Hudson, you are most welcome to visit whenever you want. It would make an old man very happy.'

That old man line yet again. Now I knew that he was teasing me.

'And next time,' he went on, 'since we are becoming such good friends, maybe you can tell me at last why Lydia Brakefield is so keen on your company. Apart, that is, for the sheer delight of your personality.'

Of course, I had no intention of revealing any such thing, but smiled.

'I hardly like,' I said, 'to bother Freddie to take me home. Perhaps your coachman...'

'You think I keep a man to drive me about. Fiddlesticks to that, Mrs. Hudson. I am no Thomas Brakefield. I'll drive you back myself.'

And so it happened, no doubt providing anyone in the village who noticed us with plenty to gossip about. Indeed, the Squire was all for coming into the shop to greet Joe, until I reminded him that it was Sunday, the shop closed, and Joe's day off, so he contented himself with handing me down from the trap. Then, giving a deep bow, remounting and driving off, waving his whip in the air.

As for me, I watched him go and then retraced my steps somewhat, for I had observed a familiar lanky figure lurking by the duck pond. The elusive Timothy at last!

CHAPTER NINE

He was looking at me with a troubled expression.

'Oh no, m'm. Thanks for thinking of me, but I couldn't leave. No. Not at all.'

It was certainly not the response I had been expecting.

'But Timothy, your life here is so hard. I saw how Mr. Brakefield beat you. This new situation would be quite different. You would have a proper room of your own, good food. Kindness.'

He edged away from me.

'No, m'm, thanking you, but t'aint possible. Not at all.'

'I know change can be scary, but, my dear boy, at least promise me that you will think about it.'

He shook his head. 'I can think and think but I'll still say no thanks, m'm. Sorry to have troubled you, m'm.'

Then, with an agonised expression on his face, he ran off even before I could give him a coin for his supper.

I was truly astonished at his reaction, but just now could do nothing more than hope he would come to his senses. Resolving to ask Ursula Considine to talk to him at her earliest opportunity, I made my way, deep in thought, back to the shop.

Because it was Sunday and the place was closed, I had to ring the bell to get Eleanor to let me in. She instantly spotted that something was amiss.

'Whatever has happened, mama? Has Squire Simister upset you?'

'The Squire? Goodness no. He couldn't have been more attentive. No, it's Timothy.'

I explained my recent conversation and how puzzled I was by the lad's refusal of my offer. Eleanor burst out laughing.

'It's hardly funny,' I said, offended.

'No, it isn't, but mama can't you guess the reason he wants to stay, despite everything.'

I looked at her askance.

'He's clearly in love with Eve.'

'Oh…'

Of course. That must be it. The lad couldn't bear the prospect of being separated from the girl, even though he must know that he had no chance on earth of winning her.

'You should get Eve to try and persuade him,' my sensible daughter remarked. 'She's the only one he's likely to listen to.'

She was right. I would have to take Eve into my confidence. But could I be sure that was what she herself would want? He was perhaps her only friend. With a heavy heart, I accompanied Eleanor upstairs.

'Mother- and father-in-law are still here,' she whispered.

Oh dear.

They were playing cards. Henrietta looked up avidly as I entered.

'Welcome back, your highness!' she exclaimed. 'Imagine,' she turned to Eleanor,' your mother hasn't been here a wet fortnight, and already she's been taken up by the gentry even though, as far as I know, the Hudson clan can make no claim to noble blood. Perhaps I am mistaken. If so, please enlighten me. What aristocratic ancestors have you been hiding from us, Martha?'

She spoke with assumed levity, although the gleam in her eye was far from friendly.

'No,' I replied. 'I am nothing special, neither on my husband's side, nor on my own.'

'So what is your trick then, madam?'

I shook my head.

'It's her "je ne sais quoi,"' George put in jovially. 'Isn't that right, mother-in-law?'

'Her what? George, please don't throw Latin at me.'

'It means "her I don't know what,"' her son explained. 'In French, mother, not Latin.'

'Oh, in French!' Henrietta scowled. 'That's why it makes no sense.'

'I suppose,' I said carefully, 'I am a novelty here, especially thanks to my connection with Mr. Holmes.'

Henrietta's expression cleared instantly.

'Of course. That's it. They all want to hear about *him*. Well, I imagine they'll drop you pretty quick when they find out you have nothing to say on that particular subject.'

'No doubt.'

'So what,' Eleanor said, treading on safer ground, 'did the Squire give you to eat? Joe claims his mother is an excellent cook.'

I regaled them with the menu, Henrietta sniffing dismissively, especially when I mentioned the summer pudding.

'Sounds like nothing special to me,' she said. 'I make summer pudding to use up stale bread. It's a poor enough thing, especially considering it's not even summer any more. You should have been here today to taste Eleanor's apple tart, Martha. Most superior.'

If Eleanor were of a fragile disposition, I quite believe she would have fainted away at such an unexpected encomium.

'The roast chicken wasn't bad either, was it, Walter?' Henrietta continued.

'Very tasty,' her husband replied.

George tried to suppress a snort.

'Have you at long last come to recognise Eleanor's culinary skills, mother?' he asked.

'I have never doubted them,' that lady replied with dignity. 'Trumps!' she said then, laying down her cards and scooping up the pile of ha'pennies.

The next day passed drearily enough. The weather had turned. Autumnal chills and rain had set in so that it was unpleasant to be out, yet there was little for me to do in the house. Eleanor and the maid being busy with the laundry, and George, of course, in the shop, I was alone in the upstairs parlour. Not able to settle to read, I took up some needlework that I had brought with me. However, the close stitching brought on a headache, and I soon laid it by, sitting back in my armchair, eyes closed, thinking troubling thoughts. I quite offended Bella the cat after she jumped on my lap, when I placed her firmly back on the floor, being not in the humour for her and her hairs and kneading paws. She walked off, tail twitching, to show her displeasure. As if I cared. I was worried about Eve and her own supposed headache, set against Randall's childish insistence that she had been locked into her room. Surely not. Surely he was making up the story out of mischief. Still, part of me believed that the father was quite capable of inflicting such a punishment. Could it be because she had taken his pony and trap without permission to convey me home? Or maybe the girl was guilty of some misdemeanour of which I was unaware.

Eleanor, entering to ask if I needed anything, perceived my disquiet, and, having been apprised of the reason, suggested I write to the girl, since we had already established a degree of closeness.

'It would be quite in order for you to inquire about her health, given that you were told she was unwell. How she replies may set your mind at rest.'

Or not, I thought. Still, I recognised that it was a good idea

'Joe can deliver it this morning on his rounds, mama,' Eleanor added, and for some reason kissed the top of my head. 'I'll bring you a cup of tea.'

94

I thereupon penned a short note, expressing concern regarding the headache which had confined Eve to the house, adding that, as she had previously expressed a readiness to visit me, I should like very much if she could do so, this very day, if possible. When I could then, I reckoned, reassure myself that she was not being badly treated, and also talk to her about Timothy. I sealed the note in an envelope, and took it down to the shop where Joe was assembling his deliveries to outlying farms.

'My daughter suggests you might drop this in to Brakefield Hall while you're out,' I said, proffering the letter.

'I'll do it,' he replied with his usual friendly grin. 'But you know I don't usually go up there, m'm. They gets their deliveries from fancy shops in Kenwardham and beyond. Not from the likes of us. Isn't that right, guv'nor?'

George nodded. He was measuring flour into packets from a sack.

'I reckon they don't want us to know what they're eating in case we talk about it in the village,' he said.

'Old Brakefield looks like a right miser to me,' Joe went on. 'I wouldn't like to sit at table with him. Probably eats the groats and peelings he gives his pickers.'

'Now, now, Joe,' George said. 'Just because your mother is a great cook.'

'Didn't they try and poach her, but she wasn't having any of it. She's devoted to the Squire, she is.'

'No peelings yesterday anyway,' I said. 'They were having salmon mousse. That's what Mrs. Brakefield told me.'

Joe snorted.

'Salmon mouse! What's that when it's at home?'

I laughed and told him to ask his mother. Then, I pressed a coin into his hand, along with the letter.

'Here's for your trouble, Joe.'

'Ah, no trouble,' he replied, pocketing the coin. 'You can trouble me like that any time, m'm.' He looked at the name on the letter. 'Miss Eve, is it. I'll see she gets it.'

I felt better after that, and went upstairs to resume my sewing.

A couple of hours later, I heard Joe return with the wagon and went down to see how he had got on.

'That ugly brute of a footman took the letter off me,' he said. 'Wouldn't let me give it to Miss Eve personal, like. Told me I shouldn't have come to the front door, and then slammed it in me face.'

'Well,' I replied, disappointed, 'you did your best. Thank you.'

I realised I had been half hoping he'd bring Eve back with him, unlikely though that was.

It was still raining, a grey drizzle, and, while I felt the need for fresh air, could not face trudging aimlessly through puddles, even with a stout umbrella. Instead, I returned to the parlour with a sigh, and spent the rest of the afternoon staring out the window at the empty street. No, I couldn't live in the countryside for anything, much as I love nature. London, despite all its drawbacks – its dirt and stench – is bustling with life at all times. No fear of getting bored or finding oneself at a loss as to what to do there. Eleanor had previously suggested to me that I might think of retiring to Bilbourne in due course, to a little cottage of my own, and, in the summer sunshine, it had seemed a pleasant and even tempting prospect. But this is how it would be for much of the time. Dull and wet and dreary. I thought with longing of my house in Baker Street, my cosy kitchen, dear Clara and Phoebe. I would write to them too, I decided. A cheerful message to set their minds at ease, despite my dark mood. Then, if the rain eased off, I could walk down to the Post Office with it.

The writing occupied another half hour. I spoke of Eleanor and George, of the Squire and Freddie, of my visit to the hop farm, without dwelling too much on the Brakefields. Re-reading it, I judged it to sound like I was having a wonderful time. I smiled ruefully to myself and sealed it up.

However, the rain was heavier than ever, and Eleanor, hearing my plan to go out, tried to discourage me.

'I can't imagine your letter to Clara can be so urgent that you have to go out in this weather to post it. You'll get soaked, mama, and what will we do then if you catch cold?'

'I'm not that feeble, Eleanor.'

She put on an innocent face.

'Of course, mother-in-law will be in the Post Office. She's bound to insist on your coming in for a chat.'

Ah.

'All right,' I replied. 'The letter can wait.'

'I thought it might.'

CHAPTER TEN

The following morning saw a watery sun peering through clots of dirty cloud, but at least it wasn't raining. Thank goodness! I should at last be able to take a walk. It would be even more pleasant, I mused, if there were a local tea house to visit, but the only place locally for refreshments outside of people's homes was the inn, the Green Man and Lanthorn. Since I had not yet ventured to that end of the village, I decided that, unless I heard from Eve in the meantime, I would take a walk that way after posting my letter to Clara and Phoebe. Not, of course, to venture inside the hostelry – that would be most unseemly. All the same, I was curious to see what that particular den of iniquity looked like. My one concern regarding this enticing plan was Henrietta, and I hoped to be able to slip into the post office, deal only with Walter, and slip out again. Any ambush by his wife would surely put paid to my expedition.

Luck was on my side. Walter informed me, as he took my letter, that his wife was out visiting.

'That's a shame,' I said, hoping he didn't discern the insincerity behind my words. 'Still,' I added cheerfully, 'I'm bound to see her again soon.'

'That you are,' he replied. 'I'll tell her you dropped by.'

'Thank you.' I was about to leave when he called me back.

'I was just wondering...' He stopped.

I waited.

'Well, you seem the kind of person who's interested in history, Martha,' he said finally.

'That's true.'

'Only I was thinking maybe we could organise an outing to that Richborough Castle I was telling you about.'

'An outing?'

'Yes.' His narrow face creased into an eager smile. 'A family day out. We could hire a charabanc.'

'That's a lovely idea, Walter, but would we need such a big vehicle for just the five of us.'

'Well, we could hardly take George's delivery wagon, and a barouche would only comfortably seat four people... I suppose that would do if one of us didn't want to come.'

He looked a little wistful, as if thinking of a particular person we might well do without, but who was most unlikely to agree to stay behind. Or maybe I was ascribing my own sentiments to my companion.

His notion certainly appealed. I was beginning to feel very confined in this little village. However, there were undoubtedly problems standing in the way of the plan's execution.

'I don't wish to make difficulties, Walter,' I went on, 'but much as I should love to see Richborough Castle, isn't it rather far? I think you said it was beyond Canterbury, on the way to Margate. It would surely take many hours to get there.'

He nodded, looking despondent. A little droplet hung from his nose, like a tear.

'Of course, we could always go part way by train and then hire a conveyance from the nearest station,' I suggested. 'That would make much more sense.'

'Henrietta hates trains,' Walter said. 'She thinks they're common.'

'I see... Oh dear...Well, surely there is somewhere nearer that we could go.'

'Well...' He thought for a moment. 'There's always Rochester Castle and Gardens, if you've never seen them before.'

'I haven't. That sounds wonderful.'

'Of course, the castle's not nearly as old as Richborough. Only Norman, you know. No Roman connection there, I'm afraid.'

'Henrietta will be pleased about that.'

He sighed. 'She will. And when she gets bored with the castle, as she is bound to do and quickly, she can at least visit the shops.'

He smiled to offset any implied criticism of his wife by the remark. Poor Walter. I could not help but think how my dear late husband, Henry, would have been as excited as myself at the prospect of such an outing, for our tastes coincided. What a shame Walter did not have a wife who shared his interests. Not only that: Henrietta displayed veritable impatience towards them. And if the rest of us found her difficult, how much more of a trial she must be to one who had to endure her all the time. Only her son seemed able to stand up to her, making affectionate fun of her pretensions and overbearing ways, a teasing she tolerated from him and him alone.

Promising to set the plan before Eleanor and George, I bade Walter farewell and left the post office, walking a little way up the road in order to view the school. It was, as had been described, a small red-brick structure of neat aspect, with two wings on either side of a higher gable. I could hear laughter and chatter through an open window on one side, and, on the other, silence punctuated by a stern female voice, presumably that of the senior Miss Clements. I imagined Jamesie and Davey Considine sitting there quiet as mice, pretending to be good students, while their little brother, Oliver, in the other class, enjoyed the kindly encouragement of Miss Phyllis. It would be interesting, I thought, to make the acquaintance of these two very different sisters.

In order to embark on my planned walk, I was obliged to go back down through the village, passing the churchyard on my way. I don't know why, but it occurred to me, while no one was around, to see if I could find the tombstone erected by Squire Simister to his late wife. If anyone should ask what I was about, I could always say that

100

I enjoy the peace and quiet of such places, which is no less than the truth.

Pushing the lychgate open, I walked in, almost immediately regretting it, since the graveyard was extensive enough, and I had no idea where Susannah Simister was interred. Nevertheless, I followed the path around the back of the church, keeping an eye open for something extraordinary, as Henrietta had suggested the monument to be. Nothing of the sort struck me, and I was about to give up, when I came upon a regular mausoleum, a veritable miniature mansion like those I had seen in Paris cemeteries, the door a metal grid that one could peer through. I did so. A stone coffin was within. Was this what I had been searching for? This incongruous and, to my mind, overblown sepulchre? I checked the name on the lintel and sighed with relief: Benjamin Brakefield was carved there in Gothic script, surmounted by some sort of arcane symbol. How could I ever have imagined that Squire Simister, from what I knew of him, would have erected such a monstrosity?

On the way back my eye was caught by the statue of an angel. I had not noticed it before, since it was partly concealed by a spreading yew tree. The statue was of pearly white marble and quite beautiful, a vase of white lilies standing in front of it. They must have been placed there recently, for the blooms showed no sign yet of wilting. The inscription on the tombstone read 'Susannah, much beloved wife of John Simister,' along with her dates of birth and death. The poor woman had been only thirty-seven years old when she died, and I said a silent prayer for the repose of her soul, then made my way thoughtfully out of the churchyard.

Passing the duck pond, I observed that my usual seat was still wet from the overnight showers, so there would be no reposing there today. In any case, my intention was a brisk walk to make up for my recently enforced inaction.

Taking the road that would eventually lead out of the village, I soon came upon the inn. It was not at all what I had expected, not den of vice at all, but a quaint place of considerable age, whitewashed, half-timbered and with a well-maintained thatched roof. Carved wooden benches, unoccupied just now, stood on either side of the old oak door. However, this charming effect was marred somewhat by the inn sign, just now swaying vigorously in the wind. From it, a grotesque face peered down at me with blank eyes through a mass of ancient foliage that sprouted from its very head, nose and mouth, ominous shadows cast over it by a candlelit lantern painted above it. Even though I remembered hearing that the Green Man, as a figure from ancient mythology, was judged a beneficent spirit symbolising rebirth, I did not care for the look of this creature at all.

Of the pickers supposed to frequent the place there was no evidence. I supposed they would only be calling to the inn at eventide, after the day's work was done. In fact, I encountered very few people at all as I proceeded out of the village – mostly women with great wicker baskets holding vegetables or laundry, or farm labourers about their business. They each one greeted me with friendly nods. Meanwhile, the road I was on wound up and down little hills dotted with the odd cottage, but with no sign or indication of anything very much else ahead of me, any townland or village. Fields, some still golden with corn waiting to be harvested, stretched on either side to distant farms. I could even discern here and there the distinctive form of oast houses that must belong to plantations other than that of the Brakefields.

I always dislike retracing my steps and had hoped therefore that I should find a road that circled back to Bilbourne. However, bearing in mind my previous misadventure, and not wishing to over-tire myself, I enquired regarding this of a toothless old woman sitting outside her shack. This resulted only in a shake of her grey locks and the raising of a gnarled finger to point back the way I had come. I thanked her and turned about.

By the time I reached the inn again, a light drizzle was descending. I had foolishly omitted to bring my umbrella, and loitered for a few moments, debating whether after all to enter and take refuge within, staring up betimes at the eerie Green Man as if he might make the decision for me.

'He looks rather like my father, doesn't he?'

I must be going deaf for I had not heard anyone draw near. Or else Freddie had crept up on me for the pleasure of seeing me jump.

'Not a bit,' I replied, recovering myself. 'I cannot see any likeness there at all.'

He laughed. 'Maybe he's more like me, then.' He wiggled his fingers in front of his face and rolled his eyes. 'What do you think?'

'Wherever did you spring from?' I asked, ignoring his antics. 'This is the second time you have surprised me.' Remembering the time in the lane.

'Ah, I have powers, Mrs. Hudson, you would not dream of.' He smiled and his eyes glinted. It struck me more than ever how very exotic he looked, his olive skin, his black hair studded with diamond rain drops, that midnight blue cloak. Quite the necromancer, in fact.

'I can well believe it,' I said.

'Well then, I am sorry to disappoint you with a rational explanation. In this instance I was simply tying up Pegasus around the side of the inn.'

'Ah.'

'So are you dropping in for a glass of beer, then, Mrs. Hudson?'

'Not at all. I was just passing.'

'In this weather?'

'It was dry when I set out.'

He shook his head. 'You should always be prepared for rain in Kent. I am afraid you have become quite corrupted by London where you can dodge into shops or tea houses whenever the heavens open.'

'You may be right,' I replied, smiling.

'Come now, the inn is sure to be almost empty. You will not offend any of the proprieties if you take shelter there until the shower passes.'

I did not fancy a tête-à-tête with the young man just then, so replied that I feared – looking up at the dark clouds – that the rain might soon get worse. I should hope to be back home before that.

'I can't tempt you then. A pity.'

He didn't look sorry at all as he turned with a sweep of his cloak to go into the inn. As I moved on, I noticed Pegasus tied up, as Freddie had indicated, at the far side of the building.

However, I had not taken more than twenty steps when the rain started to come down with a battering vengeance. There was no alternative: I should have to shelter in the inn after all. I rushed back and pushed my damp way through the door, as Freddie had done before me, and found myself in a large room as comfortably antiquated as one might imagine from the outside of the building. A beamed ceiling hung low over a stone floor sprinkled with sawdust; the once whitewashed walls were turned brown with decades of tobacco smoke. A roaring fire was set in a great stone fireplace, a kettle bubbling over it and logs of wood piled alongside. Above the mantel hung copper pots and pans that, to my eye, needed a good polish to bring out the gleam. A dresser stood at one wall, its shelves holding pewter and earthenware mugs, as well as dinner plates stood on end.

To my surprise, however, there was no sign of Freddie. Just two ancients, sitting together peacefully by the fire, one of them smoking a clay pipe, the smoke of which perfumed the air not unpleasantly. If they were astonished to see a lone woman enter the inn, they showed no sign of it. Nevertheless, I felt the need to explain my reason for being there to the stout, red-faced, many-chinned man behind the bar counter, whom, from his general air of authority, I took to be the landlord.

'Aye,' he replied. 'That rain be dreadful wet. You're welcome to stay and wait it out, m'm. Set you down by the fire and I'll bring you a hot toddy.'

'Ah, no thank you,' I replied, looking around. 'But where is Mr. Simister?'

'Who?'

Was it my imagination, or did the man suddenly look furtive?

'Mr Freddie Simister,' I repeated. 'I was talking to him outside but a moment ago.'

He shook his head. I turned to the old men.

'You must have seen him. He just came in.'

'Ah…well,' one of them replied. 'We didn't see anyone, did we, Billy?'

The other said nothing, puffing on his pipe.

'Are you sure?' I asked.

I didn't want to call them all liars, but Freddie had most definitely entered the establishment. I had heard the door bang shut behind him.

'We do be too occupied to notice things much,' the old man continued.

Doing what? I thought. Staring into the fire?

'His horse is outside.'

The landlord shrugged and shook his head again

'You sure you don't want something to drink, m'm? Against the cold?'

Perhaps that would loosen tongues, I thought.

'Well now,' I said, 'the local beer has been highly recommended to me by William at the plantation. Maybe a small glass of that.'

The landlord smiled now, his double chins quivering. 'Ah, yes, Willum Makepeace,' he said. 'A fine man, him. So he recommended us, did he? Well then, a glass of Old Devilish coming up.'

I was a little taken aback.

'What?'

105

'Don't you worry, m'm. It's mild and sweet enough for a lady. Set you down by the fire alongside Zachariah and Billy there, to dry out, and I'll bring it over to you.'

I did as he said, and smiled at the two men, old farm workers, I judged, their sun-darkened skin weatherbeaten into wrinkles.

'Would you gentlemen care to join me in a drink?' I asked, perceiving how their mugs were empty.

They looked at each other.

'Gennelmen, is it!' one said. 'Did you hear that Billy? I never bin called that afore. 'Ave you?'

The other removed the pipe from his mouth. 'I 'ave not,' he pronounced, and replaced the pipe.

'Still and all, I be inclined to accept. Thank ye kindly, m'm.'

The notion that it might not be proper to take a drink from a woman apparently did not occur to either of them.

'Two more here, Micah,' the one with the impressive cognomen of Zachariah called across to the landlord. 'You do be the lady staying in the shop, then,' he continued. It was a statement of fact, rather than a question.

'I am indeed.'

'Staying with the 'Azelgroves.'

'Mrs. Hazelgrove is my daughter.'

'Ah. That's right.'

No chance of anonymity in this village.

Just then, the landlord, Micah, brought over three foaming mugs of brown ale carefully holding two in the one hand. He set them down, and I sipped mine tentatively, while they all watched me.

'Very good,' I said nodding. It was indeed tasty enough, even though in general I am not fond of brewed hops.

My companions seemed satisfied at my response.

'I remain astonished that you haven't seen Mr. Simister ,' I said, after a while. 'I could have sworn he came in here.'

Zachariah shook his head, but Billy made a slight but unmistakable indication with his chin and pipe towards a door set at the far end of the room.

'Perhaps he came in another way,' I said. 'Is there another way?'

The landlord sighed at my persistence. 'I'll have a look out back.' Walking with evident reluctance to the said door, he tapped upon it. After a moment, it opened a crack, and he whispered a few words to whoever was within.

This proved, of course, to be Freddie, who burst over to me.

'You changed your mind, Mrs. Hudson,' he said, as if delighted, although I could tell he was somewhat nonplussed. 'Well, now, you have found out my little secret.'

'Have I?'

'Indeed, you have. You see… er… just now father thinks I am in my room studying. But I am afraid I am a bad student and sneaked out here to hide, and quaff a noggin or two. It's my refuge from law books and such weighty matters, you know.' He slapped the landlord on the back. 'Micah here is most discreet. He feared you were sent by the Squire to spy on me, isn't that right, Micah?'

The man nodded, a little uncertainly, I thought.

'You know how obsessed my father is with spies, Mrs. Hudson. Not above a bit of spying on his own account, do you see.' Freddie laughed, a little too loudly. 'Well, well, well,' he continued, rubbing his hands. 'So you are drinking beer in good company.' He sat himself down with us.

'Just until the rain eases off,' I replied.

'Of course, of course, Let it not be thought that you regularly frequent such dubious establishments as this. Ha ha… Well, Micah, bring me over a mug of the same and we can all toast each other's good health.'

For a few moments we sat in silence, while the landlord fetched the drink. The two old men seemed easy, Billy puffing on his pipe, the other staring at the fire, nodding his head at private thoughts.

Freddie, however, looked to be restless, tapping one foot on the floor. I didn't feel comfortable either. Something strange was going on.

'You'll be staying for the harvest festival, then, m'm.' Micah addressed me, as he handed Freddie his mug.

'Yes, I suppose I may as well now. It's in a few days, isn't it?'

'Along o' the pickers' feast.'

'Oh!' I was a little surprised. 'Are they not the one event?'

My companions burst out laughing.

'God bless you for a furriner!' exclaimed Zachariah. 'Not at all! The likes of us aren't let go to the pickers' feast. As if we would anyway. That's for that London lot. And them gypsies.'

He shook his head.

'I see.'

'The harvest festival, now, that's nought to do with...' Now Zachariah lowered his voice for some reason, 'with them Brakefields, d'you see, even though in past years they've made out it does.'

'Thomas Brakefield isn't too pleased,' Freddie put in, also quietly, 'that this year they're on the same day.'

'That's not usual then?' I asked.

'Not at all,' Micah added, sotto voce. Why was everyone was whispering, suddenly? 'See, hisself likes to pretend he's lord of the manor when we all know it's your father, Master Freddie.' He gave a nod that was very nearly a little bow. 'We're all for the squire here,' he added for my benefit.

'Anyways we got round the vicar to announce it for the one day,' Zachariah said.

Freddie grinned. 'I don't think the poor man realised why Thomas was glaring at him so hard, and when he did it was too late to change.'

'Quite right too,' Zachariah added. 'Why should we make ways for the likes of them? Harvest festival, 'tis a village thing. Thanksgiving service at church and then… well…'

'A frolic on the green,' Freddie said.

'All very respectable, now, m'm,' Micah put in hastily. 'You'll enjoy it.'

'I'm looking forward to it already.'

'Actually, you know,' Freddie continued, 'Thomas Brakefield might still be able to preside over both events. The feast doesn't start until the evening by which time most of the harvest festivities will be over.'

This thought seemed to plunge the assembly into gloom.

'Anyway,' Freddie suddenly shouted, making me jump again. 'Eat, drink and be merry for tomorrow etcetera, etcetera… More Old Devilish all round, Micah!' Had he already downed his drink?

'Actually,' I said, rising, 'I think I'll check on the weather for I really should be getting back.'

'I understand,' Freddie winked. 'The lovely Eleanor will be worried.'

It was true that I was anxious to leave, so I was delighted to be able to report back that the heavy shower had already passed over, and that I must be off instantly in case another followed hard on its heels. No one tried to keep me, but before I left, I took another draught of the beer, again pronouncing it excellent, to counter the fact that I had hardly drunk any of it. I was about to pay when Freddie forestalled me.

'Good heavens, Mrs. Hudson. Please desist,' he said. 'I cannot possibly permit a lady to reach for her purse in my company. It will be my pleasure to treat you all, and you too, Micah, if you have a mind to a bevvy.'

The old men nodded their appreciation, but the landlord shook his head.

'Thank you, Master Freddie, but I'll take something later with my dinner.'

'Something tasty's on the hob, I'll warrant,' Freddie said.

'Ay.' Micah slapped his belly to make a rather crude point. 'Betsy has a jugged hare in the pot.'

'I wonder who caught that. And where,' Freddie said.

Micah just grinned.

I took my leave of them then, quite certain that at least one person present was glad to see me go, however hard he had pressed me to come in earlier. It was quite a mystery.

As I set off, I noticed that another horse was now tethered beside Pegasus. It was a grey mare with a most distinctive white blaze on its forehead, suggesting the horn of a unicorn. Since the horse most certainly had not been there before, it could not belong to either of the old men, nor yet the landlord. One conclusion might be that someone had joined Freddie through another door into the back room. His excuse for being there was, after all, very feeble, as if thought up on the spur of the moment. Moreover, the secrecy, to which the others present were party, surely indicated that something unusual was up. Could the unknown visitor be a woman? It certainly looked from where I was standing as if the horse was wearing a side saddle. I was mightily intrigued, but could hardly go and peer through the back window to see if I was right. Well, at least, I consoled myself, if Freddie were caught up in some *affaire de coeur*, he would surely leave my Eleanor in peace.

CHAPTER ELEVEN

Returning to the shop, I found it in turmoil, full of women chattering nineteen to the dozen. It was a while before I understood what was going on, and it was up to Henrietta, leading the mob, finally to explain it to me.

'Whatever do you think, Martha? Lydia Brakefield has invited us all to a garden party.'

Amazing news indeed.

'In all the years that she has lived here, she has never done any such thing. Her ladyship has always turned her nose up at the likes of us. Her loss, of course, since we here in Bilbourne are as cultivated as any of your London people.' Henrietta frowned then. 'Mind you, Martha, you needn't think it has anything to do with your presence.'

'I assure you, no such notion occurred to me.'

'Well, anyway, that's how it is.'

'When you say *everyone* is invited...'

'Oh, only we ladies. The men must stay home... Apparently, you see, Mr. Brakefield will be away on business that day, so the coast will be clear of that particular unpleasantness.'

Eleanor intervened at that stage. 'I shouldn't be surprised to learn that his wife was forced by her husband to avoid us villagers all this time. The poor thing has probably been terribly lonely, and has been longing to have more to do with us.'

From what little I knew of Lydia Brakefield, it would have utterly astonished me if that were indeed the case. To me, she had expressed only scorn for the locals. But I said nothing in contradiction. It was typical and charming of my daughter to look for the best in people.

Henrietta, however, reared up. 'Well, if that is so, it's a very poor look-out for our sex. That a wife should give way to her husband on matters of public interest, politics, economicals and the like, is fair enough... And don't you say a word, Martha, for I know you and I disagree on that particular subject. But, as I've said before and will say again to my dying day, the wife should rule the household. It is her domain and if she wants to invite friends round, or do anything of the sort, then she should be allowed to do so.'

These remarks were received with general approbation by the ladies present, I considering with some amusement of what would happen if Walter ever tried to lord it over his wife. Meanwhile, amidst the commotion, poor George and Joe continued attempting to serve those who actually wished to purchase something. Very few of those present, as it turned out. All the talk revolved round what should be worn for a garden party. Sunday best suddenly seemed far too dingy, and plans were everywhere afoot for expeditions to the drapers in Kenwardham.

'When is this exciting event to take place?' I asked.

Henrietta gave me a sharp look as if to check that I wasn't mocking them. My innocent expression however, must have dispelled her suspicions.

'After harvest festival. The feast for the pickers is on the same day, you know, so by then that lot should all have gone back to wherever it is they came from, thanks be to God.'

'So soon? Goodness, that doesn't give you much time to get ready.'

Another searching look. Another of my innocent faces.

'I suppose,' said Henrietta, 'that Madam Brakefield is under the impression that like herself we all have a wardrobe stuffed full of suitable dresses and hats. However, little matter. The ladies of Bilbourne will manage as they always do... By the way, Martha, wherever have you been? You look quite bedraggled, and is that beer I smell on your breath?'

Nothing escaped the woman's notice.

'I got caught in the rain,' I said, ignoring the second of her remarks, and the looks cast upon me by the others.

'Upstairs at once and dry yourself, mama,' Eleanor said, 'before you catch a cold.'

Usually, I would be annoyed at her fussing, but just now it served my purpose. To get away from Henrietta and her 'gang,' as Eleanor dubbed the gossips of the village. As for the garden party, I could not help but wonder. Lydia Brakefield seemed the last person on earth to covet the company of such as us.

Eleanor accompanying me upstairs, as thankful as I was, I suspect, to get away from the throng below. I asked her if there had been any word from Eve, to which she replied in the negative.

'I am concerned about her,' I said.

'Well, nothing to be done there,' she replied. 'Take off that wet dress before you get rheumatism.'

'I have never suffered from rheumatism in my life, Eleanor.'

'In that case, you don't want to start now.'

She made to leave and give me privacy. However, I called her back to convey her father-in-law's suggestion that we all go on an outing to Rochester to see the castle. 'You, George, Henrietta, Walter and me.'

'What a lovely idea, mama. Of course, George and I have visited the castle gardens before. They are delightful.' She looked thoughtful. 'We can leave Joe in charge of the shop for one day,' she said. 'Although I am not sure about the post office. It would be a shame if someone had to stay behind to look after it.'

Would it really? I thought, but remarked, 'I imagine Walter was thinking of a Sunday. Immediately after church.'

'Yes, that would work well. How very nice... So many things to look forward to.'

113

She left me then, exhorting me again to change my dress and, if the wet had got through to my undergarments (if you'll excuse my mentioning them), to change them too. Good heavens! The girl badly needed a baby to employ her nurturing instincts.

I lay down on my bed in my robe and took up a book from Eleanor's little collection, since I had finished all that I had brought with me. It was an old novel by Mrs. Elizabeth Gaskell, titled 'North and South,' which Eleanor recommended highly for its depiction of the ills facing working-class people. From her little Kentish village, my daughter was developing a strong social conscience, of which I could only approve. However, overcome after my walk, I soon dropped off to sleep, the book falling from my hand.

Another day passed for me in an agony of frustration, unable as I was to forward my plan regarding Timothy. I felt it incumbent on me to write back to Mary Goodhart in Hampshire, for she must surely have been wondering at my delay in dispatching the youth. I explained no more than that there was a necessary postponement, but that I should endeavour to send better news very soon. Then, as I was kicking my heels ever more vigorously, another invitation arrived from Ursula to take tea at the vicarage on the morrow, 'for my husband so wants to talk to you about your famous lodger.' It hardly improved my spirit. The last thing I wanted to do was to chat about Mr. H with an enthusiast, who, as Henrietta had predicted, could only be disappointed by my lack of intimate knowledge (or refusal to share). At least I could hope to speak with Ursula on the subject that engaged both of us.

Thus it was that at the appointed time, I set off, on this occasion without Eleanor. She had been prevailed on that same day to accompany her mother-in-law on a shopping expedition to Kenwardham in order to purchase dresses, or, if nothing appropriate could be found, cloth for the making of them, to be worn at the forthcoming garden party. Henrietta had been quite put out that I had declined to accompany them.

'Well,' she said. 'I am glad you consider that your wardrobe includes something suitably grand, Martha.'

I didn't have the energy to explain that Clara had insisted, against my doubts that I would have any occasion to wear it, on packing the cerise silk dress I had bought in Paris, nor yet that I had half a mind to return to London immediately after the harvest festival, thus missing the garden party altogether. Just now, the vicarage invitation provided me with a good excuse for missing out on the Kenwardham shops with Henrietta. On balance, tea with the Considines was certainly the lesser of two evils.

'You know,' I told her. 'It would be most impolite to refuse the vicar's invitation.'

'I'm sure they wouldn't care tuppence about that,' she replied. 'But I can see your mind is made up, so I will say no more on the subject.' She pursed her lips. She would no doubt say plenty to Eleanor and the others on the journey.

The vicarage parlour was as take-us-as-you-find-us as it was on the earlier occasion, both the vicar and his wife seeming to notice nothing amiss as they removed books and papers from chairs for us to sit upon, or kicked (this was the vicar) a ball under the table, where it collided with a toy train, knocking it off its rails. The boys were at school, but this time, at least, I was rewarded with the presence of baby Emily, a fat, gurgling, smiling infant of near one year old, who had not yet quite managed to walk, but who could crawl with amazing speed, to the delight of her doting parents.

'See how she runs!' her father said. 'Have you ever seen a child move as quickly as that?'

I nodded, while musing how so many parents think their own children must be exceptional in every way.

Ursula went off to busy herself in the kitchen and hurry up the maid, leaving me with the vicar, who instantly called my attention to a great pile of papers now lying on the floor. These turned out to be issues of The Strand magazine, in which Dr. Watson's accounts of his and Mr. H's adventures are regularly published.

'I think I must have every one of them to date,' the vicar said, rubbing his chin in excitement. 'Now, Mrs. Hudson, you must tell me everything.'

'Everything! Goodness! That's a tall order, Mr. Considine.'

It was a great relief, then, to discover that, unlike Henrietta, he was far from wanting to be titillated by details of scandals. His interests were domestic, and ones that I could easily satisfy. What was Mr. H's favourite dinner, for instance? I explained that Mr. H seldom paid attention to his food as long as it was well-cooked. How he soon complained if his egg was too soft or too hard-boiled, insisting on a precise four and a half minutes of simmering.

'I wonder sometimes,' I said, 'why he doesn't prepare it himself. He possesses a Bunsen burner for his experiments and a good stop watch. I could provide him with a suitable pan.'

Mr. Considine chuckled merrily at that.

'But regarding his tastes in general,' I said, 'he certainly prefers traditional English food. After my travels to Ireland and France, I endeavoured to offer dishes native to those countries, without much success, though Dr. Watson appreciated my efforts. Sadly, Mr. H turned his nose up at my stirabout, my coq au vin and my tarte normande.'

'Oh my, oh my!' exclaimed the vicar, shaking with mirth, 'That's priceless, Mrs. Hudson. Quite priceless. Coq au vin, indeed. Ha ha ha! Quite priceless.'

I was pleased to be able to entertain him so easily.

'By the way, vicar,' I said. 'You must explain something to me.'

He smiled, though perhaps a little warily: was I about to ask him some esoteric point of doctrine?

'In your sermon, you mentioned wearing clothes made of nettles. I have to admit it puzzled me. Were you referring to mortification of the flesh?'

He laughed even more loudly at that, astonishing little Emily, who then clapped her chubby hands and chortled along with her father.

'Good heavens, no, Mrs. Hudson, I am certainly not one of those priests who think it necessary to punish ourselves in that way. Hair shirts, flagellation and so on... Not at all. Ha ha ha... No, you see, with very little trouble, nettle fibre can be made into a strong and attractive yarn. In fact, the jacket I am wearing now is made of it.'

I was astonished. The vicar's jacket, a dark green weave, though perhaps somewhat dusty and crumpled, was of a serviceable looking fabric.

'Touch it. Go in,' he urged.

'Will it sting me?'

'Ha ha ha.'

I leant forward, and tentatively felt the hem between my fingers. It was pleasantly soft.

'I have tried in vain,' said he, 'to persuade the villagers to set up a cottage industry to produce the cloth. Sadly, they prefer to buy ready-made stuff in Kenwardham.'

'That is indeed a pity,' I remarked. 'I love to see nature put to good use.'

'Perhaps you can use your good influences, or even...' a fanatical glint had crept into his eye, 'learn how to make it yourself, Mrs Hudson. There's an old woman I know who can give you lessons. She's the one who wove this fabric for me.'

'Well, now...' I started to say, but was reprieved by the return of Ursula. She was followed in by the maid wheeling a tea trolley loaded with the same mismatched set of porcelain cups, saucers and plates as before, a tarnished silver milk jug and a teapot with a chipped lid, as well as a high pile of sandwiches, cakes, scones, buns and biscuits.

'Good heavens!' I exclaimed. 'I hope you don't expect me to eat so much.'

'Whatever we don't manage, the boys will help put away,' Ursula said. 'The rest I can distribute among the pickers later.'

Little Emily, meanwhile, who by the look of her mouth had been busy off somewhere eating fluff, now whizzed across the room and tried to haul herself up on to the trolley, placing it and herself in imminent danger of collapse. At the last minute, her father scooped her up, along with a currant bun on which the child munched happily for the next while, sitting on his lap. It was a charming and somewhat unusual sight, the vicar in his dog collar and dusty frock coat holding the plump and rather grubby child, the top of whose head he kissed from time to time, between taking bites of his own bun. A somewhat blasphemous association occurred to me, a reversed Madonna and Child, the father and baby daughter.

Ursula poured the tea. Then offered me my choice of comestibles.

'It's so difficult to decide,' I said, eventually selecting two small sandwiches of potted meat, along with a bath bun, not because I was hungry, but because I felt it would be impolite not to try and do the feast some justice.

'Just help yourself if you want any more.'

'I was telling Mrs. Hudson about my jacket,' Mr. Considine said, returning to the previous subject. 'She is most interested in how they make fabric from nettles. I am trying to persuade her to take up the craft herself.'

Ursula glanced at me.

'I am sure Martha, like myself, is far too busy for that.'

'In any case,' I said. 'Where I live in London, vicar, nettles are very few and far between. But I should certainly be interested in purchasing such fabric if you ever get your cottage industry off the ground.'

'Ah, well,' he replied good-humouredly. 'As to that, it is the fate of such as I to be a voice crying in the wilderness.'

We chatted on then most amiably, I wondering to myself how Eleanor was faring with Henrietta in Kenwardham, more sure than ever that I was the better off, my parsonage visit proving considerably more enjoyable than I had anticipated. I liked Ursula very much, and there was an evident bond of affection between the vicar and his wife that rather reminded me of the relationship between myself and dear Henry, and latterly between my daughters and their husbands. Moreover, unlike anyone else I had encountered in the village, the couple shewed an interest in hearing about my life and opinions, which, I admit, gratified me, even though I am far from ever wishing to blow my own trumpet. I spoke of Ireland and Paris, though resisted the temptation to describe in detail my various adventures in those places, since they were perhaps rather too sensational for clerical ears. The subject of Mr. H cropped up a few more times as well – the vicar being particularly interested in the detective's chemical experiments, 'Being something of an amateur that way myself, you know, Mrs. Hudson.' At the which, Ursula made a face and shook her head.

'I fear he will blow us all up one of these days, Martha,' she said.

'I often feel the same in Baker Street,' I replied. 'The odours emitting from Mr. H's rooms are truly horrible.'

The vicar chuckled merrily at that intelligence, saying again, 'Oh my, oh my!' then adding 'But nothing I do is dangerous, though the boys love to see what happens when you add baking soda to vinegar.'

'What happens?' I asked.

'Will I shew you?' He was already preparing to get up. 'It's even better with a few drops of cochineal.'

'Not now, Oliver dear,' Ursula replied, adding for my benefit. 'It creates a red volcano, Mrs. Hudson. And a terrible mess.'

'That sounds most interesting,' I said. 'Maybe another time,'

The vicar seemed a little disappointed, although he was clearly enjoying our discourse, and displayed no inclination to leave the two of us women together. In vain did Ursula suggest that he might have business to attend to, a sermon to write, some parishioner to visit. No, he was perfectly happy to sit dandling baby Emily on his lap while; for her part, she continued to munch her way through an alarming number of buns.

'Are you going to Mrs. Brakefield's garden party next week?' I asked Ursula.

She sighed. 'I suppose I'll have to.'

I explained how my daughter and her mother-in-law had gone to Kenwardham to buy outfits for the occasion.

'Good heavens,' Ursula replied. 'It never occurred to me before, but I suppose we'll all be expected to dress up. I wonder if I have anything suitable.'

'Of course, you have, my dear,' her husband replied. 'Sadly not,' he went on, winking at me, 'made of nettles. But you have lots of pretty dresses.'

To look at his wife just now in her drab and undoubtedly worn cotton gown, with its stains, baby dribbles and what looked like dried mud, one would have to doubt it.

'If only they still fit me,' she wailed. 'I haven't been able to lose the weight I put on before Emily was born.'

At the sound of her name, that little person grinned, dropped her bun, then started to scream – and how amazing it is that a creature so small can produce so much ear-splitting noise. In vain did her father proffer another bun to her. No, it was the fallen one she wanted. In vain did he tell her it was dirty. Now Emily stretched out her arms to her mother, who picked up the sobbing mite and carried her over to the window, murmuring consoling words as they went.

'See, baba,' Ursula said. 'There's Eve.'

Emily immediately forgot her woes, and cooed with excitement, while I jumped up and hurried to join them where they stood.

'Where is she?'

In the distance, on the meadow backing on to the vicarage garden, someone was cantering on horseback.

'Is that Eve?' I asked, peering out.

'Yes, we often see her there on the common, exercising her horse.'

'What once was the common, my dear,' the vicar corrected her. 'You know it's enclosed now.'

Ursula nodded. 'Of course.'

'I'm most anxious to talk to her,' I said. 'Would you mind very much if I went out and tried to attract her attention?'

'Not at all. I'll come with you.'

With Ursula still carrying Emily, we traversed the garden where a youth was trying to look busy tidying the flower beds.

Ursula greeted him. 'On with the good work, Samuel,' she cried cheerily, 'but mind the asters. They aren't weeds, you know.'

He grinned back, brandishing his trowel.

'A simple soul,' she confided. 'The cook's boy. Weak in the head. I like to give him something to do, and out here he can't get up to too much harm.'

We reached the back fence and she waved with her free hand at Eve. It took a few moments to capture the girl's attention, but at last she saw us and brought the horse trotting over to us. I was most taken aback. It was a grey mare with a distinctive blaze on its forehead that resembled a unicorn's horn.

'Is this your horse, Eve?' I asked her after we had all greeted each other.

'Yes.' She smiled and stroked the beast's neck. 'This is Queen Mab.'

'She's beautiful,' I continued. 'And I am most impressed with your outfit.'

Eve was wearing that new fashion called bloomers, wide trousers under a short skirt. It enabled her to rise astride the horse instead of side-saddle as women are wont to do.

'Much more practical,' she said, adding with a giggle, 'Lydia hates them.'

Emily stretched out a fearless little hand to stroke the great nose that poked over the fence.

'She's looking for a sugar lump,' said Ursula. 'I didn't bring one with me this time, I'm afraid.'

'Oh, Mab gets plenty of sugar lumps,' Eve said. 'But raw carrots are her favourite.'

'I was hoping you would call round,' I told her. When she looked puzzled, I added, 'In answer to my letter, you know.'

'What letter?'

'The one Joe delivered the other day.'

She shook her head. 'I received no letter from you, Mrs. Hudson.'

'I sent it over while you were ill.'

'Ill?'

'I was told you had a bad headache. Last Sunday, at church.'

The girl looked troubled. 'Oh... well... I don't know. Maybe they forgot to give it to me. Or perhaps your boy forgot to bring it.'

I could not doubt that Joe had delivered it as he said, so the omission, deliberate or not, lay somewhere in the household.

'It concerned Timothy,' I said. 'Mrs. Considine and I are worried about him.'

'Timmy? I see... Well...'

Just then someone shouted at her from the far end of the field.

'I have to go,' she said. 'We can talk soon. I'll find a way.' With that and a wave, she cantered off.

'That's most odd,' I said. 'Why would they not give her my letter?'

'It's strange, all right,' Ursula said, musing. 'Perhaps they indeed forgot. Or perhaps they confiscated it, thinking it was from some beau.' She laughed.

'In that case, would they not have opened it and have seen that it was no such thing?'

'Hmm, well yes. I suppose so.'

'At church the other day,' I went on, 'when I asked why Eve wasn't there, her stepmother said she had a headache, but Randall claimed she had been locked up in her room.'

'You wouldn't want to believe what Randall says.' Ursula shook her head. 'That child... well...'

'Lies?'

'Makes things up.'

'I hope it's that.'

Much as I liked Ursula, I didn't consider that I knew her well enough to reveal the task Lydia Brakefield had tried to impose upon me, to spy on her stepdaughter.

Still, I asked, 'Has Eve a beau then?'

'Chance would be a fine thing for the poor girl. Not at all. Who is she ever allowed to meet? How will she ever, the way they keep her close, be able to spread her wings and fly?'

Perhaps, I thought, recalling the scene at the inn, Eve had after all found her own, perilous way of flying. Could she really have had an assignation with Freddie Simister there? It was a most troubling notion. But the grey mare was quite definitely the one I had seen tethered up outside.

Of course, I said nothing of the sort to Ursula, though I felt it quite in order to tell her how Timothy had refused my suggestion that he go away, despite the general unpleasantness of life on the plantation – how indeed I had seen him whipped by Mr. Brakefield.

'Eleanor put his refusal down to him being in love with Eve. That being the case, I reckoned only Eve could persuade him to go away for his own good, and that's what I wanted to talk to her about.'

'Ah,' Ursula replied, smiling. 'Well, perhaps the girl wouldn't be happy to see him leave either, since they are friends.'

'I had thought of that, too.'

She shook her head. 'Nothing is ever simple, is it? Well, you have done your best, Martha. That's all any of us can ever do.'

The girl on horseback had disappeared by now, and we turned back to the house.

'If you wish,' Ursula said, 'you might accompany me tonight when I go out among the pickers. You might see Timothy there. Maybe he has thought things over by now.'

'I doubt he will have changed his mind,' I said, 'but, yes, I should like that. I'm not used to idleness, and find doing nothing most wearing.'

'Oh, if that is the case, Martha,' she replied, 'I am sure I can find lots of things for you to do around here. You need never be bored again.'

Soon afterwards, I took my leave of the Considines, arranging to return that same evening to join Ursula on her mission of mercy. On the way back, I paused at the duck pond and sat myself down, not quite ready yet to face the household. I wasn't expecting anyone to join me, and no one did, so I remained there for a good while, watching the ducks at their antics, trying unsuccessfully to banish troubling thoughts.

It was only much later that something struck me, which I should have noticed at the time, given how much Mr. H emphasises the importance of observation. Perhaps, indeed, you, my readers are ahead of me. I expect at least some of you are. But whether it would have changed anything, if I had thought of it just then, is a moot point.

CHAPTER TWELVE

'You really should have come with us, Martha,' Henrietta remarked, spreading her purchases out over the parlour chairs for me to admire. 'You must admit that Madame Bertha has some outfits quite as good as any you'd find in your London shops.'

The dress she had chosen was certainly eye-catching, nay eye-watering, yellow polka dots on shimmering pillar-box-red satin, with flounces and bows in all manner of extraordinary places.

'Indeed,' I said, 'I doubt you could find anything like it either in London or Paris.'

Eleanor gave me a sharp look, but Henrietta was too pleased with her choice to suspect any double meaning.

'Yes, indeed. Bertha is a wonder,' she continued. 'I am surprised she has confined her talents to Kenwardham, when she could have made a fortune elsewhere. But her loss is our gain. Isn't that right, Eleanor?'

Without waiting for a reply, she then demonstrated the hat she had purchased, adorned with great yellow plumes to match, as she said, the dress. 'For you have to make a special effort with your headwear at a garden party, you know, Martha.'

How many ostriches, I wondered, had given their lives for that hat?

'And of course, Madame Bertha is much cheaper than dressmakers elsewhere. You wouldn't believe, Martha, what all this cost. It was almost for nothing. At least,' she gave a wink and a smile, 'that's what I shall tell Walter.'

'What about you, Eleanor?' I asked. 'Did you buy anything?'

'Oh, nothing pleased her,' Henrietta said. 'Bertha had a blue dress that would have complemented Eleanor's colouring perfectly, and would have gone well next to mine, but she wasn't having it.'

'Didn't I buy some green cloth, mother-in-law, to make up my own pattern.'

'Oh, olive green, so dull,' scoffed Henrietta. 'And anyway, as I told you, green is unlucky, but would you listen? Such a shame. Bertha's creation was such a lovely shade of royal blue.'

'Too bright for me.'

'But didn't you hear Bertha tell us how vivid colours are *in* this season, Eleanor?'

'It was too frilly. I prefer to have something simpler,' my daughter replied. 'Something that I can wear afterwards.'

'Oh, I'll wear mine afterwards. You can bank on that.'

She left shortly afterwards, to my considerable relief, and, I am sure, Eleanor's as well.

'You have great patience, my dear,' I told her.

'Maybe, but I am quite worn out now,' she replied.

I insisted on preparing the supper, despite her objections, while she went to lie down. To tell the truth, I was a little concerned, for she looked pinched, and paler than usual. Of course, she had been out all day running around with Henrietta, which probably explained it.

Having served up dishes of a plain enough fare of boiled beef, potatoes and cabbage, for George, Eleanor and Joe, who often shared supper with his employers, I excused myself to go and meet Ursula.

'Will you not be hungry, mother?' Eleanor asked. 'Can you not sit down with us first?'

I had been nibbling on and off while cooking, and so felt no pangs. In addition, I was loth to keep my friend waiting.

'Not at all,' I said. 'In any case, Ursula is taking left-overs to the pickers, so I can have a bun if necessary to keep me going.'

'Bring some broken biscuits with you,' George said. 'I keep them for my poorer customers. They're in a sack under the till.'

'I'll show you, m'm,' said the ever-obliging Joe, jumping up.

He soon produced the said biscuits, and put a fair quantity in a bag for me.

'That should do you all right,' he said, smiling, and taking a biscuit for himself with a grin.

I thanked him and, thus laden with goodies, set off for the parsonage.

It was a brisk walk up past the Post Office and school, and alongside what had been the common, to arrive at the sheds where the pickers were housed. Although Ursula had warned me, no words could have prepared me for the squalor in which those poor wretches were forced to live. Sleeping quarters consisted of a cluster of small windowless sheds without any furniture, only straw to sleep on, although pickers who had worked there before had the foresight to bring with them potato sacks or rough blankets. Within the sheds, people had lit fires for cooking and to warm themselves, which seemed extremely dangerous to me, with all that dry straw around.

When I said as much to Ursula, she just shrugged. 'What are they supposed to do? They are cold and hungry.'

'I thought they were supposed to have meals provided.'

She made a face, and led me to the shed where our friend Nancy and her two children were lying stretched out after a hard day's work, bowls beside them. Nancy stood up as we approached.

'Tell Mrs. Hudson what a delicious supper you've all enjoyed tonight, Nancy,' Ursula said.

In response the woman proffered the bowl to me. It contained what looked like dirty water with some unidentifiable lumps floating in it.

'Whatever's that?' I asked.

'Turnip soup,' she replied. 'Disgusting, it is. I wouldn't give it to my worst enemy.'

'Well, we've brought you something to cheer you up a bit.' Ursula opened her bag and took out sandwiches and buns. I contributed some biscuits.

'They're a bit broken,' I said, 'but fine otherwise.'

'Don't you worry about that, m'm. They get broke anyways when we bite into 'em.' She was suddenly energised. 'Come on, childer. See what the nice ladies have brought you.'

The boy got up, but little Sarey stayed where she was.

'Come on, Sarey, love. It'll make you feel better.'

The child raised herself with some difficulty, whimpering, and limped over to us.

'What's happened to her?' I asked.

'That monster's what happened to 'er,' Nancy replied. 'Thomas Brakefield. Went mad with 'is whip. Said she stole some apples 'cause he saw her eating one.'

We were both shocked.

'As if she could even climb into that orchard,' I said.

'Well... as to that...' Nancy looked suddenly confused.

'Was me what done it,' the boy said. 'He should of beat me.'

'Now, now, Charlie,' said his mother. 'Hush up.'

'He shouldn't beat anyone,' Ursula said. 'He should feed you properly. Then you wouldn't have to go scrumping.'

'In any case,' I added, 'there's apples and plums a-plenty in that orchard, and many are rotting because no one is picking them.'

'Yes,' Nancy said bitterly. 'But they're Brakefield's rotting apples and no one else must touch 'em.'

'It's just not right.' Ursula wrung her hands.

'Course it's not right. None of it... Dan'l be raging over it.'

'Where is he?'

Nancy sighed. 'I dunno. Gone to the Green Man, I guess. Drowning 'is sorrers or getting up some Dutch courage.'

'He isn't planning to do anything silly now, is he, Nancy?' Ursula asked anxiously.

'Said e'd like to kill the old b....d.' The boy spoke with relish.

'Charlie!'

'Well, 'e did.'

'O' course 'e won't. He's all talk, my Dan'l is. Mind you, he dotes on Sarey here, don't he, pet?' She ruffled the child's matted curls.

'Ah, she's daddy's girl, all right, ain't you Sarey?' It was the man himself, entering the shed. He swept the child up in his arms and cradled her tenderly. 'How are you, pet?'

I was perforce reminded of the scene at the parsonage just a few hours before. Father and daughter.

'Oh Lordie! Not you lot again!'

Daniel had been followed in by Stephen, the overseer. He was regarding Ursula and myself with dislike, mouthing the word 'do-gooders' with a pejorative expletive in front of it which I will not include.

'Thought you was going to the pub, Dan'l,' Nancy said.

'Bumped into Stephen here, didn't I? Said he would make it right.'

'And how's he going to do that, eh? Make them cuts and bruises disappear, is 'e?'

'Now then, Nancy,' Stephen said. He turned to us. 'This here's estate business. Nothing for you ladies to get hot under the collar about. Mr. Brakefield was perfectly justified in protecting his property.'

'Justified!' Ursula was incensed. 'Beating a small child!'

'What have this lot been telling you?' Stephen protested. 'Just a little slap, it was.'

'With a whip,' I replied. 'The action of a coward, picking on the most weak and defenceless.'

The overseer sighed and made a dismissive gesture, which incensed me.

'Listen Stephen,' I went on. 'I saw how Mr. Brakefield laid into one of his workers, another child. His rage got the better of him. He had to be restrained before he inflicted real damage.'

'Well, mebbe he got a bit carried away this time. But, you know, these people here are used to a bit of physical.' He addressed the father. 'I bet you beat the kids yourself, Daniel, when they cross you.'

'Never! Not that way.'

'If Sarey 'ad been really badly 'urt or God forbid killed,' Nancy said, 'then what, Stephen?' She paused. 'I'll tell yer what. His magistrate pals would let him off like what you did. Justified in protecting 'is property. But if my Dan'l did anything like back at 'im, they'd 'ang him in a blink. Ain't that so?'

'No one got killed, Nancy. Nothing near it.'

'Still and all,' Daniel put in, 'if he so much as touches any of mine again without very good reason, so 'elp me, I'll kill him, the b....d. I'll slit his d...d throat. Don't think I won't.'

He spat on the ground.

'Now, now, Daniel, calm yourself down,' Stephen said, laying a hand on the other's shoulder, which he shook off. 'Listen to Nancy. You do anything stupid and it'll be you who pays the bigger price.'

'So Nancy's right. If 'e kills my daughter, 'e gets off. If I kill 'im I'll 'ang, is that it?'

Stephen smiled. 'More or less. We all know life's not fair, now, don't we, folks. My advice to you: forget about it. In a few days it'll be the pickers' feast. A great fat greasy pig on the spit for you to enjoy. And in a week's time you'll be back in London.'

'I know what pig I'd like to see on the spit,' Daniel muttered.

'No more of that sort of talk or you'll be in deep trouble.' Stephen's eyes had narrowed to slits. Then he reached in his pocket.

'Take this half-crown, Dan, and no more hard feelings, heh?' He proffered the coin.

The man rejected it scornfully.

'Blood money is it, a whole 'alf-crown. So how much if he'd kilt her then, eh? A guinea? Two guineas?... Go away, Stephen, like the lackey you are, and take you take your d....d bribe with you.' He struck the coin from Stephen's hand.

The overseer bent to pick it up from among the straw stalks. I could see he was barely containing his rage.

'You're stark staring mad, Daniel Ridge,' he said. 'That child's hardly bruised.'

'Is that right?'

Daniel raised Sarey's skirt. Ursula and I gasped at the sight of her skinny little legs, red with angry weals. She buried her face in her father's shoulder.

'D'you want to see her back too, Stephen, where 'e beat her? Then tell me she's barely bruised.'

'Listen, Daniel. Do yourself a favour and leave it be....' The overseer's voice turned cajoling. 'Here, Sarey, love, if your dad don't want it, why don't you take this nice shiny coin. Buy you lots of sweeties.'

The child cringed back, against her father's breast.

'Give it 'ere,' Nancy said, ignoring her husband's dark looks. She took the half-crown and put it in the bosom of her dress.

'Blood money, like I said, and not much of it,' muttered Daniel.

'I take whatever's going,' Nancy replied.

'Good girl yourself.' Stephen gave her a broad and triumphant smile. 'Your wife's got sense as well as beauty, Daniel.'

Job done, he turned and left the shed.

It was an ugly scene, and I was sorry to be part of it, although it brought home to me just how hard life is for some, and how easy for others. Nancy's miserable bowl of turnip soup beside Lydia's salmon mousse. Good heavens, Martha, I said to myself, be careful or you'll turn into a socialist.

Having examined little Sarey's injuries, Ursula asked that Charlie come down to the parsonage with her to fetch some ointment to help them heal.

'No need, thank you kindly, m'm,' Nancy replied. 'There's a gypsy woman here give me some salve made of 'erbs, Made you feel better, di'nt it, Sarey?'

The child nodded.

For myself, I could do no more for them than press another half-crown into Nancy's hand, and then we took our leave, Ursula expressing the hope of seeing the family at church on the Sunday. Nancy nodded but Daniel shook his head as if to say what has your God ever done for us? We then continued on our rounds to other families, my purse emptying further at the sight of so much need. Most were grateful, but a few looked upon us with dislike, as Stephen had, and even resentment. To them we must have appeared as prosperous Lady Bountifuls, appeasing our consciences with a little charity.

All the time I was keeping an eye open for Timothy, but again he was nowhere to be found. No one even admitted to having seen him. I was conscious, too, that Stephen was following us, discreetly enough and at a distance, but just so that we knew he was there. What did he think we were about? Stirring up dissatisfaction among the pickers? We weren't needed for that: The Brakefields seemed to manage perfectly well without our help.

Eventually, baskets emptied, we left the camp as the sun was setting. Night comes down like a heavy blanket in the countryside, unless there's a moon to counter the impenetrable blackness. As I remarked to Ursula, I should not care to be caught outdoors without a lamp to guide me.

'Indeed not,' she said. 'City dwellers have no idea of real darkness. I myself didn't before we came to live here.'

She went on to tell me how, at the time of their marriage, her husband was serving as vicar in a slum parish in a northern city.

'When the twins came along, we were unwilling to rear them in such a place, so Oliver asked to be moved. I have always felt guilty about it. Bilbourne is such a wonderful place for children to grow up in, but I know that we are privileged, not like those poor folk we have just visited, who have no choice as to where they live. I can only imagine what Daniel and Nancy are going back to.'

'He won't do anything foolish regarding Thomas Brakefield, will he?'

'I hope not. I trust he is all bluster… so long as nothing else bad happens.'

With that sobering thought in mind, we walked on in silence down towards the village, dusk falling in a blue veil that blurred and softened the world around us. Soon, welcome lights from the cottages shewed us the path. At the bottom of the hill, we parted ways with an agreement to meet again soon. As I passed the duck pond, I glanced towards the seat under the shadowy willow branches, in the unlikely hope that Timothy would be waiting there. Of course, he was not, and I wondered if our plan to save him from this place was doomed after all.

CHAPTER THIRTEEN

Over the next days I was surprised and disappointed not to receive a visit from Eve. I had assumed, given her good nature, as well as her interest in Timothy, that she would endeavour to see me, and hoped that her absence had nothing to do with Freddie Simister. If her hot-tempered father had found out she was meeting him in secret, I dreaded to think what he might do.

On the Saturday morning, George came up to the parlour where I was reading, to say that I had a visitor, and could I come down. He said no more than that, but his face had a droll expression on it.

Eve at long last was, of course, my first thought, although I was surprised at the formality of the request. Could she not simply have run up? As it soon turned out, my hopes were to be frustrated yet again. Outside the shop stood the massive equipage that belonged to the Brakefields, the spotty young coachman in his livery aloft on the box, while within, the lady Lydia herself. She could not even exert herself sufficiently to alight.

'I hope you will take a ride with me, Mrs. Hudson,' she called through the window, adding in a mocking tone, 'that is to say if you have no other more pressing engagements today.'

She was not the companion I could have wished for, but I was curious to know what she was about. Of course, I had my suspicions.

'I will fetch my jacket and bonnet,' I replied, 'and be with you instantly.'

As I walked back through the shop, George winked at me.

'If only mother were here to see this,' he said.

'You're getting far too grand for the likes of us, Mrs. Hud,' Joe added with a grin. 'Or mebbe she wants to hire you as the new cook. Mum says they've lost another one.'

'Hush,' George said. 'Leave gossip to the women.'

'I certainly hope she's not planning to offer me any such position,' I replied, securing my bonnet with a pin. 'I am perfectly well set up at home, thank you very much.'

Mrs. Brakefield's intentions, however, moved in quite a different path. As I settled myself into the coach and we moved off, she fixed me with mournful eyes.

'I have to say I am most gravely disappointed in you, Mrs. Hudson,' she said.

'Oh dear. I am sorry to learn that.'

'I have been expecting to hear from you at every moment on the subject we discussed before.'

She paused. I said nothing.

'You know full well I have been terribly worried about Eve.'

'I told you I could not help you there, Mrs. Brakefield.'

She shook her head impatiently, and, with it, the pink ribbons on her straw hat quivered in sympathy.

'That's what you *said*, but you led me to believe that the opposite was the case.'

'If that's what you thought, then I am afraid you were much mistaken.'

'So you have nothing at all to tell me about Eve?'

In truth, the matter was posing something of a dilemma for me. If Eve were involved with Freddie Simister then, for the girl's good, a stop should be put to it at once. But although the evidence was strong, I had no actual proof that she had met him at the Green Man, only the sight of her horse outside. In addition, I strongly suspected that the motive behind her step-mother's request was far removed from Eve's welfare. I had no inkling what that motive might be, except perhaps jealousy. I could not help but be reminded of the fairy tale, in which the Queen keeps asking the mirror who is the fairest of them all. When the mirror replies that it is no longer she, but her step-daughter, Snow White, the wicked Queen plots the demise of her rival. Lydia Brakefield, I thought, with her fading beauty, would make an excellent wicked Queen.

'What are you thinking, Mrs. Hudson?' The woman was regarding me greedily.

I could hardly tell her.

'Eve has a gentle trusting nature,' I started to reply carefully, at which my companion snorted in derision.

'Is that what you think! My God, she has really pulled the wool over your eyes, hasn't she, the sly little cat.'

'Whatever about that,' I continued in measured tones, realising I could not hope to heal the rift between the two of them, 'I do not know if anyone in particular has wooed her. She revealed nothing of the sort to me, although she did say that the hermit had paid her compliments.'

Mrs. Brakefield looked at me aghast. Then burst out laughing.

'Our hermit!' she said. 'Oh dear, oh dear! The poor thing must be desperate if she is accepting attentions from that ragamuffin.'

'You mistake me, Mrs. Brakefield. Eve is distressed by, and even fearful of the man.'

She was still amused.

'Tut! He's perfectly harmless and isn't even around very often. At least not in the hermitage,' she said. 'Although, between you and me, I shall be employing him for the garden party.' She chuckled somewhat unpleasantly. 'I'm sure he will divert the ladies of the village tremendously.'

'I don't doubt it,' I replied, thinking of Henrietta, and what she would make of it all.

Mrs. Brakefield sighed.

'Well, this has been a mighty waste of time, hasn't it,' she said. 'I shall inform Beatrice Trueblood that she vastly exaggerated your powers of investigation, Mrs. Hudson.'

Beatrice Trueblood hadn't asked me to spy on anyone: the service I rendered her had been quite different. However, keen to take at least some advantage from the present situation, I replied that I was sorry to have disappointed, but that I had pressed Eve to visit me. So far, I went on, she had not put in an appearance. I did not, of course, add that the matter to be discussed was not at all what Mrs. Brakefield desired.

'I cannot force the girl,' I said.

'No, but I can,' came the daunting reply. 'She shall be with you this very afternoon.'

The coachman had evidently been instructed to take a circular route, and, having passed the inn, where today I was relieved to see no white or, more particularly, grey horses in evidence, we drove along a pleasant winding road up into the hills, beside harvested cornfields where roughly clad women and children were bent double, presumably collecting seed from amid the stubble. They straightened up as we went by, some waving at us. I waved back through the open window.

'Peasants!' exclaimed Mrs. Brakefield disdainfully. 'You should not encourage them, Mrs. Hudson, or they will take ever more liberties.'

We exchanged banalities after that, or, rather, I made uncontentious remarks concerning the beauteous countryside, the excitement among the ladies of the village regarding the forthcoming garden party, my own interest in the harvest celebrations, receiving no more than bored monosyllables in reply.

It was to my great relief that we eventually descended into the village, taking the road that passed down by the school and post office. If Henrietta were on the look-out, I did not see her.

'So this is your shop,' my companion stated, without interest.

'Not mine. My son-in law's.'

She waved a gloved hand as if to express her indifference at the distinction.

'Of course, we send for our purchases in Kenwardham or Rochester,' she said. 'So much more choice. However, I shall ask Baines to visit here and see what is on offer.'

'You may be pleasantly surprised,' I said. 'It's a well-stocked store, and the produce is all fresh and good.'

'I don't need an advertisement, thank you. Baines will check it out for herself... Well, are you going to get out, or what?'

I hope the look I gave her conveyed my view that, gentry or not, she displayed a distinct lack of good breeding. However, I doubt she even noticed.

Later that day, Eve arrived as promised, and was brought straightway up to me in the parlour by Eleanor, who then left us be. It seemed the girl had walked all the way down from the big house, and was glad of a drink of water after such exertion on a hot afternoon. She looked about herself with curiosity, and it occurred to me that she might never have been in such an establishment before.

'It's very... er...'

'Small?'

She laughed. 'I was about to say cosy,' she replied. 'I love the way you can look out of the window, and see what's going on, all the people walking by.'

All the people, God bless her! I told her that she should come to Baker Street and look out my windows there. Then she'd get a sense of 'all the people,' the motley city throng so very different from the village folk of Bilbourne.

'I should like that very much,' she said.

'You would be most welcome... But Eve, I wanted particularly to speak to you about Timothy.'

'I know,' she replied. 'He told me you want to send him away from here. But, you see, he doesn't want to go, Mrs. Hudson.'

'That's what he said, but I thought perhaps you might be able to persuade him.'

'I?' She looked confused.

'I know he is your friend, so you would probably be sorry to see him leave.'

She replied nothing to that.

'But you must surely realise what a terrible life he has here. My friends can establish him in a place where he would be well-fed, well-sheltered, with a farmer who wouldn't be cruel to him.'

'Like papa is?'

'Well, we both saw how he whipped the boy the other day, and you yourself said…'

'I know. I know. Yes, you're right. For his own good I'll try and talk him round.' She stood up abruptly. I could see there were tears in her eyes.

'Oh, I'm so sorry, Eve. I have upset you. Please, sit down again.'

'I have to go.'

'But you have only just arrived, my dear.'

I crossed to where she was standing to take her in my arms. She shrank back, as if unused to such close contact with another. Then subsided into sobs, clinging on to me.

'I wish you could find somewhere for me to go to, like that, Mrs. Hudson.'

The poor unhappy child. What could I say to her?

'Your life won't always be like this, Eve. In a few years you'll be able to find your own path.'

'Lydia says they'll fix me up with a husband, some old farmer. The only one who'd take the likes of me.'

'I'm sure she was joking.' A cruel enough jest all the same. 'Anyway, they can't force you into anything you don't want to do.'

'You don't know my father. But I'd run away before that.'

I drew her to the sofa and we sat close together for a while until her sobs grew less.

'Listen. Why don't I take you with me back to London when I go, for a little holiday? How about it?'

'I'd love that.' Then shook her head. 'But I wouldn't be let go.'

'You might. We can but ask.'

Never mind the father, I imagined Lydia Brakefield would be only too glad to see the back of the girl, if for just a short while.

'I'd only be the more sorry then, when I had to come back.'

'Is there nothing here to keep you, no one?' I was thinking of Freddie, but then realised that he too would soon be off away, in London as well.

'I have no real friends. How can I have? Only you, Mrs. Hudson. You have been so very kind.'

She raised her tear-stained face to me.

'I am sure my daughter Eleanor would love to be your friend. She's not so very much older than you are, you know. And then there's Mrs. Considine, the vicar's wife. She's a very nice understanding kind of woman. There must be others here.'

Eve gave a bitter laugh. 'I don't want to offend you, Mrs. Hudson, because it's far from what I think myself, but papa and step-mother would say that people like that are below our consideration, that we'd lower ourselves by associating with them.' She paused. 'In fact, I was most surprised when Lydia told me to come and visit you today. Obviously, she didn't know you wanted to discuss Timothy. She'd go wild if she knew I met him in the orchard.'

Of course, I wasn't about to reveal the real reason Lydia Brakefield had wanted me to meet up with Eve. However, for my own peace of mind, I needed to quiz her on the subject.

'Timothy is very fond of you,' I said.

'He's as alone as I am.'

'He likes you very much. But there must be others. You can't tell me you have no admirers, Eve. A pretty girl like you.'

140

She looked puzzled.

'Admirers? No. And I know I'm not pretty.'

'That's because certain people keep telling you as much. But you are. Very pretty… And I'm sure you've caught someone's eye…'

She wasn't having it, and shook her head.

'I thought your overseer, Stephen, attentive enough.'

She blushed then. 'Oh, Stephen,' she said. 'He's like that with all the women. He's even like it with Lydia.'

'Is that so?'

Perhaps here was the root of Mrs. Brakefield's jealousy. The unpleasant young man was certainly handsome, and might have turned the head of a woman who, as gossip had it, was loose in her morals. She might not like it if he flirted with her step-daughter.

'I hope he has never taken liberties,' I said.

'Oh no. Nothing like that. Just teasing,' she replied. 'He means nothing by it.'

'Of course, Stephen wouldn't be on the same social level as you,' I said. 'What about…' as if the idea had just occurred to me, 'what about… Freddie Simister?'

Now Eve burst out laughing. 'Freddie! That peacock! He's only in love with himself.'

Her mirth seemed genuine.

'Anyway,' she went on, 'the Simisters are our sworn enemies.'

'So I've heard.'

'All over hunting rights, or something. Riding over our land without permission.'

I was not about to discuss the rights and wrongs of enclosure with her.

'Yes, Freddie rides,' I said. 'He has a fine white horse.'

'Has he?'

'Pegasus, it's called, after the winged horse of mythology. A real beauty. Only just the other day I saw it tied up outside the inn. The Green Man, you know.'

The artlessness of her expression surely could not be feigned.

'What's strange about that?' she asked. 'Men frequent inns, don't they? Well, not papa, of course.'

Maybe not in Bilbourne, but from my recollection of his intemperate state, Thomas Brakefield easily found other means of quenching his thirst.

Perhaps the grey mare I had seen, distinctive markings or not, didn't belong to Eve at all. It seemed clear that she had no particular interest in Freddie Simister, unless she were a consummate actress, the which I doubted, even if her step-mother said she was sly. So that seemed to be that regarding beaus. I couldn't think of another who might fit the bill, and besides, Eve appeared innocent of any attachment. That was what I would report back to Mrs. Brakefield, without feeling that I was breaking any confidence.

Meanwhile, before she left, I was determined that Eve should meet my daughter properly, so I called Eleanor up from the shop and, leaving the pair of them together, went to fetch some refreshments from the kitchen.

The girl was astonished to be told that we had made the biscuits and drop scones ourselves.

'Don't you have a cook to do that?' she asked.

'Why get someone else to do it, when we like making them?' Eleanor replied.

In truth, apart from Joe, the Hazelgrove household extended only to the little scullery maid, who helped out with the heavy work. This wasn't solely for reasons of economy. Like me, Eleanor preferred to do things for herself.

I am not sure Eve was convinced, however. She took a very tentative bite out of her biscuit, as if worried that, unless it was made by a proper cook, it could not be palatable. Then she smiled and pronounced it good.

'I don't think I should be permitted in the kitchen,' she said. 'In any case, our new cook is very bad-tempered.'

Eleanor and I looked at each other, but said nothing.

I offered to accompany Eve at least part of the way back home, shewing her the seat where I had been wont to sit and chat to Timothy.

'It's a charming spot,' she said. 'I should like to sit here too, if I lived nearby.'

'The only danger is being joined by someone you don't particularly want to talk to. Your orchard is an altogether better place to enjoy solitude.'

'To enjoy solitude,' she repeated. 'I like that. That's exactly how it is.'

I walked up with her as far as the road that branched off towards the Brakefield estate. Before parting, we paused for a while on the bridge over the little river Dee. The water tumbled down picturesquely over boulders. Pale reeds grew high at the edge, waving their fronds in the breeze. A path led alongside the riverbank, disappearing under the trees with their rusting leaves. It made for a charming prospect, but I noticed a slight chill in the air. Autumn was marching inexorably towards winter.

'Tomorrow is the pickers' feast,' Eve said. 'Then they'll all be gone, and it will be quiet again.'

Little did either of us know how wrong she was!

CHAPTER FOURTEEN

The bells rang out joyfully, summoning us to the service, and we hurried thither, along with crowds of others, a rare excitement in the air. The little village church was almost unrecognisable. Usually so plain and unadorned, it was now decked out in an abundance of the fruits of the harvest, a veritable feast for the eye in the variety of shapes and colours before us, golden sheaves of corn standing to attention at either end of the altar, large wicker baskets beside and in front of it piled high with great globes of cabbage, bouquets of purple kale and knobbly stalks of Brussels sprouts; rosy apples, golden pears and purple plums; orange- and yellow-striped squashes, and marrows as fine as the one in Mrs. Jeffries' kitchen garden. Indeed, quite probably that same fine specimen was displayed here, since I spotted the Squire's housekeeper herself seated proudly with Joe in one of the pews.

The Squire himself, with Freddie, was in his usual place to the right of the aisle, and for once the Brakefields had arrived early, all four of them, and were sitting across from their old enemy. Indeed, the church was more packed than I had seen it before, and by now I could recognise many of the faces, the villagers and farmers and even some of the pickers, Nancy and her family among them. They kept to the back, the men standing as if to make a hasty exit, their duty once done.

The church bell having at last stopped chiming, the vicar, full of smiles to see such a big congregation, directed us to rise for the first hymn, whereupon the organist – Miss Priscilla Clements, the

144

schoolmistress – launched into the rousing tune, 'Come ye thankful people come, raise the song of harvest home.' Children in white surplices, including the Considines' own three boys, formed a choir, perhaps rather more enthusiastic than tuneful, but very sweet to see. All in all, it was a most delightful service. In his sermon celebrating the goodness of God in providing us with such plenty, Mr. Considine encouraged people to enjoy the forthcoming celebrations.

'All here are welcome to attend.' (With a firm emphasis on the *all*). Then he added a gentle word of caution. 'In past years, regrettably, some of you have enjoyed yourselves perhaps a little too much, and have lived to regret it the next day. I beg you to desist from overindulgence, of any sort, whether it be in spirituous liquors or… whatever.'

Henrietta, in her favourite seat beside me, gave me a nudge. For a moment I wondered if she imagined I would be one of those intemperate people, but then she whispered the ominous word 'babies,' with a shake of her head, so I knew she could not have me in mind.

Following the sermon, we shuffled up to take communion, which I have to say was a little awkward, given the obstructions caused by the fruits of the harvest, but everyone was in a good humour over it. Well, perhaps not the Brakefields. Thomas frowned deeply as he stepped up, jostled by common folk, while Lydia, resplendent in voluminous amber silks, gave an ostentatious sigh as she tried to negotiate a path round the baskets. Eve followed her step-mother, head bent, while Randall, as I observed, took advantage of their absence from the front pew to lean forward and steal a plum.

After the final hymn, 'We plow the fields and scatter,' ever a favourite of mine, there was something of a rush for the door, the reason for which soon became clear. People were hurrying towards the village green, where trestle tables with long benches on either side of them had been set up in a great circle, presumably in advance of the goodies to be heaped upon them. As we made our own way thither, I feared there might not be room for us, the spaces were filling up so quickly.

'I don't know what all these pickers are doing here,' Henrietta commented sourly. 'They have their own celebration to go to. It's a disgrace.'

'The vicar invited everyone to join in,' I reminded her.

'More fool him, if we respectable folk can't get a seat... Well, I'll soon see about that.'

She thereupon set off in determined fashion, bursting her way through the throng like a beribboned cannonball, while the rest of the Hazelgroves hurried after. For myself, I was held back by a restraining hand. It belonged to the Squire, who had caught hold of my sleeve.

'Mrs. Hudson,' quoth he, 'I trust you will join Freddie and me at our table. He is keeping places for us.'

'Thank you,' I said, 'but I cannot abandon my family.'

'Don't even think of it,' he replied genially. 'There's room for all.'

Even for Henrietta, who by now had commandeered the end of a table in a position at the back, far inferior, I might add, to that of the Squire's table, in its place of honour. She was beckoning vigorously to us to join her, and, when I crossed to tell her of the new arrangements, I was amused to observe the mixed feelings play across her face. Irritation at having to relinquish her hard-won terrain quickly giving way to satisfaction at being invited to join such an exalted party.

We found Joe already seated at the table, along with his mother.

'See what democrats we are here today,' Freddie said with a smile, as we sat ourselves down. 'Mrs. Hazelgrove, do you come and sit next to me.'

It was Eleanor he meant, and so was visibly taken aback when Henrietta squeezed in next to him with a simper.

146

'Oh Mr. Simister, reelly,' she said, putting on a genteel accent. 'I do declare you'll quite make me go scarlet.'

Freddie, to his credit, quickly recovered well, behaving towards Henrietta with perfect gallantry, as if there had been no misunderstanding at all.

The Squire meanwhile had made room for me beside himself.

'What happens now?' I asked.

'Just wait and watch.'

For what, soon became apparent. Shouts of 'Hooky, hooky, hooky,' were heard as a brightly painted wagon made its slow way up the village street, bearing sheaves of wheat, and garlanded with flowers. The boys on the wagon sported coloured ribbons in their straw hats. Even the old carthorse had bows and streamers tied in its mane.

'The last sheaves harvested,' the Squire explained.

'What the hooky, hooky all about?' I asked.

'No idea.'

'It's traditional, mother-in-law,' George said.

'I think it's just what people around here call this party,' Mrs. Jeffries added. 'The harvest home.'

I had to be satisfied with that, although my own memories of the celebration never included such a procession.

'And now,' the Squire rubbed his hands together, 'we all have to make corn dollies.'

'Oh, how delightful,' I exclaimed. 'You have quite transported me back to my childhood, Mr. Simister.'

'You know about corn dollies, then?' I could tell he was surprised.

'Indeed, I do. I spent my early years in a village not much bigger than this one, and at harvest time we children all made dollies.'

'Freddie, go and get some straw at once,' the Squire ordered. 'Let us see if Mrs. Hudson remembers how to make the thing.'

'Are you sure?' his son asked, grinning. 'It's a pagan practice, you know, Mrs. Hudson. An offering to the gods of fertility.'

'Good heavens!' That from Henrietta, shocked.

'Pagan or not,' I replied, 'as far as I remember, it's a very positive symbol, an offering for a good harvest in the following year.'

Mrs. Jeffries nodded.

'That's right,' she agreed.

'In that case, I'll take my chance.'

To be honest, even if my brain didn't quite remember, I was most keen to see if my fingers knew how to weave the stalks into the traditional spiral.

Freddie duly went to collect straw from one of the lads handing it out from the wagon, bringing back a whole bundle.

'Let's see who can make the best one,' he said. 'But you'll have to rule me out. I am all fingers and thumbs.'

In the end, only the Squire, Eleanor, Mrs. Jeffries and myself had a go. Henrietta had been put off by the suggestion of paganism, or perhaps she was simply afraid that hers would not be rated the best. After a shaky start, I soon got into my stride. Eleanor, nimble-fingered, was well able for the task, as was the housekeeper. However, I had to keep pausing to instruct the Squire, whose large paws weren't able for the delicate twisting of the stalks, which kept breaking on him.

Meantime, village girls were coming around the tables, depositing on each heaps of pies and sausages, cheeses and great loaves of bread, slabs of the traditional seed cake, as well as foaming jugs of local beer.

Henrietta addressed our girl.

'I hope you don't expect us to eat like savages, Jenny. Some knives, forks and plates, if you please, miss.'

'On their way, m'm,' the girl replied, with a wink at Joe. 'Tankards, too, so you won't have to pass round the jug.'

'Hmm… Cheeky minx.' Henrietta addressed this to Freddie, who simply smiled.

The Squire abandoned his dolly as a lost cause, while we others laid our finished efforts out for inspection.

Freddy voted Eleanor's the best, George, most kindly, for it certainly wasn't, chose mine, and the Squire Mrs. Jeffries'. Henrietta was loth to cast a vote at all, but Walter and Joe voted for Eleanor. I cast mine for Mrs. Jeffries, before I was told that, as a fellow competitor, I was ineligible.

'So young Mrs. Hazelgrove wins!' the Squire pronounced. 'Mrs. Jeffries, you must hang up yours in the kitchen, while I claim Mrs. Hudson's dolly for myself, for good luck.'

I had to agree, although I should have liked to keep the thing, ill-made though it was, for myself.

We then turned our attention to the feast, and all did justice to the great spread, which, as Mrs. Jefferies soon revealed, was provided by local farmers, not least among them, the Squire himself.

'Now, now,' he reproved her. 'We mustn't go around blowing our trumpets today. It's expected of us, you know.' He took a great slice of meat pie, oozing gravy.

'Is this one of your fine efforts, Mrs. Jeffries?'

'I am afraid not,' she said.

'Not as good as yours, mum,' said Joe, though I noticed he wasn't stinting himself.

'Ah well,' Mrs. Jeffries replied, mollified, tasting it for herself. 'Though I have to say it isn't too bad.'

The Squire then raised a tankard.

'To good food in good company,' he said, to which we all answered 'hear, hear', and shared the toast.

It was almost the last happy moment for a long time to come.

While people were still eating, a little band of musicians, fiddlers, and a boy with a tambourine, had struck up a lively dance tune.

'Gypsies,' spat Henrietta with disapproval.

'Never mind, mother,' George said, a little embarrassed. 'They can certainly play.'

'Come on, you must dance with me, Mrs. Hazelgrove,' Freddie said, grabbing her hand.

'Good heavens! Whatever are you thinking, Mr. Simister?' She snatched her hand back. I could tell, nevertheless, that she was pleased with the attention.

'The young Mrs. Hazelgrove, then.' Freddie turned to Eleanor. 'That is, if her husband will permit the liberty.'

'Whatever you like, my dear,' George said. 'You know I can't dance to save my life.'

Without waiting for a reply from my daughter, Freddie pulled her into the middle of the green, among the other dancers. I was a little perturbed, sure that she hadn't wished to join him. Still, what harm could come to her among so many.

Henrietta looked on with pursed lips. I think she was put out that Freddie hadn't insisted further on herself as a partner.

The Squire then invited Mrs. Jeffries to the floor, and though she demurred at first, it was clear she was delighted to be asked.

'Come on, Mrs. Hudson,' said Joe. 'I'm sure you'd like a twirl.'

I laughed. 'Not at all, Joe. Why don't you go off and join the young folk?'

The boy looked at George, who nodded. Needing no further permission, Joe was off and was soon seen dancing with the same Jenny who had served our food.

'Well, mother,' George said. 'Are you sure you don't want to step up?'

'I do not. I have no intention of making a show of myself in front of all these... people.' Henrietta put on her most self-righteous face. 'Anyway, I thought you said you couldn't dance.'

'I was going to suggest that father partner you.'

Luckily, Henrietta didn't notice the dismay on Walter's face, for she was too intent on watching the dancers.

'You know, George,' she said. 'I think it very wrong of you allowing Eleanor to get up with Mr. Simister. He has a bad reputation.'

George smiled easily. 'I think I can trust my wife,' he said.

'Nevertheless, people will talk. You know what they're like.'

I could hardly restrain myself from bursting out laughing. Talk about the pot calling the kettle black.

George chatted to his father then, while Henrietta and I sat in silence. I cannot speak for my companion, but I was most diverted watching the lively throng. Even Eleanor was smiling, although she cast anxious looks towards us from time to time as she spun by. At last, that particular tune was over, and she hurried back to us, her partner looking after with his usual amused smile. Then he disappeared into the crowd, presumably in search of another fair maid.

The Squire returned Mrs. Jeffries to her place and turned to me.

'Come on, Mrs. Hudson,' said he, 'You must dance, you know. You will insult me, and all present, if you refuse.'

The last time I had danced was in Paris, at the Moulin Rouge, an occasion that that provoked troubling memories. However, I let myself be persuaded, not daring to look and see how Henrietta was taking it.

As we danced around the green, I spotted Ursula Considine accompanying – for it could hardly be said that they were exerting themselves – the elderly Dr. French, who, gasping for breath, soon had to sit back down again. The sisters I knew to be the teachers, ramrod stiff Miss Clements and her merry little sister, Miss Priscilla, were dancing with two of the Considine boys, Oliver and one of the twins. Clearly Miss Priscilla was enjoying herself much more than Miss Jane, while the latter's poor partner, whether Jamesie or Davey, looked considerably less than content with his lot. Many of the other ladies who sailed by, acknowledged me, with nods and smiles. They were presumably looking forward to the garden party on the morrow. I hoped they had all managed to acquire suitable dresses. And hats.

'My goodness,' the Squire said, 'you seem to know a lot of people here, Mrs. Hudson, even though you only arrived a short time ago.'

'It's thanks to the shop,' I replied. 'It's a regular meeting place for the ladies of the village, and I sometimes sit on a stool there, rather than stay upstairs by myself.'

As we took yet another turn around the green, I was surprised to see that Freddie's new partner was Eve. Her head was down and she was blushing, but smiling, too. The Squire saw them at the same time as I, and muttered, 'Silly fool!' though whether he meant his son or Eve I could not say. I feared he might be planning to intervene, so I tried to smooth things over.

'Thank goodness the younger generation don't bear the same grudges as their parents,' I said.

I am afraid I made things worse.

'You know nothing of the matter, madam,' he replied.

I was surprised at his sharp tone, but kept my peace. For myself, I wondered if Eve had after all misled me regarding her feelings for Freddie. Whether she had indeed ridden Queen Mab to the inn to meet her beau that day.

However, there wasn't time to speculate further, for we suddenly became aware of a row taking place at the far end of the green, angry voices drowning out the music which soon stopped altogether. The Squire excused himself to investigate, and I followed after him.

Daniel Ridge, very much the worse for drink, had, we soon discovered, accosted Thomas Brakefield, and started threatening him. Blows had even been exchanged, with Mr. Brakefield coming off the worst, until Stephen, the overseer, had intervened to pull the picker away. He was now holding him firmly by the arms, while Daniel shouted curses.

'You'll pay for this, Ridge,' Mr. Brakefield was saying, wiping blood from his nose. 'It's hard labour you'll be doing for the rest of your sorry life.'

Nancy stepped forward then. 'Isn't it hard labour he's been doing all his life so far, with little reward for it either.'

'Shut your mouth up, woman,' Mr. Brakefield snarled. 'You're as rotten as he is, the lot of you are. ignorant pigs from the stews of Clerkenwell.'

'And who was the ignorant pig whipped my five-year-old daughter?'

'Your daughter was a sneaky little thief, like the rest of you.' Brakefield, too, I could tell, was influenced by liquor. 'Thieves and vagabonds.'

He raised his fist to Nancy, and was about to strike her, when the Squire intervened, gripping the man's arm.

'Good heavens, Brakefield,' he said. 'You can't just go around beating up women and children, you know. This is a supposed to be a celebration, and you aren't wanted here. Go back to your lair and lick your wounds.'

There were murmurs from the crowd, who were clearly in agreement.

The man then rounded on the Squire.

'Take your hands off me, Simister. By God, I'll have the law on you for this. On the lot of you who support him.'

'I think we have witnesses enough here this time to forestall any false claims on your part, Brakefield. Respectable witnesses who can't be bought.' The Squire towered over his adversary. But the latter hadn't finished. He gave a great ugly laugh.

'So now you're adding defamation to the list of charges against you. And another thing you can add, how your wayward son, with your connivance, has been trying to seduce my daughter.'

There was a gasp from the crowd, whether because it was so outrageous or because they suspected it might be true.

Brakefield shook off the other's hand, the Squire himself clearly shocked, and suddenly speechless.

'I have a feast to attend to. In my lair, as you call it. But you haven't heard the last of this, John Simister. Oh no. Not at all.' He strode off, grabbing Eve as he went, dragging her roughly after him.

Suddenly I became aware of Timothy among the onlookers, an expression of sheer hatred on his face. Then, before I could reach him, he darted off after them.

At last Stephen let go of Daniel and swaggered away himself, smiling, after making a cut-throat gesture across his neck with his forefinger, whether directed at the Squire or at Daniel or at both of them, only he could tell.

'Good Lord,' Freddie said, coming up to us, 'I only danced with the girl. Is that a crime these days?'

'You know what you've done,' the Squire muttered, and walked off, leaving me standing.

The musicians, who had temporarily broken off their melody, now resumed with a lively polka.

'Come now, Mrs. Hudson,' Freddie said. 'You can't refuse me.' Then, just as I was about to, he added in a whisper, 'Think how it will look if we cave in to the man. The show must go on, as the ringmaster said when the tiger escaped and ate the little boy.'

I laughed then, and he took me round the waist, though happily not too close. As we danced and after what had just happened, I felt I could ask him, 'Is it true?'

'What?'

'Are you Eve's beau?'

He seemed genuinely astonished.

'That little mouse! Good heavens, no. It was just that she looked so forlorn, sitting there by herself. I took pity on her.'

'Well, I'm glad to hear it,' I said.

I did not feel I could quiz him further about the owner of the grey mare outside the inn and concluded that I must have mistaken the horse, and that any questions about it would make me sound like a real village busybody.

When the dance was finished, I thanked my partner, who gave a deep, and possibly ironic, bow. Then I returned to our table. The Squire was gone and everyone else seemed in a humour to leave. The fun had gone out of the day.

However, as we were making our way home, I was accosted by the vicar's wife, who drew me aside, the others going on ahead.

'I am most fearful for the Ridges,' Ursula said. 'Who knows what revenge Thomas Brakefield has in mind, but he will for certain not let it go. He was humiliated in public.'

'Whatever can we do?'

'I am minded to go to the Hall and try to intercede for the family. Would you come with me, Martha?'

'Under the circumstances,' I replied, 'would not your husband, as a man of the cloth, be a more suitable companion?'

'Yes, if he were here. However, he has been called to the bedside of a dying parishioner, and I have no idea when he is likely to return. You are friendly with Mrs. Brakefield, and an outsider, so surely her husband cannot take umbrage at you.'

'I rather fear he has already.' I described my earlier encounter with him at the oast house, and then the scene at the church when I excused myself from dining at the Hall because I had already promised the Squire. How enraged he had seemed.

She sighed.

'I don't want to go alone,' she said.

The last thing I wanted was another confrontation with Thomas Brakefield. However, my feelings must be put aside for the good of Nancy and her family.

'I am certainly willing to go with you as long as you don't think it will make matters worse,' I said.

She took my hand. 'Oh, thank you so much.'

I had to return home first to tell Eleanor that I was going on an errand with Ursula Considine, not wishing, with Henrietta all ears beside her, to provide further particulars. Eleanor gave me a searching look, no doubt suspecting the truth. However, she asked no further questions. Her mother-in-law was less inclined to silence.

'Goodness, Martha, after all that leaping and hopping about, I should have thought, at your age, and after being so very ill, that you would wish to go and lie down.'

I decided to make a joke of it.

'Yes, indeed. I am very old,' (nearly as old as you are, I thought), 'but somehow the leaping and hopping seems to have put new life into me. I shall see you all later.'

CHAPTER FIFTEEN

A great pig was roasting on a spit, fat falling off it into the open fire below with little explosions. Stephen, a crown of hops on his head like some pagan deity, stood beside it, sharpening a long knife on a stone, preparing to cut slices of the meat, to hand around to the eager pickers. The smell of the roasting pork was most enticing, and, although my appetite had already been well satisfied at the harvest supper, I should not have refused a taste.

Ursula was not of the same mind.

'It's enough to get one to give up eating flesh,' she said, with a distasteful grimace at the grinning head of the beast.

I was aware of the growing movement towards meat-free eating, or vegetarianism, as I believe it is called. Although I myself could not imagine adhering to such a diet – can hunger be sated with vegetables alone? – I was interested in hearing more on the subject. Now, however, was not the time, and we hurried past the revellers in search of Thomas Brakefield. By dint of a number of inquiries, we found him at last in the stables, in the process of saddling up a jittery-looking black horse. Perhaps the man's own over-excited, and, might I say, inebriated state, had infected the animal. Mr. Brakefield glowered at us as we approached, at me, I feared, in particular.

'What do you want now?'

Gently and politely, Ursula urged for leniency towards Daniel Ridge.

'The man was wrong to strike you, it was a moment of madness,' she said. 'But think of his wife and children, sir. Would you leave them destitute?'

'He should have thought of his wife and children before he punched me, madam. The man's behaviour was intolerable. I am leaving this minute to fetch the constable from Kenwardham to take him into custody.' He gave a sharp laugh. 'Ridge will face the full consequences of his actions, believe you me.'

Ursula tried again. 'Remember St Paul,' she said. ' "*Be ye kind to one another, tender-hearted, forgiving one another, even as God, for Christ's sake, has forgiven you.*" You are a Christian. Do the Christian thing, I beg you, Mr. Brakefield, and have mercy.'

'The Bible, madam, as I remember it, also says "*An eye for an eye and a tooth for a tooth. Justice is mine, I will repay.*' "

Ursula was about to argue further, but with a dismissive gesture, he turned his back on us and finished saddling the horse. The man would never, by the look of him, have relented, but I am afraid I hammered the final nail in the coffin of any hope of reprieve. My only excuse that I was very angry indeed.

'So you permit yourself freely to strike those weaker and less powerful than yourself, Mr. Brakefield, but cannot take a deserved beating yourself.'

He wheeled round, pulling his horse with him. I stepped back as the beast breathed hotly into my face.

'A deserved beating is it, madam? By God, you deserve a beating yourself for those presumptuous words. I wonder your husband hasn't put you in your place before now.'

With that, he strode off into the yard.

Had he bothered to linger, I could have told him, that my dear late Henry would never have raised a hand against me, no more than against any other of God's creatures. He abhorred cruelty in all its forms. But I suppose Thomas Brakefield would simply have seen that as weakness.

Ursula sighed.

'I am sorry for that,' I said. 'I could not restrain myself.'

'It would not have made any difference, Martha. You saw how obdurate he was.' She shook her head. 'That poor family.'

'We should warn Daniel,' I urged. 'He and Nancy should leave before the constable returns.'

'Mr. Brakefield has surely anticipated his flight. Daniel is no doubt soundly locked up somewhere.'

'Then we must release him.'

She looked at me aghast.

'How can we do that? We don't know where he is.'

Stephen will know, I thought, and for a big enough bribe he might tell.

'I shouldn't be surprised,' I continued, 'if Brakefield Hall has a dungeon. Such a thing would surely have amused old Benjamin.'

My remark puzzled her – she had never had occasion previously to visit the Hall – until I described how the construction of the edifice had been inspired by Gothic novels.

'You will see for yourself tomorrow,' I added.

'Tomorrow?'

'The garden party.'

'Good heavens. I had quite forgotten.'

Ursula Considine must have been about the only woman in Bilbourne not to have the forthcoming garden party at the forefront of her thoughts. It was one of the things I liked about her.

Just now, however, we had more important matters to concern us. I suggested we look for Nancy.

'We should try to find her, and explain how things stand.'

Retracing our steps to the feast, we found crowds of pickers sitting on the ground tearing apart chunks of meat with their teeth, no plates or knives and forks provided here, just slabs of bread. It was an unedifying sight, the glistening juices running down their chins and on to their garments. Great tankards of beer beside each one of them, children included. I feared ugly scenes would erupt later that night.

Of Nancy or the children, however, there was no sign, so while Ursula searched further afield, I approached Stephen, who was still busy carving the pig, now reduced to a gory carcass. The overseer was red-faced from the heat, and sweating like a blacksmith. He held out a lump of pork to me.

'Want some, m'm?'

I shook my head. My appetite had quite vanished.

'I am looking for Nancy,' I said. 'Have you seen her, Stephen?'

He laughed.

'I seen her all right. She be locked up with the children, safe as houses.'

I was horrified. 'Locked up? With Daniel?'

'Not a bit. No need for that. He ain't a-going to run away and leave his family now, is he? That's what Mr. Brakefield says.'

Holding the family hostage. How barbaric!

'Where are they?'

He gave me a sly look.

'Now, Mrs. Hudson, m'm, that'd be telling, wouldn't it.'

I reached inside my reticule for my purse.

'Forget it,' he said, understanding my intention. 'My job's worth more to me than your pennies.'

'I don't intend pennies,' I replied, pulling out some sovereigns.

'Nice, my lady.' He gave me a winning smile. 'But no thanks.'

'At least tell me they're all right.'

'Right as rain… though, now I come to think on it, rain ain't that right, is it?' He laughed, but did he also relent then just a little? 'Don't worry, m'm. They be safe, unharmed, and comfortable enough for the likes of them. Anyways, we'll be letting them out soon as the constable arrives. Meantime, I'll make sure they don't go hungry.' He gestured at the pig. 'Plenty still on this big old girl. Sure you don't want some?'

I left him, smirking at me, and went looking for Ursula, whom I soon discovered, along, surprisingly enough, with young Timothy. Like many of the pickers, he too sported a crown of hops. Another tradition, I supposed. The boy reported that Daniel was roaming about, mad with rage, looking for his wife.

''E says 'e'll kill that Brakefield before letting hisself be taken,' Timothy said, I am afraid with some relish. ''E's got a knife. A big 'un.'

Things were even more urgent than I had feared. It was imperative to find Nancy and the children as quickly as possible.

'Listen, Timothy,' I said. 'Would you keep an eye on Stephen for me, and when he leaves with some meat, follow after. He's taking it to Nancy. But don't let him see you. Then, come back at once and tell me where he went.'

Timothy grinned. 'Will do, m'm.'

I gave him one of the coins I had intended for the overseer, but he tried to hand it back.

'No need for that, m'm. I'm glad to 'elp.'

'Take it anyway. And maybe another day we can talk about that other matter.'

'I 'aven't changed me mind on that, m'm. I'm staying put.'

'Very well…' I wasn't about to argue just then. 'We'll wait here for you.'

He nodded and crossed over to Stephen.

'More pork, Tim?' I heard the overseer say. 'By God, you can put it away, you can.'

He gave the lad a piece of meat, and Timothy, with a wink at us, sat himself down nearby to eat it

'Let's hope Stephen doesn't wait too long to visit the prisoners,' I said to Ursula.

She looked worried.

'Oh dear, Martha,' she replied. 'You may be used to this sort of thing, but I am not. As the vicar's wife, I quite honestly don't think I should be involved in this.'

'If that is how you feel,' I replied. 'Go home. I'll be fine here.'

In truth, I wasn't at all sure of that. The pickers, having eaten their fill, were now concentrating on drinking, and were becoming more and more raucous. A trio of men had started playing a wild tune on their fiddles – were they not the gypsies from our own harvest feast? – and some couples got up to dance. Suddenly, two men came rushing over with an empty hop basket. Amid much merriment, they cast around, clearly searching for someone. Finally, they settled on one of the women, a comely lass with dark ringlets, crowned with hops. Seizing her, they put her in the basket and ran off again.

'Good heavens!' said Ursula. 'What now?'

'Don't worry, m'm.' An older woman had sidled up next to us. smiling. 'It's a tradition. No harm to it.'

Indeed, more men with baskets now came running up to abscond the women, amid much screeching and laughing. No harm to it, according to our new companion, though I rather doubted that, and preferred not to imagine what might be going on in the shadows. So intent were we on the spectacle before us that it was some minutes before Ursula jogged my arm.

'Stephen's gone' she said.

She was right. There was no sign of him, though Timothy, enthralled by the antics and laughing his head off, was still sitting in the same place.

'Timothy!' I cried.

At that, he looked around, saw his quarry had disappeared and clapped his hands to his head. Then he rushed off, though whether in the right direction or not, I had no means of knowing. I would just have to wait.

Again, I urged Ursula, if she felt uncomfortable, to go home.

'Won't you come too?' she said. 'It's most unlikely we can do anything more here, you know.'

'I have to try,' I replied.

I must admit that I found her abandoning, not just me, but the Ridge family, surprising, even given her desire to uphold the standing of the vicar. In truth, I was disappointed. For myself, I could not leave. Thomas Brakefield must not be let win without a struggle.

After Ursula had gone, the old woman next to me was happy to pass the time enlightening me on the various traditions around hop-picking. It turned out she had been coming there for the past forty or more years.

'To this very place?' I asked.

'Yes, indeed. Well, see, I'm local born and bred. Not one o' them Lunnuners... I started 'ere when Mr. Benjamin was alive. 'E was worse than this one in some ways and better in others. Our living quarters was much worse, m'm.' (How could they have been? I wondered). 'Didn't feed us at all. And 'is overseer was stricter 'n Stephen. Still, he left us be, more. There'd be none of this Dan'l Ridge business in them days, for Mr Benjamin would never have mixed with the likes of us.'

Nell, for that was her name – like my sister, I told her – rambled on. I was only half listening but grateful, since it passed the waiting time.

'Don't you find the work too hard, at your age?' I asked.

'Bless you, m'm. It's either this or the workhouse for me and I surely don't 'ave to tell you which I like best.'

Stephen was back. He gave me an insolent nod, as if he had foreseen my plan and foiled it. However, of Timothy there was no sign. I waited some more, but still the lad failed to return. Had Stephen spotted him and...? Well, I hated to think what might have happened next. Moreover, if Timothy had come to harm, it was all

163

my fault. However, it seemed there was nothing more to be done here, and, like Ursula, I might as well go home defeated.

I said goodbye to Nell, pressing a sovereign into her hand.

She was astonished, maybe hoping for a sixpence or a shilling at best.

'God bless you, m'm,' she said. 'And give you success in your endeavours.'

Instead of letting me go, she pulled me by the hand away from the throng.

'I do recall,' she said, when we were safely in the shadows, 'of a place where Mr Benjamin's overseer put people to punish them. Could be there you'd want to be looking.'

So she had overheard our conversation.

'Where is it?'

Leading the way, Nell went not towards the hall, as I had anticipated, but towards the oast houses. It was hard to see the way, and I was glad of her company, although I am afraid I had a few doubts as well. What if, having seen the contents of my purse, she was leading me off to rob me? She was older than I, but hard physical work had no doubt made her stronger.

Reaching the nearer of the oasts, she pushed open the door and went in. After a moment's thought, I decided to follow her and trust to her good intentions. It was not quite dark within, a lamp hanging from a hook. As my eyes grew accustomed to the gloom I saw several great pockets, as William had described them, stacked up at the far end of the room. I wondered if William, the drier, was still around, or was his work here done? In any case, there was no sound at all beyond our own.

Nell meantime was pointing me towards a corner faintly illuminated by the lamp. I saw nothing there but a stack of empty bags, and my misgivings returned.

'Under that,' she said. 'Help me move 'em, m'm, if you please.'

Once we shifted them out of the way I could see the top of a trapdoor. I shivered with anticipation as Nell lifted the cover and peered down.

'Nance,' she called. 'It's Nell. You there?'

I looked down, too. And indeed, huddled at the bottom were the poor prisoners I had been seeking.

'Thank God!' I said.

'Amen to that,' Nancy replied. 'I thought we was going to be left 'ere to die in the dark.'

A problem faced us now: the pit was deep and there seemed no way for them to climb out.

'There's a ladder somewheres,' young Charlie called up to us.

If there was, it was nowhere to be seen, just a long length of sturdy rope, tied to a post.

'Can you let the rope down 'ere, Nell?' Charlie asked. 'Then me and Sarey can climb up it.'

I doubted this, but the old woman found that the rope indeed extended into the pit. In no time, the boy had scaled it, like a little monkey.

'Come on up, Sarey,' he urged, calling to his sister. 'You can do it.'

She tried, bless her, but the effort was beyond her.

'She be still 'urting from the whipping,' Nancy said. 'Can't you pull 'er up, Charlie?'

The combined efforts of us all finally brought the frightened child out of her prison. However, the mother was another matter. I could not see how we could manage to get her out, big woman that she was.

'There should be a ladder,' Charlie repeated. 'That's 'ow he got us down 'ere, the blighter.'

He searched around.

'Can't be far.' He lifted down the lamp and went to check outside. Meanwhile Nell comforted the child, who was trembling and sobbing.

'Monsters,' she said. 'Doing this to a wee'un.'

'Doing it to anyone,' I said.

Charlie found the ladder, at last, apparently lying on its side again the outside wall. But just as we were about to lower it to Nancy, we heard a noise. Someone was outside. Was Stephen back, or, perish the thought, Thomas Brakefield himself? After our efforts, was all lost?

But it was only William looking grave.

'What the devil's going on 'ere?' he asked.

A reply was unnecessary. He could see for himself. The question was, whose side was he on?

'I never reckoned,' he said slowly, 'this damn 'ole would be put to use again.' He shook his head. ''Ere, lad.' He took the ladder and lowered it into the pit. 'Should 'ave sealed it up years back.'

He didn't ask why Nancy had been incarcerated. Maybe he knew already, or maybe he didn't want to know. I think it had to be the latter, for, as Nancy climbed out, he said, 'Well, I'm off. Was never 'ere.'

He left us alone then.

Nancy already knew from Stephen that Thomas Brakefield had gone to fetch the constable to arrest Daniel.

'You know what 'e says to me, the rat? You be a fine woman, Nance, says 'e. Won't be long afore you find another 'usband.' She spat. 'As for that Thomas Brakefield...' She cursed him roundly in words I prefer not to reproduce.

'You must find Daniel and leave at once,' I said. 'Thomas Brakefield will hardly pursue you to London.'

'Ha! 'e might, if 'e knew where to look. We'll make sure 'e don't.'

166

She gladly took the coins I had left in my purse and then, to my astonishment, with tears in her eyes, gave me a hug.

'You're all right, m'm,' she said. Then hugged Nell too, before, with Charlie carrying Sarey, hurrying off into the night. Nell and I meanwhile put things back as they were before, in case Stephen returned to check on his charges. At least it might delay him a little.

As we were going out the door, I gave a sudden start. Something had slithered past me, something black and sleek.

'It's only Satan, m'm,' laughed Nell. 'Come on, let's get away from 'ere quick.'

If only I could remember whether a black cat crossing one's path heralded good luck or bad. Time would tell.

CHAPTER SIXTEEN

The following morning, I expected to hear all sorts about the doings of the night before, but no one said a word about it, not at breakfast, nor in the shop, where I deliberately stationed myself on my usual stool. Perhaps the local gossips hadn't yet got to hear of it, but I was puzzled. The presence of a police officer in the vicinity would surely have come to someone's notice by now, but all the talk was of the harvest festival of the previous day, of the forthcoming garden party, and how lucky it was that the weather was so fine.

'It would have been just frightful if it were to rain,' one matron said, to general agreement.

I nodded, too, but my thoughts were all of Daniel and Nancy. I could only hope that they had got clean away, assuming they would have had the sense to go in the Maidstone direction, rather than take the road to Kenwardham, where they might encounter Thomas Brakefield returning with the constable.

On the previous night, I myself, wishing to avoid the risk of meeting Stephen again and raising his suspicions, had got Nell to point me a back way to the village, thereby avoiding a return through the celebrations. Luckily it had been a clear night, and I could make out the road well enough even in the dark without a lantern.

'God bless you, m'm!' the old woman had said, as we parted company.

'You too, Nell.'

I liked to think that she would have helped me find Nancy even without the spur of the sovereign I had given her.

I decided not to say anything to Eleanor about my involvement in what had happened. She would have disapproved heartily and maybe even have thought that locking me away, like Nancy, wouldn't be such a bad idea. Instead, after a very light luncheon, anticipating all sorts of goodies on offer at the Hall, we adjourned to our respective bedrooms to change into our party clothes. As I have indicated already, I considered that my cerise silk would be most suitable for the occasion. It would, of course, clash violently with Henrietta's post-box red gown, but I was petty-minded enough to be amused at the thought. How Eleanor, for her part, had found the time, between all her other duties, to fashion a simple but elegant dress from the olive green fabric she had purchased but a few days since, was quite beyond me. She had managed it, however, and very well it looked on her too, with her reddish locks. For headwear, we both sported black straw hats embellished with ribbons that matched our gowns, and, all in all, were most pleased with ourselves. George and Joe, when we descended to the shop, were also gratifyingly awestruck.

'Who can these fashionable ladies be, Joe?'

'Never seen the like, governor. Must be up from Lunnon.'

'At the very least.'

The obliging young lad was happy then to drive us to the Hall, picking up Henrietta on the way.

'Good heavens, Martha,' said she, settling in beside us. 'I thought you were not bothering to dress up.'

'Oh, this old thing,' I replied. 'Just something I bought a while back in Paris.'

'Well,' she said, clearly put out. 'I suppose it will do, although to my mind it is rather youthful for you at your age.'

She rustled her scarlet ruffles, like an indignant parrot.

As we drove into the long driveway that led up to the hall, she once more remarked what a pity it was that our conveyance did not carry the Hazelgrove crest.

169

'Mrs. Brakefield could not fail to be impressed,' she said, although the lady in question would hardly be standing on the doorstep waiting for us where she could see it. The only person who might have observed the insignia of gentility would have been the footman, Jobbins, and he, convinced of our inferiority, was unlikely to take any notice.

Indeed, that unappealing flunkey soon appeared on the threshold and waved us round the back. Evidently, we were not to be permitted to set foot in the house.

Still, to be fair, Lydia Brakefield had gone to a deal of trouble, or at least had instructed her servants so to do. A tent had been pitched on the lawn, and visible inside were tables, ready, as we hoped, to be laden with all manner of delicacies. Our hostess, already busy greeting the many guests who had arrived before us, stood resplendent in white, under a lacy white parasol, and, although she was perfectly gracious, her manner was as cool as her dress. She welcomed me, and, I think, looked rather approvingly at my gown and at that of Eleanor. For poor Henrietta, however, she hardly contained her scorn, regarding her up and down with something approaching mirth, from the frills at the hem, up the polka dots, to the ostentatious yellow ostrich feathers waving in the breeze.

'How perfectly delightful,' she murmured vaguely. 'Refreshments will be served shortly, ladies. In the meantime, please feel free to take a turn around the grounds, and be sure to visit the grotto. Mrs Hudson knows where it is, I think.' She gave me a complicit look. 'Perhaps she has already told you of it.'

'No.' I replied. 'I wanted to surprise them with everything here,' adding 'Is Miss Eve around at all?'

Lydia Brakefield pouted then. 'Eve is sulking in her room.' Without explaining further, she turned to greet the next arrivals.

Henrietta was looking up at the back of the hall, its eccentric turrets and gargoyles even more evident here than at the front.

'I cannot say that I should like to live here,' she said. 'I am sure it must be haunted.'

'It's not really old,' I assured her. 'All this was added on by Benjamin Brakefield, who seemingly had a great love of Gothic horror tales.'

'So then maybe,' Henrietta replied, tartly, 'it is Mr Benjamin's ghost that haunts it.'

'It might well be,' I said. 'Luckily none of us are likely ever to find out.'

'So anyway, where, Martha, is this grotto you know so well?' Henrietta was clearly, though unjustly, put out by a supposed intimacy between Lydia Brakefield and myself

'If I can find it again, 'I said, 'it is through here.' I led the way along the winding paths of the woodland.

My companions exclaimed at the grotesque statues, the ruins, the waterfall – Henrietta pretending terror at the sight of the crocodile. However, nothing could have prepared them, or indeed myself, for the grotto. Of course, I had seen it before but, on that occasion, it was lacking its inhabitant.

As we approached, Henrietta shrieked out, 'There's a creature inside and it moved.'

In the shadows of the cavernous opening stood a figure that, indeed, hardly looked human. As warily we approached, there emerged an incredibly tall, hirsute individual whose emaciated appearance was only partially concealed by the bearskin he was wearing, much of his chest, one shoulder, one skeletal arm and both legs from the thigh down exposed. He was also filthy, his hair and beard hanging down in matted clumps. As Henrietta recoiled, the man laughed in triumph, revealing black stumps of teeth. Wherever, I wondered, had Lydia Brakefield found this apparition, another of her freaks? No wonder Eve was scared of him.

'It's the hermit,' I said. 'He lives here, or that's what Mrs. Brakefield wants you to think.'

171

On cue, the man fell to his knees and, adopting a position of prayer, started some sort of pig-Latin chant in a high warbling voice. It was all quite horrid, even blasphemous, since this was no genuine man of God.

We had seen enough, but as we turned to go, the man leapt forward and caught Henrietta by the hand.

'An offering for the poor hermit,' he babbled. 'An offering, good lady in the pretty red dress, for the love of God.'

A beggar, to boot. I rather felt this was the man's usual occupation.

'Does Mrs. Brakefield not pay you enough?' I asked sharply.

'Ah now, lady in pink, blessings be upon you, I live on the charity of God-fearing folks like yourselves.' This in wheedling tones.

I was loath to give the man anything, but Eleanor reached into her reticule and brought out a sixpence, which she thrust at him, dropping it as, relinquishing his hold on Henrietta, he stretched a claw towards her.

'Blessings on you, beautiful lady in green,' he said, scrabbling for the coin, and ogling Eleanor with an open and unchristian leer.

We hurried away.

'You shouldn't have given him anything, Eleanor,' Henrietta said. 'The vile thing.'

'I was afraid he might keep hold of you forever if I didn't.'

'He has quite soiled my glove.' Henrietta brushed her hands together vigorously to remove the supposed stain.

As we made our way back to the civilised part of the grounds, we met several ladies of Henrietta's acquaintance heading towards the grotto.

'Don't say anything,' she whispered to us. 'Let it be as much a surprise to them as it was to me,' adding in something of a contradiction, 'and by the way, Martha, I think it very wrong of you not to have told us in advance what to expect.'

'I never saw the hermit before,' I replied. 'I understand Mrs. Brakefield only employs him when there are visitors. It amuses her.'

'The poor devil,' said Eleanor, which I felt to be almost too charitable of her.

The tables in the tent were by now groaning under the weight of all manner of good things to eat, tiny sandwiches of potted meat or shrimp cut into neat triangles, biscuits of all sorts – I spotted Queen drops, garibaldis and gingerbread. There was cake, too – Victorian sponges oozing jam and cream, a marzipan-clad Battenberg with that characteristic pink and yellow stained-glass window effect, a rich Dundee topped with almonds. However bad-tempered the Brakefield's new cook might be – according to Eve's report – she was certainly well up to the mark where baking was concerned. In addition, fruits of all sorts, shining apples, pears and plums presumably from the orchard, were piled into dishes beside smaller bowls of almonds and hazelnuts. To drink, claret-cup and lemonade, or tea and coffee, were on offer. There were even ices, in little paper cups, melting quickly in the warm air. All in all, a spread that surely no one, not even Henrietta, could fault.

The ladies of the village, in their motley finery, were seated on garden chairs and benches, the platters on their laps piled dangerously high. Some of the younger women even sat on the grass on thick colourful rugs. It presented a most charming picture, something indeed for an artist to portray, perhaps one of those 'Impressionists' I had encountered in Paris. No one was paying attention to the black bank of cloud massing over us, except when it briefly masked the sun.

Henrietta, meanwhile, was looking about herself for a chair, which she soon found beside some of her gang, while my daughter and I were delighted to spot Ursula Considine, a little less dishevelled than usual. Indeed, she looked quite charming in a pretty sprigged muslin gown, tiny blue flowers on white. Her hair even contrived to stay tidy under her bonnet, with only a few stray curls.

She looked askance at me, and I conveyed to her in a few whispered words, how I had found Nancy and her family and had urged her to leave with Daniel at once.

'What about the constable?' she asked.

I shook my head.

'I have heard nothing at all about that.'

'Perhaps Mr. Brakefield had second thoughts after all.'

'Maybe,' I replied. Though of that I had my doubts. He was not a man for second thoughts.

Our conversation was interrupted at that point by old Mrs. Gracie, button-holing my companion regarding the harvest fruits in the church, which apparently were to be distributed among the deserving poor of the parish. Apparently Mrs. Gracie, fine black silks and all, regarded herself as one such. Ursula gave me a resigned smile and let herself be led away.

'This is all very pleasant,' Eleanor remarked, when I joined her where she was standing with some friends.

I agreed, although I could hardly enjoy the day, however, agitated as I was by what had happened at the feast, and still wondering if the Ridges had escaped. It was hardly something I could ask Lydia Brakefield, but, as I automatically sipped my lemonade and nibbled my biscuit, it occurred to me that I could, in all innocence, ask Stephen, if I could find him. He would hardly associate me with the fugitives. Making an excuse to my companions, who in any case were chatting most amicably, I slipped away, back through the Gothic woodlands towards the plantation. I was careful to avoid the grotto this time, and so became a little lost along the winding paths.

Pausing to get my bearings, it was with some astonishment, since I had thought myself entirely alone, that I heard someone utter my name in a hushed whisper.

'Timothy!' I said. 'Whatever are you doing here?'

The boy looked more ragged, more dirty, more everything than usual, that agonised expression seemingly become fixed on his face.

'Miss Eve,' he said, 'she left the ribbon on the gate, she did, but she ain't come.'

'I believe she is in her room.'

'I mus see 'er, I mus...' His eyes were quite wild.

'What has happened?'

He shook his head vigorously but said nothing more.

'Well,' I went on. 'I suppose I can try and tell her you're here.'

'Please, m'm. If you can.'

It was not an errand I particularly I wished for at that moment, but there was a desperate neediness about the lad that I could not ignore. Stephen could wait.

'Has she spoken to you about going away?' I asked.

'Oh yes, m'm. I mus go away, I mus. Right now.'

'That's great news,' I replied. 'I will write directly to my friend and tell her, and then...'

He grabbed my hand.

'I done it, m'm. 'Twas me what done it. You heard me say it.'

'What have you done, Timothy?'

He just shook his head.

'Please get Miss Eve.'

'Very well. But before I go, do you happen to know if the Ridges got away, or if Mr. Brakefield caught up with them.'

'Brakefield!'

Timothy started shaking, like one afflicted with St Vitus Dance. The lad must have been truly badly abused for the mere name of his persecutor to engender such a reaction.

'I am just hoping the family got away safely.'

''E coul'nt catch 'em.'

'Thank God for that. Very well, Timothy, I'll endeavour to give Miss Eve your message.'

I was not at all sure that I should be acting as a go-between for the pair, but the lad was in such distress I felt I could only try and help him. At least, now he had agreed to go away from this place, so Eve must have done a good job of persuading him.

'Remember, m'm, I told you, 'twas me what done it.'

Nodding, though I had no idea what he was talking about, I made my way back as quickly as I could, forgetting to avoid the hermit, who spotted me, and cried out his appeal for alms. I rushed on, ignoring him. Still, I could not help but think it shewed a cruel and warped sense of humour to employ the wretched man thus?

How to reach Eve proved my next problem. The servants were clearly under orders to prevent any interlopers into the Hall, and barred my way, despite my pleas. They also refused to send a message on my part to the girl. There was nothing for it but to search out Lydia Brakefield and request permission from her. I found her seated on a swing, languidly rocking back and forth, looking utterly bored. while a group of village ladies clucked around her. At the sight of me, she rose and, without apologising for abandoning her companions, who looked after her with some astonishment, walked over to me.

'You have come to save me, Mrs. Hudson,' she said, hardly bothering to lower her voice. 'My eternal gratitude.'

I laughed. 'Whyever did you invite us all, if we trouble you so much?'

'I really don't know.' She sighed. 'I suppose I was bored with being bored, and thought this might help. But these women... they are impossible, quite unable to rise above the banal, the provincial. Their conversation, if that is what it be, wears me out. You don't know how lucky you are to live in London.'

'I think I do,' I replied.

We were making our way under the shade of a lime tree walk, leaves turning pale gold, some already falling to provide us with a rich carpet. At least there was nothing remotely Gothic here. It was quite charming and I said as much, my companion responding with

176

apathy. I decided – nothing ventured, nothing gained – to broach the subject close to my heart.

'Mr. Brakefield is still away, then?'

'Goodness, yes. He would not have put up with this for a moment.' She relented a little. 'Of course, he knew of the party. He didn't approve.' She smiled. 'But I persuaded him. It would be to our advantage, I told him, for us to be on good terms with the villagers, especially…well…' She paused. 'He finally consented. "You may go ahead," said he then. "As long as you leave me out of it." '

I poked at some fallen leaves with the toe of my shoe.

'He seemed highly incensed yesterday,' I said. 'The last time I saw him, he was off to Kenwardham to fetch a constable.'

'Was he?' She looked genuinely surprised. 'Well, he never returned with one. What was that all about, anyway?'

'I believe one of the pickers had struck him.'

At that, she burst out laughing.

'Oh yes, indeed, a capital offence. I do hope he got a bloody nose.' Then, seeing my shocked expression, added, 'To tell the truth, Mrs. Hudson, I am surprised more pickers haven't resorted to violence… My husband has a temper he often cannot control.'

This was nothing new. I had seen it up close for myself.

'No,' she went on. 'He has gone to Rochester on business. I expect him back tonight, or more probably tomorrow.'

Well, I was glad of that for the sake of the Ridges. Mr. Brakefield's rage must indeed have abated. Perhaps Ursula's soothing words had acted upon him, after all. I asked my hostess then if I might go and visit Eve.

'I doubt she is in a humour to see anyone. She refused to talk to me this morning, or to come down to the party. I have had to tell the ladies she is unwell. It is most provoking. However, she likes you and may admit you.'

She called over the unprepossessing maid I had seen before, and instructed her to bring me up to Miss Eve's room.

'You have, I suppose, made no further discoveries regarding her affections,' she said, in front of the hovering servant.

'I have found no evidence of any such. However, I think she is lonely and could benefit from meeting more people of her own age.'

'I have said it to her father on many an occasion. I even suggested we should send her away to finishing school, preferably abroad. All he replied was that she is his daughter not mine, and that I should limit my concerns to Randall.'

She looked across the lawn to where the boy himself, with his long-suffering nurse, was gleefully kicking a cake as if it were a football.

'So much spirit,' she said proudly.

I nodded, not of course expressing my real opinion, and followed the maid into the Hall.

CHAPTER SEVENTEEN

Silence answered the maid's first knock upon the door. Then, when she persisted and knocked louder, an abrupt 'Go away!' was heard.

'It's Mrs. Hudson, Eve,' I called out.

Another silence. and then 'I suppose *you* can come in.' Words spoken listlessly.

She was seated looking out of the window, and failed to turn as I entered. It was a gloomy room, north-facing I judged, and thus without any direct sunlight. At least, apart from an ugly iron chandelier, the room was spared the gothic excrescences evident elsewhere in the house. A framed print on the wall sentimentally depicted the Madonna and Child, which rather surprised me. I had not thought Eve particularly pious. Perhaps she liked the loving way the mother was cradling her baby on her lap. The poor unloved girl, I imagined, must miss her own mother. Otherwise, the room was extremely untidy, with clothes strewn over chairs, even the floor, piles of books and notebooks heaped everywhere, even on the bed. Some roughly executed sketches and watercolours adorned the mantelpiece, surely the work of Eve herself. Among the studies of flowers and rural sketches I discerned a couple of profiles. Was that Timothy? It touched me to think of him posing for her in the orchard.

'How are you, Eve?' I asked.

'Are you enjoying Lydia's party, Mrs. Hudson?' Her voice shook a little.

'Well enough. Why won't you come down?'

'I don't want to.'

'Whyever not? It's very pleasant in the garden, you know. Lovely and sunny. With some delicious cakes.'

'Oh, cakes!' She made a dismissive gesture.

'People are asking for you. They want to meet you.'

She turned then, a tear-stained face.

'They will all look at me, judge me. I couldn't bear it.'

'Judge you in what way?'

'In comparison to *her*, to themselves.'

Oh, the self-centredness of the young.

'I am sure they will not. They are very kind... well, most of them.'

She shook her head.

. 'I suppose *she* sent you.'

'Your stepmother, you mean?'

'Lydia. She can't bear having to make excuses for me, can she? You may think she doesn't mind what people think of her, but she cares enormously. Even what the villagers think.'

'I know nothing about that. She certainly didn't send me. I came about something quite different.'

I glanced at the image on the mantel.

'Timothy is waiting to see you.'

She gave me a sharp look then.

'You met him? Where?'

'In the wood. He looked to be in a terrible state.'

'What did he say?'

'Just that he saw the ribbon on the orchard gate and thought that you would be there.'

'Oh that... I forgot to take it down... That's all he said?'

'Well, there was something else strange.' I paused.

'Yes?'

'He told me he did it.'

'Did what?'

'That he wouldn't say. But he was most agitated… Have you any idea what he means?'

'No.'

'At least, he's agreed to go away, Eve. That can only be good news. I thank you for persuading him at last.'

'It is for the best.' She turned back to the window. There was nothing much to see from this side of the Hall, a stretch of lawn, a small wooden summerhouse surrounded by trees, and beyond it, the edge of the estate and a lane running past that led I knew not whither.

'You will miss him. You will miss Timothy.'

Was that the cause of her tears?

'Mm… Yes.'

'So will you come down now?'

She shook her head again.

'Not now. I'll find him later when everyone has gone. If you see him again, tell him to wait in the stables.'

I could have replied that I was not her messenger. But there was a desolation about the girl that made me want either to give her a hug or leave her in peace.

'If there is something troubling you, my dear, you know you can always talk to me.'

'There's nothing, Mrs. Hudson. Nothing new. Oh, how I hate this place.'

She turned back to the window.

I understood that I was dismissed, and left her, still staring out.

Timothy was anxiously waiting for me on the very outskirts of the woodland, in danger of being spotted. Caring nothing for that, he looked beyond me, as if expecting to see Eve coming after me. All I could do was to pass on her message.

'No,' he said. 'That's no good. I must see 'er now and then go away.'

'I'm sorry, Timothy, she won't come down until everyone has left. Anyway, you can't leave immediately, for I must inform the people in Hampshire that you are on your way. Come to the shop tomorrow, or...' perceiving his reluctance, 'meet me by the duck pond, if you prefer, and then we can make arrangements for your journey.'

He gave me that look again, and then, heaving a great sigh, rushed off, soon disappearing entirely from my sight among the trees. Shaking my head in some wonderment, I made my way back to the ladies. Ursula introduced me to the two Miss Clements – the elder tall and stern, the younger small and plump and gentle-looking, calling to mind the Jenkyns sisters, Miss Deborah and Miss Matty from Mrs. Gaskell's charming little book, 'Cranford.' They were both evidently anxious to make my acquaintance, but I am afraid that, on this occasion, I was distracted, and my conversation failed to sparkle. To tell the truth, I could not wait to return home, to write and tell Mary that Timothy had at last agreed to leave Bilbourne.

'Will you not join us in a game of croquet, Mrs. Hudson?' Miss Priscilla was asking eagerly. 'I see that the servants have set up a court for us.'

Indeed, they had, driving hoops into the flattest part of the lawn, and bringing out balls and mallets. Already some of the ladies were playing.

I tried to demur, but in vain. I must join in. However, I played so ill that I was soon let go, my partner, Miss Jane, entirely disgusted with me. I made my apologies, pleading a touch of the sun, and wandered off round that side of the hall where Eve's room was situated. Maybe I could send her a signal that I had spoken to Timothy.

She was no longer seated at the window I thought must be hers, and I turned down towards the summer house. It was a pretty octagonal structure, and would provide, as I thought, a pleasant place in which to escape both from the heat of the afternoon and from the chattering of the ladies. But as I approached, I heard low voices from within. A man and a woman. I was not inclined to intrude on their privacy and was about to depart, when the woman spoke louder.

'You should not have come. Why did you come, today of all days? After what we have done! Do you want us discovered…? Oh God help me!' and she burst out of the little building, quite distraught. On perceiving me, however, she pulled herself together as best she could.

'Why, Mrs. Hudson,' cried Lydia Brakefield, for it was she. 'Whatever are you doing here? I thought you were with Eve.'

She had raised her voice louder than necessary, I think in warning to whoever was within to stay there. For once, she looked flustered, as well she might if discovered in a compromising rendezvous. I hope I was able convincingly to simulate ignorance of the circumstance, giving her a reassuring and bland smile, and letting myself be led away.

'Eve wanted to be left alone,' I said. 'And so I thought I would explore your beautiful grounds further.'

She was still trying hard to recover her aplomb. 'I understand you so well, Mrs. Hudson. May I call you Martha, for we are friends now, are we not...?' Was I then permitted to call her Lydia? She did not say. 'Yes, indeed,' she continued. 'Like me you wanted to escape from all those dreadful people… Ha ha ha!… Of course, I don't really mean dreadful. They are your friends and relations, and are quite charming, in their way, but a trifle wearing all the same.'

All the time, she was hustling me further from the summer house.

Suddenly stopping in her tracks and quite pinching my arm, to halt me too, she looked me in the eye – oh, hers were so very cold. 'You have discovered my secret, Mrs. Hudson,' she said.

Whatever was she about to confess? And did I want to hear it?

She laughed. 'Yes, yes, for sure. You see you have caught me rehearsing.'

'Rehearsing? Do you mean, a play?'

'Indeed, I do. A monologue, in fact. I go to the summerhouse to practice my lines, because, for now, I don't want anyone knowing about it. I want to surprise them all.'

'Oh really,' I replied. 'How very interesting! What is the monologue about?'

'Have you heard,' she asked, 'of Alice Arden?'

I admitted I had not.

'Well, I won't say any more about it.' She smiled, trying to be coy. 'If you are still here when I am quite ready, I shall be delighted to invite you to the performance.'

I nodded and expressed my pleasurable anticipation.

'Have you acted before?' I asked.

'Ah, well. Not as much as I should like.' She looked away from me towards the Hall. 'It is an appealing prospect, is it not, to be able to throw aside one's own personality for a while, and take on that of another?'

She had quite come back to herself now, and held my gaze.

Of course, I didn't believe a word the woman said. At least, she might well have it in mind to perform a starring role in some sort of amateur dramatics – I think I have mentioned that I suspected she might have been on the stage before her marriage. However, in this case, I was quite certain she was trying to cover up the truth, that she was meeting a man, not her husband, a man with whom she was on intimate terms. I admit I am irredeemably curious, and would have given a lot to creep back and see who he was. However, Lydia Brakefield kept a firm hand on my arm as we marched back to the other ladies, long enough indeed for the man to get away.

The weather was changing fast. What I have heard described as an Indian summer, when unseasonable warmth occurs in the autumn, often turns out to be prelude to a storm, and indeed the dark clouds, which we had all ignored at the start of the garden party, had now massed ominously above us. Just as Lydia and I rejoined the others, a jagged flash of lightning was immediately followed by an ear-splitting clap of thunder, and fat drops of rain started to fall. The lady herself was soon hurried into the Hall by Jobbins, wielding a huge umbrella, but the rest of us were left to manage as best we could. We huddled under the tent, more terrified that our beautiful gowns would be spoilt, than we feared the clashing clouds above us.

Thankfully the downpour, though heavy, lasted but a few minutes. There was then considerable muttering that our hostess had left us in the lurch.

'She could have brought us inside,' Henrietta was complaining. 'The place is big enough, after all.'

For once I had to agree with her, although I understood too how much the possibility of an invasion by the ladies of Bilbourne would have horrified our hostess. Once in, how would she easily have got rid of us?

The party thus broke up earlier than we had been expecting, although for my part I was glad to depart. Without Joe and our equipage, however, we would have to make our way back on foot along a road now running with water and mud. Oh, our poor finery! As we were preparing ourselves for the trek, however, I was, to my surprise, approached by Jobbins. Apparently – disdain etched on his ugly face as he conveyed the message – Mrs. Brakefield had ordered the coach to take me and my party back to the village. I was about to refuse. What about all the other ladies? No such arrangements, it seemed, were to be made for them, and I did not like to be singled out as special. However, Henrietta quickly intervened, accepting gratefully on our behalf. She then urged the Misses Clements to join us, while I invited Ursula Considine. There was then really no room comfortably for all of us, though Henrietta, despite taking up two-thirds of the space on one side, still insisted we could all pile in. It was quite impossible and I was for walking back despite my fears for my cerise silk. An argument ensued, Eleanor, ever mindful of my welfare, insisting I be driven. In the end Ursula and herself opted to go back on foot.

'This is very nice,' Henrietta remarked, as we drove along. I almost expected her to give queenly waves to anyone we happened to pass. 'Although,' she continued, 'I still think madam could have brought us inside against the wet. And where was the girl? It was very strange that she did not come and greet us.' She looked at me. 'What do you think, Martha?'

'Miss Eve is very shy and self-conscious,' I replied.

'I am self-conscious myself,' Henrietta said. 'Are we not all conscious selves? That excuse won't do, Martha. It will not do at all.'

She regarded me accusingly, as if it were my fault that Eve was the way she was. Well, I could not really excuse the girl either.

'In any case, I don't think her shy,' Henrietta continued. 'She is just sulky and sly. Thinks she's above us, like the rest of the Brakefields. But I could tell you a thing or two about that little miss, if I was so minded. However, as you well know, I hate idle gossip... Still, the family should know what she is really like.'

She gave me a self-righteous look. I am afraid the vague suspicion I had been harbouring, that Henrietta might have been behind that letter, sent by 'a friend' to Lydia Brakefield, accusing Eve of consorting with an unsuitable man, was only reinforced by her words and her look. Perhaps I was wronging her. I hoped so.

'And as for that little brat of a Randolph, or whatever his name is,' Henrietta remarked, 'he could do with a taste of your switch, Miss Clements, to put manners on him.'

Miss Clements nodded. 'Randall is a much over-indulged child. I believe he has a private tutor, God help the poor fellow.'

'Does he?' I asked. I didn't know that.

'Oh yes,' Miss Clements said. 'A Mr. Symons from Kenwardham.'

'A most pleasant person,' added Miss Priscilla. 'At least, he was most polite to me when I met him... by chance, you know.' She had gone quite pink.

'They do say,' Henrietta added, ignoring her, 'that Mrs. Brakefield... well, not to put too fine a point on it... takes a particular interest in the young man.'

'Who says?' asked Miss Priscilla. 'I hadn't heard that.'

'No more have I,' her sister added, pursing her lips, and giving Henrietta a disapproving look. It seemed the Misses Clements were not part of the 'gang' of gossips.

I was most interested in the intelligence, however, if that's what it was. Perhaps this tutor was the person who had met Lydia Brakefield in the summer house.

'Of course, Mr. Symons isn't allowed to live in' Henrietta remarked with a knowing smirk.

'No? That's most unusual,' I said.

'You have seen how they keep themselves to themselves.' Henrietta was undaunted by Miss Clements's stern eye. 'And *he* wouldn't trust another man in the house with *her.*'

'Tut,' said Miss Clements.

'Mr. Symons has a room with old Mrs. Gracie in the village,' Miss Priscilla explained. 'And goes home, as he told me, to his mother and sisters at the weekends. Which is why, you know, we never see him in church.'

She gave a little sigh. I rather felt Miss Priscilla had something of a particular interest in the tutor herself.

'They had one governess after another before him, but they all left,' Henrietta said. 'No one could put up with the boy... You can stop here,' she called out to the liveried lad driving the coach, for, perhaps fortuitously, we had reached the post office with the school house above it, where the sisters lived.

'You getting out here too?' The coachman turned to ask me rather brusquely, seeing as I had not moved.

'No,' I said. 'Drive me down to the shop, if you please.'

He sniffed. It did not please him at all, but he had to do it.

I was glad Eleanor had insisted on my taking a ride, for I now found I was quite worn out.

George was most surprised to see me.

'I was going to send Joe up shortly for you all.'

'We left early after the shower,' I said. 'Eleanor is walking down with Mrs. Considine.'

'Walking!'

George called Joe and told him to go in haste and meet Mrs. Hazelgrove and friend. I was a little surprised, since they had to be well on their way by now, but was touched, at the same time, by his consideration for his wife.

CHAPTER EIGHTEEN

The next day passed, and the next and the next with neither sight nor sound of Timothy, and I was getting ever more concerned. Maybe the lad had changed his mind. If so, there was nothing more to be done: I could hardly force him to go away against his will. It was surprising all the same, since he had seemed so insistent himself on leaving. In the meantime, a balmy Thursday evening found the Hazelgroves and myself taking tea in the upstairs parlour of the shop. Since my return to Baker Street had at last to be imminent, the proposed outing to Rochester castle, which must take place before then, was taking shape. The following Saturday was the proposed date for the excursion, Sunday having been firmly ruled out by Henrietta, because on that day the shops would all be shut.

'It would be such a waste of time and effort to go all that way for nothing,' she said.

'For nothing, mother!' George exclaimed laughing. 'But it is the castle we are going to see, not the shops.'

'And I am sure the castle is very pretty. Indeed, I think I must have seen it before.'

'You have, mother, several times.'

'Then it is most strange to be going there again. Although I suppose it is all for Martha's sake, since she won't ever have visited it.'

I confirmed that was indeed the case.

However, if we were not to go on the Sunday, a problem arose regarding both the Post Office and the grocery. They must remain open. Since the departure of the pickers, the store had become noticeably quieter, and Joe could safely be left in charge. The post office was more of a problem. Henrietta's suggestion that Walter stay behind was greeted with universal protest. He, who had suggested the outing in the first place, could certainly not, the rest of us agreed, be left out.

'We'll need father to explain the full history of the castle and all its intricate architectural details to us,' George said, with a straight face.

'Hmm. Well, anyway, I'm not staying back to look after the office, while you're all off enjoying yourselves.' Henrietta did not brook contradiction.

There was a pause. Goodness, I thought, why does everyone feel the need to defer to this silly woman? Of course, I kept my thoughts to myself.

'I don't mind not going,' Eleanor said at last. She had, it seemed, helped out at the post office on occasions in the past.

I was about to object – why should my daughter be deprived of an outing? She had looked washed-out for some time, and I could not help but wonder if she were sickening for something. A change would surely do her good. But something in her demeanour suddenly struck me. Could there be a more joyous reason for her condition? At that moment, I caught her eye, and an understanding seemed to pass between us.

'I should quite honestly prefer,' she continued, 'to spend the day sitting in comfort, rather than be rocked about in a carriage for hours.'

'Well, that's settled, then,' Henrietta said with satisfaction, while Walter asked Eleanor if she were quite sure, and, finding that she was, thanked her warmly for what he could only see as an extraordinary instance of self-sacrifice. Surely, it would be a great deprivation for her not to take up the opportunity to visit a ruin, even if it were not a Roman one.

For George's part, he made no attempt to dissuade his wife, the which made me even more suspicious of the truth. Instead, he being delegated to arrange our transport, and the older Hazelgroves taking their leave, I remained upstairs with my daughter.

'Is it what I think, Eleanor?' I asked her when we were alone.

'It is too soon to be sure, but I believe so. Oh, mama, let it be true.' She threw herself into my arms, and I hugged her tight.

'You are right not to risk the journey to Rochester,' I said, 'although I should have loved your company.'

'Be sure to visit the gardens. They are very beautiful.'

I assured her that I would, for I love gardens even more than picturesque ruins. We spent a while, thereafter in joyful contemplation of the future, though my daughter impressed on me the need for discretion on the subject until all was certain. I understood what she meant without her spelling it out. If her mother-in-law got an inkling of the possibility of a grandchild, we should never hear the end of it, nor would the rest of the village.

The next day, being again pleasant, and myself in need of exercise, I decided to try again for that circular walk that had defeated me before, although, to vary it, starting from the opposite direction. This time, Eleanor furnished me with a hand-drawn map of the district, including all the roads and points of interest, so that I could not possibly get lost again, bless her thoughtful heart.[5]

I duly set off, taking with me this time a little basket in which to collect blackberries. Glancing at the seat by the duck pond as I passed, I hoped as usual, though did not truly expect, to see Timothy there. It was occupied, but by a mother and child, who were feeding the ducks. I greeted them and continued on my way. In a year's time, that might be Eleanor and her baby. The prospect made me smile.

This time, my walk took me up the hill past the post office and school in the direction of the Hall, but, well before I reached that, I

---

[5] Eleanor's map can be found at the beginning of this account

came to the pretty little stone bridge over what the locals liked to called a river but which to me looked more like a stream. They called it the Dee, not an original name for I knew of at least one other river, if not two, of that name. Not in Kent, though, so I supposed that was permitted. I noticed how it was shallow enough to paddle over, if one had the mind, though, shod as I was, I took the more conventional route. I had, nevertheless, to chuckle at how the very thought of removing my shoes and stockings and lifting my skirts to enjoy the refreshing cool of the flowing water on my bare feet would have shocked the respectable denizens of the village. Paddling is an activity I remember with great pleasure from my girlhood, before civilisation perforce tamed me. I supposed that the local children, let out from school at last, would love to come here too, and I paused on the bridge, as if to hear ghostly echoes of their cries of delight. Perhaps, indeed, continuing my earlier musings, a few years on, Eleanor's child would come here too, and the thought filled me with joy.

The path that led along the riverbank, though enticing, looked muddy, and I feared for my skirts. In any case, it wasn't the route indicated by Eleanor. Instead, therefore, I continued by the highway. At a fork in the road, I took the one that branched off away from the Hall, trusting this time to make the circle successfully. Thus, while pausing frequently to collect juicy fruits from the hedgerows, I yet kept a sharp eye out for the turn back to the village. Rather sooner than expected, there it was, a little lane down to the left. The walk was thus much shorter than I had anticipated and I was reluctant to curtail it so soon. I would continue, I decided, along this other road, and then, before I became too fatigued, turn back. In any case, I was much stronger now than when I had first arrived, and would surely not succumb to weakness again.

Indeed, I was through the woodland and out at the side of the wetlands again before I knew it. As before, I looked across that treacherous marsh towards the village church in the far distance, and, as I looked, I thought I saw something moving, not the waving reeds, or thin saplings, something more solid. I blinked and it was gone, whatever it was. A bird, I supposed, unless it was a lost sheep that would never find its way out again.

It occurred to me that I was now very near Blossomfort Hall, and wondered if it would be presumptuous of me to call in and see if I might try my luck with the famous maze. Had Squire Simister not told me I was welcome to return any time? Etiquette be darned. I would call in if only to beg a glass of water.

The flustered little maid, who answered my knock – Mabel wasn't it? (I pride myself on remembering the names of servants) – informed me that both the Squire and Master Frederick were away out, but that she would inform Mrs. Jeffries of my visit. She brought me into the hallway where soon I was joined by that admirable dame herself. I was able to inform her that Joe was well, and added that he was a treasure the Hazelgrove household quite relied on, which brought a smile of pride to her face. Mabel, standing behind her, blushed beetroot red at the lad's name, causing me to suspect she must like him rather a lot, too.

Mrs. Jefferies was all for me going into the parlour to drink my water, but I assured her that I would be more comfortable with her in the kitchen.

'The Squire will be sorry to have missed you,' she said, as we sat down together.

'I hope you enjoyed the Harvest Feast the other day,' I offered.

'Oh yes, indeed, even despite that upset with Mr. Brakefield.'

I recalled the angry accusations made to the Squire, and the dignified way in which they had been received.

'He is a most short-tempered man,' I replied. 'And, it seems, unloved by the pickers.'

'I understand he was struck by one of them, and so threatened to bring down the law on him.'

'Yes, Daniel Ridge it was. Mr. Brakefield had soundly whipped his little girl after accusing her of stealing an apple,' I said. 'Daniel's response, if not to be condoned, was understandable.'

Mrs. Jeffries shook her head. 'And now,' she said, 'he's gone missing.'

'Daniel Ridge?' Yes, back to London, I hoped.

'I meant Mr. Brakefield.'

This was news indeed.

'I saw him that night,' I said, 'intending to head to Kenwardham to fetch the constable.'

'Well, he never came back.'

'Not then, perhaps. Mrs. Brakefield told me he had business to see to in Rochester. I assume it has kept him there.'

'That must be it, although William is greatly puzzled. His master has never stayed away so long before without sending word.'

'Do you mean William the drier?'

'He's my brother,' she explained. 'He calls by sometimes to see how I am, and give me all the news. Of course...' she added hurriedly, 'the Brakefields know nothing of that. They'd not approve of him coming here, into enemy territory, as William likes to call it.'

'I won't tell them,' I promised, smiling.

Not to delay her from her duties – I could see that she had been preparing pastry and meats for a fine beef pie – I took my leave.

So distracted was I by the news regarding Thomas Brakefield and his continued absence, that I realised I had quite forgotten to ask if I might visit the maze. No harm. I was sure permission would have been granted, and I duly made my way to the back of the house where the thing was situated. The dark yew hedges loomed up, looking quite sinister. Undaunted, I entered.

The Squire had been right. It was a true labyrinth. Time and time again I went down a path I thought must lead me to the centre, only to come up against a dead end. Moreover, and more seriously, I could not remember how to find my way out again, and felt rather foolish. No one knew I was here. What if I became stuck, unable to get out? I should have brought a roll of thread, like Theseus, or pebbles like Hansel and Gretel. In the fairy tale, the second time the children are left in the forest by their wicked stepmother, they drop crumbs of bread, to help them find their way out again. I ate a blackberry, thinking I should have left a trail of fruit, so now remedied my previous neglect by dropping a blackberry or two whenever I came to a turn. It might not help me get out, but at least I should not venture down paths I had already traversed. Of course, in the tale, birds eat the crumbs and the children are left stranded. I trusted such a fate would not be mine. Still, I was becoming quite worn out with all the twists and turns, and started to curse the tricky designer of the maze. At one of the dead ends was a stone bench and I sank on to it with some relief, studying the yew hedge to see if there were any possibility simply of breaking through it. However, it was too dense.

Suddenly I became aware of voices approaching, and was about to call out, when something in the intimate tone of their conversation caused me to change my mind. Good heavens! I realised that once again I was privy to a discourse between Lydia Brakefield and a man whose voice this time I soon recognised as that of Freddie Simister. Whatever was she doing here – in enemy territory, as William dubbed it – and with him? Was he the man from the summerhouse? Had it been she who met him at the Green Man? On that occasion, Queen Mab, I now remembered, had worn a side-saddle, while Eve, as I had witnessed, rode astride. It was something I should have noted before: Mr. H for certain would never have been guilty of such an elementary oversight. Now everything was starting to make sense. Was it not most probable that Lydia Brakefield had 'borrowed' her step-daughter's horse in order to arrive at a secret assignation? Indeed, anyone knowing that the horse belonged to Eve might well assume, as I had done, that the girl was the mystery horsewoman. Had not Thomas Brakefield himself accused Freddie in front of us all at the Harvest feast of trying to seduce his daughter?

However, if Freddie were indeed the man from the summerhouse, her attitude towards him had changed considerably. Now she was all sweetness, and he, as I could hear even without listening, was responding in kind, and I could not doubt but that they were embracing. Oh dear, what an invidious situation I found myself in. What if they came into the maze? How would I explain myself? But the soft voices soon receded, and I was left with the old dilemma. How to get out for I had no notion now of reaching the centre, only of escaping.

My ruse with the blackberries worked to some extent, and I was able at least not to retrace my steps up blind alleys. After a few more false attempts, I was out, thanking God, and hurrying away as fast as decorum allowed, hoping not to be spotted.

I think I managed it, and was soon on the road with only the long walk back ahead of me. Plenty to think about, all the same, to fill the time. Lydia Brakefield and Freddie! Lydia Brakefield and an unknown! The gossips, it seemed, were right to some extent. The woman was voracious, while Freddie was clearly acting as his father had predicted and 'sowing his wild oats'. I could not approve of either of them.

Sighing and shaking my head I trudged on. The hedges here were heavy with blackberries and I paused to replenish my basket, while not delaying too much, for Eleanor would be concerned if I did not return soon. After a while I heard the clip-clop of hooves. Were they ahead of me or behind me? If the latter it might be Lydia Brakefield or Freddie, neither of whom I wished to meet just then. However, I soon realised that the sounds were approaching from the direction of the village, and was soon most relieved to perceive the Squire himself come around the bend of the road upon a fine chestnut steed.

'Mrs. Hudson!' said he, pulling up beside me. 'The very woman! Was I not just down in Bilbourne inquiring for you?'

'Inquiring for me, Squire? For what reason, pray.'

'Do I need a reason other than to see your charming countenance?' He laughed heartily. 'In fact, as Mr. Horace Walpole might have put it, it is all most serendipitous.'

'Is it?' Whatever was the man on about? Still, I was glad he was too distracted to wonder at my presence on the road coming from Blossomfort Hall.

'I learnt from your estimable son-in-law,' he continued, 'that you are planning a trip to Rochester castle on Saturday.'

'Yes, we are.'

'Splendid, splendid!' He gazed down at me. I waited. 'Hmm, well, I should be most glad to put my equipage at your service. I am sure it is far more comfortable than anything to be hired in the village.'

'That is most kind,' I replied.

'Of course,' he continued, 'the only disadvantage from your point of view is that I must insist on accompanying you, as your coachman, since, as you know already, I do not employ one.'

What could I say? Only that I should be delighted for him to come with us, rather wondering, at the same time, what Henrietta would make of it.

'That's settled, then!' He suddenly seemed to realise where we were, and his big friendly face creased into a frown. 'But have you been at Blossomfort?' he asked.

'I am out picking blackberries,' I said, conscious that my basket was still rather emptier than it had been before I entered the maze. 'I was presumptuous enough to call in for a glass of water before I set off back again.'

'Good heavens! Water again! Come Mrs. Hudson, you must join me for something stronger.'

It was with some difficulty that I persuaded him I must return, for I was expected. Eleanor, I said, would worry if I failed again to come back at a reasonable time. The truth of the matter was, however, that I dreaded meeting Freddie. Of Lydia Brakefield I felt sure there would now be no sign.

Before the Squire and I parted company, I broached a subject which concerned me.

'Mrs. Jeffries told me that Mr. Brakefield has gone missing.'

'Did she, the trollop?' He slapped his thigh. 'Not at all. The scoundrel is no doubt lying dead drunk in some low hostelry in London, excuse my bluntness, Mrs. Hudson. It has happened before, you know.'

He suddenly seemed disinclined to prolong our conversation, and with a flamboyant wave, cantered off down the lane away from me, while I tramped on back home, occasionally replenishing my basket of blackberries, and wondering, with a little smile, what anyone entering the maze would make of the scatterings of fruit on the paths.

I had other matters to think about, however, and resumed my musings about Lydia Brakefield. She was, of course, a beautiful woman and Freddie a youth with a roving eye. However, she was also married, even if wed to a monster, and considerably older than Freddie, to boot. Whatever were they thinking of?

CHAPTER NINETEEN

On the Saturday morning of our excursion, we were once again blessed with unseasonably fine weather, although caution this time led us to bring with us a quantity of umbrellas and overcoats in case of a sudden change. Moreover, picnic baskets aplenty had to be crammed into the landau wherever there was spare space, since all of us – Eleanor and I, Henrietta and indeed the Squire, too, thanks to the good offices of Mrs. Jefferies – had provided enough comestibles to feed a small army.

The Squire looked somewhat astonished, as well he might, at the sight of Henrietta, decked out in the finery she had worn to Lydia Brakefield's garden party, scarlet satin dress with its scatterings of yellow polka dots, ostrich feathered hat and all.

'For you know, Martha,' she had whispered to me, 'it is not as if I have many occasions to wear such style, and I am sure the Squire would expect one to make an effort.'

She looked somewhat disparagingly at my simple bonnet and rather plain brown serge suit, which I had deemed most comfortable for a long drive, followed by a walk and a picnic.

At least she could not complain that the Squire did not pay her attention.

'Dear lady,' he said, helping her into the landau, 'How absolutely charming you look. I quite feel we must have been transported to Paris. Longchamps in the Bois de Boulogne, don't you know.'

Henrietta didn't know, but wasn't about it admit it, and gave me a triumphant look.

'And you, Mrs. Hudson,' helping and complimenting me too. 'Needless to say, you always look impeccably well dressed for any occasion.'

Then, while Walter sat up with Squire Simister, Henrietta and I, along with George, settled inside the landau with some difficulty, given the lady's desire not to crush her gown or squash her hat. Just as well, I thought, that Eleanor was not present, for the three of us, together with the baskets, blankets, umbrellas and overcoats, quite filled up the interior. Still, it was a pleasant enough trip, the Squire urging his two horses along at a spanking pace, not to my mind outside the bounds of comfort, even though Henrietta winced exaggeratedly at each bump in the road, her ostrich feathers repeatedly hitting against the roof of the cabin.

At last, the distinctive skyline of Rochester became visible, the towering Norman castle and the spire of the ancient cathedral, the Squire driving round to the river entrance to the gardens.

'I recall this now, George,' Henrietta said. 'Yes, you are right. I was here before. The castle is indeed very big and, in truth, rather horrid looking.'

I could not disagree. The high stone edifice loomed before us, its many windows like hollow eyes staring out ominously. A shiver ran down my back. Walter, however, was delighted.

'What a prospect!' he exclaimed, in an unusual burst of eloquence. 'I never tire of visiting it. And such a bloody history, it has.'

'I trust,' the Squire said, turning to smile at us, 'you will not frighten the ladies with your tales.'

'I hope we are not so delicate,' I replied, sure of myself, and of Henrietta too, who would likely relish whatever gruesome details her husband could provide.

She, however, was gazing with wary eyes to the very top of the castle.

'We aren't going up there, are we, Walter?' she asked.

'Of course, my dear. That is why we are here.' He rubbed his hands together. 'You could have stayed home, you know.'

Ignoring this last, she looked at me. 'I fear a climb like that would quite wear you out, Martha,' she said.

'Not at all,' I replied. 'I am quite agog to see it.'

First, however, it seemed, we must make inroads into our provisions, for the journey had left Henrietta quite famished. The Squire found a boy to watch our equipage, promising him a sixpence and a slice of pie on our return, and we made our way up the broad tree-lined approach to the castle, passing wooden seats where visitors could take their rest, enjoying the fresh air and the view. Indeed, I think many were even more diverted by the sight of Henrietta in her finery, whispering and pointing at the unwitting lady as she passed by in stately fashion, leading the way as the rest of us staggered rather under the weight of the baskets and blankets.

Circling round, we at last found a satisfactory spot near the bandstand to sit and have our picnic.

'A shame,' quoth Henrietta, 'that the band isn't playing just now, for I do so love music. Do you not, Squire?'

'It depends what is played,' he replied. 'I should not like it to be so loud as to drown out conversation.'

'Oh Lord, no. I hate it loud.'

Meanwhile, George was laying the blankets on the grass for the gentlemen, while Henrietta and I were vouchsafed the comfort of a bench, and soon we were making inroads into Mrs. Jeffries' veal pie, our own roasted chicken, and Henrietta's potted shrimp sandwiches. All the others drank ale, but I preferred some refreshing home-made lemonade, claiming that anything stronger would send me to sleep.

'You are right to resist, Martha,' Henrietta remarked, quaffing away. 'You have not the head for drink. I have noticed it before… Not that I myself partake in excess, of course,' she added hurriedly, simpering at the Squire. 'However, I do enjoy a good local beer on occasion.'

'Quite correct, Mrs. Hazelgrove,' he replied. 'We must support local industry. And may I compliment you on these sandwiches. Did you pot the shrimp yourself, I wonder?'

'Goodness, no. I should not know how... It's from George's shop.'

If the Squire was, as I thought, teasing her, she was happily unaware of the fact, and simply thought he was being attentive.

The emptied picnic baskets closed up, the blankets folded, we headed towards the castle at last.

Oh, if I could only recall what Walter told us of the history – of Bishop Odo and Bishop Gundulf, of the Barons' war and all the various sieges, the fine details of the architecture (Norman, I gathered), the use of Kentish ragstone as a building material – but I am afraid my mind kept wandering. Still, who could forget the details of the siege of 1215 when the inhabitants of the castle were forced to eat horseflesh or worse, when those unfortunates sent away to relieve the garrison were captured and had their hands and feet amputated by the besieging forces, how King John ordered pigs to be slaughtered and set on fire below the tower to bring it tumbling down.

'Pigs! Pigs!' squealed Henrietta, in unconscious mimicry of those unfortunate creatures.

'It must have smelt delicious,' quoth the Squire.

'Isn't that how the Chinese first discovered roast pork, when a house burnt down with a pig in it.' This from George. 'At least according to Mr. Charles Lamb.'

'So who first discovered roast lamb, I wonder?' The Squire laughed at his own joke.

To Henrietta's great relief and Walter's disappointment, we were not after all able to climb the winding stone stairs of the castle, it being deemed too dangerous. All that was allowed, after the Squire had slipped a coin into the hand of the guardian of the place, was entry up some wobbling steps to the first floor, where we could view the towering walls, sinister and dark, hanging over us. One could so well imagine the terrible deeds perpetrated here, that, despite my earlier enthusiasm to explore, I found that I too was relieved that we could progress no further.

'There must be ghosts here,' Henrietta remarked, awestruck.

'Indeed and there be,' the guardian told us. This somewhat disreputable-looking individual, his warty face red from drink, was keeping a watchful eye on us to make sure we ventured no further than permitted. 'Lady Blanche de Warrene it is, shot dead in error by her lover, Sir Ralph de Capo. And wasn't he just trying to save her from the embraces of the dastardly Sir Gilbert de Clare.' He shook his mane of greasy hair. 'Ah yes. Lady Blanche walks the ramparts still, in her white dress, her black hair streaming behind her, the deadly arrow still impaled in her bosoom.'

He grinned, revealing a sparse mouthful of yellow teeth.

Henrietta's eyes bulged.

'Have you seen her yourself?' she whispered, as if the ghost might hear her.

'Many times, m'm, many times.'

We all looked up then, as if trying to catch a glimpse of the poor woman ourselves.

'Only at night, m'm,' the guardian went on. 'Only at the midnight hour, like.'

'You will have to come back later in that case, Mrs. Hazelgrove,' the Squire said, laughing.

'Oh no, Squire. I'd be too terrified. Unless… unless a *man* was with me.' She gave him a meaning look.

Poor Walter, I thought, although that gentleman seemed quite unperturbed, far more interested in scanning the upper floors.

'Observe,' he was saying excitedly to George, 'the scalloped capitals, the chevron ornaments. Splendid, splendid.'

George obediently murmured his appreciation, although I am almost sure that he had no more notion of what constituted a scalloped capital or a chevron ornament than I had.

After the castle, we felt we should also like to visit the ancient cathedral. At least most of us did, Henrietta expressing a contrary determination to go round the shops, 'for was that not in part why we were here?' But of course, she would not go alone, and challenged me, as the only other female present, with a look. What could I do? Against my will, I accompanied her, arranging to meet up with the rest of the party later. Unexpectedly, however, it proved a pleasure, wandering through the charming medieval streets, peering into the various quaint emporia, even though I had no particular desire to purchase anything, and particularly not from the dress shops that Henrietta favoured. Instead, while she was off examining hats, gloves and bags, I betook myself to a book shop next door, where, after browsing the shelves, I purchased a copy of 'The Mystery of Edwin Drood,' by Mr. Charles Dickens, which, as the vendor told me, was set right here in Rochester, where the famous author himself had once lived.

'Though sadly Mr. Dickens died before he could finish the book,' he said. 'You will have to imagine what the ending might be.'

How intriguing, I thought, although when I told Henrietta about it, she sniffed with disdain. In her view, if it was a waste of time reading a novel, how much more foolish one with no ending.

'But Martha, you will never find out who marries whom, and isn't that the whole purpose of a story? I am sure I could find more useful ways of occupying myself.'

After a deal of no doubt useful time spent poring over the offerings of the dress shop, she had come away with one of those essential female accessories, a small cotton handkerchief, edged with lace.

'Although you know, Martha,' she added, 'I did not care at all for the attitude of the assistant. It is the woman's job, surely, to present to me anything I wish to see. She seemed quite surly when after all I settled for the handkerchief, and only, you know, to buy something.'

My sympathies being entirely with the poor put-upon shop assistant, I said nothing.

We had previously arranged to meet the rest of the party for tea in a charmingly old-fashioned establishment on the High Street. However, since I still wished to see the cathedral, I forwent the refreshments and slipped off, having assured Walter, who no doubt wished to instruct me on the various points of architectural and historical interest both outside and inside the building, that I was quite content to go thither unaccompanied. My chief reason, indeed, was less from any particular interest in the place, than to find a haven of peace and quiet away from Henrietta's constant babble. I certainly found it within that holy place.

The organist was evidently practising for the evening service, and I was soothed and indeed delighted by his playing, the beautiful sounds lifting my spirits to the soaring vaults. Sitting myself in a pew, I said a silent prayer to God that all would be well, that Eleanor's baby would be born strong and healthy, and that the lost would be found at last.

The journey back was blissfully quiet too, apart from Henrietta's gentle snores that became louder every time we went over a bump in the road. Walter and I, either unwilling to disturb her, or wrapped in our own thoughts, kept silent too, admiring the scenery, to the accompaniment of a faint murmur of voices from the Squire and George, who had taken his father's place up on the box. Walter indeed was sitting back with a beatific smile on his face, no doubt revelling in the memory of so much history and architecture, even if it wasn't Roman.

CHAPTER TWENTY

I must now return to the very start of my present account, for it was just after we arrived back in Bilbourne that Eleanor, come hot foot from the Post Office, broke terrible news to George and myself.

'If Timothy has not been found, whom then are you talking about' I asked.

'Why, who else has been missing?' she replied. 'Thomas Brakefield, of course.'

'Found dead, you say?'

'Found murdered,' she added.

'How very shocking!' George exclaimed. 'But are you quite sure of that, my dear? Perhaps it was an accident.'

Eleanor shook her head.

'I don't know the full details. They are said to be too horrid... but it seems it happened several days ago. Probably on the night of the harvest festival.'

Since then! All the time we were out and about feasting and enjoying ourselves, the poor man – for, no matter what his faults, he assuredly did not deserve such a fate – was lying cold and dead.

'Please find out what you can?' I asked George, who looked at me askance. 'It is not out of idle curiosity, I assure you. I have a special reason to want to know.'

'They say the constable is sending to London to arrest Daniel Ridge,' Eleanor added.

'Daniel, yes of course, they would think of him,' I replied. For my part, however, I could not help but recall Timothy's anguished and cryptic words, 'I did it'.

'The fact of the matter is that there is no shortage of people who wished the man dead,' George remarked grimly. 'It could be Daniel Ridge, but it could just as well have been our friend, the Squire.'

'Hush,' Eleanor said, shocked.

'I am just saying that it is foolish to jump to conclusions regarding Ridge's guilt.'

I quite agreed.

It wasn't difficult, in the end, to discover exactly what had happened to the man, despite a worthy wish on the part of the vicar, in particular, to keep the full gory details from ladies who might be thought too tender-hearted to bear them. In point of fact, the village gossips fell upon the intelligence with hungry relish. We in the house heard all about it from Joe, his uncle William being the one who had found the body. It was in the second oast house. His master seemingly had been stabbed many times, and his body then stuffed into one of the pockets awaiting transport to the brewhouse of Kenwardham.

'Twas the terrible stink, do you see,' Joe reported, with most unfortunate glee. 'That's what alerted uncle. That and the leaks.'

One could only imagine what state the corpse was in after several days in that heat. It was all the more surprising, then, that it hadn't been discovered earlier, as I remarked.

'See, Mrs. Hud,' Joe explained. 'The second oast had already been emptied of drying 'ops, Uncle Will 'ad no good reason to go into it until 'e was required to move the last pockets. In fact, I do believe it was Satan who led 'im to the thing.'

'Satan?' exclaimed Eleanor, shocked.

'The cat,' I said.

The next day, being Sunday, we made our way to church, along with more villagers than usual, all no doubt keen to find out what they could about the murder, and gawk at the family of the victim. The remaining Brakefields, however, were conspicuous by their absence, to the evident disappointment of many.

'We all reckon it was *her*,' Henrietta said in a loud whisper, the 'we' presumably referring to her gang. 'Lydia, the wife. Anyone could see she detested him. And now she won't even show her face.'

'So you reckon, do you, that Mrs. Brakefield would have the strength to lift a grown man into one of those pockets?' I asked. 'He'd have been a dead weight.'

'She had an accomplice, of course, Martha.' Henrietta sneered. 'One of her many lovers.'

I was silent. After all, from what I knew, it could not be entirely discounted. Freddie Simister was sitting up in the family pew next to his father. I studied the back of his raven head, but it told me nothing. And then there was the unknown from the summerhouse.

It proved hard to concentrate on the vicar's predictable exhortations to pray for the Brakefields in their hour of sorrow, to pray too for the Ridge family, remembering that all are innocent until proven guilty, and to avoid spreading unsubstantiated rumours. I could not help but run a list of those with motives through my head, recalling, as well, what the Squire had remarked about Thomas Brakefield's unsavoury acquaintances away from Bilbourne. Pray God, I thought, it is some stranger to us here who has done the deed, unlikely, given the circumstances, though that was.

As we left the church, I was accosted by Ursula Considine, who requested most particularly that I take a walk with her. 'For I have something to discuss... in private,' she added, since Henrietta shewed every indication of tagging along.

'I will see you back at the house,' I told the latter firmly.

'Very well, Martha. As you please.'

Mightily offended, Henrietta took Eleanor by the arm in proprietorial fashion, and walked off with a toss of her head.

Meanwhile, Ursula and I made our way in silence to the duck pond, and sat ourselves down under the willow.

'I am most afeared for Daniel.' Ursula at last got to the point. 'He has no one to speak for him.'

'I know. It is all too convenient to lay the blame on him, a poor man and an outsider.'

'Nancy arrived at the vicarage late last eve in a frightful state. It seems they have already taken Daniel off to Maidstone to await trial. The woman is beside herself and assures me that Daniel had nothing to do with the murder… Martha, you have so much more experience than I in such matters. Would you come and talk to her?'

Of course, I agreed, on the condition that it would have to be after Sunday dinner.

'For it will be considered very strange,' (by Henrietta, though I did not say it), 'if I am much delayed. And you must know,' I continued, 'that, as for my experience, it has been more a question of luck in the past, than any great ability on my part to solve crimes. I leave detecting skills to my eminent lodger.'

'You are too modest,' Ursula said. 'But in any case, it will be comfort to Nancy to talk to you.'

Henrietta wanted, of course, to know why the vicar's wife had carried me off in such, as she said, an extraordinary fashion, but I just mumbled something vague about Ursula's fears that Daniel might be found guilty of something he did not do. I certainly did not mention the presence of Nancy at the vicarage.

'It's as I said.' Henrietta was triumphant. 'None of us believes in that fellow Ridge's guilt. It is clear as day that the wife is behind it.'

'Not the Squire then?' George asked with assumed innocence.

'Of course not. Squire Simister is far too much of a gentleman to commit murder.'

He had become a firm favourite with her following the outing to Rochester.

'So, mother, you don't think the Squire and Mrs. Brakefield together...'

'George!' exclaimed Henrietta. 'Shame on you.'

'Well, it all sounds very Alice Arden to me,' George remarked.

'What!' At the name I almost jumped out of my seat.

'Alice Arden, mother-in-law. A local woman who finally succeeded in murdering her husband after multiple attempts, or at least engaged lovers and others to assist her, including, I might add, a landowner who had a dispute with her husband over enclosed commons. Just like our dear Squire.'

Henrietta squeaked another protest.

'Now, now, George!' said Eleanor.

'He was called Thomas too,' Walter added. 'Thomas Arden.'

'He was indeed,' George agreed.

'How very strange,' I said.

'I must say I never heard of it.' Henrietta sounded put out. 'Walter, why did you not tell me of it?'

A local scandal, and she in ignorance!

'I do believe Shakespeare or someone wrote a play about it,' her husband replied.

'Oh, you mean it's ancient history.' Now, at last, Henrietta could dismiss it.

I said nothing. I was not about to reveal to all and sundry that Lydia Brakefield had claimed to be rehearsing a monologue from that very play when I discovered her in the summer house with an unknown man. If I did, the news would be broadcast over Bilbourne within the afternoon.

'This lemon meringue pie is quite delicious, Eleanor,' I said instead, to change the subject.

'It isn't bad,' Henriettta conceded, 'but Eleanor, are you not eating any yourself?'

'She has probably poisoned it, mother,' George remarked. 'Murder is catching, you know.'

'Heavens!' Henrietta put down her fork.

'George, don't tease,' Eleanor said. 'I am a little off my food, mother-in-law. That's all.'

I had heard my daughter rushing to the bathroom each morning recently to be sick, and understood only too well the reason. Oh, how we poor women are made to suffer for the privilege of continuing the race! However, if Eleanor wanted her mother-in-law to be kept in the dark over that particular piece of intelligence until it could longer be hidden, I was happy to concur with her wishes.

Although I was now impatient to be off, it was not proving easy to get away. I had intimated to Eleanor my desire to visit the vicarage after dinner, but there was little either of us could do in the face of Henrietta's insistence on a post-prandial game of cards. I played ill, annoyed at once again having to submit, out of politeness, to the silly woman's tyrannical whims. She meanwhile returned, over her hand, to the subject of the murder, speculating on who might be Lydia's accomplice, from Freddie Simister, indeed – 'you can tell from his jackets that he is not to be trusted' – to Mr. Symons, the music teacher – 'a dark horse'.

I remarked that I had not yet met this latter gentleman.

'I suppose some might find him pretty,' Henrietta said. 'A small man, smaller even than you, Walter, with hair that waves a little too much to be natural.'

George guffawed. 'Well,' he said. 'I suspect William Makepeace. The murderer always returns to the scene of the crime, you know.'

'Don't be ridiculous.' Henrietta slapped down her winning hand and pulled the pile of farthings towards herself. 'William would hardly be in cahoots with the likes of Lydia Brakefield.'

She may well have been right about that. Still, I thought, I should like to talk to William as soon as possible.

At long last, Henrietta having succumbed to the effects of a heavy meal, and with the help of a large glass of port – 'for my weak digestion, you know' – was slumbering soundly but not soundlessly in an armchair, while George and his father were engaged in a game of chess, and I was able to slip away unnoticed.

Poor Nancy! She fell into my arms as if I were some sort of saviour.

'I knows you and Mrs. Vicar 'ere will free my Dan'l. You will, won't you?'

I got her to sit down, and took a seat myself. We were in the kitchen, away from Mr. Considine and the children. Since the cook had the afternoon off, we were left undisturbed.

'Nancy, 'I said. 'You must understand that things look bad for Daniel. He attacked Mr. Brakefield and threatened him in front of witnesses.'

'But you don't believe 'e did it, do you, m'm?'

I paused. 'I want to believe he didn't do it, Nancy,' I said, and then, when she jerked away in angry response, I added, 'Of course, I don't know him the way you do. In order to convince me and others, I want you to tell me everything you remember from the night of the feast.'

She looked at me for a long moment, as if assessing my reliability.

'You can trust Mrs. Hudson, Nancy,' Ursula said. 'She is on your side.'

The woman then recounted much that I already knew, including the quarrel at the harvest festival that had led her husband to strike Thomas Brakefield.

'My Dan'l 'ad drink in 'im, sure enough, but, drunk or sober, wouldn't have kilt the man, though God knows 'e 'ad cause enough. Poor Sarey still ain't right after the beating that monster gave 'er.'

'What did Daniel do after the row?' I asked. 'Did he stay with you all the time?'

She hesitated. Then shook her head.

'He weren't with me,' she said.

'Did he go off to drown his sorrows some more?' suggested Ursula gently.

'Not a bit of it, Mrs. Vicar. Knowing what the master was about, sending for the constable, Dan'l was busying hisself finding how we could leave the place afore morning. That's 'ow Stephen got us.' She threw up her hands. 'I should have known 'im for the black-hearted devil 'e is. Instead, 'e pretended to be on our side. "Dan'l's waiting for you at the oast house, Nance," says he, all soft and chummy like. But when we got there, he pushed Charlie into the 'ole first and little Sarey after. Then 'e said, 'I suppose you'd better join your darlings, Nance." And 'e pushed me in, too. By God, if I'd had a knife with me, I'd have driven it into 'im there and then, the devil.'

'He came back with some food, didn't he?' I asked.

She frowned. 'If you think that makes 'im less of a devil, think again. Didn't 'e want to check we could breathe down there, in case they 'ad *'im* up for murder. Not,' she added, 'that 'e wouldn't be capable of it, villain that 'e is. And 'im so 'ot with her ladyship.'

'What?'

She laughed. 'All the pickers knew it. 'Ow when 'er 'usband was away, she'd come down to "inspect" the works, and then order Stephen to "discuss" it with 'er in private, like. Oh, we all knew the nature of them discussions right enough. Stephen didn't even make a secret of it, swaggering and preening 'isself.'

Ursula looked rightly shocked. For my part I was more surprised.

'That was dangerous, surely. If Mr. Brakefield had got to hear of it...?'

'Our word against theirs? They'd have said we was lying out of spite. Anyway, the old bloke...'

She stopped.

'What?'

'Nothing.'

'Come now, Nancy. I need to know everything.'

'Well… they say – now I never saw it meself – they say old Thomas liked the youngsters. The very young ones. Not as young as Sarey, thank God.'

Ursula gasped, while I was sorely disillusioned. I had thought such corruption confined to the more sordid parts of the city, that the countryside at least remained unsullied.

'Anyways.' Nancy went on. 'After you let us out from our prison, m'm, old Nell went off to find Dan'l, while we hid in the shadows. Lucky for us Stephen didn't come back afore Dan'l found us. From there we made our way on foot back to London, sure that no one would bother to come looking for us there, especially since we moved our lodgings. Someone must have ratted on us, m'm, for the constable found us quick enough.'

'You were surprised to hear that Thomas Brakefield was dead?'

'Not really, m'm. If anyone deserved a knife in the guts it was 'im. But my Dan'l didn't do it. I can swear on the Bible itself to that. On me two children's lives.'

'The time you were apart from Daniel, do you know where he was or who he was with? There may be witnesses who could vouch for him.'

'I wish there was, m'm. But…' she glanced at Ursula, ''e wasn't sure 'isself. I suppose a'ter all there was a bit more ale involved. See, 'e was looking to getting away, but then, when we all went missing, 'e got into a right old state looking for us, especially after Stephen told 'im he'd never find us. Drove 'im a bit off 'is head, it did.'

Enough to kill? But surely Thomas Brakefield was gone by then. Unless, of course, he came back for some reason, as I suppose he must have done. Oh dear. I felt no nearer getting to the bottom of the mystery, even though Nancy had given food for thought in a new direction. Stephen! Was it him in the summerhouse, then, and not Freddie? What had Lydia called to him as she ran out? If only I could remember her exact words: 'after what has happened?' 'after what we did?'

Something else occurred to me.

'Now, you were in the first oast house, Nancy, and Mr. Brakefield was found in the second. It's unlikely, I suppose, but did you see or hear anything while you were hiding there, waiting for Daniel?'

She thought. Then shook her head.

'Ah well...' It was a long shot.

''Cept young Timothy. I seen 'im?'

'Doing what?'

She shook her head.

'Nothing. Waiting, like, seemed to be.'

Timothy who had also disappeared! Timothy who had said, 'I did it?'

CHAPTER TWENTY-ONE

As I prepared to leave the vicarage, having promised Nancy to do what I could – at the very least to throw doubt on Daniel's guilt, 'For they'll 'ang him for sure, m'm, if no one does nothing' – I was taken aback to meet Lydia Brakefield coming in. She was clad in the requisite black mourning that, however, did not suit her, draining her skin as it did of what little colour it had, and making her look her age for once. A more charitable person than I might have said she was still in shock, but I am afraid, like Henrietta, I could see her husband's death only as a release for her.

She seemed as surprised as I was at our meeting.

'Mrs. Hudson!' said she, stopping short, 'whatever brings you here?'

Clearly she had forgotten that we were now supposed to be on first name terms.

'Ursula Considine is a friend of mine,' I replied, rather annoyed at having to explain myself.

'A friend, ah, yes. A friend,' repeating the word as if unaccustomed to it.

I recalled then how she herself had told me previously that she had no friends in Bilbourne, a sad admission I had thought at the time. Now I was thinking, no women friends, at least.

At that moment, Mr. Considine emerged from his study.

'Mrs. Brakefield, my deepest condolences,' he said, taking the lady's hands in his.

'Thank you.'

216

She pulled back, as if stung by the touch. Mr. Considine, gentleman that he was, showed no sign of noticing. Or maybe, quite simply, he didn't.

'You are here to discuss the...er... funeral arrangements, I believe. Your manservant indicated as much earlier.'

'Yes,' she replied, for some reason looking at me rather than at him. 'I preferred to come here rather than oblige you to visit the Hall, vicar.'

'It would have been no trouble at all to me, dear lady. But come into my study. I am afraid it is a little topsy-turvy at the moment, but I am sure I can clear a chair for you.'

Despite the awful circumstances of the visit, I could barely repress a smile at the thought of the topsy-turveyness of the study, and what the fastidious Lydia would make of it.

'Mrs. Hudson,' she added, 'I wonder would you join us?... No offence, vicar, but I should appreciate the support of one of my own sex at such a time.'

'Surely Mrs. Considine...' I started to say. She put her hand out to me in such an appealing way that I could not refuse.

'You and I,' she said. 'Well, I think we might almost call ourselves friends, too... Martha.'

Of that I was not convinced. However, I felt sorry for her, even while not entirely trusting her goodwill or discounting the accusations levelled against her by Henrietta and her gang.

'Come along then, Mrs. Hudson,' the vicar said, perhaps a little relieved not to have to endure a tête-à-tête with the lady. 'I am sure we can find space for you, too. In any case, Ursula will be busy putting the little ones to bed for their afternoon nap. You know how it is, ladies, they like mama to read them a bedtime story.'

Now I was fairly sure that Lydia Brakefield had never read Randall a bedtime story in the boy's life, but she nodded anyway.

'I am most anxious,' said she, once settled in the chair that had been cleared of papers for her, 'to expedite the funeral, since Randall and I will be leaving here immediately afterwards.'

'Leaving? Are you then selling the plantation?' asked Mr. Considine asked.

'It is not mine to sell,' she replied with some bitterness.

'Oh?'

'Mr. Brakefield has willed it to Eve.'

Both the vicar and I were quite struck dumb by the intelligence.

'I have known the terms for some time,' she went on. 'Thomas claimed that it had been his first wife's wish to provide for their daughter, but I don't believe him. At least, not to provide in that way... No, he thought it a great joke...' scowling at the memory. 'He was a spiteful man, you know.'

The vicar made a dissenting gesture, though I have never quite understood the stipulation that one should not speak ill of the dead, so many of them richly deserving harsh words.

However, Lydia, observing the gesture, relented a little.

'Perhaps,' she went on, 'had Thomas lived, he would have amended the will. We will never know now.' She looked at us in turn. 'Of course, for Randall's sake, he hasn't left me destitute. There will be enough for my son and me to live on in reasonable comfort. I intend going to Italy. One can live there quite well on little.'

Now I understood why she had come to the vicarage, rather than receive Mr. Considine in the Hall. It was not her place any more. But surely, I thought, Eve would not be so unkind as to drive out her stepmother before, as they say, her father was cold in his grave. I wondered how recently Lydia had become aware of the terms of the will, or if this awareness indeed dated from before her husband's demise. If she were telling the truth, it might have a bearing on whether nor not she had been involved in his murder. She was surely covetous enough to wish to wait for him to change the will back in favour of herself and her son. But on the other hand, her passionate nature might have spurred her to a quick revenge for slighting them. It was all most thought-provoking, and yielded no clear signal.

The funeral arrangements, concerning the which Thomas Brakefield had left instructions, were quickly settled after that. It was to be an ostentatious enough affair, complete with horse-drawn carriages bedecked with blackened ostrich feathers, as befitted a lord of the manor, which is how the man had seen himself. He had also stipulated that all who attended the service should be given a half crown coin, clearly a bribe to ensure that a man as unpopular as he should not lack mourners. He was, of course, to be buried in the family mausoleum, beside his father and first wife, of whose name, I realised now, I had never heard mention.

The business over, and the vicar left to his devices in his study, Lydia requested, with some urgency, that I accompany her back to the Hall.

'Perhaps you can talk some sense into Eve,' she said, 'for she will not speak to me.'

'Talk to her about what?' I asked.

She regarded me as if I were utterly stupid.

'I should of course wish to know something of her plans, now that this fortune has descended upon her.'

'Eve knew nothing about it in advance, then?'

'Apparently not. My husband swore me to secrecy, so I presume he did not confide in her. And I certainly should not have told her, for she would surely have gloated at the news and held it over me.'

I was as keen to talk to Eve as my interlocutor was keen that I should so do. However, it would be necessary to tell Eleanor where I was gone, since, knowing my daughter, she would worry if I were long away. Ursula, emerging from the kitchen where I assumed Nancy was still ensconced, and observing my companion's impatience to be off, most kindly offered to send her maid round to the shop to tell them.

'Our friend will be looked after,' she said to me, and I nodded, understanding that she meant Nancy.

'You and all your friends!' Lydia said, with an edge to her voice, as we settled into the coach. 'How it must drain your energies keeping up with them all.'

'How is Alice Arden getting along?' I asked, all innocence.

'What?'

'I suppose your projected play must be cancelled now.'

'Oh that. Yes…yes…'

'Such a shame. I was looking forward to seeing it.'

She studied my face, but my expression, I trust, was one of bland insouciance.

'The murder of one's spouse rather puts paid to idle entertainments, Mrs. Hudson.'

The tide of friendship seemed to have ebbed again.

'Just as well, perhaps. Such a grim history.'

'You know it, then.'

'I heard of it recently.'

Silence. Then, 'I am not stupid. I know what people are saying.' She gave me a fierce look. 'I can assure you here and now that I had no hand whatsoever in the frightful murder of my husband.'

'I am most relieved to hear it.'

She gave a bitter laugh. 'If only I thought you believed me…' She caught my hand. 'Oh, my marriage was unhappy, a sham, Martha. Everyone knew it. But believe me or disbelieve me, I am committed enough in my obedience to the sixth commandment not to take that path.'

If only, I thought, you were equally committed to the seventh commandment, madam.

'But do you find it likely,' she went on, 'that Daniel Ridge killed my husband?'

'I am inclined to think him innocent.'

'I see.'

We continued the way to the Hall in silence. When we alighted, Lydia instructed the coachman to be ready to take me back down to the village again shortly, to which the insolent youth snorted, as if to say, who are *you* to give me orders now? Or perhaps I imagined it.

As we approached the house, I noticed a large laurel wreath hanging on the front door, a grim reminder that someone who lived within had recently died.

'I shall be in my parlour,' Lydia said. 'Be sure to call in before you leave again, Martha.'

To tell me what Eve said, hung unspoken in the air between us.

I nodded. 'If only she will admit me,' I said.

Eve was not to be found in the house, however. Jobbins informed us that she had gone out shortly after Mrs. Brakefield left, he knew not whither. Perhaps, I thought, as newly installed mistress of all, she was inspecting her domain. Or perhaps she was simply taking refuge in her beloved orchard. I would try there first.

A cold wind had sprung up on the heights, ripping through the branches of the trees and sending showers of leaves flying hither and thither like demented spirits. Winter was coming.

I glanced at the grotto as I passed it. Thankfully there was no sign of the hermit. I supposed the man would never be employed there again.

As I entered the orchard, I called out Eve's name. There was a sudden loud rustling noise, perhaps even a murmur of voices, and then the girl appeared before me, pale and drawn and frowning. Her first words echoed those of her stepmother, and sounded equally unfriendly.

'Mrs. Hudson, what are you doing here?'

Was I mistaken, or did the rustling noise continue elsewhere as she spoke?

'I have come to see you, my dear. I am so sorry for everything that has happened.'

'My stepmother sent you, I suppose.'

'She did, but I assure you, Eve, that I am here on my own behalf, and will not tell her anything you want kept from her.'

'Oh God!' she said, softening suddenly. 'Let us sit down.'

She led me in the opposite direction to the one from which she had come, and found us a wooden bench.

'You are not cold?' I asked for she was underdressed for the season in a light cotton frock and carried no shawl.

She gave a dismissive wave.

'Has Lydia told you of my good fortune?' She spoke the words as if a curse had been visited upon her.

'That you are to inherit the Hall and plantation,' I said. 'I confess I was most astonished.'

'As was I, as you may imagine. I don't know what to think of it.'

'You father loved you after all.'

'Loved!' she gave a shriek of mirth. 'I suppose you could call it that.'

Not quite sure what to make of that particular response, I continued, 'Your stepmother has asked to know what your plans are... since you seem disinclined to speak to her about it.'

Eve seized my hand. 'Mrs. Hudson,' she said. 'What plans can I have as yet? I am quite bowled over. I need someone to give me kind advice. Would you be able to do that?'

'I fear I am not well-equipped for that particular task,' I replied. 'Perhaps a friend of the family...'

Eve interrupted with another of those horrible laughs.

'Friends!' she exclaimed. 'We have none.'

Just as her stepmother had said.

'Your father must have had a solicitor. Perhaps he...'

She made a dismissive gesture.

'Actually,' she said, 'I was wondering...what about Squire Simister?'

Now that was unexpected. My face must have shown my surprise.

'His quarrel, Mrs. Hudson, was with my father, not with me,' she continued. 'Could you perhaps ask him to call on me? I have heard that he likes you.'

Whoever told her that? William perhaps.

I thought about it.

'The Squire is a good-natured man, and, if willing, would be a well-chosen adviser,' I replied. 'I shall be most happy to approach him on your behalf.'

At that, she fell into my arms.

'Thank you so much. Oh, I have felt so alone, Mrs. Hudson, so surrounded by enemies.'

'Enemies! That's a strong word.'

'Lydia hates me.'

'Well, you will not have to see much more of her. She is planning to go abroad after the funeral.'

Suddenly Eve's face lit up with a broad smile.

'What wonderful news! Oh, thank you so much for telling me.'

Odium existed on both sides, it seemed.

'Any word from Timothy?' I asked.

'Timmy?...' she looked furtive. 'No. Nothing at all.'

'He wasn't with you just now, then?'

'No.'

'Only, I thought I heard someone.'

'Probably a bird or a rabbit,' she said. 'I was quite alone. Thinking.'

'You see, Eve, I cannot help but worry that he might be involved in your father's death.'

'That's not possible. I heard... I heard they had caught the man.'

'They have arrested Daniel Ridge, but I do not think him guilty.'

'He must be. Everyone heard him threaten papa in front of everyone. He attacked him.'

'All the same...'

'You are wrong.' She flushed angrily.

'I know you like Timothy. And yet I cannot forget his words, "I did it."'

'He could have meant anything.'

'So where is he, to explain himself?'

'I don't know.'

Her mouth set in a stubborn line. I could not press her further, and soon took my leave, promising to speak to the Squire on her behalf at my earliest opportunity.

On a whim, on my return through the woodland, I approached the grotto, to have a closer look at it, now that its horrid incumbent was gone. On entering, I perceived that the cave extended far back into the side of the mound into which it was set. When my eyes accustomed themselves to the darkness, I discerned a rough bed within, covered with a blanket, some drinking and eating vessels, and even a loaf of bread on a small table. Of course, it could all belong to the hermit, who after all had been there not many days since. However, the bread was not at all stale, as I should have expected it to be under those circumstances. Strange.

I made my way back towards the Hall. As I came out on to the lawn, I spied William in conversation with one of the gardeners. Here was an opportunity to ask him some questions, and I approached him for that purpose.

He was more than happy to accede to my request, and asked if I was returning to the village, as he was going that way himself. I said that I was, since I had no desire either to speak again to Lydia or to ride down with the young churl of a coachman, who was waiting by his equipage for that purpose. It was rude of me, I know, to sidle off like that, but at least I went up to the youth and asked him please to tell his mistress that I would talk to her again soon, pressing a coin that he didn't deserve into his hand.

He took it with more of a nod of respect to me than he had evinced before, and then William and I set off. I soon broached the subject of his discovery of the body.

'Twas an 'orrible business, Mrs 'Udson. Not fit for the ears of a lady like yourself.'

'I can assure you, William,' I replied, 'that I am no stranger to such horrors. And I have a particular interest in learning the precise details,'

Perhaps he took me for a sensation hunter like so many other of the village ladies. It occurred to me, as he started his account, that he must have told it many times already. How he first noticed the oozings from the bottom of a particular pocket, stacked with all the others, and, on investigating, found it to contain the stinking, rotting, maggot-ridden corpse of his master.

'You know yourself 'ow 'ot it was in that there oast 'ouse, Mrs. 'Udson,' he said. 'Speeded up the inevitable.'

'Yes, yes,' I replied. Truly, I could have dispensed with those particular details. 'But you see I am more interested in how he came to be placed in the pocket in the first place. How the body could have been disposed of there.'

'Ah, well, I been a-thinking of that, too. I reckon 'e must 'ave been attacked on the platform above the pocket, and shoved in from there. Would 'ave been too difficult otherwise, 'eaving the body up them steps. Would 'ave left traces, too, and there weren't none.'

'I see,' I replied. 'Can I ask, were there any traces of such an attack up on the platform itself, then?'

He gave me an appreciative look. 'I see you like to act the detective, Mrs. 'Udson. Like meself. Yes, I pointed the bloodstains out to the constable. O'course, someone had tried to get rid of 'em by the look of it, rubbing hops on top of them. But blood soaks into bare wood in a special kind of a way.' He rubbed his hands together. 'To my mind, someone lured 'im up on that platform for the sole purpose of doing 'im in.'

'A premeditated attack then?'

'If that means planned in advance, I should say so. Yes, indeed.' He shook his head. 'Faults 'e 'ad in plenty, the master, but to end like that. No, 'tisn't right.'

'So do you think Daniel Ridge could have done it?'

William scratched his bald head.

'He could. But I don't think that would 'ave been 'is way. Not like that. And how would 'e 'ave persuaded the master to go into the oast house with 'im?'

'Unless Mr. Brakefield, seeing him go in, followed him there, and then a fight broke out.'

'Possible I s'pose. But why would Daniel go to the oast 'ouse, in the first place? Nothing for 'im there.'

'No. Unless he knew his wife and children were imprisoned in one of them.'

'No, no one much knowed of that there hidey-hole. I'd forgot about it meself.'

Reaching the village, we parted company. I rather suspected he was on his way to the Green Man and Lanthorn to tell his tale over again and to quench the thirst that had come upon him, after I gave him a coin to thank him for his time.

CHAPTER TWENTY-TWO

'My dear Mrs. Hudson,' the Squire was saying. 'Of course, I will talk with the poor girl.'

This conversation was taking place the following afternoon in the Hazelgroves' little parlour, Joe having obligingly gone out of his way on his rounds to deliver the missive I had sent to the said gentleman, requesting an interview.

It had rather astounded me to see the Squire roll up in his pony and trap, even before Joe had returned. I had been sitting on my usual stool, engaged in knitting a tiny jacket, when he burst into the shop in his customary explosive way.

'You wanted me, Mrs. Hudson,' he exclaimed, causing Betsy Warren to gawk openly over her purchases of tea and flour, while George smirked in an annoyingly knowing way, as I, in some confusion, showed the Squire upstairs to the parlour.

'What a delightful little room,' he remarked, without any hint of condescension, as he threw himself onto a chair that creaked ominously in response.

It was true enough. Eleanor's tasteful touches had rendered the parlour a delightful place, and my own needlework among hers was evident everywhere in the embroidered cushions and antimacassars.

'It is so typical of you, madam,' he now continued warmly, when I had explained the reason for his summons, 'ever to be thinking of others. I had hoped, however...' He gave a little smile, 'that your request to meet was in the nature of a more personal desire.'

'It is always a pleasure to see you, Squire,' I replied in level tones.

'A special pleasure, I hope,' he went on, meaningfully.

Oh, these gallant gentlemen! I do not deceive myself into thinking my charms anything special, and yet it seems wherever I go, whether in Ireland, Paris or the Home Counties, some man or other starts paying court to me. I liked the Squire well enough, but found him a little exhausting, forever thundering on about something or other. Just now he filled the parlour to overflowing with his great bulk and his booming voice, which from time to time exploded into a laugh, his lion's mane trembling with mirth.

'Old Tom Brakefield will be spinning in his grave when I turn up at his pile,' he said, perhaps forgetting that the unfortunate victim had yet to be entombed. 'I shall go there on the instant. I trust you will give me the honour of accompanying me.'

I hesitated, not having thought of any such thing.

'She is such a very young lady,' he continued with a delicacy I had not suspected in him, 'a girl, indeed, that, since she does not wish to include her stepmother in her dealings, must surely welcome one of her own sex in support.'

He smiled at me. John Simister really had a very warm smile, as if the sun had just burst forth. Under its influence, I did not feel I could refuse him, and, indeed, what he said made good sense. Eve might well appreciate my attendance. We duly set off together.

As luck would have it, Henrietta was standing outside the Post Office as we passed, in close conversation with two of her cronies. Feeling conspicuous enough, I was glad it was the neat little pony and trap the Squire had brought, and not the landau. Still, they all three turned and stared at us quite openly.

'Good afternoon, ladies!' he called out to them, flourishing his whip, while I gave a little wave.

'I am afraid,' he continued in jolly tones, 'that, being seen driving off with an old reprobate like me, Mrs. Hudson, will quite destroy your reputation in Bilbourne. Those three witches will see to that. Ha ha ha!' He gave his poor pony a great swish with his whip on its hind quarters and the beast leapt forward as if to take off into the skies.

I could not condone his language or behaviour. Had he forgotten already that one of those 'witches' was my daughter's mother-in-law, a woman, indeed, he had so recently flattered with his attentions? Perhaps he did not recognise Henrietta without her polka dot gown and ostrich feathered hat, for she was today wearing only a drab grey housedress and workaday bonnet.

Mouths hung open at the Hall, too, as we drove in. Two gardeners stopped what they were doing and leaned on their spades for a better look, a groom froze in his tracks and the cross-eyed maid, about some errand in the courtyard, dropped the basket she was carrying.

The Squire hailed them all heartily, calling over the groom to look after his equipage, and having helped me down, strode to the front door, on which the laurel wreath still hung. He rapped loudly on the demon-headed door-knocker, after commenting, 'Looks quite like the old boy himself, doesn't it, Mrs. Hudson?'

The old boy meaning, I presumed, Thomas Brakefield. Since the Squire wasn't looking for a reply, I gave none, not approving one whit his levity.

Jobbins, when he finally opened to us, was no way less astonished than the rest of the servants.

'I have come to call on Miss Eve, at her request,' the Squire stated.

''Ave you indeed? Well, we'll see about that,' Jobbins muttered. He would have closed the door on us, I am sure, only the Squire had already inserted his big boot inside the step.

All the same, we were left to stand in the hallway, while Jobbins went off to inquire whether the Brakefields' arch-enemy was to be admitted or no. He soon returned, however, clearly disappointed at not being able to eject us, and we were shown into what had so recently been Lydia Brakefield's own sunny pink parlour, where Eve very soon joined us.

'Thank you for coming so speedily, Squire Simister,' she said. There seemed a new confidence about her. Indeed, she was dressed in an elegant suit of mourning, far from the frills she had worn before, and looked to be quite the young lady. Unlike her stepmother, black became her. For once, the Squire was struck dumb. He too was clearly surprised, having thought to be dealing with someone little more than a child.

'But Mrs. Hudson,' she continued. 'I did not expect you as well.'

'The Squire reckoned you would be more comfortable if I were present,' I replied.

'Did he?' She smiled at him. 'That was most thoughtful. However, I should prefer for you to leave us. You see, what I have to discuss is of a very private nature.'

I was somewhat taken aback, nay offended, if I say true. Yet I could not argue. The Squire, perhaps sensing my chagrin, started to remonstrate.

'It is my fault, Miss Brakefield, that Mrs. Hudson is present...'

'Yes, and I am sorry for it. However, I am afraid I must insist... You know your way about, Mrs. Hudson. I am sure you can find something to do while I talk to the Squire.'

There was nothing for it. I had to bow out as gracefully as I could and leave them alone. Then to think where to go and what to do. I could hardly wander over the house uninvited, so I took myself out into the grounds again, and made my way round the side of the Hall to where the summerhouse was to be found. There was no sign today of Lydia, and I could not help but wonder where she might be. However, a shrill voice I recognised as that of Randall was within. It seemed a lesson was underway and that the pupil was not happy about it.

'Stupid!' the child was shouting, in a temper tantrum. 'I'll tell mama how cruel you are. Then you'll be for it. I'll tell mama.'

A man's voice in reply was pitched soft and low, attempting to pacify.

'Your mama particularly wants you to study Latin, Randall,' he said.

'She doesn't. You're lying. Anyway, it's stupid. No one talks your stupid Latin any more...'

'When you are in Italy...'

'They don't speak Latin in Italy. Stupid! Anyway, I don't want to go to stupid Italy...'

A great sigh, and then, 'Let us try one more time. Amo, amas, amat, amamus...'

'To hell with your amamuses!'

Upon which shocking note, the little brat burst from the summerhouse, crashing into me.

'Who are you?... Oh, I know, that old woman from the shop... You're stupid too.'

With that, he ran back towards the Hall.

The man who now emerged from the summerhouse was miniature in stature, with tiny feet and hands, and neat little features expressing dismay. This must be the tutor, Mr. Symons, whose hair, Henrietta said, waved too much to be natural. It was also finely spun, and of as golden a hue as Rumplestiltskin could have wished for. All in all, a pretty young fellow clearly ill-equipped to deal firmly with his charge.

'Oh dear!' he said. 'Oh dear, dear, dear!'

'You have your hands full with that boy,' said I, sympathetically.

'I do indeed, Mrs. er...' He raised his eyebrows in inquiry.

I introduced myself. 'The old lady from the shop,' I added with a smile.

'I apologise on his behalf... What Randall needs...' he started to say, and then stopped.

'A good slap,' I said. 'Although I know his mother would not agree.'

'I do not believe in corporal punishment, Mrs. Hudson.' Mr. Symons shook his head. 'But some non-corporeal punishment is certainly called for. Were it up to me, I should deprive the child of his favourite sweetmeats or toys at the very least, and make him sit in the corner, enjoined to silence, which if he breaks will only prolong the ordeal. However...' He gave another great sigh.

'Well, since I understand Mrs. Brakefield will be leaving this place soon, your own ordeal must surely be soon at an end.'

'I am afraid that she has requested me to accompany them, as the boy's tutor.' He looked miserable.

I laughed at that. 'Surely you don't have to agree. You're a free man.'

'Would that it were so simple, Mrs. Hudson,' he replied. 'Mrs. Brakefield pays excessively well. I should have difficulty finding a position as good. And I have responsibilities. A widowed mother and unmarried sisters to support.'

I nodded in sympathy.

'I am the youngest, do you see,' he continued, clearly happy to unburden himself, 'and my sisters... well, it seems unlikely that, without a marriage portion, any of them will find husbands, though they are all sweet-natured girls, if not in their first youth.'

'Are they all totally dependent on you?'

'They are. Well, Milly does a little dressmaking and Lilly makes the most delectable jams which she sells through a local shop, while Tilly is truly artistic. Her watercolours rank, in my humble opinion, with those of James Miller Mackay. But of course, she would never get the same recognition as he, being a woman, you know.'

'What euphonious names they have.' What's yours, I thought? Billy?

He gave a little tinkling laugh.

'Oh, that's their own fancy. It's Millicent, Lilian and Matilda really, but since childhood, they have rhymed themselves together like that. They are very close, you see. And lovely girls. It is such a pity...'

'Could they not take up some position to support themselves?'

'Oh goodness!' He laughed again. 'My mother would have a fit at the mere suggestion, Mrs. Hudson. We may be poor, she would say, but my daughters are still ladies. To think of them as governesses, or worse, typists, or worse still, in trade, working long hours in some ghastly shop!'

My sympathies for the family instantly evaporated, for I cannot bear snobbery.

'I am afraid, Mr. Symons,' I said coolly, 'I cannot agree with you. I look forward to a modern world in which women are able to take their place beside men, on an equal footing, in the workplace as well as everywhere else. I pray I may live to see such a world, or at least that my daughter, who, by the way, runs a shop, may do so.'

'Oh dear,' he said, blushing. 'Oh dear, oh dear, oh dear... I must apologise now on my own behalf, Mrs. Hudson. Although you understand that the opinion I expressed was not necessarily mine, but that of my mother.'

'Well,' I replied, somewhat mollified, 'I am sorry for you in your predicament. I should not like to be tutor to that boy. Though I suppose at least you will have the chance to see Italy.'

'Mm,' he replied, evidently not overjoyed at the prospect. 'When I told mother about it, she was not too pleased.'

'You have told your mother?' I asked, a little puzzled.

'Yes. When I was home, it must have been a month ago.'

Now I was even more confused.

'Do you mean that Mrs. Brakefield has been planning to go to Italy for some time?'

He reddened again.

'Oh dear,' he said. 'I shouldn't have mentioned that. It was supposed, you see, to be a secret.'

I smiled.

'Don't worry,' I replied. 'Mrs. Brakefield herself told me of her plans to go abroad.'

He looked relieved.

'Of course, it is a great opportunity for me. All the same... I should prefer... ah well...' He ran tiny fingers through the waves of his flaxen hair. 'Mother is afraid my complexion will be spoiled under the southern sun.' He laughed ruefully.

I could not imagine, looking at and listening to him, that this milksop was the person Lydia Brakefield had met in secret in the summer house on the previous occasion, unless he was a terrific actor. Of course, I could not yet rule him out, either. What was of much more interest to me was the intelligence that already, a month before her husband died, Lydia Brakefield had been planning to go away. Perhaps there was nothing to it. Perhaps Thomas was even to go with her. And yet, and yet...

At that moment, the Squire came round the side of the house accompanied by Eve.

'There you are at last, Mrs. Hudson!' he boomed. 'Parsing Latin verbs with the resident scholar, no doubt!'

Eve, for her part, was now all sweetness and light.

'I must apologise for my abruptness earlier,' she said, taking my hand in hers. 'I must have sounded very rude indeed. I just hope you can understand how shaken I am by all that has happened. The burden of responsibilities so unexpectedly thrust upon me... The Squire here has proved a great support. I feel much relieved.'

I could not be cross with her, she looked so penitent.

'Please come and take some refreshments within, before you go back,' she said.

'That would be most pleasant if the Squire has the time.'

'All the time in the world, dear lady,' he said.

I turned to say farewell to Mr. Symons, and found that young man staring at Eve with what could only be described as puppy-dog adoration. Aha, I thought. Now I know why you have stayed on in such an unpleasant situation, and why you are so reluctant to leave. Just like Timothy, in fact, and yet so unlike.

'Mr. Symons.' She smiled at him. 'Please join us too.'

He started to babble. 'I...I...my duties... Randall... you know...'

'As you will.'

He looked downcast, as if disappointed that she had not exercised her new powers to insist. The young man shuffled behind us as we three ambled up towards the Hall again, Eve and I on either side of the Squire, arm-in-arm with him.

We were back in Lydia's parlour. A black cat was stretched out on a cushion on the window ledge. It lazily turned green eyes upon us as we entered, and for a fanciful moment I wondered if a spell had been cast and the absent lady of the manor had been transformed into this feline.

'Is that Satan?' I asked, instead.

'No, I wanted him, of course, but he's too wild to be let into the house. That's Lucifer...' Eve laughed. 'William got him for me. Such a darling.'

The cat, as if knowing it was being spoken of, stretched out its paws, and clawed at the silk cushion it was lying on. Lydia wouldn't like that one little bit, I thought.

'Satan? Lucifer?' The Squire exclaimed. 'What devilish work is here?'

'I've always wanted a cat and now I can have one,' Eve replied, adding, rather sadly. 'In fact, I suppose I can have anything I want.'

'Where is your stepmother?' I asked.

'In Kenwardham. With the undertaker, arranging for the cortège.' She sighed. 'I still cannot believe papa has gone for ever. I keep expecting him to come through that door.'

'Let us pray he is looking down on you,' I said.

'Or looking up from down below.'

'Squire Simister!'

'I refuse to be a hypocrite, Mrs. Hudson. The man was a monster, the way he treated everyone, including his family. This poor girl! Hell isn't hot enough for the likes of him.'

'Hush, you are talking about Eve's father.' I had to remonstrate with him.

'It is all right,' she replied. 'The Squire's view of papa, alive and now dead, is, of course, no secret to me. I respect you for your honesty, Squire. And I have to admit papa had his faults. All the same...'

'I am sorry,' he said. 'Mrs. Hudson is right. I should not have spoken like that. Forgive me. I am a bumbling idiot.'

She gave him one of those smiles of hers that transformed her face.

'You are yourself, Squire,' she replied, 'and that is very special.'

The cross-eyed maid brought in the tea then, giving Eve a wary look, at least as far as one could tell. I wondered if she was worried about her situation under the new mistress of the house.

'Thank-you, Agnes,' Eve said.

At least she treated the servants with a courtesy that had not been shown by her predecessor.

'I have to say, Eve, that you look very well in that gown,' I told her, as she handed me my cup.

'Thank you. This is something of my mother's. I had nothing suitable.'

Her dead mother's dress! I was somewhat taken aback to learn it.

'It fits you very well.'

'People are always telling me how like my mother I am.'

'Yes, you are, my dear,' the Squire said. 'Very like. She was a beautiful woman. Such a shame...'

We sat in silence for a little while, perhaps thinking of our dead. At least, I know I was thinking of dear Henry, so prematurely snatched from me.

We chatted some more about inconsequential things. I asked, without expecting enlightenment, whether Eve had received any word from Timothy. She shook her head, avoiding my eye. I could not help but wonder about that scene in the orchard – the evidence of occupancy in the grotto – and yet if she did not wish to tell me anything, I could not make her. And perhaps, after all, I was wrong. My sister Nelly always insists I have a too fertile imagination.

'Who is Timothy?' the Squire asked.

'A boy who works here,' Eve said. 'We haven't seen him for some days. More tea?'

At last, we took our leave. The Squire, as we drove back, was in ecstasies.

'To think that sweet wench is spawn of old Brakefield,' he said. 'Incredible!'

'I trust you managed to help her sort out her affairs. It's a big responsibility to be laid on such a young woman.'

'Indeed, it is. What she needs is a good manager for the plantation. But I think she has one already.'

'Stephen?' I hoped it was not so.

'No, not him. I wouldn't trust that fellow an inch. Anyway, between you, me and the gatepost, I rather think young Stephen has quite another position in mind.' He chuckled, but did not elaborate. 'No, I was meaning William Makepeace.'

I was surprised. 'The head drier? Mrs. Jeffries' brother?'

The Squire guffawed.

'You fear nepotism at work here, Mrs. Hudson? Keeping jobs in the family, what?' he said. 'Not really: The girl suggested him herself. They are good friends and she trusts him. William is rough around the edges, of course, but very practical. I'm sure he'll do well… It's an odd business, all the same.'

He shook his locks.

'You mean the will? Disinheriting the wife and son?'

'I suppose I can understand the wife, People say, well, you probably know what they say… But the little boy…'

'Have you met him?'

'Ho ho, Mrs. Hudson. I know what you mean. Still, blood is thicker than water. My own son might not be all I'd hoped for, but I'd never consider depriving him of his birthright.' He furrowed his brow. 'Unless, of course, in Randall's case…'

'Unless what…?'

He looked at me sideways.

'In the words of the bard of Avon, Mrs. Hudson, it is a wise father that knows his own child.'

'Oh!'

I understood him now. A shocking suggestion indeed, yet one that would explain the disinheritance of the boy. I paused to think. The Squire evidently misinterpreted my silence.

'Ah now, Mrs. Hudson, I have upset your womanly sensibilities, crass fool that I am.'

I smiled at him.

'No, Squire. I am sufficiently a woman of the world to recognise the possibility at least of Mr. Brakefield believing the child not to be his. True or not, true or not.'

We continued the rest of the short journey in silence, each of us with our own thoughts. Once arrived at the shop, the Squire was quieter than usual as he helped me down. He made no move to enter with me, and I did not try to detain him. Truth be told, I was fatigued, and craved the peace and quiet of my bedroom, indicating as much to Eleanor on my way upstairs. I lay myself down on the bed and closed my eyes. What veiled and terrifying passions, I thought before I dozed off, lurk beneath the charming carapace of the English countryside. As for Thomas Brakefield's murderer, I was no nearer identifying him or her than ever, and meanwhile poor Daniel Ridge rotted in prison awaiting his trial.

CHAPTER TWENTY-THREE

The date for the delayed funeral of Thomas Brakefield was set at last, the police having released the body to a funeral parlour in Kenwardham. It had been generally accepted that, so long after his demise, and in such sorry circumstances, Mr. Brakefield could hardly be removed to the Hall.

'Just imagine the stench!' Henrietta remarked, pulling a face. 'A florists' shop full of flowers couldn't make that corpse smell sweet.'

As usual, she did not mince her words.

She had also somehow come to be au fait with the arrangements. The cortège, as she told us, would set off, with the coffin in one horse-drawn carriage – complete with those black ostrich feathers – the family following behind in two others. Lydia and Eve apparently by mutual agreement would not travel together, the which rather shocked the population of Bilbourne, as represented by Eleanor's mother-in-law.

'Still, I suppose it is hardly surprising they aren't talking,' she added, with a sniff of disapproval, 'given the terms of the will.'

By now, everyone knew that Eve, rather than Randall through Lydia, would inherit the estate, and speculation as to why was the constant subject of chat in George's shop. When asked for my opinion, I always shook my head in ignorance. Unspoken through delicacy, but at the forefront of general opinion, was, given Lydia Brakefield's reputation, the dubious parentage of Randall.

'Thomas found *something* out, *something* most untoward,' accompanied by knowing nods, was as far as decorum permitted speculation to be voiced.

The Indian summer weather broke on the day of the funeral, which dawned dull, wet and cold. The event itself was similarly dismal and dispiriting, although I suppose it could hardly be other, given the tragic circumstances surrounding it. Few people bothered to wait along the route to follow the procession as it arrived, although, given natural curiosity as well, of course, as the monetary incentive, many more turned up at the church. An ancient man hailed me as I entered. Puzzled at first, I finally recognised him as Zachariah from the Green Man Inn, along with his friend Billy, for once bereft of his pipe. I greeted them back.

'We're only here, m'm, to make sure the old blackguard,' (Zachariah using a stronger term hardly suitable for church or anywhere else) 'is well and truly dead.'

He chuckled and Billy nodded in agreement. However, I reckoned that, in their case, the promise of that half crown was not to be ignored either.

Inside the church it was even colder than out, and I was glad that I was able at last to wear my good black bombazine, which was guaranteed at least to lessen the chill. Our discomfort was further exacerbated by the long wait for the arrival of the funeral party. I imagined those gloomy carriages bumping over the rutted road from Kenwardham, the living, no more than the dead, silent within.

At last, the church doors opened to a further blast of cold, and the organist struck up the opening chords of the hymn, 'The Day Thou Gavest Lord is Ended.' We rose to sing it as the coffin, elaborately carved in mahogany and with brass handles, was brought in by the servants of the Hall – Mr. Symons, Jobbins, Stephen, William and two of the gardeners – to be positioned in front of the altar. Lydia, following behind with Randall, placed on it a wreath of roses of such a dark red that they seemed almost black. She and the boy then made their way to their usual pew, he for once overawed into manners by the occasion. The pallbearers then took their seats immediately behind them. Eve, however, having placed her own wreath of lilies beside the roses, crossed to the other side of the aisle, and sat herself beside Squire Simister and Freddie. Henrietta gave me a sharp nudge.

'See that,' she whispered, as if I might possibly have missed it. 'Well, I never! Words fail me.'

If only they did!

The congregation was further enlarged by several self-satisfied-looking stout gentlemen in sombre suits, who, it seemed, had also formed part of the procession from Kenwardham. They joined Lydia in the front pew.

'That's the solicitor.' Henrietta pointed to one of these. 'Mr... Mr... Oh, I forget... What's his name, George?'

Her son shook his head, and pressed a finger to his lips to try and enjoin her to be quiet.

'Well,' she said, undeterred, 'it will come to me. I suppose the others are those judges and people Brakefield hung around with. Not many of them, though, are there? I doubt he was very popular with them, either.'

While George shot her an exasperated look, the Reverend Considine gestured to us all to be seated. He then proceeded with the service, conducting it with his usual bland dignity, and all might have passed off in the ordinary way, if suddenly, in the middle of the homily, the doors had not crashed open again. Everyone turned to look at the latecomer. It was Nancy Ridge. She came running up the middle aisle, carrying Sarey and dragging a reluctant Charlie behind her.

'You shoun't,' she shouted. 'You shoun't send that devil off with a Christian burial. 'E deserves to rot in 'Ell, he does, for what 'e done to us.'

'Nancy!' exclaimed the vicar. 'Calm yourself. Please. Remember where you are.'

'I knows where I be. It's 'im 'as no business in this sacred place.'

Ursula had risen from her seat, and now hurried over to the distraught woman. Nancy was not to be quieted, however.

''E beat my girl. Look at 'er. She ain't right yet, poor Sarey ain't. And for what? For eating an apple what was anyways left to rot in 'is old orchard. And now my Dan'l is going to 'ang for killing 'im, something 'e didn't do. And you're giving this AntiChrist a Christian burial! You should be ashamed.'

She spat at the coffin, then turned on us.

'One of you 'ere knows who done it. For sure. Maybe 'twas even one o' you.' She glared around at us. 'If so, speak up. Speak up in the 'Ouse of the Lord. Confess now and spare an innocent man and 'is family.'

By now, Stephen had rushed over, grabbing her, intending to drag her away. She kicked out at him.

'Take your dirty hands off o' me, Stephen Norris,' she said angrily as he tried to restrain her. 'You won't be throwing me and mine down that pit again. Not never, boy.'

'Nancy! Stephen! Desist, I implore you!' The poor vicar found himself quite out of his depth. But suddenly Nancy fell to the floor weeping, the fight quite gone out of her. Ursula pushed Stephen aside with surprising force, and raised the poor woman up.

'This won't help your Daniel,' I heard her say softly.

Nancy sobbed on the other's bosom and then let herself be led away, the children trudging behind her, Sarey noticeably limping. They left the church then, and I supposed Ursula took them to the vicarage, kind-hearted woman that she was.

'Well now...' said Mr. Considine, clearly nonplussed. 'Where were we?' He flicked the pages of his prayer book, trying to rediscover his place. This took a few moments, but, once having found it, he then rushed over the rest of the homily. It was evident that the vicar could hardly wait to be done with the whole sorry business, concluding the service in almost unseemly haste. Henrietta tut-tutted beside me, but what could the poor man do? Hardly celebrate Thomas Brakefield's life or praise him after that. For form's sake, he muttered some platitudes regarding Thomas's fine character, 'despite having something of a quick temper,' a reservation that hardly covered the facts. He dwelt for a moment or two on the grief of the family, although, from where I was sitting both Lydia and Eve looked stony-faced, not a tear between them, while Randall, back to his old bad self, was fidgeting and pulling faces.

The service was over at last – all eight verses of 'Abide With Me' sung while the massive coffin was carried out into the sodden graveyard. The congregation shuffled after, causing something of a blockage at the narrow doorway, when those at the front paused to raise their umbrellas aloft against the now pouring rain. Eventually we were able to follow the coffin to the Brakefield mausoleum, the tradition that women be not present at the graveside for fear of hysterical outbursts, seeming not to apply in this country place.

Given the varying heights of the pallbearers – tall, muscular Stephen alongside tiny Mr. Symons, massive, aged Jobbins paired with wiry little William, the progression of the coffin made for an inelegant sight. Whoever decided on that particular arrangement must have a warped sense of humour, I decided, only the two gardeners at the rear being of a similar height.

Slipping and sliding on the mud, on two occasions nearly dropping their burden, the which would have provided a grisly yet comical climax to the occasion, they managed at last safely to reach their grim destination, Thomas to be lodged with his father, Benjamin, and unnamed first wife, for all eternity.

Dust was joined with dust, and ashes with ashes, in the usual way, and the thing was finally done. I had little appetite to go on to the Hall afterwards, but felt that I must, if only to give support to Eve.

243

A fleet of coaches was lined up to take us thither, though half of them remained unoccupied, many people, having pocketed their bribes, heading off home instead. Henrietta, of course, was determined to see the thing to the bitter end, and piled in beside me, along with the two teachers, the Misses Clements, the school having been closed for the day as a mark of respect. It was quite a squash, especially since we were all encumbered with umbrellas, and Miss Phyllis kept apologising, I am not sure for what or to whom particularly, since she was the smallest of all of us.

During the short journey, Miss Jane sat frowning, while Henrietta launched into a discussion of the events of the last while.

'What a scandal!' she remarked with satisfaction. 'Bilbourne has never seen the like before.'

'The poor vicar,' said Miss Phyllis.

'He should have been far more forthright with that Nancy woman,' Henrietta continued. 'God knows, I had no great love for Thomas Brakefield, yet even he deserved to be sent to his Maker with dignity.'

'Yes, I suppose, but…'

'It's for the Lord God Almighty himself to decide what to do with him after that, Phyllis,' said Henrietta. 'Whether he goes up,' she raised her eyes to what I suppose was heaven, 'or down.' Hell apparently being located just under our feet, for she tapped hers on the floor of the coach. 'Don't you agree, Jane?'

Miss Clements senior frowned even more deeply to be addressed with such familiarity.

'It is not for me to say, Mrs. Hazelgrove,' she replied.

'My point exactly,' Henrietta stated with satisfaction, as if the teacher were agreeing with her. 'We are all in the hands of God.'

I stared out of the window at the countryside, bleak in the driving rain.

'Who'd have thought a few days ago at that garden party,' Henrietta resumed, as we drove through the gates of the Hall, 'that we'd be returning here so soon, and under such different circumstances.'

She shook her head piously.

'Yes, indeed,' Miss Phyllis agreed.

We hurried the short distance from the coach, sheltered somewhat from the downpour by our umbrellas. Happily, the front door stood open, so we had no need to wait on the step or make use of the devil's head door knocker to gain entrance. Depositing our dripping gamps in an elephant's foot, positioned for the purpose ('Oh, the poor elephant,' said Miss Phyllis), we were directed by Agnes, the cross-eyed maid, to the large dining room. I had not had occasion to visit this gloomy chamber before. It was not made more cheerful by the drapes drawn over the arched windows, the swathes of black crepe festooning the walls and covering the mirrors, the ominous face of the stopped grandfather clock. The room, indeed, embodied the tastes of the erstwhile owners. An iron chandelier surmounted by predatory-looking griffins hung from the vaulted ceiling. The cast iron fireplace, embellished with medieval motifs and figures was empty of the blaze that might have relieved the chill. Only the mahogany table, set on a dark wood floor, promised a little cheer, heaped as it was with meat pies, cheeses and fruit cake, as well as those little biscuits called ladies' fingers, for some reason considered suitable for funerary feasts. Sweet wine had been poured out into many more glasses than there were mourners to drink them, but Lydia, unperturbed, was behaving as if there were nothing amiss, greeting the few people present quite as if she were still lady of the Hall.

Eve, meanwhile, was sitting awkwardly by herself. I was about to go over to her, when she was approached by the man Henrietta had indicated as the solicitor, a stout individual of an unhealthily purple complexion.

'Hargreaves! That's him,' Henrietta exclaimed so loudly that people near us turned to look. 'I knew the name would come to me.'

After the pair had exchanged a few words, Eve, shaking her head, rose and left the room. The solicitor looked after her, thoughtfully.

I wondered if I should go after her, but, since she had shown no special inclination to talk to me, I decided to leave her be for now. Instead, I chatted with the Squire, who apparently felt he had licence to step into hostile territory, now that the enemy-in-chief was no more. Freddie was present, too, not, I noticed, acknowledging Lydia in any particular way. Instead, having inquired of me if my lovely daughter would be joining us (she would not, it being a working day in the shop), he paid court to Miss Phyllis, who giggled and blushed like a girl, while Henrietta stood by smiling hopefully, awaiting her turn. She must have quite forgotten the disapprobation with which she had spoken of the young man in the past.

'What do you make of this heap, Mrs. Hudson?' the Squire was asking me. 'Not very homely, is it.'

'No, indeed. I should not at all like to live here.'

'Poor Eve,' he went on. 'I cannot imagine her standing it for long. If it were mine, I'd pull the whole ugly lot of it down and start again.'

'That sounds quite drastic, Squire. And expensive. You must recall the pink sitting room we were in before and admit that it, at least, is quite charming.'

He slapped his forehead. 'Of course,' he said. 'I had quite forgot it. In fact, I should like to go there now, away from all this. Can we slip out?'

I did not see why not, though a discreet exit was hardly in the Squire's nature, and he seized a couple of slices of pie as well as a glass of wine to sustain him on the journey. We then crossed the hallway and entered into Lydia's erstwhile refuge. There, curled up on the chaise longue, looking wan and strained, was the new lady of the house herself, Lucifer, the cat beside her, shredding another silk cushion with his claws.

'Oh,' I said, 'we must apologise for disturbing your solitude, Eve.'

I made to back out again.

'No, I am glad to see friendly faces. Please stay.'

We sat ourselves down, the delicate chair creaking under the Squire's bulk. I noticed that in here, as well, the mirror was covered with black crepe, but that, otherwise, there was no attempt made to mark the passing of the master.

'You see,' Eve was saying, 'I feel so very alone.'

'You should not, my dear,' the Squire replied gently. 'You have us. You have me.'

'Thank you. You are very kind.'

Casting about for something to fill the ensuing silence, the Squire continued, 'That was quite a scene in the church just now. Most shocking.'

'Understandable though,' I said. 'Poor Nancy!'

'Poor Nancy!' Suddenly Eve, face flushed, was incensed. 'It was horrible.'

'Yes, but...'

'It was her husband, Mrs. Hudson – if indeed married such low wretches be – that killed poor papa!'

'We don't know that for sure, Eve,' I said.

'Who else could have done it? Who else?'

'It seems your father had many enemies...'

I had not looked at him, but the Squire burst out, 'Me, for instance!'

He sat with his big hands firmly placed on his large thighs, as if about to leap up. 'Though I didn't do it.'

'Of course not, Squire. I never thought you did.' She smiled across at him.

'Mrs. Hudson isn't so sure.'

They both looked at me then.

'You are correct, Squire,' I said. 'I should not like to rule anyone out at this stage. Though, on balance, I consider you are probably innocent.'

He stared at me aghast for a moment, and then guffawed with laughter.

'That's honesty for you,' he said.

'Of course, the Squire is innocent. What a preposterous suggestion!' Eve glared at me.

'All I mean is that many people, apart from Daniel Ridge, had motive and opportunity. In any case, it seems to me that the deed was planned and thought through to some extent. Hardly Daniel's way, surely. If he were guilty, would he not have merely struck out and left the body where it lay. I have learned from William that Mr. Brakefield was almost certainly lured into the oast house and up on to the platform. It would be the only way in which he could have ended up in the hop pocket.'

'Oh, you have been talking to William, have you? I suppose you think he might have done it, as well.' Despite her mother's elegant black dress, Eve no longer looked like a young lady, more like a sulky child.

'William would hardly have explained the means to me if he were guilty,' I said.

'Unless he wanted you to have that very reaction.'

Surprised, I replied, 'I very much doubt he is that devious, Eve.'

'So, Mrs. Hudson,' the Squire said,' you are determined to act detective, are you? Indeed, I understand you have had some success at unravelling crime in the past.'

'I have been lucky on occasion,' I concurred.

'Goodness, Eve,' he said. 'We must watch our step with this lady.'

'Nothing will persuade me that any other than Daniel Ridge had a hand in papa's death.'

She gave me a challenging stare.

'Not even Timothy?' I asked, softly.

'Timmy! Never!'

The Squire was puzzled. 'This Timothy again. Remind me who he is.'

'One of the labourers,' she told him.

'Mr. Brakefield treated him very cruelly,' I explained.

'Timmy is as innocent as the Squire here. I'd swear it on my mother's grave.' Eve insisted.

'And yet,' I said, 'after the deed was done, though before it was discovered, Timothy told me "I did it."'

'Really!' The Squire turned to me, astounded.

Eve made a gesture of impatience. 'He could have meant anything, Mrs. Hudson, as you very well know.'

'He could have meant anything, only now he has disappeared.'

'This is most serious, Eve.' The Squire slapped his hands on his thighs. 'You must admit it.'

'If you knew him, you would not suspect him. He has probably run away out of fear that the crime would be laid on him.' She shot a glance at me so sharp that, were it an arrow, might have struck me down. 'As you, Mrs. Hudson, are now trying to do.'

'I am as fond of Timothy as you are,' I replied, 'and was trying, as you know, to remove him from this place. But, as to his guilt, and again as you well know, Eve, he disappeared after the murder must have taken place but before your father's body was discovered. That surely suggests that he was involved.'

The Squire was looking from one of us to the other.

'The boy must be found,' he said, 'if only to exonerate himself.'

'He is innocent,' Eve said again, drawing a hand over her forehead. 'I don't want to talk about it anymore.'

I felt ashamed. The poor girl. Of course, such a discussion must distress her mightily. I rose to go.

'My apologies, Eve. I should not have raised the issue,' I said. 'I will leave you in peace.'

I looked at Squire Simister, expecting him to join me.

Instead, he said, 'Actually, Eve, now I have you, if you are willing just now, I should like to discuss further those matters we touched on before.'

'Ah,' she said. 'Yes, but...' She looked at me without rancour. It seemed her anger had passed.

'We have no secrets from Mrs. Hudson, do we?' the Squire continued, winking at me.

'I suppose not.'

She cast her eyes down, and busied herself stroking her cat. Then looked up at me again.

'I shall leave you,' I said, reading the wish in her face. 'Having no desire to impose on your privacy.'

'Thank you for your understanding, Mrs. Hudson. I am foolish, I know...'

I took my leave, not able to imagine, however, what could be so very secret in her dealings with the Squire. Perhaps she took me for one of the village gossips. Now, after the fraught dialogue that had just taken place, I had no desire to return to the company of those ladies. Agnes was just then crossing the hall, laden with a tray, and I asked her if there was a quiet place where I could sit for a while.

She stared at me for a moment, as if I had addressed her in a foreign tongue. Then, indicating another door with a twitch of her head, said, 'Liberry.'

The library proved to be yet another gloomy room, though at least its walls were covered with bookshelves and not dark panels and grim portraits. I picked a volume of poetry somewhat at random, and sat myself down in a comfortable chair facing the window. Instead of opening the book, however, I stayed looking for a long time out across the lawn towards the woods. A mist of rain veiled the scene, quite the metaphor for my thoughts regarding the solution of the crime.

CHAPTER TWENTY-FOUR

I could not settle, beset by troubling thoughts. It was not the afternoon for an excursion, especially not in my good black bombazine. However, I could not help but think of the last occasion on which I had visited the woods, and of the evidence of occupancy I had observed in the grotto. A mad notion now possessed me to investigate further.

Forthwith, and with a degree of caution, I left the library for the hall, retrieving my umbrella from the elephant's foot stand. The front door was now closed, but I was able to open it and slip out without making too much noise. I could not say that the rain had eased off, but at least it was no heavier than before, and I was glad of the diligence of the gardeners, who had shaved the grass back almost to the skin of the lawn. As I recalled it, the parlour in which Eve and the Squire were sitting was situated on the other side of the house, and in the dining room where the mourners were feasting on the funeral fare, the curtains remained drawn as a mark of respect. I had little fear, therefore, of being observed, although it would be awkward were I to be challenged. The need for fresh air which I had used as an excuse before would hardly convince in the present weather.

Without any such hitch, however, I soon reached the cover of the woods, and proceeded as swiftly as possible, given that the path was strewn with slippery leaves, treacherously disguising a profusion of puddles. My umbrella proving something of an encumbrance, continuously caught in low-hanging branches, I gave up on it, and folded it together. Although the trees were still thick with leaves, these provided only a partial protection against the rain, and drops kept landing on my neck and snaking down my back. I began to regret my impetuosity. Still, since I had come so far, I continued on.

At last, I reached the grotto. It looked to be empty, but, so as not to make the arduous venture a complete waste of time, I decided at least to check if there were further signs of a recent presence, and duly made my way in.

If anything, it was gloomier and more cavernous than before, and it took some considerable time for my eyes to adjust. As they did, I became aware that I was not, after all, alone. What looked to be a human form was crouched against the far wall as if attempting to disappear into it.

'Who's there?' I asked, trying to sound authoritative. Let it not be the hermit!

Silence. Then, 'Me, m'm.'

'Timothy?'

I had suspected as much, and was not unduly surprised.

'Don't be afraid.' I said. 'You know me. Mrs. Hudson.'

He stepped forward. Now his face reflected the dim light from without. He looked ill.

'What are you doing here, child?' I asked gently. 'This is no place for you.'

He said nothing.

'Timothy?'

'I was worried about you. Mrs. Considine was worried.'

'Had to,' he said at last.

'Why?'

'You know why.' He almost shouted this time. 'You know why. 'Cause I did it. I did it.'

'What did you do?'

'I kilt him. I kilt the old devil.'

'Mr. Brakefield?'

'Yes! O' course!'

He waved his arms in agitation.

'All right.' I kept my voice calm. 'But why did you do it?'

''Cause he's an old devil, that's why.'

The boy burst into tears. I stepped forward to hug him, but the poor child drew back.

'Did he beat you again? Is that why?'

He continued to sob.

'Now listen, Timothy,' I told him, taking him by the shoulders. 'You'll have to own up.'

He shuddered, and tried to pull away, but I held him fast, even though I knew he was stronger than me and could have pushed me away if he really tried.

'No,' he said. 'I can't.'

'Listen to me, Timothy. An innocent man is in prison for something he didn't do. If you won't come forward, they'll hang him. Hang him by the neck until he is dead. Daniel Ridge has a wife and young family. Do you want that on your conscience?'

He looked up at me then, puzzled. I doubted he knew what 'conscience' meant.

'Do you want him to take the blame for your action? To hang for what you did?'

'No, m'm.' He looked miserable.

'Then you must speak up.'

'I don't want to be 'anged, neither.'

'Maybe,' I said, 'we can convince the judge that you were provoked...' Another word he didn't understand. 'That you were defending yourself.'

Even as I spoke, I knew how unlikely this sounded. Hadn't I thought myself, like William, that the attack was planned? Moreover, with all the judges being old associates of Thomas Brakefield, what chance would this poor lad have of pleading his case?

'Let's sit down.' The crude bench served as both seating and a bed. 'And you can tell me exactly what happened.'

We sat, myself between him and the opening of the grotto in the slight hope that I could halt him if he tried to run out. I noticed a fresh loaf, a pie like the ones at the funeral feast, and a jug possibly of ale on the table. For now, I decided not to ask where they had come from, who had brought them.

'So, Timothy,' I repeated. 'How did you come to kill Mr. Brakefield.'

At the word 'kill', he shook his head. Then said, 'I just did.'

'In the oast house?'

'Yes, m'm.'

'And then you put him in the pocket.'

He nodded, eyes fixed on the floor.

'All by yourself?'

He looked up then, of a sudden, fear in his face.

'Yes, m'm.'

'You know, you can tell me the truth, Timothy. I'm your friend.'

Silence.

'Is it Miss Eve who brings you food and drink?' I asked.

He neither denied nor confirmed it.

'She's a good friend to you.'

He nodded vigorously at that.

'But it's cold. And you can't hide away in here for ever.'

'I'll be going soon.'

'Going? Where?'

'To Amerikay.'

'Is Miss Eve arranging it?'

He seemed to make up his mind.

'She says it's for the best.'

I gave out a great sigh.

'Listen to me, Timothy. If you go away like that, Daniel Ridge will certainly be hanged and his wife and children left without a father. You don't want that, do you?'

He shook his head.

'Now I don't want you to suffer any more than you already have. What you did was very wrong, but Thomas Brakefield was a cruel man and I'm sure he drove you to it. I suggest you write down a confession that I can take to the authorities after you have gone away. You will be safe in America and Daniel Ridge will be set free.'

Timothy shook his head again.

'Whyever not?'

'I can't write, m'm.'

I smiled then. 'You can tell me what to say, and I can write it for you. Then you can sign it, or,' seeing his renewed distress, 'make your mark.'

At last, he nodded. 'That's good,' he said. 'Yes, let's do that thing. Thank you, m'm. I don't want Dan'l to suffer for what I done. No, I don't. Even though…'

'What?'

'…Nothing.'

I did not tell him just then that he would have to sign his mark in the presence of a lawyer. My word alone, I was sure, would never serve to establish the truth of the document.

'In the meantime,' I asked, 'are you happy enough to stay here?' I shivered, and I was dressed more heavily than he was. 'It's very cold.'

'It does me all right,' he said.

I had nothing to give him except a coin, which would not prove very useful under the circumstances, since he would hardly be going to a shop or the Green Man and Lanthorn any time soon to spend it. I gave it to him anyway, for the future, as well as a packet of violet lozenges that I carried in my reticule to refresh the breath. All I had on me in the way of edibles.

He took these as if they were something precious. I doubted if the poor soul had seen the like before.

'You're kind to me too, m'm.'

'Give me a hug, Timothy, before I go,' I said.

As we embraced, I felt the tension in his skinny body. Was it the first hug he had ever received?

Making my way back through the soggy wood, having promised to return soon to the boy, I was so wrapped up in my thoughts that I inadvertently stepped into a puddle so deep that the water came up over the top of my boot and quite soaked through my stocking. What a sight I should be, returning to the Hall! I decided instead to walk back to the village, thereby evading the inevitable interrogation by Henrietta and others. I particularly wanted to avoid Eve, for now. Although I had many things to ask of that young lady, the day of her father's funeral was not an appropriate occasion.

By the time I at last reached the shop, I was thoroughly chilled. Eleanor took one look at me and hurried me up to my room with stern orders for me to change out of my wet things, while she prepared a bath for me, as well as a hot drink.

'Really, mama, sometimes I think you are not fit to be let out on your own.'

I said not a word about Timothy, but let her think the state I was in was simply from walking back.

'I could not stay there,' was my only explanation.

Sometime later, as, thoroughly warmed up, I lay in my bed, I heard the unmistakeable strident tones of Henrietta below. After a moment, thuds sounded on the stairs, and all too soon that same lady burst into my bedroom, Eleanor behind her, throwing her hands up as if to say 'I tried to stop her to no avail'.

'Goodness me, Martha,' Henrietta exclaimed. 'There you are. We thought you had gone missing like old Brakefield. The Squire was quite beside himself.'

'I am sorry you were worried. I should have told you I was going home.'

'Indeed, you should. I am surprised at you being so thoughtless. Miss Eve was most put out.'

'Was she?'

' "Wherever can she have gone?" She kept saying. The maid told her you were in the library but of course you weren't… It was all the Squire could do, you know, to stop Miss Eve going out in the rain to look for you herself.'

'Ah.'

'Mind you, the grieving widow couldn't have cared less. "Don't make a fuss, Eve," she said, "Mrs. Hudson will turn up." As of course you have, but how could she know that, with murderers about? I was thinking of that horrible man in the woods and what he might have done to you.'

'The hermit, do you mean? He isn't there anymore.'

'Oh really, and how do you know that, pray?'

I bit my lip.

'I was told they only employ him when they have visitors,' I replied.

Henrietta's expression was all smugness.

'And if we aren't visitors, what are we?'

'I meant for parties. His presence would hardly be required for a funeral.'

'How do we know that for sure?' She gave a shudder. 'Now I think of it, isn't he the most likely person to have done away with Mr. Brakefield? He should be found immediately and arrested.'

The conversation was taking a dangerous turn.

'So Lydia Brakefield has been cleared of the crime now, has she, Henrietta?'

'Not at all. She probably did it *with* the hermit. Yes, indeed. That's the most likely.' She smiled in satisfaction. 'There. I've solved it. You aren't the only detective around here, Martha.'

At that moment, sensing my weariness, Eleanor took charge and shunted her mother-in-law out of the bedroom, with the promise of coffee and some of her favourite biscuits.

'As if I could eat any more, Eleanor, really! After all they gave us up at the Hall!'

Later, my daughter informed me that Henrietta did more than justice to the plate of macaroons placed before her.

Meanwhile I lay thinking. There was something that troubled me about Timothy's confession, although I could not say just then what it was. At some point, I dozed off. In my dream the hermit came rushing at me out of the oast house, waving an umbrella, shouting 'I killed him and now I'll kill you too.'

CHAPTER TWENTY-FIVE

The following morning, I asked George if he knew of a lawyer I could approach on a delicate matter.

'What, Martha. Are you changing your will again?'

I wasn't in the mood for his foolish jokes, and, frowning, said nothing in reply.

'There's a good man in Kenwardham I've used myself,' George continued, somewhat subdued.

'No one nearer than that?'

I felt the matter should be expedited as soon as possible, and had been hoping again hope for someone in Bilbourne itself.

George shook his head. 'Well, there's Hargreaves, of course. The Brakefield's solicitor. He's based in Rochester, but might still be around.'

'No,' I said. 'He won't do.'

I had not cared for the look of the man, who in any case was too involved with the principal parties.

Then Eleanor interjected, blushing slightly for some reason as she spoke, 'Isn't Freddie Simister studying law? If all you want is advice, mama, he might be able to help.'

'That's an idea,' George added. 'Of course.'

They both looked at me expectantly.

'He won't do, either,' I said. Freddie Simister, of all people! 'I need someone fully qualified.' Adding, 'It's to witness a document.'

'You *are* changing your will, mother-in-law.'

'Don't be silly, George!' This from Eleanor.

'I cannot say anything more at the moment,' I told them. 'Except that it is important I find someone as soon as possible.'

'That sounds ominous,' George said.

My son-in-law has the sort of fresh round face suited to smiles and good humour. When he tries to look serious, the result is slightly comical, and just now, despite myself, I burst out laughing at the sight of his expression. It was, of course, no laughing matter, but I could not tell them that it was quite literally a case of life and death. At least my apparent good humour dispelled their suspicions, and we continued eating our breakfast.

'It has to be a lawyer, does it, mama?' Eleanor asked, after a while. 'I mean, surely anyone of standing can witness a signature.'

Of course, she was right. How single-minded I had been.

'The Squire, for instance,' she ventured.

I shook my head. 'No, not the Squire.'

Why did I say that? Because he was too close to Eve? But why should that matter? Surely, he would be the perfect choice. And yet, and yet...

'Dr. French?' suggested George.

The elderly general practitioner who had looked after me when I first arrived. He was a possibility, although very doddery and feeble. Moreover, I didn't know him well enough to trust him to keep silent.

'Or Mr. Considine, perhaps?' Eleanor broke into my thoughts.

The vicar would, of course, be the perfect choice, if only I could be sure that he would agree to be party to my plan to let Timothy escape the law. Of course, I need not tell him more than that he was to witness a confession, but how could I then face him and his wife afterwards? After Timothy had disappeared, this time for ever? All the same, it seemed to me that Mr. Considine was my best option.

'That's a good idea, Eleanor,' I said. 'Yes, I will go and see the vicar at once.'

'Don't get soaked again,' she warned me. 'Be sure to take your umbrella.'

A light drizzle was falling. Nothing like the deluge of the previous day. Eleanor fussed too much.

'He's out, m'm,' the maid told me. 'Mrs. Vicar, too. Visiting a parishioner that's poorly.'

No, she could not say when they would return, but added that I was most welcome to wait.

I sat for a while in the parlour, impatiently twiddling my thumbs, but could not settle. Standing up, I examined the bookshelves, but found nothing there to absorb me, so moved to look out over the wilderness that passed for a garden. With the renowned fickleness of English weather, the rain had stopped, and it had turned into a bright, if blustery day. I hoped it would clear my muddled head to go outside, so I duly made my way through the French windows to where the cook's simple son – Samuel wasn't it? – was occupied in some very desultory and ineffectual gardening. I smiled at him.

'Weeds,' he said, holding out to me some plants that he had just pulled up.

'No...' I started to reply, but he was clearly so delighted with himself that I did not have the heart to tell him he had uprooted some perfectly good stalks of chard.

I wandered to the fence with its view over the enclosed meadow, and wondered if the new owner of all this would return it to its former state of common land. Even as I considered this, a horsewoman came into view in the far distance. I soon discerned it to be Eve herself, astride Queen Mab. I was most surprised. The girl had only buried her father on the previous day, and etiquette surely demanded a period of mourning and isolation. However, she was her own mistress now, and, I suppose, could do as she pleased.

I watched as the mare cantered across the rough terrain, the rider soon urging her mount into a veritable gallop, tearing off into the far distance and then coming back round again. It was quite a vision: the girl's loosened hair streaming behind her, even as the mare's

261

mane and tail streamed, now and again the pair seeming to fly through the very air itself over some obstacle. Impossible not to share their exultation in movement. The joyful freedom of it.

At some point, Eve must have caught sight of me, or at least have gained an awareness that someone was watching her, for she reined in the mare and caused her to come trotting over to where I was standing on the other side of the fence. Her face was flushed with the exertion of the ride, and it struck me how lovely she looked with those loose tresses hanging down golden over her shoulders. A veritable wood nymph, or perhaps something painted by one of Lydia's favourite Pre-Raphaelites. All the same, hardly appropriate for one in mourning.

'Mrs. Hudson,' said she. 'This is indeed serendipitous.'

The Squire's word!

'How so?' I asked.

'I have a great need to discuss a certain matter with you.'

'Timothy?'

'Hush! Not here.'

She glanced over to where Samuel was demolishing a bed of autumn planted garlic, as if the poor lad were capable of eavesdropping.

'Will I come to the Hall?' I asked.

'Better not.' She thought for a moment. 'Could you meet me later at the bridge by the river? We can walk and talk there unobserved.'

I was slightly puzzled. 'Why there?'

She smiled. 'Oh, I want to save you having to come all the way up the hill again,' she explained. 'And, you know, I like to escape from the Hall and Lydia's spies when I can.'

While not sure about the spies, I could understand wanting to get away. If the place oppressed me on my brief visits, how much more must it weigh on someone who lived there all the time, and I could not help but wonder whether her father's legacy would prove more of a curse than a blessing for Eve.

'You are visiting the vicar?' she continued.

'In connection with the same matter, in fact. But he is out. I await his return.'

'I see.' Queen Mab was shifting restlessly under the girl. 'Have you discussed Timothy with anyone else?'

I told her no. She looked relieved.

'Then I wonder, she continued, 'could I ask you please, not to say anything about it, until we have spoken.'

'Very well. If you wish.' Surely a few hours more or less could make no difference.

She smiled again. 'Good. And, in addition, please don't even mention to anyone that you are meeting me…You must think I am being very mysterious, Mrs. Hudson, but I promise, it is in the interests of all concerned, especially our friend. You know whom it is I mean… I will explain everything later.'

I trusted she would, for I was most perplexed. Perhaps it was her age that required her to call so often for secrecy. I remembered my own girls when they were as young as she, although their little mysteries were as nothing to Eve's.

Returning to the house, I informed the maid that I would wait no longer, but would call back another time. After that, I wandered for a while in the graveyard, still trying to make sense of Eve's urgent request. Did she know that Timothy had confided in me, and did she therefore fear I might alert the authorities to his guilt, thus preventing her arrange his escape? Perhaps she thought I was planning to ask Mr. Considine what in all conscience to do about it. Well, I could not hope to read the girl's mind, and soon gave up, soothed by the company of the dead in this peaceful place. What matter, in the face of eternity, all our human cares?

I paused at the monument to Susannah Simister, now near neighbour of the man who, according to rumour, had hastened her demise. Passing by his resting place, that same Brakefield mausoleum, grim in its Gothic way, I saw how the wreaths left by

Lydia and Eve were already beginning to wilt. The sight dispirited me, and I left the graveyard to its dead. I was tempted to sit for a while in my old peaceful spot by the duck pond under the willow – its pendant leaves now turning a pale shade of gold that reminded me of Eve's hair. My God! The girl haunted my thoughts whether I would or no. However, I feared being accosted by someone I would rather not talk to, and instead went straight home. For the same reason, rather than sit in the shop, I betook myself to the upstairs parlour and spent the rest of the morning quietly sewing.

Over a light mid-day meal, taken with my daughter alone, since Joe was out on his usual delivery round and George could not leave the shop, Eleanor asked me how I had got on with the vicar.

'Not at all,' I said. 'For he was not there.'

'I suppose then you sat with Ursula, for you were away a long time.'

'No, she was out, too,' I explained. 'I waited, and then gave up.'

'I expect they were visiting old Nell Pardon. Apparently, she took sick last night and isn't expected to live out the day.'

'Nell!' Was that the woman who had helped me find the Ridges in their prison? I hoped not, though it seemed possible.

'I'll try them later,' I said.

The pretence would give me a reason to go out and meet Eve, without breaking my promise not to speak of it.

CHAPTER TWENTY-SIX

A mist was rising from the river beneath the bridge, floating through the branches of the overhanging trees, and imbuing the spot with an eerie beauty. Perhaps I was early, for there was as yet no sign of Eve, and I rested my arms on the parapet to wait. The dim light cast flickering shadows over me. The days were drawing in. Already nearly twilight at five o'clock.

'There you are, Mrs. Hudson. My apologies for the delay.'

She was on foot but for some reason still in her riding dress, comprising a short tunic over bloomers. I suppose such garments are much more comfortable than the constricting garments we women are conventionally supposed to wear. Eleanor, indeed, quite espouses the ideas of the rational dress movement, although I am old-fashioned enough to be a little shocked at such laxity. However, under the present circumstances, it was neither here nor there. At least, Eve's hair no longer hung loose, but was tied up in a neat coiffure.

'You have come from riding,' I remarked.

'Yes. I know some people would frown at my apparent carelessness in the face of papa's death, but, you see, Mrs. Hudson, when I am on Queen Mab, I forget everything else. All the bad things... Now come,' she said, taking my arm. 'Let us walk and talk.'

The path she took was the one that led alongside the river. I had not ventured that way before and remarked on the fact.

'Not many come this way,' she said. 'We are unlikely to encounter anyone here.'

I had to ask her. 'But why all the secrecy, Eve?'

She gave a bitter laugh.

'I suppose it is the way I have been brought up. To hide and dissemble. You can have no idea, Mrs. Hudson. No idea at all.'

How very sad, I thought. What a lonely child she must have been.

'I hope you know,' I said, 'that you can tell me anything, my dear. I will keep your secrets, I promise.'

'Will you? All of them? I wonder.'

She seemed disinclined to say more, and we continued on in silence for a while. So much, I thought, for walking and talking.

'It is lovely here,' I remarked, at last, for something to say.

It was, if you like lonely and remote. Dark trees hanging over the rushing water, a slippery carpet of leaves underfoot. Rusting bracken at the edges of the path. The scent of decay.

'Is it lovely? Oh, I suppose you would think that, coming from the city.' She sighed. 'It is all too familiar to me, I am afraid.'

She was in a strange mood. Under her apparently cool exterior, I could sense repressed excitement.

'Eve, we really need to talk about Timothy,' I said. Surely this was the reason we were meeting.

'Yes. Yes, we do.'

'He told me things.'

'I know.'

'That he killed your father.'

'I know that, too.'

'How very strange, then, that you still want to help him escape?'

She let go my arm and turned to face me.

'My father was a monster, Mrs. Hudson. A devil. The world is well rid of him.'

What terrible words for a daughter to utter!

'That's as may be,' I replied. 'Only God knows all, and it is for God to exercise vengeance, Eve, not man. Not us!'

'You don't understand anything.'

'I know that an innocent man is likely to pay with his life for something he didn't do.'

'Ridge, is it!' I was shocked to hear the disdain in her voice. 'A wretch like that! If not guilty of this deed, I am sure he has done similar, or worse.'

'What could be worse than murder?'

She shrugged.

'And,' I pursued, 'whyever would you think that?'

'Oh, I know his sort, Mrs. Hudson. A low-life. A degenerate from the slums.'

'No, he is just a poor man trying to do his best. Daniel Ridge is a loving husband and father.'

'Can there be such a phenomenon among his ilk?'

Her father's prejudices had clearly infected the girl. I decided not to try and argue that particular point further just then.

'Nevertheless, I had a plan,' I said, 'to clear Daniel Ridge by revealing the true culprit.'

'Is that so?' Her voice was cold.

'That was why I was visiting the vicar this morning, Eve. I wanted to ask him to witness Timothy's confession, which I could then present to the judges.'

'So that Timothy can hang in Ridge's place, I suppose.'

'No, not at all... Have you not told the boy you would arrange for him to flee to America?'

'Ah yes. I did.' A strange expression crossed her face for a moment. A sly, shifty look, or did I imagine it? It passed as quickly as it came, and her face turned blank. 'Well, it's a good idea you've had... But would you and the vicar not then risk the force of the law for abetting a fugitive?'

'Not if we had no idea he was about to flee.'

She laughed.

'You are quite the Jesuit, Mrs. Hudson. In fact, it is a pity that Mr. Considine is not of the Catholic faith, for he could then plead the seal of the confessional.'

'So what do you think?'

'What do *I* think? That it may be rather too late for all that.'

'Too late? How? Daniel has not yet come to trial. A date has not even been fixed. Not too late, surely.'

She halted. We were in a tunnel of trees, and I could not now well read her face.

'You are a woman of considerable perception, Mrs. Hudson. I think you will not long delay in working it all out.'

We stood silent for a moment, sere leaves falling around us, the mist thickening on the river.

'Tell me,' she continued at last, 'what did you make of Timmy's confession?'

'In what way?'

'Did it convince you? Truly?'

'Well...' I thought about it. 'Why should he lie? Although I suppose I have the same doubts that I had regarding Daniel Ridge's guilt.'

'In what way exactly?' She was clutching my arm again, and almost pulling me along. Again, that barely repressed excitement.

'The murder surely had to be premeditated,' I said. 'Now, although Daniel and Timothy both had good reason to hate your father, would they possess the cunning and even malevolence to plot his death in that way? And how would either of them have lured him into the oast house in the first place?'

'That's easily dealt with. Timothy must have followed him in.'

'I think not. Why would he do such a thing? In any case, around the time your father said that he was leaving to fetch the constable from Kenwardham, I saw Timothy at the feast, and even asked him to watch and follow Stephen for me, in the hope that he would find out where Nancy and the children were being held'

She stared at me.

'You asked him to do that?'

'Yes. And Timothy readily agreed to it. There was nothing strange in his demeanour at that time. No premonition that he was contemplating murder. He was sitting calmly enjoying his roast pork along with everyone else.'

She considered my words for a few moments.

'Well, there you are then.' Her voice was become triumphant. 'He followed Stephen to the first oast house, where, as we all know now, Nancy and the children were imprisoned. Then Timmy saw my father enter the second oast house, and, as I said, followed him in and killed him.'

'That's possible, I suppose, though unlikely. Why would your father go there in the first place, when he was impatient to leave for Kenwardham? Why would Timothy suddenly be filled with an overwhelming rage against your father at that precise moment? It would be quite out of his character. He's a gentle boy.'

'Maybe they met outside the oast house. My father started on at Timmy in his usual way and Timmy decided he had had enough. Perhaps whatever few wits the boy possessed had been scattered by ale, and he wasn't thinking properly.'

A note of pleading had entered her tone. She wanted me so much to believe it. I started to doubt my doubts. After all, what other explanation could there be? And yet, did I not know already, deep down? Had I not guessed it the moment I saw her at the bridge? Or even earlier? I was on dangerous ground, and yet could not leave well alone.

'So did Timothy bring a knife with him?' I continued. 'I certainly didn't see one on him earlier, and there was nowhere among his rags for him to conceal it.'

'Oh, I don't know... Perhaps he found one lying about.'

'That doesn't make any sense, does it?'

'So, in point of fact, Mrs. Hudson,' she said – her voice ice cold now – 'you don't believe Timmy's confession?'

'Eve, I don't know what to think. I ask again, why would he lie?'

'Indeed. Why?'

Her gaze was intense.

'Unless, of course,' I said carefully, 'he was protecting the real killer.'

'Why would he do that?'

'Because it was someone he loved very much.'

She regarded me, long and hard.

'Ha!' she said at last. 'Now we arrive at it.'

Did she mean the truth of the matter, or the location? A bend in the path had brought us, to my surprise, to the edge of the wetlands by another route from that which I had taken before. How was it possible? A sudden dread came over me.

'It was you killed your father, Eve,' I said, unable to stop myself.

'I knew it. Timothy *did* tell you.'

'No, Eve, you have told me. You have led me to the truth. I should have accepted Timothy's confession, had you not sown doubts in my mind.'

'You would have come to that point by yourself eventually. A woman like you. An amateur detective.'

There was no praise in her tone, only scorn.

'Why did you do it, Eve? Was it for the inheritance?'

She burst out laughing then, a horrible sound shattering the damp silence.

'I knew nothing about that. As if I even wanted it!'

'So what then?'

'I cannot say it.' She was racked with anguish. 'I had no choice.'

'My poor girl.'

I tried to clasp her in my arms, but she broke away.

'Don't touch me. I can't bear it… I couldn't bear it.' She turned to me, a challenge on her pale features. 'My father, Thomas Brakefield, violated me, Mrs. Hudson,' she said finally. 'Many times. Since I was small. Because I looked like my mother, he said.' She laughed in that terrible way again. 'Well, I couldn't go on with it, so I told the disgusting old drunkard to meet me in the oast house. He had been about to leave, as you say, for Kenwardham, but couldn't resist the temptation to have me one more time. But when he tried to embrace me, I pulled out a knife… He was so surprised…' That fearsome laugh again. 'I stabbed him over and over and over. He squealed like the pig he was.'

Despite the horror of it, it was almost a relief to hear the truth at last.

'And Timothy was there too?'

'That was – what's the Squire's word again? – serendipitous? It was almost as I said before, Mrs. Hudson. Timmy must have been following Stephen at your request, but saw me entering the oast house and came after me. I told him to hide and wait. He didn't know what I was planning, but helped me dispose of the bloody corpse after.' She gave a girlish giggle. 'It was a good notion, wasn't it, to dump the filth in one of his own pockets? It was just a shame that William found it so soon. I was hoping they'd bear it off to Kenwardham with the other pockets. What a shock they'd have had in the brewery when they opened it up!' She giggled some more, evidently and horribly pleased with herself.

'Something still puzzles me,' I said, endeavouring to keep emotion out of my voice following this shocking confession. 'What ever happened to your father's horse? We all assumed he had ridden off on it, and that was why no search was made earlier.'

'Alas, poor Nero! A fine steed. But of course, he must not be found.' She looked out over the wetlands. 'That's a hungry place, Mrs. Hudson.'

'You drove him into the wetlands?'

'Timmy did. He knows his way about it, you see. How to get in and out safely. How to avoid the boggy parts that eat up anything that falls into them.' I wished she would stop that chilling giggling. 'I should have put papa there, too. Then all this unpleasantness would have been avoided. If he had disappeared completely, people might even have assumed he had met his end somewhere else. In Rochester, perhaps. In London...' She frowned. 'But then, of course, without a body, Randall might have inherited, after all. Much as I don't want it for myself, I couldn't have that, could I?'

She had lied. She had known about the will, after all. But before I had time to reply – and what indeed could I have said? – I became aware of movement ahead of us through the gloom, that soon realised itself into the form of a man and a horse. A boy, rather, for it was Timothy himself, leading Queen Mab.

'Ah, here cometh the knight in shining armour, or more appropriately of the sorrowful countenance. He who wishes to take the blame for what I did. What a hero! What a foolish knight he is, after all.'

Her voice was full of contempt.

My God, I thought. How misled we had all been! Or not all of us. I have to confess that Henrietta, with her assertion that Eve was sly and not to be trusted an inch, had got it right for once. Lydia, too.

Timothy could not have heard her disparaging remarks, delivered as they were in low tones, and, had I repeated them now, he assuredly would not have believed me. His adoration was absolute, as evidenced in the gaze he directed upon her.

'Well now,' Eve went on. 'This is very sad.' She didn't sound sad at all. 'I had hoped not to have to do this, Mrs. Hudson, but I am afraid you cannot be let reveal what we have just discussed.'

'After what you have told me,' I said, 'I am sure any judge would look upon you kindly.' Did I really believe that, given the premeditation? 'But you know, my dear, that I cannot stay silent.'

'Exactly. So this is where it ends. Poor foolish woman that you are, poking your nose in everywhere... Timmy, you know what to do. Into the hungry bog with her.'

The boy, to be fair, gaped at her in horror.

'No,' I cried. 'Timothy, you are not a killer.'

'Be quiet,' she said, and suddenly struck me so hard across the face that I fell back on to the ground, almost under the hooves of the restless mare. I feared that the beast, sensing the disquiet, might trample me, where I lay, and tried to rise. The boy looked at me with pity, but made no attempt to help me up.

'Timmy,' Eve said in wheedling tones, 'this woman knows everything. She will hang us both if she is allowed to live. You don't want me to hang, do you Timmy? Remember all I have done for you.'

'Miss Eve...' he said at last. 'I cannot. I cannot do it...'

She approached him then and put her two hands on his shoulders. Then pulled him towards her and kissed him on the lips.

'One last thing, for me,' I heard her whisper. 'My love...'

When I regained consciousness, for I must have been struck again with some force, I found myself in the middle of the treacherous wetlands, on a tiny mound, next to a thin sapling. Timothy was beside me. He was whispering, wind in the reeds.

'I couldn't do it, m'm, what she said. You bin good to me, you 'ave.'

He moved away.

'Are you leaving me, Timothy?' I asked. 'Better you kill me quickly than leave me to die here.'

'Hush now. Like you said, I'm no killer, m'm.' He bent down again, and whispered in my ear. 'You'll be safe as long as you stay put, m'm. And quiet, so she don't 'ear you.'

No use telling him I would soon surely succumb to cold and hunger. He left me, then. I could make out his lanky form treading a careful way back, and tried to memorise his path, but it was too twisted, and anyway the encroaching darkness soon hid him from me entirely.

'Is it done?' Eve's sharp voice carried across the bog.

He must have told her that it was.

'Good,' she replied, laughing. 'Well done... So now, off to America with you.'

I heard a surprised gasp, followed by a low moan, a frightful choking sound. I could only imagine with dread what had just happened. Then horse's hooves clopped off into the distance. Followed by a deep silence, the silence of death.

Night had fallen, although the gibbous moon that peeped out from time to time from behind clouds, relieved the complete darkness, and I could make out the forms of trees in the distance, one in particular, long and with thin branches like clawing fingers. I did not like to look upon it.

It was damp where I lay, and a foul stench rose around me. I could not help but imagine all the corpses that had perished here slowly releasing their putrefaction into the atmosphere. However, I am not a woman who easily gives in to despair. I was still alive, after all, and decided to stay where I was until dawn gave me a better idea of my surroundings. If Timothy brought me in, I reasoned, he must have carried me. Surely his passage would be marked with broken reeds, and with care I might find my way out again. Meanwhile, I clung to the little sapling. It gave me hope, growing in this place against all the odds, and I spoke to it, thanking it for its presence and support.

My brain was buzzing with what had happened, the dark treachery and villainy of Eve, undoubtedly her father's daughter. Even if he had violated her, as she claimed, it was no justification for such a bloody retribution. And why did poor Timothy have to be sacrificed, as he must have been? Did she not trust even him to keep silent for ever?

274

How much time passed, I cannot say. I was hungry, thirsty and cold. I had not my reticule with me, and imagined that it must lay somewhere else in the bog. However, searching my pocket, I found therein part of a packet of violet lozenges, the same I had given to Timothy, for I had no other. He must have returned them to me out of pity, while I lay unconscious, and I shed a tear at the realisation.

More time passed. I shivered with the chill, hoping soon to see the pale light of dawn, while reason told me it must still be a long way off. Despite myself, my eyes kept being drawn to the tree with the clawing fingers, as if some poor soul were trying in vain to scramble out of the bog. Was that to be my fate? No, it could not be. I was not yet ready to quit this world. Many were the prayers I sent heavenward that night, prayers for myself and for Timothy, though I feared it was too late for him.

By now I was clinging fast to the sapling, so as not to slip off the little mound. My skirts were sodden, and I could feel them pulling me down. When would dawn come? There was not even a glimmer of light yet in what I took to be the east. For all my brave thoughts, hopelessness and despair hovered, vulture-like, around me.

Suddenly, I became aware of pin pricks of light in the distance that soon resolved into a procession of torches breaking through the darkness, and of people calling out my name. How could this be? Was I delirious, or had Timothy somehow survived to raise the alarm? I hoped so. I called back as loudly as I could.

The rescue took a long time. The two sturdy farm lads who came for me, clearly only too aware of the dangers of the wetlands, proceeded slowly. But they were coming! By some miracle, I was saved.

'It was young Samuel, the simpleton,' Eleanor told me much later, after my hot bath, when I was tucked up in bed with a steaming bowl of soup. 'He overheard Eve arranging to meet you at the bridge, and, when you failed to return and we all became anxious, told his mother of it. The cook informed Ursula, so now at least we knew where to start looking. From the bridge there are only two roads you might have taken. The main road leading up to the Hall, or the one branching off it that eventually leads to Blossomfort. We found no trace of you on either, nor at the Hall itself, so then the men proceeded along the river path.'

'What did Eve say when you asked her about me?'

'She told us she had spoken to you briefly at the bridge, and that you had then gone your separate ways. She assumed you had returned home.'

'Ha!' I replied. 'I wonder does she know yet that I was found alive.'

'What do you mean?'

I then explained in full what had happened. At first, Eleanor thought I was delirious, it sounded so unlikely, and called George in to hear what I had to say. I repeated my account as calmly as I could.

'Did you find Timothy?' I asked.

They looked at each other.

'It is as you feared, mama. The poor boy lay at the side of the road, stabbed to death.'

Left there like a heap of rubbish. She had no care for anyone.

'Eve must be apprehended at once,' I said. 'She is either mad, or the veritable embodiment of evil. In either case, she is quite likely to inflict more destruction on those around her. I would fear particularly for Lydia and the boy, whom she hates.'

'I'll send for the Squire,' George said. 'He is the only person here with the necessary authority.'

'He will probably not believe you,' I warned. 'He is very fond of Eve.'

'He must believe it.'

'Tell him that she must be guarded for her own protection.'

He nodded and hurried out.

Eleanor embraced me with emotion.

'Oh mama, what if we had lost you?'

'I should be most distressed,' I replied. 'For I must, at least, be around long enough to welcome my new grandchild into the world.'

CHAPTER TWENTY-SEVEN

It was a few days later, and a group of ladies – Henrietta's gang and others – were assembled in the vicarage parlour, enjoying tea and cake, and hungrily discussing recent events.

'I still can hardly believe it of Eve,' the younger Miss Clements was saying. 'She always seemed such a sweet girl. So quiet and demure. She must have gone stark staring mad.'

There were murmurs of agreement. Her sister, however, shook her head.

'Still waters run deep, Phyllis. Always beware the quiet ones.'

'Eve was ever a sly and dissembling minx,' Henrietta put in. 'I told you that, Martha, but you wouldn't believe me. She pulled the wool right over your eyes.'

'It's true,' I replied. 'She quite took me in.'

They were all, of course, agog to learn the full horrid details of my ordeal and the rest of it. However, while I was happy enough to talk about my experiences in the wetlands – the fear, the cold and damp, the joy of seeing the torches approaching, the voices calling my name, the realisation that I was saved and would not perish there (Miss Phyllis shivering in sympathy) – I wasn't about to gratify them regarding what I had subsequently learnt. I was especially not going to tell them what Lydia Brakefield had revealed to me in a conversation we had had the previous afternoon at the Hall. According to her, how Eve's claim that her father had violated her was a complete fabrication.

'Do you know that for sure?' I asked.

'Mrs. Hudson,' she replied. 'My marriage was a sham. My husband did not care for women, if you get my meaning…' She looked at me as if debating the necessity to explain further. 'He was what the Marquis of Queensbury, referring to Mr Oscar Wilde, rather amusingly mis-called a "somdomite".'

'Ah, I see.'

'You know, I even suspect that the poor boy who was killed had been forced by him. He wouldn't be the first.'

The idea filled me with dismay. 'Oh, I hope not. Poor Timothy… But why would Eve claim such a thing, if it weren't true?'

Lydia's smile was chilling.

'Because she so much wanted it to be true… Oh, Mrs. Hudson, you are shocked, but let me explain. Even as a small girl, Eve always hoped in vain that her father would pay attention to her. Once she reached a certain age, this must have shifted into sexual desire. In fact, those private notebooks she kept scribbling in attest as much, as has now been discovered. She led such an isolated life, you see. I wanted to send her away to school for her own good, but her father wouldn't have it, wanting to keep us all where he could control us. She, of course, hated me for it, thinking I plotted to separate her from the only person she wanted to be with.'

These were murky waters indeed.

'What I think may have happened was something like this,' she continued, 'although I doubt Eve will confess to it. Because they were close, Timothy might well have hinted to Eve what her father had done to him, and so, overcome with jealousy and disgust, she hatched her plan. Perhaps she told Timothy to waylay her father before he left for Kenwardham, and lure him to the oast house for the usual purposes. Instead of Timothy, however, Thomas was confronted with Eve, who, when he rejected her, took out a knife and… well, you know the rest.' She paused. 'He was not a nice man, Mrs. Hudson. But that was a terrible end.'

I had taken Lydia to be a silly vain woman, which in some ways she was, and yet I pitied her now, for the life she had been made to lead.

'So it is true, then,' I said. 'Randall cannot be your husband's son.'

'Oh, as to that, I can assure you he is. My husband did what he considered his duty by me at the beginning of our marriage, to have a son to continue the line, you know. It is only in recent times, that extreme loneliness has driven me to find comfort elsewhere, wherever I could.' She put a weary hand to her head in one of those theatrical gestures to which she was prone. 'No, it simply came to suit Thomas to think my depravity had existed from the start. Eve may believe his will proves that he really loved her, but it is no such thing. It was simply spite against me that caused him to change it.'

I could well believe it. And though I could never condone her loose behaviour, I could understand it.

'So what are your plans now?' I asked. 'I suppose you will inherit after all, as next of kin. Will you stay on here?'

'Heavens, no. There are too many horrid memories. I am selling up as soon as possible, and then Randall and I will go as planned to Italy. The only difference being that we will be able to live in considerable luxury there, instead of scrimping and saving.'

She touched her hair, as if preparing at last to make an entry into the world.

No, I was not about to titillate the Bilbourne gossips with Lydia's explanation. It might not, in any case, be the correct one. I was not fully convinced either by her version, or by that of her stepdaughter. When I met Timothy at the feast, his carefree manner had certainly not given the impression that he was involved in any sort of a plot against Thomas Brakefield. It seemed to me more likely that Eve's account, as far as it went, was largely true. That she had lured her father to the oast house, maybe with a suggestion that all was not well there. If, for instance, he thought thieves were robbing him, he would certainly have hurried to check it out before leaving for Kenwardham. If Timothy, looking for Stephen, had seen Eve entering the oast house, he might well have followed after, to see what she was about. There, witnessing her stab her father to death, out of love for her he had been persuaded to help her dump the body in the pocket. His guilt, combined with his desire to protect her, had led him subsequently to confess to me. It was the best explanation of the facts that I could come up with.

There were more unanswered questions, however. Did Eve bring the knife with her? If so, the murder must have been premeditated. I had not noticed knives lying around when I visited the oast house, but neither had I been looking for them. Nonetheless, if Eve had intended to confront her father for whatever reason, if he had rejected her, then possibly, enraged, she might have grabbed some weapon she found there. But this explanation seemed weak to me. Much more likely that she had planned the whole thing, though I doubted she would ever reveal the full truth. To that extent, it must remain a mystery.

If I doubted Eve's story of violation, I had no great faith in her ladyship's newfound candour either. Her story might be true, or partly true, or a fiction, or even something she believed in order to explain her husband's indifference to herself. 'What is truth?' Pontius Pilate had asked of Our Lord. In this case, I sympathised with him. Truth, I am afraid, is so seldom absolute.

So what of Eve? Following my revelations, the Squire had taken control of the situation. Indeed, I believe that Eve had confessed to him as she had to me, perhaps hoping that his goodwill would cause him to let her go free. I could imagine her bitter tears, explaining how her father had ill-used her. I could imagine the Squire's fatherly sympathy. And yet he was a man of probity. She was taken off to Maidstone jail, and, in due course, Daniel Ridge was freed, to the unbridled joy of Nancy and the children. I know that because, once returned to London, I took it upon myself to visit them, and indeed, have made it my business to help them out in all sorts of little ways. Dr. Watson even examined little Sarey at my behest, and was able to treat her bad leg, so that she is now quite well again, while the boy, Charlie, was pleased to take up the position with the farmer in Hampshire that I had hoped would be Timothy's. Nancy tells me he is doing well, and that next summer, the whole family will go there to work, instead of to Bilbourne.

Because Eve confessed, there was no trial as such, though she managed to charm the judge to the extent that, having claimed a conversion to the Roman Church, she was sent to an enclosed convent, rather than to prison. I only hope the nuns keep sharp knives out of her reach.

But here am I again violating the chronology of my tale. Dr. Watson would not approve. I have to end, or almost, with a conversation I had with Squire Simister before I left Bilbourne. Following my ordeal, I decided the countryside to be far less restful than town, and so was anxious to return home as soon as possible. I could not, however, avoid an invitation to dine with the Squire at Blossomfort, alone, as it turned out, since Freddie had taken himself off at last to London to resume his studies, or at least to do what young men of wealth do in that great city. Apparently, his frolic with Lydia Brakefield, was nothing more than that on both sides. I was happy to accept the Squire's invitation, hopeful that he might reveal something of his interrogation of Eve, and throw light on parts of the matter that still puzzled me. He was reluctant to be too forthright, however, saying only that he pitied the girl from the bottom of his heart.

'I am sure it was her father who twisted her into what she became. I can even start to understand the violence she inflicted on him – knowing as I do so well what a throughgoing blackguard he was. However, her murder of Timothy and her attempted murder of

282

your good self, put her beyond the pale. We were all fooled by her, were we not, Mrs. Hudson?'

'Indeed, we were.'

'Ha ha,' he went on. 'She even tried to persuade me that it was likely you who stabbed Timothy to death, and then ran into the wetlands to escape. Of course, that was eventually discounted especially when we found Queen Mab's hoofprints all over the scene, proving she was there.'

I was astounded. 'I am glad to hear that,' I said. 'I am glad to hear that you *eventually* discounted it.'

'But I have not invited you here to talk of Eve.' He raised his glass, obliging me to do likewise. 'To us!' he said, adding, 'I have another special reason, Martha...' He gave me a knowing smile and a wink.

Oh dear, I thought. Oh dear, dear. dear.

'Your charming daughter has informed me that she hopes you will decide to stay on in Bilbourne, especially given the forthcoming happy event. I mean, of course, the birth of another grandchild.' He raised his glass again, and clinked it against mine.

'Well, as to that...' I started to say.

'It would give me the greatest pleasure, Martha,' he went on. 'Indeed, I am hoping that you will agree to stay here. At Blossomfort, in fact.'

'Oh, Squire Simister...' Why does this always happen to me? I cannot understand it.

'You see,' he continued, 'Mrs. Jefferies has decided the workload here is too much for her. She wants to retire, to spend her remaining years... oh, I don't know, growing roses, keeping bees, or whatever people do in such circumstances. So, therefore, a position will be vacant here as cook housekeeper, and I can think of no better person than your good self to take it up.'

He sat back, a satisfied smile on his face, as if he had paid me the greatest of compliments. I stared at him, aghast.

'Your housekeeper…?'

'And cook. I understand you to be a great woman in the kitchen.'

I burst out laughing, then. His smile turned to a look of puzzlement.

'Oh, Squire!' I said. 'Forgive my levity. But you see, I have my own house in London. I am independent, and landlady to the two men I admire most in the whole world. Thank you kindly for your offer, but I am afraid I must turn it down.'

How forlorn he looked. How relieved was I that he had not proposed another position to me that I would have had to reject. To explain how I was still devoted to the memory of my dear Henry.

'Your last word on the subject?' he asked.

'Absolutely.'

'Well, what can I say. The two women I had hoped would share my lonely life from now on, out of my reach.'

'The two women?'

He looked rueful. 'Call me an old fool if you like, but before all this blew up, I had asked Eve Brakefield to consent to become my wife.'

My jaw must have dropped and my mouth hung open, for now it was his turn to laugh in the face of my astonishment.

'Whatever did she say to that?'

'She accepted me. I couldn't believe my luck. A beautiful young woman like that. Of course, now I realise what a lucky escape I had. She would probably have pushed me down a well, or poisoned my soup.' He shook his head. 'I suppose I will have to marry Mrs. Jeffries instead, to keep her here.'

As far as I know, he did not do so, or not yet. Or she turned him down. Meanwhile, I went home, much to the relief of my lodgers. Dear Clara is competent enough in general, but not up to my standards when it comes to mealtimes. Without wishing to blow my own trumpet, I am, as the Squire rightly said, 'a great woman in the kitchen.'

In the fullness of time, I returned to Bilbourne for the confinement of my daughter Eleanor. I found the place mightily changed. Lydia and Randall had gone to Italy, the latest scandal entertaining the village being that Stephen Norris, the overseer, had gone with them, last seen decked out in finery way above his station. Well, good luck to them. At least, it cleared up for me at last the probable identity of the lover in the summerhouse, unless there were others of whom I knew nothing. They dragged with them, as well, the reluctant tutor Mr. Symons, no doubt also broken-hearted over the revelations regarding Eve. The plantation had been sold and a new owner had taken over, keeping on William Makepeace as drier-in-chief.

'Mr. Grimshaw seems a decent man,' George said. 'He has restored the common land to us.'

I was delighted to renew my friendship with Ursula Considine, who told me that she missed me a lot.

'There are so few people here I can really talk to, apart, of course, from your daughter.'

That was good to hear, both from Ursula's perspective and that of Eleanor.

I forthwith invited Ursula to visit me in London, the which invitation, she accepted with alacrity. Indeed, I expect her at Baker Street before the summer comes around again.

Meanwhile, all went well with the birth, thank God, and Eleanor and George are now parents to a bouncing baby boy, Henry.

'Named for me,' Henrietta commented, giving me a triumphant look.

'And for Eleanor's father,' George said.

'Oh, him as well, I suppose.'

We had a good chuckle at that, and clustered round the infant's cradle, cooing over him as mothers and fathers and grandparents have done since time immemorial.

ACKNOWLEDGEMENTS

Grateful thanks as ever to my publisher, Steve Emecz and his team for their continued encouragement and support. To Brian Belanger for another great cover.

Thanks too, to my faithful readers, Ann O'Kelly, Phyl Herbert and Patricia McCarthy for their always useful comments.

And to my friends, Bill Bourne, Ken Ward and Bill's wife Dee, for permission to use their names for the village, town and river in the novel.

A trip in 2022 to the Kent Life open-air museum near Maidstone enabled to me to visit a working oast house during the September harvest, pick hops myself and chat to some women who remembered their time as pickers when they were children. I am indebted as well to George Orwell's accounts, in diaries, articles and subsequently in his novel *The Clergyman's Daughter*, which describe vividly the hard time pickers had of it in the 1930s. I doubt it had changed much since the 1890s, when *Death in the Garden of England* is set. Another very useful source was *Hops and Hop-Picking*, a history by Richard Filmer.

Mrs. Hudson's ordeal in the wetlands is based on something that happened to me while staying at the Tyrone Guthrie Centre, the lovely artists' retreat at Annaghmakerrig, County Monaghan. Luckily for me, and unlike my heroine, I was able to summon salvation by mobile phone. Many many thanks to the local guards and the firemen who carried me out.

Susan Knight is the author of three previous Mrs Hudson books, issued by MX publishing. The short story collection, *Mrs Hudson Investigates* (2019) and the novels *Mrs Hudson goes to Ireland* (2020) and *Mrs Hudson Goes to Paris* (2022). She has also contributed a number of stories, narrated by Dr. Watson, to the *MX Books of New Sherlock Holmes Short Stories*. In addition, she is the author of three other novels and two short story collections, as well as a non-fiction book of interviews with immigrant women living in Ireland. She lives in Dublin.